K... Ellis ... born ... h...

Wesley Peterson murder myst...
Plantagenet mysteries and the A........ ..., ...t
in the aftermath of the Great War.

She has twice been shortlisted for the CWA Short Story
Dagger and for the CWA Dagger in the Library award.

Visit Kate Ellis online:

www.kateellis.co.uk
@KateEllisAuthor

Praise for Kate Ellis:

'A beguiling author who interweaves past and present'
The Times

'[Kate Ellis] gets better with each new book'
Bookseller

'Kept me on the edge of my seat'
Shots magazine

'Ellis skilfully interweaves ancient and contemporary
crimes in an impeccably composed tale'
Publishers Weekly

The
Mechanical
Devil

Kate Ellis

piatkus

PIATKUS

First published in Great Britain in 2018 by Piatkus
This paperback edition first published in 2018 by Piatkus

1 3 5 7 9 10 8 6 4 2

A CIP catalogue record for this book
is available from the British Library.

ISBN 978-0-349-41312-9

Typeset in New Baskerville by M Rules
Printed and bound in Great Britain by
Clays Ltd, Elcograf S.p.A.

Papers used by Piatkus are from well-managed forests
and other responsible sources.

Piatkus
An imprint of
Little, Brown Book Group
Carmelite House
50 Victoria Embankment
London EC4Y 0DZ

An Hachette UK Company
www.hachette.co.uk

www.littlebrown.co.uk

For Eloise, who loves books.
And many thanks to Paul Whitcombe,
who allowed his name to be used for a good cause.

1

The car was red, the colour of fresh blood. Andrea clutched the steering wheel tightly as she peered at the road ahead, focusing on the tarmac; hardly aware of the rolling fields either side dotted with sheep, living beings against the vast expanse of Dartmoor.

Andrea had never picked up a hitch-hiker before, always heeding the urban myths about serial killers and knife-wielding madmen. But that was before she'd seen the girl standing at the side of the road, sticking her thumb out hopefully; too vulnerable and young to leave in the middle of nowhere at the mercy of God knows what . . . or who.

'Where did you say you were going?'

'I didn't,' the girl said. 'I'll tell you when to drop me off.'

Andrea took her eyes off the road for a moment to glance at her passenger. 'Everything OK?'

'I'm fine.' The girl's reply was dismissive, as though her mind was on something else. She was in her late teens with pouting lips, straight blonde hair and jeans too tight for comfort and she clutched the strap of the rucksack she'd flung at her feet in the footwell as though it contained something precious.

They reached a village; a small place with a cluster of

cottages, an ancient stone church and a single thatched pub with whitewashed walls. According to the sign exhorting motorists to drive carefully, the place was called Lower Torworthy and its church tower stood stark against the pale-grey sky.

'Drop me here.' The girl's words sounded like an order rather than a request.

'Are you sure?'

'I said so, didn't I?'

Andrea pursed her lips in disapproval; so much for gratitude. She stopped the car just beyond the pub and switched off the engine.

Without a word of thanks the girl climbed out, hoisted the rucksack on to her shoulder and slammed the car door behind her.

'Rude little bitch,' Andrea muttered to herself, craning her neck to watch the girl striding confidently down the road past the church. When she saw her stop by an old-fashioned red telephone box she started up the engine again and set off slowly.

She glanced in the rear-view mirror and saw a car following her: a large white SUV looming far too close and blocking her view of the road behind. The thing looked threatening, like some predatory shark closing in on her sleek Mercedes SLK. Experiencing a moment of panic, she spotted a parking place ahead and signalled to turn in, hoping to lose her pursuer. As she pulled into a little lay-by the white car sped past and she relaxed.

Andrea turned off the engine. The lay-by afforded a magnificent view over Dartmoor. From there she could see undulating fields sloping downwards into a valley and the wooded land beyond rearing up to meet the sky. She looked at her watch. She wasn't due at Princebury Hall until seven and if she arrived too early she'd be killing time. She picked up the brochure lying on the passenger seat and thumbed through it with a smile of anticipation. Then, after ten minutes, she decided to stretch her legs so she climbed out of the car and stood by the metal gate in the drystone wall admiring the vista and enjoying the unexpected moment of solitude. It had rained earlier that day; she could smell the moist earth and for a brief time the tangled complications of her life receded. She gazed into the field, wondering about the section of stone wall at the far end protruding from the ground like a skeletal arm waving from the grave. Andrea was never normally curious about such things but the wall looked old and there was an archway in its centre; the remains of an old doorway perhaps.

'Lovely, isn't it.'

Startled, she swung round to see a lean middle-aged man with receding hair and a dark beard looking at her earnestly. In his walking boots and outdoor attire, to Andrea he might as well have been a member of an alien species.

'Yes, it is,' she answered politely and made a show of looking at her watch because she had no wish to continue a conversation with this intrusive stranger. He seemed to take the hint and let himself into the field, clanging the gate behind him.

The roar of a motorcycle passing on the road shattered the peace of the moor as she watched the stranger pick his way over the uneven grass towards the ruined wall. She was about to return to the car when a loud crack sent birds fluttering upwards, crying in alarm.

She turned in time to see the stranger in the field fall to the ground like a rag doll dropped by a petulant child and for a few seconds she stood paralysed with shock. It was clear the stranger needed help but before she could unfasten the gate a second shot rang out and she felt a blow to her chest that sent her staggering backwards.

Then the green world turned black.

Extract from draft PhD thesis written by Alcuin Garrard

July 1995

The importance of Sir Matthew's meticulously kept parish records cannot be overemphasised. Having been discovered in the archives of Exeter Cathedral, where fortunately they escaped the bombing of the city during the Second World War, they provide us with a valuable insight into the life of a small Devon parish before Henry VIII's decision to deny the authority of the Pope caused political and social turmoil throughout the land.

There is evidence that Devon, geographically distant from the 'powers that be' in London, was largely resistant to the changes in church practice demanded by the authorities and Sir Matthew's records (incidentally, the title 'sir' was used routinely by priests in those days) give us a vivid picture of how events almost 300 miles away in London caused dramatic upheavals to the comforting rituals of village life.

His account of his parishioners' joys and woes are compassionate and sympathetic and his interest in science shines through his words, especially his attempts to harness it for the benefit of his flock.

However, various contemporary documents suggest that the apparently benign priest started a chain of events that was ultimately to release a force of evil beyond his control.

2

'She's been missing for a week now.'

DI Wesley Peterson watched the chief superintendent's face and saw concern there. CS Noreen Fitton was a tall angular woman wearing a uniform so crisp it might have been taken from the packet that morning. She looked formidable but Wesley had always found her a reasonable boss.

'How old is she?'

'Seventeen – turns eighteen next week. She was in the sixth form at Widedales School but she refused to go back at the start of this term.' She rolled her eyes and Wesley guessed she found the idea of a girl with such privileges throwing it all away exasperating.

DCI Gerry Heffernan was slumped in the seat beside him, a frown of concentration on his chubby face. 'If there's one thing I know about teenage girls it's that they can't resist sharing the ins and outs of their lives with their mates,' he said. 'Has anyone had a word with them?'

'Uniform spoke to some of them but they weren't much help.'

Gerry sighed. 'Is there any reason to believe she's in danger?'

CS Fitton shook her head, her severe bob undisturbed

by the movement. 'She was attending a residential drama course near Neston. Her father hoped it would help her decide what she wanted to do with her life. He wanted her to go to university but ...' Her words trailed off and she took a deep breath. 'Anyway, a week ago she packed her bags and left without a word and nobody's seen or heard from her since.' She paused. 'And she's not answering her phone.'

'We can track her phone if necessary,' said Wesley.

'It's switched off.'

'What about her financial transactions?'

'She hasn't accessed her bank account either.'

Wesley and Gerry exchanged looks.

'Want me to set things in motion?' Wesley asked.

For a few moments the chief super stared at the neat pile of papers on her desk. Something was worrying her and Wesley suspected that she hadn't yet told them the whole story.

'If you don't mind me asking, ma'am, why is this being dealt with at such a high level? Am I right in thinking this isn't an ordinary missing persons inquiry?'

Noreen Fitton sighed. 'You are, Wesley. Jocasta Ovorard's father is Jeremy Ovorard, who happens to be a junior minister in the Home Office. He wants us to treat this as a priority. TV appeal, the lot.'

Wesley saw her point. Jeremy Ovorard was a ubiquitous presence on the region's media, supporting local charities and discussing the problems of the area. He was charming and popular – and his seat was regarded as safe so long as he was the incumbent.

'She's probably gone off with some unsuitable lad,' said Gerry.

'You may well be right, Gerry, but her father insists this is out of character which worries me. If she doesn't turn up in the next twenty-four hours I think we should make a TV appeal.'

'Will you be doing it, ma'am?' Gerry asked hopefully.

There was an awkward silence before she answered. 'I was thinking more of you, Wesley.'

Gerry grinned. 'Well, he is better-looking than me and he speaks proper.'

The chief super's face turned uncharacteristically red. 'Er ... I think if a black officer makes the appeal it'll reassure the public that the police service is representative of the community we serve. That's so important in this day and age, wouldn't you agree?'

'I'm sure he'll be chuffed to do it, ma'am,' Gerry said with a hint of mischief.

Wesley did his best to keep his expression neutral, even though he felt like groaning. He hated the glare of publicity; and being used to make his superiors look virtuous.

'Mr Ovorard's coming in to see me first thing tomorrow,' the chief super continued. 'He's beside himself with worry. So is his wife.'

The mention of the wife sounded like an afterthought and Wesley wondered whether this meant she didn't share her husband's concern. If this was the case, did she know something he didn't about their daughter's whereabouts?

'I'll set the ball rolling, ma'am,' Wesley said. 'If you've got the missing girl's details ...'

Without a word the chief super passed him a sheet of paper.

'Jocasta's father describes her as a "free spirit".'

'An awkward little madam, then,' said Gerry.

Fitton smiled. When she did that she looked quite human, Wesley thought.

'She's a missing daughter, Gerry. You have a daughter of your own so you can imagine how that feels.'

Wesley knew that Gerry was all too familiar with daughters and their problems. He had one daughter, Rosie, who'd been far from easy since her mother's sudden death and he'd recently discovered the existence of another called Alison, who lived up in Liverpool. And if anything happened to either of them Wesley knew he'd react exactly like Jeremy Ovorard MP.

Dr Neil Watson of the County Archaeological Unit ended the call, intrigued by what he'd just been told.

As Neil had been supervising a survey of medieval graffiti at Lower Torworthy's ancient parish church he was the first person the vicar, Oliver Grayling, had thought to contact regarding a problem of a historical nature.

Grayling had begun with the usual pleasantries before revealing the reason for his call. Workmen mending a water main near the boundary of the old churchyard had made a strange discovery. A lead box; very heavy and probably ancient. Would Neil like to see it?

It was mid-September and Neil had a pile of post-excavation reports to write up. But the vicar's mention of an ancient lead box tempted him away from his paperwork and, without hesitation, he made the half-hour journey down the lonely Dartmoor roads to the church where he found Grayling waiting for him in the porch. He was a fresh-faced man in his forties, clean-shaven with neat brown hair and the look of an ageing choirboy.

'Thanks for coming, Neil. Hope I haven't dragged you away from anything important.'

'What have you found?'

Without answering, Grayling led the way into the church where several large arrangements of fresh flowers brightened the gloom and the pervading scent of lilies mingled with the smell of wax polish. Neil followed the vicar into the vestry tucked away at the side of the building, a small, north-facing room lined with wooden cupboards the colour of dark toffee.

The box lay on the desk in the centre of the room where many a happy bride and groom had signed the marriage register. It was made of lead, battered and misshapen, and it was the size of a small child's coffin. Neil's heart sank.

'It was found just beyond the boundary of the churchyard. Unconsecrated ground. My first thought was that it might be an unbaptised baby but it seems too big and ...'

'There's only one way to find out and that's to open it. But I'd like to do that at the university if that's OK. If there are human remains inside ...'

A look of indecision passed across Grayling's face before he told Neil to do whatever he had to. But as Neil made the necessary phone calls he saw the vicar staring at the strange box as though something about it was worrying him.

3

'Jocasta Ovorard definitely hasn't used her phone since she disappeared. Or her bank card. I've double-checked.'

Wesley sat himself down on the chair by Gerry's desk, which was strewn with files and paperwork in no particular order.

Gerry took off his reading glasses and peered at his colleague. 'And it's a whole week since she was last seen.' He paused. 'A lot can happen in a week.'

Wesley studied the photograph of the missing girl Uniform had provided. She was pretty ... and young. She probably wouldn't have thought of herself as vulnerable but Wesley had been a policeman long enough to know that youthful confidence was no protection against the bad people out there.

'According to the missing persons report, she was last seen by her fellow students on her drama course. We need to speak to them.'

'No time like the present,' Gerry said, looking at his watch. 'And if we get nowhere there's always that TV appeal.'

'You'd be better at it, Gerry.'

'You heard Aunty Noreen, Wes.' Gerry always gave the

chief super that homely title, as though it rendered her less formidable. 'She wants you. You can't wriggle out of it.'

'If the girl's friends can shed some light on the matter it might not be necessary.'

Gerry grinned revealing a wide gap between his front teeth. 'They're studying drama. Learning how to lie for a living.'

'If they're only studying they might not be too good at it yet.' Wesley was confident he could pick out a liar. He'd had plenty of practice.

The Tradington Barn Centre for the Performing Arts, part of the Tradington Hall Arts Complex, provided courses for aspiring actors, singers and dancers and had a reputation locally for catering for those unable to find a place at more conventional drama schools or music colleges. From what he'd already learned about Jocasta Ovorard, he suspected she'd been dabbling in the world of drama rather than nursing any burning ambition to take to the stage.

After driving through the pretty Elizabethan town of Neston eight miles upstream from their base in Tradmouth, Wesley reached the grounds of Tradington Hall a mile out of town, glad that the Barn Centre was well signposted. As he drew up outside, he guessed the place had been the main storage barn for the extensive Tradington Hall estate in centuries gone by. The interior was cavernous, fully modernised and smelled of new timber.

They made for the office where a helpful middle-aged woman pointed them in the direction of Drama Studio Two. She assumed a suitably worried expression and said she hoped Jocasta would turn up soon. They were all terribly concerned about her.

Wesley thanked the woman politely but gave nothing away.

'Wonder how much it costs to send a kid here,' said Gerry quietly as they walked down the corridor towards the studio. 'Can't be cheap.'

'You're probably right but don't let your prejudices show, will you.'

'Me, prejudiced against kids with rich mummies and daddies who've got nothing better to do than cause us grief? Never.' Gerry, who went out of his way to give second chances to young tearaways from the local council estates, had a blind spot when it came to the privileged.

Wesley bit his tongue and said nothing. The sign beside a tall wooden door at the end of the corridor told him they'd reached their destination and when he pushed the door open he found himself in a large space, painted matt black. There was a stage at one end constructed from moveable sections where a group of young people sat in a circle: three boys and three girls dressed in uniform black. They all looked round as one when the two policemen entered the room.

'Sorry to interrupt,' said Wesley before making the introductions. 'You've probably guessed we're here about Jocasta Ovorard. Her father's reported her missing. Anybody know where she might be?' He tilted his head to one side expectantly and waited.

After a few seconds of awkward silence a small, thin girl with red hair and freckles cleared her throat. 'I share a room with her.'

'Where's that, love?' Gerry asked.

'We're staying in the main hall during the course.'

'It's residential,' one of the boys chipped in. He had a

top knot, a wispy beard and a worried look on his face as he held out his hand. 'Craig Carswell. We're all worried about Jo so if there's anything we can do to help ...' The boy had chosen all the right words but Wesley couldn't help wondering if his concern was genuine.

'Who knows Jocasta best?' Wesley asked.

Craig Carswell looked as if he was about to speak but thought better of it. Then the red-haired girl raised a nervous hand.

'If I can speak to you first then,' he said with a reassuring smile. 'Then we'd like to have a word with the rest of you – and your tutor.'

Craig Carswell rolled his eyes. 'We don't see much of her. She leaves us to our own devices.'

Gerry had wondered whether to get some uniforms over there to conduct the interviews but in the end they decided to take three students each, one at a time in the adjoining common room which, as luck would have it, was empty.

Wesley decided to save the red-haired girl whose name was Kimberley, until last. She told him in a nervous rush that this was her first encounter with the police; nothing like this had ever happened to her before. Wesley asked to see the room she'd shared with Jocasta, doing his best to put her at her ease.

As they walked over to the main building he asked her questions, making it sound like a friendly chat. She was soon telling him what had brought her there and what her ambitions were and by the time they'd reached the main house she seemed more relaxed.

'Tell me about Jocasta,' he said as they walked across the cobbled courtyard.

Kimberley stopped walking and thought for a few moments before she answered. 'I don't think she was happy. She'd been at boarding school but she'd quit because she couldn't stand it any more – said they treated her like a child. She'd always enjoyed drama so she thought she'd give this a try.'

'And?'

'We've only been here four weeks but she'd already started skiving off workshops and rehearsals. I don't think it suited her. Not really.'

'What did she do when she skived off?'

Kimberley shook her head. 'She never said.'

'She had a phone?'

'Of course,' she said as though she thought it a stupid question – like did she have a head?

'She hasn't used it since she disappeared.'

Kimberley looked shocked. 'That's not like her. She was on it all the time.'

'Who to?'

'No idea.'

'Did she ever mention a boyfriend?'

'Not to me but that doesn't mean she didn't have one. She didn't give much away, if you know what I mean,' the girl said, a note of sadness in her voice.

Wesley suspected Kimberley had tried to befriend her room-mate but had been knocked back.

'When did you last see her?'

'A week ago. Around lunchtime. She didn't turn up for the afternoon session and when I got back to the room her things had gone.'

'Were you worried?'

'Not really. She didn't like it here – didn't really fit in.

And if she took her things she can't have been abducted or anything like that, can she?'

She led him up a narrow staircase to the student rooms. The set-up reminded Wesley of an Oxbridge college: a stone-built medieval house centred around a courtyard with doorways at regular intervals leading up to the accommodation. The room Kimberley shared with Jocasta was anything but luxurious. Perched in the eaves, it was poky and institutional.

With Kimberley's permission he conducted a search of Jocasta's half of the room but it proved fruitless. The missing girl had clearly taken everything of interest with her when she left, leaving only a few unwanted clothes dangling sadly off hangers in her wardrobe, some dog-eared paperbacks and an assortment of half-used toiletries.

Wesley felt that he knew no more about the missing girl now than when he'd arrived. Then Kimberley spoke. 'I don't know whether this means anything.' She took a book off the shelf above her bed, pulled a sheaf of A4 sheets from between the pages and handed them to Wesley.

It was a play script; something modern he didn't recognise.

'I'd lost mine so I borrowed hers. I was going to get it photocopied and give it back to her but she'd gone before I got the chance. She's drawn something on the back, see.'

Wesley turned the sheets over. Sure enough there was something on the reverse of the script: a doodled sketch of a motorcycle, hardly the work of a talented artist but recognisable.

'Did she show any interest in motorbikes?'

Kimberley shook her head. 'No. Not at all.'

'Did she ever mention knowing someone who owned one?'

'Like I said, she never discussed her private life.' She glanced round, as though she was afraid of being overheard. 'But I got the impression she had a secret.'

4

When Wesley and Gerry returned to the police station they made their way upstairs to CS Fitton's office to report their findings, such as they were. Wesley had made a copy of the doodle the missing girl had drawn on the back of the script. It struck him as being an unusual thing for a girl who'd expressed no previous interest in motorbikes to do and he wondered again whether she had a secret boyfriend who owned one. But the sketch gave no clue to the make or model, or to the identity of the rider.

When they reached the chief super's office they found she wasn't alone. A tall man in a grey suit was sitting in her visitor's chair sipping tea from a china cup. He had neat silver hair and a smooth round face and his open-necked shirt suggested he was off duty. At first sight he possessed the confident demeanour of a man used to giving orders – and having them obeyed. But then Wesley saw an uncertainty in his eyes, as though for the first time in his life he was feeling vulnerable.

The chief superintendent sprang up to make the introductions.

'Mr Ovorard, this is DCI Heffernan and DI Peterson. They've taken over the investigation into your daughter's disappearance. Gentlemen, this is Jeremy Ovorard, Jocasta's father. DI Peterson will be making the TV appeal with you, Mr Ovorard.'

As they shook hands Wesley experienced a sudden flutter of panic. They had nothing new to tell him, other than the fact his daughter hadn't made any particular friends at the Drama Centre and was regarded as stand-offish. This wasn't what any parent wanted to hear, let alone a parent whose child was missing.

'We've just been speaking to her fellow drama students at Tradington,' Wesley began. 'I'm afraid she didn't confide in anybody there, although the fact that she took most of her things with her suggests she left of her own accord, possibly to meet somebody.'

'That's what I was told before. That's why this hasn't been taken seriously.'

'I assure you we are taking it seriously, sir,' said Wesley.

'Are you absolutely sure she didn't have a boyfriend, Mr Ovorard?' Gerry interrupted.

'I would have known,' the man answered quickly.

Wesley and Gerry looked at each other. Surely no father could be that confident of knowing his teenage daughter's deepest secrets.

'When did you last see her?' Wesley asked.

'About a month ago when she left for the course. I called her a couple of days later to ask how she was settling in and she said she was fine.'

'You haven't spoken since then?' Gerry's question was sharp.

The MP examined his fingernails. 'I've been in London. Besides, girls of that age don't want their fathers interfering, do they.'

Gerry smiled. 'You're right there. How did you learn she was missing?'

'The Drama Centre contacted me to say she'd gone. That's when I notified the police.'

'What about your wife? Has she spoken to her recently?' Wesley asked.

'No.'

'You're sure about that?'

'Of course I am. Look, I gave you my daughter's number. Have you traced the calls she made before she disappeared?'

'It's being dealt with but I'm afraid these things take time. Service providers aren't always quick at getting back to us.'

Ovorard looked sceptical, as though he suspected Wesley was making excuses. But he'd told the truth. The miraculous speed with which results appeared in cop shows gave the public a false impression of the frustrations of real investigations.

'I've arranged for the appeal to go out on the evening news,' Noreen Fitton said. 'Will your wife be appearing with you, Mr Ovorard? It usually helps if both parents—'

'My wife's far too distressed to be paraded in public like that,' Ovorard snapped, as though she'd made an indecent suggestion.

'I understand,' Fitton said.

There was an awkward silence before Wesley spoke again. 'Does Jocasta know anyone with a motorbike?'

'Not that I'm aware of,' Ovorard answered before standing up. 'I'll see you all this evening then.'

'Unless we find her in the meantime,' Wesley said with an optimism he didn't feel.

21

'The appeal will take place in the conference room upstairs at five thirty.' Fitton turned to Wesley 'Don't be late.'

'No, ma'am.'

'What did you make of Ovorard?' Gerry asked as they made their way back to the CID office.

'He might seem full of confidence but he's worried sick. He's used to being in control.'

'Funny he didn't want to involve his wife. Most mothers would be round here hammering our doors down if their kid went missing.'

'He said she was too upset – which is understandable.'

'I know, but something doesn't feel right.'

Wesley didn't reply. He'd had the same feeling himself.

'I'd better prepare for my big performance,' Wesley said.

'Break a leg, darling,' Gerry said with a giggle, replacing his Liverpool accent with the plummy tones of an affected actor.

Wesley groaned. He hated being the centre of attention but a girl was missing so he'd do his best, for her sake.

It was a coffin and it most likely contained the remains of a child. The thought made Neil Watson feel slightly sick.

He placed the box gently on the back seat of his car and as he drove to Exeter he was aware of its presence; the sad remnants of a little life cut short. He wasn't a superstitious man – quite the opposite – but the sight of a child's bones at an excavation got to him every time.

Instead of taking it home and transferring it to the university the following morning, he made a detour and left it at the lab before returning to his flat. Now the box was no longer in his custody he felt more relaxed and while he made himself something to eat he turned on the TV news.

When he heard the sound of a familiar voice pleading for anyone who knew anything about the whereabouts of a missing girl to contact the police as soon as possible, he abandoned his feeble attempt at cookery and returned to the TV. The concerned face of his old university friend, Wesley Peterson, filled the screen, so he sat down and turned up the volume.

Belinda Crillow, newly returned from her evening run in the nearby lanes, sat alone in the neat front room of her cottage surrounded by photographs of the dead: parents; grandparents; cats she had owned and cared for over the years.

She was forty-five – young by modern standards when sixty-year-olds regularly cavorted in nightclubs, or so the TV would have you believe. Whenever she looked in the mirror she saw an attractive woman with large eyes and shoulder-length brown hair, and her indifference to food coupled with her daily run meant that she was slim, verging on skinny. Someone – she couldn't remember who – had once said that you can't be too rich or too thin, although it didn't make her feel any better

She had little in common with her colleagues at the council offices and the last relationship she'd had with a man had ended three years ago when he'd left her for a former girlfriend. The friends she'd mixed with in earlier years now had their own lives and families, and her half-hearted attempts at online dating hadn't been a success. That had been before the break-in eighteen months ago: before she'd returned to her flat in Tradmouth to find it ransacked and vandalised. The intruder had been more intent on destruction than theft and the violation had left her shaken and too terrified to return to the place that had once been her sanctuary.

Determined that nothing like that would ever happen to her again, she'd moved to a cottage on the edge of a small hamlet a mile and a half out of town. Nobody visited her these days but, even so, she still kept her home spotless, cleaning each evening when she returned from work; polishing and hoovering until there was nothing more to be done after she'd eaten, washed up and tidied away.

The TV helped to break the silence of her life; that and the radio she put on first thing in the morning while she was getting ready for work. The voices were company, the only company she had when she wasn't in the office. Now her tasks were done she rearranged her carefully positioned cushions and made herself comfortable on the sofa to watch the news, which she found strangely comforting. The reports of mayhem in the world outside made the cottage feel like a safe haven.

The local news had just started and one of the headlines caught her attention: a missing girl – the daughter of an MP. Her photograph flashed up on the screen; a girl with pouting lips and the careless beauty of youth. Belinda thought she could see contempt in her eyes; maybe even cruelty.

Then the girl's image was replaced by that of the officer dealing with the case and Belinda shuffled forward in her seat, her heart thumping. It was him – the good-looking black detective inspector she'd met after the break-in when the certainties of her life had been shattered. He had been patient and sympathetic, taking his time to reassure her – unlike some of his colleagues – and his caring manner had imprinted itself on her memory; the only bright thing in a dark time. He'd been the only one who'd seemed to understand how she was feeling – that it wasn't just a matter of property but of her very existence.

She heard a sound that seemed to come from outside; a scraping as though someone was at the back door. She froze, suddenly fearful. What if someone was out there? What if her ordeal was about to start all over again?

5

As soon as Pam Peterson had welcomed Wesley home with an absent-minded kiss on the cheek, the cat Moriarty appeared in the hall demanding food. Their son, Michael, was supposed to have fed the animal but, being in the grip of adolescence, his former reliability had vanished beneath a sea of surging hormones. Pam sighed and made for the kitchen with the cat in hot pursuit, rubbing up against her ankles in an impressive display of cupboard love.

'Did you see the press conference on the local news?' There was a hint of anxiety in Wesley's voice, like an actor awaiting the critics' reviews after a daunting first night.

'You came over well,' Pam assured him. 'Just the right blend of concern and professionalism. Any news of the girl yet?'

'No, but it's early days.'

Wesley watched his wife as she dished out the food, unable to shake off the unease he'd felt about her health since she was diagnosed with breast cancer in the spring. Her treatment had been successful but the episode had left Wesley with a nagging awareness of the fragility of life. Before joining the police he'd studied archaeology at university and he'd come across medieval depictions of the Wheel of Fortune – the people of the Middle Ages had known only too well that fickle fate can change everything in an instant.

After they'd eaten Wesley and Pam relaxed on the sofa together. Today had been one of her days back at work, teaching at the local primary school, and the fear that she was doing too much too soon weighed on Wesley's mind.

'I suppose this missing girl case means you'll be working late?' she said as Wesley took a sip of the red wine he'd just poured for himself.

'Can't be sure but we're hoping she'll turn up soon.' He hesitated. 'Although she hasn't used her phone or bank card since she was last seen.'

'It's hard to separate girls her age from their phones, so that *is* worrying.'

Before Wesley could reply the doorbell rang three times. The visitor, whoever it was, sounded impatient and Wesley hurried off to answer the door. A minute later he returned, followed by a woman with long black hair, dyed to conceal the grey. She wore a blue velvet coat over a long skirt and her flowing scarves concealed a figure she was constantly trying to keep under some sort of control.

'It's your mother,' Wesley announced with patient resignation as Della Stannard flopped down beside her daughter in the space Wesley had just vacated.

'She can see that, Wesley. Any wine going?'

Wesley had heard Pam describe Della as a force of nature, amongst other things, and he knew there was no getting rid of her once she'd made up her mind to stay. After he had filled a glass for Della he topped Pam's up, knowing she'd need it to deaden the impact of her mother's unexpected arrival.

'I saw you on the TV news,' she said to Wesley once she'd taken a large gulp of wine. 'You could have sounded more assertive but, other than that, you didn't do too badly.'

Wesley thanked her for the half-hearted compliment and waited for her to come to the point of her visit.

'I've come to do you a favour, Pam,' she began. 'I've met this man through the internet. He's called Ben and he's not bad-looking – got a good head of hair and all his own teeth, which is an important consideration when you get to my age.' She looked downwards like a coy young girl, something Wesley found disconcerting. 'He's very charming.'

'So are a high proportion of serial killers,' said Wesley.

Della ignored him as though she hadn't heard.

'So what's the favour,' said Pam warily.

'I asked Ben to go with me to a residential course on Dartmoor,' Della continued. 'I booked us both in for a week ... starting tomorrow.'

'What kind of course?'

'Motivational. How to change your life and discover your inner power.'

He saw Pam roll her eyes. 'Right.'

'Anyway, Ben called to say he couldn't make it so there's a spare place going and I wondered if you'd like to come.' She looked at Pam expectantly. 'It's highly recommended.'

'And highly expensive?'

'I've already paid so it won't cost you a penny.'

'You actually paid for this Ben?'

Della's face reddened. 'Well, if you're worried that I'm spending your inheritance ...' She took another swig of wine.

'Tell us more about the course,' said Wesley, a natural smoother of waters. Della had lived alone since the death of

Pam's father and Wesley sensed a deep desire for company behind all the bluster and frenetic activity. Sometimes he thought he understood her more than Pam did.

'It's at Princebury Hall up on Dartmoor. The man who runs it's called Xander Southwark. He served time in jail for fraud, but then he turned his life around.'

'How do you know?' Pam muttered under her breath. Wesley gave her arm a nudge.

'It's all in the brochure. I haven't met him yet but I've heard he's inspirational.' She looked at her daughter hopefully. 'Are you interested in coming with me?'

Pam shook her head. 'Sorry, I'll be working. Then there's the kids and ... '

'Your loss,' Della said, holding out her glass for a refill. 'I'll just have to go on my own.'

Wesley knew Della was reluctant to acknowledge that she'd now reached the age when, should she have the misfortune to be mown down by a bus, she'd be described in newspaper reports as 'a pensioner'. He suspected she wanted to visit Princebury Hall to inject some excitement into her life, but her new man's no-show had changed all that. She hadn't been able to hide her disappointment when Pam passed up the chance to take his place and he guessed the refusal had hurt her more than she'd admit.

'Be careful,' he said, not quite sure why he'd chosen those particular words.

The red Mercedes was parked in the lay-by as though its occupants had stepped out to take in the view. Tourists weren't usually out this early unless they were the outdoors type, Dan Noakes thought as he climbed down from his battered Land Rover to open the gate in the drystone wall first thing the next morning. Dan's family had kept sheep here for over 100 years and as he was on his way to the village shop, he thought he might as well pull in and walk through Manor Field to check on his woolly charges.

The sheep were in the top field so he hadn't had cause to come this way for a few days and as he steered the Land Rover into the field he studied the grass, assessing its grazing potential. He shut the gate behind him and his border collie jumped down from the passenger seat.

But instead of awaiting his master's instructions the dog hared off to the right, stopped behind the wall that separated the field from the road and barked urgently. Dan knew something was wrong and he assumed one of the sheep had wandered into Manor Field and got itself into trouble. Sheep weren't the most sensible of creatures.

He shouted to the dog to leave whatever it was alone and the dog obeyed, standing guard over his find, still barking the alert.

'What is it, lad?' the farmer said as he trudged nearer. The dog stopped barking and stood panting, satisfied he'd done his duty.

The woman lay on the grass behind the wall, staring at the sky, but her eyes, pecked by crows, were now black holes sunk in the pale oval of her face. Her arms lay neatly by her sides and the farmer's first thought was that someone had taken the trouble to arrange her like that; almost a respectful laying out.

He took his mobile phone from his pocket but before he could check for a signal, the dog dashed off again, skidded to a halt by the section of old wall further up the field, and resumed his barking.

A feeling of dread slowed Dan's steps as he trudged

over to investigate and when he reached the dog he saw a bearded man lying on his back beside the ruin, hidden from view of the road. His eyes too were gone and the bullet wound in his forehead resembled a third eye, hollow and bloody. Dan stared at the second corpse for a while, wondering if he was in the middle of a nightmare. But he could feel the breeze on his face and smell the damp earth so he knew this was real. When he checked his phone there was no signal so he stumbled back to the Land Rover, waited for the dog to leap up beside him, and headed for the village, his foot down on the accelerator as far as it would go.

Wesley had only just arrived at the police station when the news came in. Two people had been found dead in suspicious circumstances on Dartmoor, just outside a village called Lower Torworthy. The scene had been sealed off and the CSIs and Dr Bowman, the Home Office pathologist, were on their way.

Gerry emerged from his office, scratching his head. A girl was missing – a girl with a high-profile father at that – so a pair of unexplained deaths was something they could do without.

Wesley knew there was a possibility they had to consider. 'Could the female be Jocasta Ovorard?'

Gerry shook his head. It was the first thing he'd asked when he'd taken the call. 'The dead woman's a lot older. Probably in her early forties.'

'Cause of death?' Wesley asked as Gerry reached for his coat.

'The farmer who called it in says they were shot.'

'Double suicide?'

'It's possible.'

'Anything come in overnight on Jocasta?'

'Lots of sightings – all being followed up. Your appeal's brought all the cranks and attention-seekers out of the woodwork as usual.'

Wesley suddenly felt guilty that he hadn't arrived earlier, even though since Pam's illness Gerry had told him he needn't come in before he'd helped her get the kids ready in the morning. But if Jocasta Ovorard didn't turn up soon and the shootings up on Dartmoor proved to be murder, all that would have to change.

6

The field was cordoned off with blue-and-white police tape and Wesley and Gerry were given the customary crime-scene suits to wear to prevent contamination of any evidence. Gerry always said he felt like a snowman in his and Wesley said nothing to contradict him.

They watched in silence while the CSIs busied themselves in two separate areas roughly fifty yards apart. There was a look of earnest concentration on Dr Colin Bowman's face as he knelt by the drystone wall between the field and the road and they waited until he'd finished work before making their way through the inner cordon. For the first time Wesley could see the focus of Colin's attention – an expensively dressed woman with well-cut blonde hair and bright red nails. She looked as if she'd taken care of herself and if the flashy red Mercedes parked on the verge near the gate belonged to her, she hadn't been short of money either.

When Wesley had been told it was a shooting, he had expected to see shotgun wounds – from the rural weapon of choice – but the neat hole in the woman's forehead had been caused by another sort of weapon, a rifle or perhaps a revolver. There was a hole in her chest where a bullet had penetrated and when Colin turned her over Wesley saw that her back was a mass of dried blood.

She'd been shot in the chest from some distance away, Colin pointed out, hence the large exit wound in her back. Then she was shot in the forehead at closer range – presumably because the killer wanted to make sure she was dead.

Colin turned the head to give them a view of the exit wound, a mess of blood and brain matter. 'I'm pretty sure she didn't die here,' he said. 'She's been moved and someone's gone to the trouble of arranging her body neatly, which seems odd because this bears all the hallmarks of an assassination.'

'Time of death?'

Colin wrinkled his nose. 'All I can say is that she's been here a while – four or five days perhaps but that's just a guess.'

'We were told there's a second victim,' Wesley said and Colin pointed to the section of ruined stone wall at the top end of the field where the CSIs and the police photographer were at work.

'It's a middle-aged man dressed like a walker. Identical MO and dead about the same length of time,' said Colin. 'The only difference being that he was shot in the back whereas this lady was shot in the chest which suggests she was facing the killer and he was either running away or had no idea the assassin was there.'

After asking Colin how soon he could fit in the post-mortems, Wesley and Gerry walked over to view the second body. As they approached Wesley saw a pair of legs in walking boots sticking out from behind the wall, the sole remnant of a building, long ago left to fall to ruin.

Again the body had been neatly arranged and Wesley turned to the constable on guard who was young; straight out of training school by the look of it. From his queasy expression Wesley guessed it was probably his first murder case.

'Any ID on either of the victims?' Wesley asked.

'The red Mercedes SLK parked in the lay-by next to the field is registered to an Andrea Jameson – address in Tradmouth, sir,' said the constable, making a great effort not to look at the corpse on the ground. 'The car's unlocked and there's a handbag inside. The ID found in it backs that up.' He pointed in the vague direction of the second body. 'There's no ID on the man but if he was out walking he probably didn't carry any with him.'

'We'll check all the local hotels and B and Bs,' said Wesley. 'He must have been staying somewhere.'

'Unless he's local, sir,' the constable chipped in.

'Well, Wes, what do you think?' Gerry asked as they made their way back to the car.

Wesley considered the question for a few moments. 'Both victims were obviously killed by the same perpetrator, but they don't look like a couple to me. She was smart. Make-up, manicure and expensive clothes. She was even wearing high heels – on Dartmoor.'

'I noticed that. But there's only one shoe. They're still looking for the other,' Gerry said.

'Whereas he was obviously the outdoor type: backpack, anorak and walking boots – all good quality but well worn. The two victims don't go together.'

'There must be some connection,' Gerry said with a sigh. 'We'll have to set up an incident room in the village.'

'I'll organise a team to conduct house-to-house interviews. Someone must have seen the victims – or the killer.'

Gerry nodded. 'Once the press get hold of this it'll be big. Mafia-style assassination outside a quiet Dartmoor village – they'll lap it up.'

'And the minister's missing daughter?'

'Her and all.'

Neil Watson was taking no chances. The lead coffin – for he was now sure that's what it was – had been safely stored at the lab at Exeter University overnight and he'd used his extensive contacts to assemble a team of experts to open it and examine the bones inside.

The box had been placed on a stainless-steel table and Neil watched while his colleagues manipulated the soft grey metal. They worked with care and silently, as if out of respect for the child they were sure it contained. Even though hundreds of years had passed, the death of a child was cause for solemnity rather than the usual speculation and banter.

Neil wondered how well the little body would be preserved and he held his breath as the split in the lead widened to reveal the contents.

Margaret, the forensic anthropologist, bent over to peer inside the box. 'I don't understand,' she muttered before asking her colleague to enlarge the hole.

As the aperture widened Neil stood on tiptoe to get a better view. He could see something inside the box: not bone or mummified flesh but wood covered with paint – muted vegetable colours like the rood screen in Lower Torworthy church.

'Is it a wooden coffin?' he asked.

Margaret shook her head. 'It looks like a carved figure of some kind. I've never seen anything like it before.' She nodded to her colleague, who proceeded to widen the hole in the lead until eventually the lid of the box was peeled back completely.

For a while they all stared at the thing lying inside. It was a carved man with a bald head and prominent ears, two feet tall and wearing what looked like a monk's habit. Its face was finely carved and disturbingly real, with a hooked nose and full painted lips. The wooden clothing was coloured brown and its eyes stood out blue against the painted flesh.

'It must be the statue of a saint,' someone suggested. 'Maybe they buried it during the Reformation when the authorities were destroying anything they considered superstitious?'

Neil nodded. It was a good theory: a precious local saint saved from desecration by a pious priest and his flock.

Margaret signalled for it to be lifted from its resting place and one of her assistants obliged. But as he laid the thing carefully on the table a flap at the side of the figure came loose and dropped on to the steel surface with a clatter.

'What have we here?' said Margaret. Human remains were her province but she'd been caught up in the excitement of this strange discovery.

Neil picked up the flap. It fitted back into the gap in the wooden image perfectly. Whoever had created this unusual statue had been a master of his art. He removed the flap again and when he peered inside the figure he saw something that made him catch his breath.

'What is it?' Margaret asked.

Neil looked round and saw that everyone's attention was on him.

'There's some kind of mechanism inside. Let's get it on its feet.'

Karen, the civilian receptionist on the enquiry desk at Tradmouth Police Station, watched the woman step through the automatic doors and hesitate, as though she wasn't quite sure where she was. Her glossy brown hair framed a heart-shaped face and her white trousers and striped top flattered her figure. She was wearing dark glasses even though the sky outside was grey.

'Can I help you?'

The newcomer stopped suddenly and stared as if she'd only just realised Karen was there.

'I have to see Detective Inspector Peterson,' she said in an urgent whisper.

'He's not in at the moment. Is there anyone else who can help you?'

The woman shook her head vigorously. 'No. I have to speak to him. Urgently. What time will he be back?'

Karen rang up to the CID office. After a hushed conversation she turned to the woman apologetically. 'I'm afraid he's been called away to a case but I'm sure someone else from CID will be able to help you if it's urgent ... '

'No. It's Inspector Peterson I need to see. I'll come back.'

As the woman turned to go she took off her dark glasses to reveal a patch of livid bruising around her eye and the moment of revulsion Karen experienced was immediately replaced by curiosity.

'That looks nasty. How did you get it?' Karen knew it was none of her business but she'd come across domestic violence before and, in her opinion, it should be nipped in the bud whether or not Inspector Peterson was available to deal with it.

'That's why I want to see Inspector Peterson,' the woman said, her voice shaking. 'I've been attacked.'

Extract from draft PhD thesis
written by Alcuin Garrard

July 1995

In the coroners' inquest records for 1518
there is a reference to a Matthew At Wood
of Lower Torworthy who gave evidence at an
inquest in March of that year. Later records
give the priest Sir Matthew's surname as
At Wood so it is likely this is the same
person.

According to the records a Matthew At Wood
was fishing with his cousin in the river
near the village when the cousin fell into
the water. Matthew stated that the river was
swollen by recently melted snow and was so
fast-flowing that all his attempts to rescue
his cousin were in vain.

Matthew was questioned closely about the
incident but it seemed that nothing could be
proved against him.

7

Colin Bowman conducted both post-mortems at Tradmouth Hospital and the results were pretty much as expected. Both victims had been shot and the bullets had passed through both bodies, causing small entry and larger exit wounds. Colin suspected some kind of rifle had been fired from some distance away to inflict the body wounds, perhaps using a telescopic sight. However both victims' foreheads bore characteristic signs of tattooing around the entry wounds, which confirmed that the head shots had been made at a closer range. They had been felled like hunted animals then finished off, and the thought made Wesley shudder.

Once Wesley and Gerry had finished at the hospital they returned to Lower Torworthy, where things were moving fast. Computers and phones had already been set up in the church hall which was serving as the incident room for the time being. A team was out conducting house-to-house inquiries in the village and the surrounding area and every aspect of Andrea Jameson's life was being investigated, starting with the contacts on the mobile phone found in her handbag.

'Strange she left her handbag in the car,' Rachel Tracey

observed. She was standing next to Wesley in the field where the bodies had been found, watching the CSIs still at work behind their flimsy barrier of blue-and-white tape. 'I never would.'

'Of course not. You've got more sense.'

Rachel looked at him, half smiling at the gentle teasing in his voice.

'Did Dr Bowman say anything interesting at the post-mortem?' she asked.

'As I expected, the cause of death was gunshot wounds. The first to the body probably killed them, then the perpetrator put a bullet through their brains, just to make sure.'

'Vicious.'

'Too right. The bullets passed through the bodies so I've ordered a fingertip search of the area but it might take a while.'

'Professional job?'

'Looks that way. We're thinking both bodies were moved, presumably to delay discovery and give the killer time to leave the area before anyone could raise the alarm.'

'He could be miles away by now.'

Wesley knew Rachel was right. The assassin could be anywhere, even out of the country. He looked around. 'Unfortunately there's no danger of being caught on CCTV here in the middle of nowhere, which could be why he chose this spot. Wonder how he got the victims here. Did he follow one or both of them? Did they arrive together or did they arrange to meet here?'

'And what's the relationship between the two of them?'

'They might not have known each other. Maybe the killer lured them both here at the same time for some reason. Any luck identifying the male yet?'

Rachel shook her head. 'Nothing so far. A few people from the village noticed the red car parked there but nobody reported it abandoned. It's been there since tea-time on Friday according to one witness, which might help pinpoint the time of death. It's a tribute to the honesty of the locals that the handbag wasn't nicked.'

Wesley grinned. 'Almost restores your faith in human nature.'

His phone rang and Rachel watched as he answered it.

'I'm sorry, I'm busy at the moment. I'm sure someone else can help you.'

There was silence as he listened to the reply and even though they'd known each other so long and been through so much together, Rachel couldn't read his expression. He apologised again and repeated his assurance that his colleagues could deal with whatever it was and ended the call.

'Who was that?' Rachel was curious by nature – that was why she'd joined CID in the first place.

'A woman was attacked while she was out jogging and her assailant gave her a nasty black eye. She came to the station but I wasn't there so she rang.'

'She had your number?'

'She was the victim of a nasty burglary about eighteen months ago and I must have given her my card and told her to call me if she remembered anything.' He shrugged. At that moment he had more important things to think about.

'Did she describe her attacker?'

'She said he was wearing a balaclava.'

'Worrying.'

'Yes. But I'm sure someone at the station can deal with it.'

They began to walk back to the car. Rachel had parked it some distance from the red Mercedes, which was now being hoisted on to a low loader to be taken back to the police garage for examination.

'If they think the victims didn't die where they were found, where were they killed?' Rachel said.

'When we know that we might get somewhere. It's rained a bit since Friday so evidence might have been lost.'

Wesley could see the team of CSIs scouring the ground around where the Mercedes had been. They'd be looking for any traces of blood that had survived the rain – or the missing bullets, preferably both. He heard one of them shout and raise his hand. He'd found something.

They stopped to watch. It seemed an age before a small CSI with ginger hair came over to speak to them.

'It looks as though something was dragged into the field through the gate; we've found fibres on the stone gatepost. It's possible the female victim got out of the car to stretch her legs and enjoy the view, then boom.'

'Boom?'

The CSI's freckled face reddened. 'It looks as though the killer opened the gate so he could get her in the field and hide her from view. We found her missing shoe in under-growth near the car. There are drag marks near where the male was found so it looks like his body was moved too. All we need now is to find the rounds that killed them.'

Wesley thanked him and asked to be kept updated before turning to go.

The woman who'd called had sounded distressed and he felt uneasy about passing her on to one of his under-lings when she'd asked specifically for his help. But he had Jocasta Ovorard's disappearance and a double murder to deal with; he couldn't be everywhere at once.

*

When the flap on the side of the wooden figure fell off Neil could see the mechanism inside: intricately crafted cogs and wheels, preserved in good condition thanks to the protective lead. There was a handle too that he suspected would wind the thing up, but nobody had dared touch it yet. Someone suggested consulting the university's mechanical engineering department. Or perhaps a clockmaker would be more appropriate.

What puzzled him most was the age of the thing. All the experts who'd stared at it and handled it reverently had agreed that it looked medieval. Sixteenth century at the latest. During his archaeological career he'd heard tales of mechanical figures created to guard tombs but he'd never actually come across one of these early robots so his inclination had been to dismiss the accounts as fantasy or wishful thinking. Now, however, he was beginning to think there was something in the stories after all.

It was eleven o'clock when he decided to drive over to Lower Torworthy. He needed to tell Oliver Grayling about the strange discovery; after all, the thing had been found just outside the boundary of his church.

He could have phoned ahead but he fancied the drive. Being stuck in the office with a pile of site reports never appealed to him, especially when the weather was fine. Once in Lower Torworthy he drew up in the small church car park beside a police patrol car. There were two more in the lane, their garish blue-and-yellow checks standing out against the village backdrop like clowns at a funeral. As he emerged from the car he could see uniformed officers coming and going from the small church hall fifty yards down the road. Lower Torworthy, unlike many villages of similar size, boasted a village shop and a gaggle of people,

45

mostly elderly, were hanging around outside exchanging gossip. He hadn't listened to the local news that day but he guessed something dramatic had happened in this place that, with recent funding cuts, normally wouldn't see a policeman from one month to the next.

He scanned the scene for his old friend Wesley Peterson but there was no sign of him so he tried the church door. If anyone knew what was going on it was bound to be the vicar.

The door was unlocked and he was about to push it open when he saw a motorcycle – an impressive Harley Davidson – propped against the church wall to the side of the porch. Perhaps the Reverend Grayling was a biker, he thought. He couldn't picture it somehow but sometimes people surprise you.

He stepped inside the church and when his vision adjusted to the gloom he saw a figure by the pulpit. The man was burly, not in the first flush of youth and built like a rugby player, with a shaven head and a baby face. He wore a black suit and a clerical collar which belied his worldly appearance.

'Hi,' Neil said as he strolled to the front of the church. 'Is Oliver around?'

The man gave Neil a smile that didn't spread to his eyes. 'He's out . . . seeing a parishioner.'

'We've not met. I'm Neil Watson. County Archaeological Unit.'

'Er . . . John Davies. Curate,' the man said, ignoring Neil's outstretched hand.

'The village is crawling with police. What's going on?'

'I heard there's been a shooting.'

'Must be more than a shotgun accident to warrant all this fuss.'

'Sorry, don't know,' Davies said quickly, fidgeting nervously with the collection box he was holding.

'I wanted a word with Oliver about that lead box the workmen found. You've heard about it?'

'Er ... yeah.' He didn't sound altogether convincing. 'If I see him I'll say you were looking for him.'

Neil turned and made for the door. As he left he looked back and saw the curate watching him.

Wesley's desk had been placed next to Gerry's on the stage of the new incident room. During his time in Devon he'd worked in several temporary incident rooms set up in church halls, all so similar they blended into one in his memory. There was always the stage used for local amateur dramatics, play equipment in the corner for the parish toddler group, and chairs stacked round the edges of the room for use at meetings, together with the folding tables used at jumble sales and fetes. Over the years he'd come to appreciate these symbols of the continuity of English rural life.

From his elevated position on the stage he could see his colleagues talking on phones and tapping information into computers. A large whiteboard had been placed against the far wall, dotted with photographs of the victims and the crime scene together with Gerry's scrawled comments. A second board near the stage listed tasks to be undertaken that day. The whole set-up looked incongruous against the Bible scenes painted by infant hands that decorated the other walls.

Because of the double murder, the disappearance of Jocasta Ovorard was now being dealt with by a team left behind at Tradmouth Police Station. After the TV appeal reports of sightings were still coming in from all parts of the country. Witnesses had claimed to have seen Jocasta in Edinburgh, in Aberystwyth, in Manchester and in Yorkshire and each report was being followed up by the local force.

The girl's disappearance had been niggling away at the back of Wesley's mind since he'd made the TV appeal, sitting between the chief superintendent and the girl's father who'd exuded exactly the right mixture of parental worry and political gravitas ... until they were off air when his mask of confidence slipped to allow a glimpse of the man beneath; on the verge of panic and frustrated by his own helplessness. It had been an uncomfortable half-hour and it had left Wesley drained. He was also uncomfortable about the mother's absence from the inquiry and he couldn't help wondering whether Ovorard had told the truth about her being too upset to speak to the police.

His thoughts were interrupted by a CSI who placed a plastic box containing the contents of Andrea Jameson's car on his desk, together with a list of calls made on the victim's phone. Then the man put a smaller box beside it: the contents of the male victim's pockets. As soon as Gerry saw it he came over, rubbing his hands in anticipation.

'Right, Wes, let the dog see the rabbit.'

Wesley stood aside and watched as the DCI lifted the lid of the smaller box.

'Our man travelled light,' he said with a disappointed frown as he viewed the contents of the box. A handkerchief – clean, a watch and a packet of indigestion tablets. A small rucksack contained an Ordnance Survey map of the area, a first-aid kit, a pen and notebook (blank), a penknife, a torch and a beer mat but no phone. Wesley picked up the beer mat and smiled to himself. It bore the name of the Shepherd's Arms; the pub in the village which, according to the sign Wesley had noticed outside, provided en-suite rooms.

Wesley turned his attention to the second, larger box and inside he found an expensive leather handbag with its contents beside it in a plastic bag. There was a mobile phone, an iPad and a glossy brochure for a place called Princebury Hall. It took Wesley a few seconds to realise why the name was familiar.

He stared at the brochure. Andrea Jameson's death in the field bore the hallmarks of an execution-style killing. And she had a connection with Princebury Hall – the place where Della had planned to take Pam.

8

Each time Wesley tried to call Della he reached her voice-mail and he was beginning to feel uneasy. If Princebury Hall was linked to something dangerous, he feared that his mother-in-law wouldn't have the common sense to walk away . . . fast. It was one of Pam's days off work so he called her at home, only to find that she hadn't heard from her mother since she set off for Princebury Hall. When she asked why he wanted to know, he was non-committal. The name of the hall had come up in their inquiries – that was all.

As soon as he'd finished speaking to Pam, his phone rang again and the caller display told him it was Belinda Crillow again. He hesitated before answering. Then he pressed the key and heard her voice. She sounded breathless, as though she'd been running.

'I've had a phone call from him.'

'Who?'

'The man who attacked me.'

'I thought you told my colleagues you didn't know who he was.'

'Yes, but . . .'

'If he called you he must have your number.'

'I . . . I suppose he must. What if he knows where I live?'

Wesley's initial irritation started to melt away. The woman was terrified. 'Tell me exactly what he said?'

'He didn't say anything but I knew he was there.'

Wesley closed his eyes, relieved. 'So you can't be sure it was him? It might have been a call centre. They sometimes—'

'I know it was him. I could hear him breathing. I think he's watching me.' He could hear the panic in her voice; the panic of a woman being stalked by a stranger in the shadows. 'Please. I need to see you.'

'Have you seen anything suspicious?'

'No, but—'

'I'm sorry, Ms Crillow, but I'm in the middle of a murder inquiry at the moment. I'll ask one of my colleagues to call round and take a statement from you.'

'If you came round yourself – if he saw you there – I know he'd stop.' She sounded desperate and this made him feel bad.

'I assure you my colleagues are just as capable of—'

'It's that girl, isn't it? That MP's daughter you were talking about on the TV. You're running around looking for her just because of who her father is while I'm in real danger and—'

'Like I said, Ms Crillow, I'll get on to my colleagues right away. I'm up on Dartmoor at the moment so someone on the spot will be in a better position to help you.'

He felt guilty about fobbing her off again but he had no choice.

Next he made a quick call to the station and DC Rob Carter answered. Rob was bright and hadn't yet come to terms with the fact that most police work is dull and painstaking. Wesley knew he'd be bored by now with sifting through the information coming in on Jocasta Ovorard, so the task of identifying Ms Crillow's tormentor might provide just the challenge he needed.

'She's vulnerable,' Wesley reminded him. 'She was the victim of a particularly nasty robbery eighteen months ago and she lives alone. This recent attack has shaken her so be sympathetic, eh, Rob.'

As soon as he'd finished the call he turned to Rachel and she gave him a warm smile. She'd seemed more relaxed recently, maybe because her wedding to farmer Nigel Haynes was exactly a month away.

'Everyone listed on Andrea Jameson's phone's been contacted,' she said.

'And?'

Rachel perched herself on the edge of his desk. She was wearing a short skirt which rode up to reveal an expanse of thigh. Wesley did his best to focus on the sheet of paper she was holding.

'Andrea was thirty-eight and ran her own business – party planning. She was divorced. No kids.'

'You've spoken to the ex-husband?'

'He lives in New York and hasn't been over here for six months. He's out of the frame.'

'Not necessarily. If he hired someone to get rid of her . . .'

'He's a surgeon.'

'So?' Wesley came from a medical family and, from the gossip he'd heard, he knew members of the caring professions didn't always behave in an exemplary manner.

'The divorce was amicable and nothing's known against him. And she hasn't been making any financial demands.'

'So he says. We can't rule him out just yet.'

Rachel looked sceptical. 'Apparently her business is doing well. She has lots of dealings with the Tradmouth and Millicombe yachting and second-home-owning sets and she owns an apartment overlooking the river in Tradmouth. The new development down by the marina.'

'Nice.'

'As far as family's concerned there's a widowed father in Plymouth who's remarried recently and a brother up north. Both have been spoken to and nothing rings any alarm bells. Everyone we've talked to speaks well of her. She's hard-working. Generous. Popular.'

'Too good to be true?'

Rachel shrugged.

'I want all her friends and contacts interviewed in person. Nobody likes to speak ill of the dead over the phone, do they. And we need someone to do the formal ID.'

'I'll see to it,' said Rachel, scribbling in her notebook.

'What about men?'

Rachel leaned forward. 'One of her friends, a woman called Sally, says there's a man she's been seeing for a while. His number's on her phone but we just reached his voice-mail. Left a message but he hasn't got back to us. Sally said she was due to go on a motivational retreat at Princebury Hall on Friday and the boyfriend was joining her there.'

'What's his name?'

'Jason Fitch. Married, no kids. Owns an IT company. I found his home number and when I called a woman – presumably his wife – answered and said he was away on business. She asked why I was calling but I said it was just routine. Didn't want to give too much away at this stage.'

'Have we an address for him?'

'Dukesbridge. Posh new development.'

'Has someone contacted Princebury Hall?'

'Yes. Both Andrea and Jason were expected on Friday evening but neither of them turned up.'

'Well, we know why Andrea didn't make it but is Jason Fitch our mystery man in the field with her? He didn't look like her type but ...'

Rachel shook her head. 'Her friend Sally met him once so I asked for a description. Fair hair. Six foot. He's not our second victim.'

Before Wesley could reply DC Paul Johnson clattered up the steps at the side of the stage, his lanky runner's frame moving fast. From his keen expression, Wesley could tell he had news.

'House-to-house came up with something interesting. A girl fitting Jocasta Ovorard's description was seen being dropped off near the Shepherd's Arms by a woman in a red Mercedes around six p.m. on Friday. Sounds like our victim's car.'

The mention of the Shepherd's Arms reminded Wesley that the village pub had to be visited as a matter of urgency. The man in the field had been carrying a beer mat bearing the pub's name so it was a fair bet he'd frequented the place – and if their luck was in, he might even have been staying in one of its en-suite rooms.

'I was talking to your curate earlier.'

Oliver Grayling looked puzzled. 'I thought Philip was out all morning.'

'The man I met was called John Davies.'

Oliver frowned. 'You must have misunderstood. Maybe this John Davies just called in to see the church. We have

54

a very impressive rood screen and some nice memorials in the DeTorham chapel.'

Neil shrugged. Like the vicar said, he'd probably misunderstood.

'I wanted to tell you what we found in the lead box.'

The vicar's face clouded. 'A child's remains, I presume.'

Neil waited a few seconds before making his revelation. 'No. It was a carved figure – probably early sixteenth century.' He leaned forward. 'And the best bit is there's a mechanism inside. It's an automaton.'

The vicar opened his mouth to speak but no words came out.

'It's rare to find one so old. It's an exciting discovery.'

'Why bury it like that?'

'My guess is that it was hidden during the Reformation when images and statues were being destroyed on the King's orders, which didn't go down too well around these parts. You can't blame the priest and parishioners for wanting to preserve something they regarded as precious.'

Oliver Grayling glanced at the safe in the corner of the vestry. 'The parish records from the sixteenth century aren't here. You could try the cathedral archives.'

As Neil left his instincts told him that whoever had hidden the automaton so well would hardly have recorded the fact in the parish records and that any evidence would probably have been destroyed centuries ago.

9

The new sighting of Jocasta Ovorard in Lower Torworthy was causing considerable excitement in the incident room. It raised the possibility that their two major cases were connected, but Gerry didn't want to share this fresh development with Jeremy Ovorard until they knew more.

Jocasta's photograph had been shown to everybody in the village and a couple of elderly ladies claimed they'd seen a girl matching her description walking down the road towards the telephone box, a rucksack slung over her shoulder. In addition, a man out walking his golden labrador thought he'd seen her on the back of a motorbike driving away from the village although he couldn't swear to it.

If, as Wesley suspected, there was a link between the village of Lower Torworthy and the disappearance of Jocasta Ovorard, this raised the possibility that the vanished girl was connected in some way to the murders. But had Jocasta met the same fate? If she had seen Andrea's killer the possibility couldn't be ruled out.

His musings were interrupted by Paul Johnson.

'I've got more on Jason Fitch, sir. Seven years ago he married a Sharon Ball.' He paused as though he was saving the best for last. 'Sharon has a brother called Kyle. Ex-army. And when I say "ex" I don't mean he left of his own accord.'

'Chucked out?'

'Spent most of his career in the glasshouse and he's got a record for GBH and ABH. He'd probably know where to get hold of a firearm and he'd certainly know how to use it. Lives in Plymouth.' He paused. 'And according to his local station he's got a nickname – the Hit Man.'

Wesley raised his eyebrows. 'In that case we'd better bring him in.'

But before Wesley could find Gerry and tell him about this promising new development, Trish Walton appeared by his desk giving Paul a sideways look. The pair had been an item at one time and recently Wesley had noticed furtive conversations between them. If the flame had been rekindled no doubt Rachel would enlighten him in due course.

'I've been to the Shepherd's Arms like you asked, sir,' said Trish, slightly breathless. 'The dead man was definitely staying there.'

'Thanks, Trish.'

Gerry had just emerged from the kitchen at the side of the stage, hands in his pockets and completely relaxed as though he didn't have a double murder and the disappearance of a teenage girl to worry about.

'Andrea Jameson's fancy man, Jason Fitch, has a brother-in-law with a history of violence and a knowledge of firearms,' Wesley said as he hurried down to meet him. 'If he's taken exception to his sister being made a fool of he might have taken it into his head to get rid of her rival. The brother-in-law's called Kyle Ball and he lives in Plymouth where he's known as the Hit Man. I'm having him brought in for questioning.'

'Let's hope it's that straightforward so we can start concentrating our resources on this missing girl. I've had Aunty Noreen on again. Mr Ovorard's not happy with our progress.' He rolled his eyes.

'Are we telling him about the Lower Torworthy connection?'

Gerry thought for a moment. 'Not worth worrying him with that till we're sure.'

'Jocasta was last seen near the Shepherd's Arms and Trish has just confirmed that our male victim was staying there.'

'Then we'd better drop in. We can get something to eat while we're there,' Gerry added, rubbing his large stomach. 'Kill two birds with one stone.'

Wesley didn't answer. They didn't have time to dally longer than necessary in country pubs, attractive though the prospect was. But this particular establishment was only yards from the incident room and who knew what they could learn from the staff and regulars.

The Shepherd's Arms was a quintessential English pub with whitewashed walls and a thatched roof. As well as a neat reception desk in the passage to deal with the residential side of the business, there was a tempting array of hand pumps on the polished mahogany bar and as they walked in everyone turned to watch them for a few seconds. The clientele was mixed: holidaymakers enjoying sustaining sandwiches and locals who'd just popped in for a pint. An assortment of dogs – mostly labradors and border collies – lounged at their owners' feet, and water bowls had been provided by the management for their refreshment.

A capable-looking woman in her forties appeared behind the bar with a smile of professional welcome on her face. Her air of confident authority told Wesley that she was the landlady.

Once Wesley had made the introductions, the landlady, whose name was Yvonne Stirling, led them into a back room, issuing orders to her bar staff en route to keep an eye on things.

'I've been expecting you,' she said after inviting them to sit. 'The officer told me one of my guests had been shot. I find it hard to believe it could be anything but a tragic accident.' Her words sounded businesslike, as if she was more concerned for the effect on her trade than the unfortunate man's demise.

Gerry shifted in the stiff leather armchair he'd chosen, trying to get comfortable. 'What can you tell us about him, love?'

'He booked a couple of weeks ago by phone and turned up last Wednesday. He said he wasn't sure how long he was staying but he paid in advance for a fortnight.'

'Is that usual?'

'Some people prefer it.'

'Did he say why he was here?' Wesley asked.

Yvonne looked at him as though she'd only just noticed him for the first time. 'To do some walking, he said. We get a lot of walkers staying here. He seemed a pleasant sort of man. Quiet. Very ordinary really.'

'When did you last see him?'

She thought for a few moments. 'I think it was last Friday at breakfast. Full English.'

'You didn't think to report him missing?'

For the first time Yvonne looked flustered. 'I did wonder whether I should but often serious walkers decide to stay in a bed and breakfast further up the moor for a few nights before coming back. They usually tell me if that's what they're planning to do but I thought he might have forgotten, although I must admit I was a bit concerned, because the moor can be a dangerous place. There are rivers and mine shafts, not to mention the mires. I feel bad about not saying anything now.'

'You weren't to know.' Wesley could tell she was upset. 'He will have given you an address.'

As if she'd anticipated the question she had the hotel register to hand and passed it to Wesley, pointing at the relevant entry.

The name was Ian Evans and he'd given an address in Dorchester. It would be up to the local police to visit his address and break the news to any relatives they could find. Wesley didn't envy them the job.

'Did he mention what he did for a living?'

'He wasn't really the chatty sort. They're all different – walkers. Some like to talk, others would rather commune with nature.'

'Can we see his room?'

She led the way upstairs and unlocked a door at the end of a wide carpeted passage. The floorboards creaked under Wesley's feet. It was an old building and not altogether symmetrical which, in his view, added to its attraction.

Wesley took Jocasta Ovorard's picture from his pocket and handed it to Yvonne. 'Have you ever seen this girl? She was spotted getting out of a red car outside this pub a few days ago.'

'One of your constables has already asked,' Yvonne said as she handed the picture back. 'Sorry. I didn't see her.'

'Did Ian Evans speak to anybody else while he was staying here? Or did he have any visitors?'

'Not that I saw. He was out walking most of the time. He ate here in the bar on Wednesday and Thursday – we serve till nine – and he was definitely on his own. I tried to make conversation but he didn't want to talk. I got the impression he was shy.'

Yvonne opened the door for them and left them to it. The room was bright and airy and the bed neatly made. There were fluffy white towels in the bathroom and the only evidence of Ian Evans's recent occupation was a closed suitcase on a stand in the corner and a wash bag in the bathroom. Wesley opened the case, which contained only underwear, socks and nicely ironed handkerchiefs, before turning his attention to the wardrobe. The clothes inside were hanging neatly – trousers at one side, shirts at the other – suggesting that Ian Evans had been a meticulous man. Wesley thrust his hand into the pocket of a linen jacket dangling from a wooden hanger and his fingers came into contact with a mobile phone, which explained something that had been puzzling him. The killer hadn't taken his phone; it was more than likely the victim had just forgotten to take it with him. Perhaps he'd planned to return to the pub before embarking on a longer walk. Alternatively, he might have realised the signal was patchy in the area and left the phone behind; one less thing to carry.

He passed it to Gerry, who dropped it into an evidence bag. Someone would be given the job of getting in touch with all his contacts. In the meantime, they continued the search but found nothing of any note.

'It's as though he hardly existed, Wes.'

'As someone observed when we found him, he travelled light. He was here to walk so he only brought the bare minimum.'

Gerry looked round. 'Know what I'm thinking, Wes? He was collateral damage. Someone wanted Andrea Jameson dead and he got in the way: wrong place, wrong time. Unless he was meeting Andrea. There might be a connection between them we haven't found yet.'

'There's no Ian on her phone, and none of her contacts live anywhere near Dorchester. I think you might be right about him being collateral damage. We know Andrea had at least one potential enemy – the Hit Man.'

'What about Jocasta?'

'If she was in Andrea's car there's a chance she witnessed the murder.' He paused. 'Which means she might have been eliminated as well and we haven't found her yet. I think we should get sniffer dogs in and make a thorough search of the area.'

'You're right, Wes. Sod the budget.'

Extract from draft PhD thesis
written by Alcuin Garrard

July 1995

In common with many men of science, Sir
Matthew's intentions were good and his sole
aim would appear to be the healing of sick
members of his flock. He was a pious man
who believed in the power of prayer, so the
idea of a praying machine would have made
perfect sense. Although it is a concept we
might find bizarre in modern times, pre-
Reformation Devon languished in the beliefs
of the Middle Ages and only a very few –
who had come under the influence of what
was then known as the 'new learning' –
would have considered these beliefs
superstitious.

There is mention in the parish records
of 'Sir Matthew's workshop and the items
therein' which begs the question of what
a country priest might have made in this
'workshop' of his. There is reference in
October 1531 to a machine made of wood and
iron and the records state that payment was

made to a clockmaker in the city of Exeter
for work of miraculous delicacy.

It is possible that those who knew the
true nature of Sir Matthew's 'miraculous
machine' were sworn to secrecy. And later
developments would suggest that certain
aspects of Sir Matthew's work needed to be
hidden from inquisitive eyes.

10

After leaving the Shepherd's Arms Wesley returned to Tradmouth Police Station, intending to go through everything he'd learned so far without the inevitable interruptions of the incident room. As Gerry had stayed in Lower Torworthy Wesley grabbed the opportunity to shut himself away in the boss's office with his notebook and his thoughts.

Through Gerry's glass door he could see the team outside in the main CID office, working on the Jocasta Ovorard case with new urgency. Earlier Wesley had asked Rob Carter whether he'd made any progress with the attack on Belinda Crillow but Rob had answered in the negative: Ms Crillow hadn't been able to identify her attacker so it was hard to know where to begin. The only clue, if you could call it that, was that she thought the attack was linked to the break-in at her last address eighteen months ago; and nobody had been caught for that particular crime. It had been one of Wesley's failures.

A couple of hours passed before Wesley received a call to say that nothing out of the ordinary had been found on Ian Evans's phone; just calls from family, colleagues and friends from his walking club. Also someone had called at

Kyle Ball's Plymouth flat but there'd been nobody at home and, according to the neighbours, Ball hadn't been seen for a few days. Another visit had been paid to Jason Fitch's address but again there'd been no answer.

The delays were frustrating but Wesley decided to use the time productively by following another lead. Andrea Jameson hadn't turned up at Princebury Hall and neither had Jason Fitch but Wesley reckoned he might learn something from visiting the place himself. Besides, Della was there so there was a chance she might be able to supply some inside information – although he wasn't getting his hopes up.

He was clarifying things in his mind when Gerry's phone rang. When he answered he heard the voice of Jeremy Ovorard MP.

'I need to speak to you,' he heard Ovorard say. 'I've just finished a constituency meeting so I can be with you in twenty minutes.'

Wesley experienced a sudden surge of panic. He had no reassuring news for the man and the possibility that Jocasta had been murdered like the others was weighing on his mind. But at least this impromptu meeting might allow him to gain some further insight into the missing girl's life. Last time he and Ovorard had met they'd both been focused on the TV appeal and there were questions he hadn't had a chance to ask.

When Ovorard arrived he took him into one of the interview rooms; the one reserved for witnesses and vulnerable victims. It was comfortable, with tea-making facilities and soft furnishings, unlike the spartan interview rooms used for questioning suspects.

Ovorard's former confidence seemed to have vanished.

He was fidgeting nervously with his shirt cuffs and for the first time Wesley found himself warming to him.

'I take it there's no news?' he said after refusing Wesley's offer of tea.

'We're doing our very best, Mr Ovorard. Every police force in the country is on the lookout for her and there have been sightings. I assure you every one is being followed up.'

'But you've made no real progress?'

'There's been a promising sighting on Dartmoor.' Wesley thought it best not to mention the link with Andrea Jameson. There was no point worrying him before they knew anything for sure.

'Dartmoor?' Ovorard's voice squeaked with surprise. 'That couldn't be Jocasta. The countryside "freaks her out", as she puts it. Has the Met been alerted?'

'They've been notified, of course. You think she might be in London?'

'It's possible.' Ovorard's reply was guarded.

This was the first mention of the capital and Wesley wondered whether the girl's father knew something he was reluctant to share with them. 'Does Jocasta have friends in London?'

'Not that I'm aware of. When she wasn't at school she always stayed in Morbay with her mother while I was in Westminster. I have a small pied-à-terre near Parliament but it's hardly suitable for a family.'

'I presume you've checked she isn't there?' If her father had a place in the capital, he thought, it was surely possible that Jocasta had gone there to sample the bright lights for a change. Perhaps the girl seen in Lower Torworthy hadn't been her after all.

The MP's face reddened. 'Er ... someone's already checked. She's definitely not there.'

Wesley nodded. It would have been a happy solution to the case but it wasn't to be.

'What about Jocasta's boarding school? Did she have any friends there?'

'I doubt it. She described the other girls as "sad" and I don't think she meant they were unhappy.'

'Has Jocasta ever mentioned a place called Lower Torworthy?'

'I don't think so.'

'What kind of girl is she?' he asked gently.

Ovorard didn't answer for a while and Wesley couldn't shake off the feeling that there was something he wasn't sharing with the police. Then he broke the silence. 'She led her own life.'

It seemed a sad thing for a father to say about a daughter. 'So you aren't close?'

'Not particularly. I'm away a lot.'

'She must be closer to her mother?'

'Perhaps.'

'I really would like to speak to your wife. Or maybe she'd prefer to talk to a woman officer ... '

The man's expression suddenly hardened and he pressed his lips together in a stubborn line. 'As I said before, she's too upset to speak to anybody.'

'Are you absolutely sure your daughter doesn't have a boyfriend?'

'I've already told you. No.'

'Teenagers have secrets from their parents. It's all part of growing up. But if those secrets are dangerous you have to worry. Is there any chance Jocasta's become involved in something she'd rather you didn't know about?'

When Jeremy Ovorard got up and walked out Wesley knew he'd touched a nerve.

Neil had spent the afternoon putting the finishing touches to the site report for the large rescue excavation in Exeter he'd headed earlier in the year. The medieval graffiti survey in Lower Torworthy church was ongoing.

St Bartholomew's was rich in carvings made by parishioners over the centuries, especially in times of trouble. Some reckoned these protective symbols to ward off evil represented foolish superstition but Neil suspected they'd fulfilled a deep need in rural people of the past, who'd had no control over nature or their own destiny in the often harsh Dartmoor landscape.

But it was the mystery of the little wooden automaton that was at the forefront of his mind. He'd been in touch with Annabel, who worked in the archives in Exeter and usually knew where to lay her hands on any historical documents he needed in the course of his work. Annabel hung round with the county's hunting and shooting set. She was way out of his league socially but their professional relationship had always been mildly flirtatious so he felt obliged to switch on the charm whenever he called her – not an easy thing for a man most at home squatting in a muddy trench.

Annabel had promised to search for any fifteenth- or sixteenth-century records that mentioned Lower Torworthy but she hadn't been particularly optimistic. So much precious medieval stuff had been destroyed by the Luftwaffe during the Baedeker raids, she'd told him sadly.

He returned to his Exeter flat feeling restless and mildly depressed. Since Lucy Zinara had left in the spring to take charge of a dig in archaeology-rich Orkney, he'd lived there alone and, although he'd never admitted it to anyone, including Lucy herself, he found himself longing for her return. Archaeology isn't a solitary occupation and all was well during the day while he was working. But when he returned to his empty flat the loneliness hit him. In his younger years the camaraderie of the dig had been all he needed but now he looked on his friend Wesley Peterson with something approaching envy. Wesley had a wife and two growing children and Neil was starting to wonder whether he'd missed out, something that wouldn't have occurred to him just a year ago.

After he'd eaten his ready meal on his knee in front of the TV he eyed his phone, tempted to call Lucy, just to hear her voice, but something made him hold back. The last thing he wanted was to make her feel pressured.

Then to his surprise his phone began to ring and he saw Wesley's name on the caller display.

'Hi, Wes. How's it going? Found your missing girl yet?' He suddenly realised his friend was investigating the disappearance of somebody's child and his cheerful enquiry probably sounded insensitive.

But Wesley hadn't seemed to notice. 'Still ongoing, I'm afraid.'

'I saw you making that TV appeal. Fine performance.'

'Thanks.'

'I've been working in Lower Torworthy and I saw all the police activity. Double murder they said on the news. One of yours?'

70

'Afraid so. Two people were shot in a field outside the village.'

'So I heard. That particular field features in the Historic Environment Record, you know – site of an old manor house. But I don't suppose that has anything to do with your case.'

'Probably not.' There was regret in Wesley's voice. Neil knew that archaeology still interested him, although these days he didn't have time for it.

'We've set up an incident room in the church hall,' Wesley continued.

'I saw all the activity. I looked out for you but there was no sign.' Neil paused. 'I haven't seen you since that strange dig at Newfield Manor.'

'Sorry I haven't been in touch but I haven't had a moment. Look, Neil, I need a favour.'

'Name it.'

'Can you put me in touch with a local metal detectorist? Someone absolutely reliable. Our CSIs reckon it'd speed up their search of the crime scene.'

'There's a bloke called Charlie Perks who lives about a mile from Lower Torworthy. He's helped us out on a lot of digs in the Dartmoor area. His equipment's state-of-the-art and he's completely reliable. Always hands anything of interest to the local finds liaison officer.'

'Honest then.'

'Absolutely. I'd give you his number, only I often have trouble getting hold of him. He hasn't got a landline and his mobile signal is temperamental to say the least so it's probably best if I ask him to call you.' He walked across the room and took his contacts book from the pocket of his favourite digging garment – an ancient, many-pocketed combat jacket hanging in his tiny hallway. 'I've got his address and I can call in tomorrow morning. Unless you want to ...'

'No, the request's probably better coming from you. Thanks. I owe you one.'

'I haven't told you about my latest find yet.'

'What is it?'

Neil knew he'd aroused his friend's interest.

'A workman from the Water Board, or whatever they call it now, found a lead box in a trench they were digging just outside the wall of the churchyard and he thought it might be a burial.'

'Was it?'

'Not exactly. I'd expected to find a child's body and I had Margaret and the team lined up to deal with it in the lab. But when the box was opened we found a wooden figure. At first we presumed it was the statue of some saint, buried during the Reformation. Then the side fell off and we saw a mechanism inside. It looks like some sort of early automaton. We're consulting the Mechanical Engineering Department at the university.'

'Amazing.' Wesley sounded impressed. 'When I've got a moment, I'd love to see it.'

'Any time.'

'Thanks. Sorry, Neil, I've got to go.'

Afterwards Neil stared at the phone for a few seconds. Wesley had sounded harassed and he realised he hadn't asked after Pam. Her diagnosis in the spring had cast a shadow over their friendship as the unwelcome glimpse of darkness intruded into Wesley's life. Neil had known Pam since their student days – they'd once gone out together before she chose Wesley – so her illness had shocked him too.

He was clearing away his dirty plate when he heard the scraping of a key in his lock. He watched as the door opened slowly. Then he smiled.

11

As soon as his interview with Jeremy Ovorard was over Wesley returned to Lower Torworthy to report back to Gerry. It was 6.30 already and he knew it would be a late night.

'Ovorard became a bit touchy when I asked whether Jocasta had a boyfriend and he still doesn't want us to talk to her mother.'

Gerry leaned forward. 'Suspicious?'

'Probably just being protective. Even so, I'd like to speak to Mrs Ovorard sooner rather than later.' Wesley examined the sheet of paper he'd scribbled notes on; things he needed to remember. 'I'm arranging for a local metal detectorist to help the CSIs locate the bullets. He comes highly recommended by Neil and it'll speed things up. Neil's fixing it up tomorrow.'

Gerry scratched his head. 'Good idea. While you were out I heard from Dorset. Someone's been round to Ian Evans's address in Dorchester. He lived with his old mum so we need to pay her a visit.'

'Before we do I'd like to visit Princebury Hall. For all we know Jason Fitch might have turned up after all.'

'Can't you phone to check?'

'I'd rather go and see for myself. If Andrea Jameson and Jason Fitch have stayed there before someone might be able to tell us something about them. You can't see people's faces when you're talking on the phone – can't tell when they're lying.'

'One of the DCs has already been up there.'

'I know, but it's only a couple of miles away. Come on, Gerry, the fresh air will do you good.'

'I take it there's still no sign of our so-called "Hit Man"?'

'Afraid not.' Wesley had given the matter some thought and concluded that no bona fide hit man would be so indiscreet about the nature of his business. But, due to the calculated nature of the recent murders, the name still buzzed in the back of his mind like an annoying wasp.

Gerry gave a loud sigh and hoisted himself out of his seat. 'Right then, Princebury Hall it is. Isn't your mother-in-law up there at the moment?'

'Yes.'

'Then with any luck she'll have some inside info for us.'

Wesley led the way out of the incident room, stopping at desks to check whether anything new had come in. But it hadn't, and there was still no word of Jocasta Ovorard from the police station at Tradmouth.

'Someone needs to speak to Jocasta's classmates at her old school,' Wesley said as they climbed into the car. 'Her father said she had no friends there but she might have told him that for reasons of her own.'

'Mmm,' said Gerry. 'They can be very secretive at that age. We'll put it on our list. Where is the school?'

'Near Ilfracombe.'

'Not that far then.'

The light was starting to fade and as Wesley programmed

Princebury Hall into his sat nav it struck him that the surrounding landscape – the rolling fields laced with drystone walls beneath the vast grey sky – would be desolate in winter. He wondered whether Xander Southwark still ran his courses in the unkinder months.

Half a mile outside the village they passed the murder site, cordoned off with crime-scene tape, and as Wesley drove on a thin mist started to descend, blending with the twilight and forcing him to switch on the headlights. They met no other vehicles but from time to time a small animal appeared in the beam and scurried off into the dusk.

Princebury Hall stood two miles from Lower Torworthy, meaning Andrea Jameson had almost reached her destination when she met her death. It was tucked into a hollow in the landscape, shielded from the road by trees. Wesley's headlights picked out the new-looking sign beside a stone gate which bore the words Princebury Hall Well-being Centre.

'I could do with some well-being,' Gerry muttered beside him.

'Couldn't we all.'

Wesley continued up the drive until the Hall appeared before him. It was a large stone house with tall chimneys and a long oriel window to the left of the central doorway. Wesley, who'd always taken an interest in architectural history, could tell it dated from the sixteenth century and that it had been a high-status home in times gone by.

Figures in tracksuits milled in and out of the well-lit main door and as he brought the car to a halt a group of people – all young, slim and dressed in dark-blue polo shirts bearing the Hall's embroidered logo – watched his arrival with curiosity.

'I'll have to be careful or they'll put me on carrot juice,' said Gerry in a loud whisper.

'Might not be a bad thing,' said Wesley, glancing at his boss's protruding stomach.

He led the way in and asked one of the polo shirts, a bearded young man whose badge announced that his name was Dylan, where he could find Xander Southwark. Dylan was gushingly helpful as he accompanied them up a wide oak staircase to an office on the first floor. The door was open and as Dylan slid away the man sitting behind the desk rose to greet them, pushing a pile of paperwork to one side. Even at this time of day when most people were looking forward to an evening of relaxation, he was on duty. At least he and the police had that in common.

Xander Southwark had a ponytail and a golden tan. When he stood Wesley noticed that he was tall and muscular with an unmistakable air of authority.

'I've already spoken to your colleagues about Andrea,' he began. 'Terrible business.' He bowed his head for a moment as though he was paying his respects. Then he emerged from behind his desk and closed the office door before inviting them to sit on a sofa in the corner. As he made his way to the chair opposite Wesley noticed he walked with a pronounced limp: a single flaw in the picture of health and vigour.

'I understand Ms Jameson had arranged to meet someone here,' Wesley began. 'A Jason Fitch.'

'Jason booked in at the same time as Andrea but he never arrived. He didn't phone to cancel either, which isn't like him at all.'

'You know Jason Fitch?' Wesley noted the use of first

names – although perhaps it was that sort of establishment.

'He's visited us before, yes, although I wouldn't say I know him well. I find it best to keep a professional distance from the souls we help here. It must be the same in your line of business.' He smiled, showing a row of perfect teeth.

'What can you tell us about him?'

'He's stayed with us a total of four times and on three other occasions he booked and had to cancel at the last minute, which often happens with busy people. I understand he has his own business.'

'Can you tell me anything about his personal life?'

'I can't discuss that, I'm afraid. Our clients rely on our discretion, so unless you have a warrant I can't help you.' He paused as though he was making a decision. 'But I can tell you he's been here with Andrea twice.'

'What about the other two occasions?'

Southwark hesitated. 'Er . . . he was with another lady.'

'We'll need her name.' Wesley took out his notebook.

'Sorry, that's confidential.'

'This is a murder inquiry, sir,' Wesley said, aware that the words sounded like a cliché from a TV cop show. 'And we can be discreet too.'

Southwark considered the matter for a few seconds. 'My assistant will provide you with Andrea's details but I'm afraid that's all I can give you until you obtain a warrant.' He sounded pleased with himself, as though he was enjoying getting one over on the police.

'Is it true you've served time in prison?' said Wesley with scrupulous politeness.

Xander Southwark smiled. 'I make no secret of it. Acknowledging what I did in the past helps me to help others. I've overcome adversity and so can they. As well as healing and meditation we specialise in life coaching and counselling here at Princebury Hall. People come to us with problems and, hopefully, leave with solutions.'

Wesley recognised a sales pitch when he heard one.

'What were you inside for?' Gerry's question was blunt but Wesley knew it was meant to be.

'In my former life I was a solicitor and I stole money from my firm's client account. I'd run up heavy debts and convinced myself I could borrow the money to tide me over then pay it back before anyone noticed but there was an audit and … I learned my lesson in jail and began a new life. I help my clients to do the same.' The smoothness of his answer made Wesley suspect that it was a story he'd told often.

'Where did you get the cash to buy this place?'

Southwark gave Gerry a curious look.

'If you must know it was an inheritance and the rest of what I needed came from an understanding bank whose faith in my project paid off, I'm delighted to say.' Southwark handed a glossy brochure to Wesley. 'You have a stressful job, Inspector. I'm sure you'd find one of our courses beneficial.'

When Gerry grunted he was handed a brochure too.

'What can you tell us about Andrea Jameson?' Wesley asked. 'She's dead so you won't be breaking any confidences.'

'She was a businesswoman who ran a successful company in Tradmouth, but I'm afraid that's all I can tell you.' Southwark stood up. 'If you'll excuse me I have a counselling session in ten minutes.'

'Did you get the impression he was keen to get rid of

us?' Gerry said as they walked across the thickly carpeted landing to the staircase.

Before Wesley could respond he spotted a familiar figure flapping towards them. Della was wearing a voluminous bright yellow kaftan; it wasn't her colour. She came to a sudden halt when she saw them and Wesley thought she looked embarrassed, something he'd never expected to see.

Gerry nudged his arm. 'Aren't you going to say hello?'

'Hello, Della. How's it going?'

'Are you here to check up on me?'

'Don't flatter yourself, I'm here on an investigation. I've been trying to call you.'

'We're not allowed phones. Besides, I'm told the signal's rubbish.'

Wesley looked round and lowered his voice. 'These counselling sessions – do people tend to reveal their innermost secrets, that sort of thing?'

The question appeared to take her by surprise. 'Xander says we have to be completely honest or we'll never overcome our past.'

'Are the sessions recorded?' Gerry asked.

'What's wrong with that?'

'Nothing.'

Gerry turned to go and Wesley did likewise.

'Is that all?' She sounded disappointed.

Wesley told her to enjoy her course and they left her on the landing. When he glanced back he saw a forlorn expression on her face, as though they'd just abandoned her.

'What do you reckon?' Gerry asked as they walked back to the car.

Wesley considered the question for a while. Xander

Southwark had refused them access to the address of Jason Fitch's other lady friend and he was sure he'd known Fitch a lot better than he'd admitted. 'I think we might need that search warrant.'

12

The following morning Rachel Tracey set off for Jocasta's old school, her colleague and house-mate DC Trish Walton beside her in the passenger seat. Wesley had observed that no teenage girl is an island; Jocasta Ovorard was bound to have confided in one or more of her former classmates.

Rachel knew that people didn't go out deliberately to get themselves murdered in the run-up to her wedding but the timing was lousy. With the double murder and Jocasta's disappearance she'd be working long hours for the foreseeable future so she wouldn't see much of Nigel, let alone have time to do all those little jobs that fell to a bride these days. She was lucky her mother was only too happy to shoulder some of the burden. Even so, Rachel felt she was missing out on something – although she wasn't quite sure what it was.

'Thought about your hen night?' Trish said, breaking the amicable silence.

'Not really,' Rachel replied in a tone that discouraged further enquiry.

Trish remained silent as they drove over the moor towards their destination. Travelling across the top of

Dartmoor, avoiding the sheep and ponies wandering on to the road, brought it home to Rachel how large the county of Devon was. The landscape up there looked barren and sinister, with few trees and great granite tors looming from the swirling, patchy mist, quite unlike the kinder country-side around Lower Torworthy. Her hands tightened on the steering wheel as she navigated her way along the empty road and by the time she reached the school she felt quite unnerved, although that might have been because she hadn't been sleeping too well of late.

Widedales School stood a couple of miles outside the North Devon seaside town of Ilfracombe and the huge red-brick Gothic building looked as if it might once have been a hospital or an asylum; the sort of place the Victorians considered the height of fashion and modern taste regarded as monstrosities.

The school secretary was younger than Rachel had expected and as she led them to the headmistress's study she made polite conversation about the vagaries of the Devon weather. Trish answered pleasantly but Rachel couldn't be bothered. Her own schooldays had been spent in her local comprehensive and she didn't feel comfort-able in a place she associated with stuffy privilege. She knew Wesley's parents, both doctors who'd come from the Caribbean to train for their chosen profession, had sent him to a well-known public school in London but, in general, she didn't like the sense of entitlement those kind of places engendered. Wesley, to her mind, was the exception.

The headmistress, a tall, gaunt woman with a well-cut suit and a crushing handshake, answered their questions with apparent candour but revealed little about her former student. When they asked to see her classmates, she looked uneasy.

They were provided with tea and biscuits while the girls who, presumably, knew Jocasta best were singled out and rounded up from their various lessons and free periods. Forty minutes later they were faced with a queue of seven sixth-form girls. To Rachel they all looked grown-up, beautiful and confident. She was sure she hadn't been like that at their age and found them a little intimidating.

They interviewed the girls one by one in the empty staffroom and the first six all told the same story, almost as though it had been rehearsed: Jocasta was stand-offish and considered herself above them. Unsurprisingly this hadn't gone down well and they made no secret of their dislike. No wonder, Rachel thought, she'd been keen to leave and embark on her drama course – although it didn't look as if she'd made many friends there either. As she listened to the classmates' damning verdicts she began to feel a little sorry for Jocasta Ovorard.

The final girl they interviewed was called Finola and as soon as she told them she'd actually shared a room with Jocasta, Rachel felt more hopeful. If Jocasta had confided in anybody it would be her room-mate. She and Trish had shared many confidences over a glass of wine in the living room of their cottage.

Finola was small and pretty with a generous mouth and turned-up nose. She looked nervous so Rachel gave her an encouraging smile, like a dentist assuring a patient that the treatment wasn't going to hurt a bit.

'I understand you shared a room with Jocasta,' she began.

The girl nodded.

'Would you say you knew her best of all the girls here?'

Her narrow shoulders lifted slightly in a wary shrug. 'Probably.'

'Tell us what she's like. And be honest. She's been missing for a while now and her parents are very worried so anything you can tell us might help us find her.'

Finola cleared her throat. 'She hated it here. The others gave her a hard time.'

'Why was that?'

'I guess she only had herself to blame. She was always going on about her big plans: drama school then an acting career. She said she had contacts. She sneered at anything they said. Louise wants to read philosophy at uni and Jo said that was really stupid. Harriet's brilliant at maths but she said that was really boring. She was always trying to bring people down.'

'What about you?'

'Once I realised she was doing it because she was insecure, I felt sorry for her to tell the truth.'

Trish had been sitting beside Rachel taking notes but she broke her silence and asked the next question. 'What was she insecure about?'

'Something to do with her parents, I think. Her dad's an MP and he's often in London which she said suited her fine 'cause he's a creep.'

'Funny thing to say about your own dad.'

'You're right. She always changed the subject whenever he was mentioned.'

'Did she say anything else?'

There was a long silence. 'She did say once that she could never take any friends home.'

'What do you think she meant by that?'

'She didn't elaborate but there was something about the way she said it . . . ' She thought for a moment. 'Maybe it was because of her mum. I think she had problems . . . with her nerves. Mind you, Jo might have been making it all up to add a bit of drama to her life. People do that a lot here.'

'What do you know about her mother?'

'Only that Jo didn't get on with her either.' There was a long pause. 'She said her mum had other interests.'

'Such as?'

Trish and Rachel waited for her to continue and after a few seconds their patience was rewarded.

'She said her mum had a boyfriend. In his late twenties and a bit of a hunk,' Finola revealed with a sly smile. 'Jo said she hated him but I knew she was lying. I think she fancied him herself.'

'Know his name?'

'Sorry.'

'Did Jo have a boyfriend?'

'I think there was somebody but she never confided in me. Sometimes she used to disappear at weekends and come back with a smug look on her face. This place is like that prison up on the moor and just as hard to escape from – but there are ways if you're really determined. And if anyone was determined it'd be Jo. She hated it here and I don't blame her.'

'You've stuck it out,' said Rachel.

'I'm interested in my grades. I want to read medicine at Cambridge.'

'Good luck,' said Trish as the girl stood up to leave.

'What did you think?' Trish asked once Finola had left the room.

'I think someone needs to have a word with the mother and her toy boy – if he exists,' Rachel replied with a grin.

'What about Jeremy Ovorard?'

Rachel didn't answer.

After Lucy Zinara's arrival the previous evening she and Neil had spent the night in bed making up for the lost summer months, breaking off their reunion only to go out and buy a midnight kebab, something that made Neil feel like a carefree student again.

Lucy had asked after Pam Peterson. Neil said she appeared to be doing really well and that he'd seen a lot of Wesley while he'd been in charge of a strange, privately funded dig at Newfield Manor near the village of Whitely, although that was weeks ago. Time flew, he said, which must be a sign of advancing age. Lucy had laughed at his joke – always a good sign.

The Orkney dig was finished and somebody else was writing up the reports so for the time being Lucy was free. Neil, however, had work to do. He had to go over to the university to see what was happening with the wooden figure he'd told her about, and after that he'd arranged to meet his group of volunteers to continue the graffiti survey at Lower Torworthy church. He told Lucy there was a chance they might bump into Wesley there because there'd been a shooting near the village and the place was swarming with police, dismissing the dramatic event with a wave of his hand. Archaeology excited both of them more than murder.

When Neil and Lucy arrived at the university the little monk, as Neil now thought of it, was standing on a steel table in the centre of the lab; a relic of the medieval world incongruous against the utilitarian surroundings.

Lucy walked round the table, examining the figure from all angles. Its side was open and the mechanism inside visible. It looked to Neil as though it had been cleaned up since he last saw it.

'I've never seen anything like it,' she said.

At that moment a large middle-aged woman in a shapeless navy-blue dress entered the room. She made straight for Neil, her hand outstretched.

'Dr Watson. I was told to expect you. I'm Dr Fletcher. Susan. Department of Mechanical Engineering. Interesting thing you've got here – from an engineering point of view – although I suspect it's more a clockmaker's province than mine. In fact it was a clockmaker I know who helped to get it going. It's surprisingly intricate for such an early date. Sixteenth century, you say?'

'Late fifteenth or early sixteenth – certainly pre-Reformation.'

She nodded. 'It's well preserved. My clockmaker friend went into rhapsodies when he examined the mechanism – said it was quite beautiful. I said it was a shame it couldn't be seen and appreciated but he pointed out that in a less enlightened time than our own that wouldn't be considered important as long as God could see it. Do you want to see it working?'

Neil looked at Lucy. 'Of course.'

Dr Fletcher turned the figure round carefully and depressed a lever in the open side. As soon as she replaced the wooden cover the thing began to move.

It shuffled forward, a little unsteady on its wooden feet, and raised its arms, all the time moving its hinged mouth as if in silent prayer. After it had moved forward a foot or so it turned and began to beat its breast. Then the head turned from left to right and the left arm was raised in blessing. Dr Fletcher allowed the routine to be repeated twice more before she removed the wooden cover and pressed the lever to stop it.

'I know it's always hard to pin you archaeologists and historians down to facts but I must confess I'm curious about this little chap,' she said. 'Do you know why it was made?'

It was Lucy who answered. 'A couple of years ago I read about something like this in a journal. It was a mechanical friar made for Philip the Second of Spain in the sixteenth century – a sort of prayer machine. The theory was that Philip had it made to pray for the recovery of his son.'

'Did it work?' Dr Fletcher asked. Neil could hear scepticism in her voice.

'He recovered but it didn't do him much good. He was mentally unstable and his father had him locked up; he died in solitary confinement. That particular machine's in Washington DC – in the Smithsonian collection.'

'So how did a similar one get to rural Devon?' she asked.

'That's something we want to find out.'

Neil was gratified by Lucy's use of the word 'we'.

'I showed it to someone from the History Department,' Dr Fletcher continued. 'He said he was sure that someone was researching something similar back in the nineties but he couldn't remember any details. It might be worth following up.'

Neil looked at his watch. Much as he'd like to investigate further, he had to be at Lower Torworthy.

*

Jason Fitch lived just outside Dukesbridge in a modern detached house on the main road into the town. The house stood apart from its neighbours and had new grey-framed windows and a small, glass-fronted balcony above the front door. Wesley guessed it had only recently been built with no expense spared and Gerry observed that Fitch's work in IT must be considerably more lucrative than working for the police.

They parked down the road because they didn't want to give Fitch prior warning of their visit if he was lying low indoors. But when they knocked on the door all they heard was distant birdsong, passing traffic and the faint buzz of a neighbour's lawnmower.

'He's not in, Wes. Must have gone away.'

'Like his brother-in-law.'

'All patrols are on the lookout for our so-called Hit Man so he's bound to be picked up before long.' Gerry had always had an optimistic streak.

'I'm having a look round the back,' Wesley said, making for the side gate. Luckily it was unlocked and they found themselves in a large garden with an immaculate lawn.

'Philandering isn't his only hobby then,' said Gerry.

'Perhaps his wife's the gardener – or they get someone in.'

Before Gerry could reply Wesley heard a voice.

'Can I help you?' The tone was scrupulously polite with an undercurrent of challenge.

When Wesley looked round he saw a grey head poking over the wooden fence to their right. If there's one thing any detective likes, it's a nosy neighbour.

When they introduced themselves the man gave a knowing smile.

'Do you know where we can find Mr and Mrs Fitch?'

'I saw them piling suitcases into the car on Sunday, which surprised me because they hadn't mentioned they were going on holiday. I usually keep an eye on things for them, you see.' He suddenly frowned, as though he feared they were there to impart tragic news. 'Has something happened? An accident?'

'Nothing like that. We just need to talk to them,' said Wesley.

'Mrs Fitch's brother was with them on Sunday.'

'Would that be Kyle Ball?'

'I don't know his name but he's a stocky man with lots of tattoos,' the neighbour said with disapproval. 'I tried to speak to him once and he was quite rude.'

'Did he go with them?'

'No. He stayed behind for a bit then he drove off.'

'You didn't happen to overhear what they were saying, I suppose?' Wesley asked. Gerry was listening carefully, awaiting the answer.

'Not really. But I could tell Sharon – Mrs Fitch – was upset about something. Giving Jason a hard time, she was. Wouldn't have liked to be in his shoes.' The man raised a hand as though he'd just remembered something. 'Of course they might have gone to the cottage in Littlebury. Jason inherited it from his grandmother and they often go there at weekends out of season when they're not renting it out to holidaymakers.'

'Know the address?' Gerry asked hopefully.

The neighbour shook his head.

Extract from draft PhD thesis written by Alcuin Garrard

July 1995

Sir Matthew's records contain a detailed account of the day-to-day work of the church. Offerings brought by his pious flock were stored under the watchful eyes of the churchwardens and later distributed amongst the needy or used for the upkeep of the church. Money was also raised at the church ales, social gatherings held in the church to celebrate holy festivals – of which there were many.

Sometimes new images of saints were made for the church. In 1528 Sir Matthew commissioned a new carved and gilded image of St Sidwell – a venerated Exeter saint – and placed it above the side altar where she soon became a focus of devotion. After this it seems that Sir Matthew, who refers to himself several times as 'the son of a carpenter like Our Lord himself', began to make images of his own. Eventually he started experimenting with new techniques

and ideas and this culminated in the
creation of his 'little monk'.

However, there is no indication that he
foresaw the trouble his innocent innovation
would ultimately unleash into the village of
Lower Torworthy.

13

Rachel was satisfied that their visit to Widedales School hadn't been a waste of time. They now knew that Jocasta Ovorard didn't get on with her parents and kept them away from her friends and she wondered whether this had something to do with her father; the man she described as a creep. But if there was anything untoward about Jeremy Ovorard surely every tabloid journalist in the land would be after him. There was always somebody out there ready to blow the whistle ... eventually. Rachel thought it more likely that a teenage girl with problems was kicking out against her family, something she'd seen happen many times.

They'd also discovered that her parents' marriage was unhappy and that her mother might or might not be involved with a younger man. According to her husband, Jocasta's mother was too upset to talk to the police but now Rachel wondered if there was another reason for her reluctance. She knew Wesley wanted to speak to the mother – and now there might be her lover to consider – although she also knew that any approach would require tact.

The echoing acoustics in the incident room made her

head throb so she retreated to the kitchen behind the stage and took a couple of paracetamols. The DCI and Wesley hadn't yet returned from Jason Fitch's house in Dukesbridge so she decided to get some fresh air.

She stood outside the church hall for a while watching the comings and goings at the Shepherd's Arms opposite. Ian Evans, the shooting victim, had been staying there and she knew that Dorset police would have broken the news to his mother by now. They'd have to talk to his family in due course and she suspected that she'd be given the job. She had a reputation for being good with bereaved relatives, although facing other people's grief was something she always dreaded.

A man wearing an old waxed jacket and cloth cap had just emerged from the front door of the pub with a border collie at his heels. He had the leathery complexion of one who spent his life out of doors and Rachel recognised him at once. He looked across at her and when she waved Dan Noakes raised a hand in acknowledgement before crossing the road to join her, the dog trotting at his heels.

'Sergeant. Have you found who killed them yet?'

Rachel bent and patted the dog, who gazed up at her with soulful brown eyes. She loved dogs; she'd lived with them all her childhood on her parents' farm and missed having them around now she was sharing with Trish. Of course once she was married to a farmer that would change and they'd become part of her life again. At times she wondered whether she was looking forward to that more than the actual wedding.

'We're following several lines of inquiry,' she said. 'Did you know one of the victims was staying at the Shepherd's Arms? Did you ever see him there?'

Dan shuffled his feet. 'I didn't take a good look at him in that field, maid. Didn't seem proper to stare.' He paused. 'You got a picture?'

Rachel had pictures of both victims in her pocket. Ian Evans's image had been provided by his mother and sent through by Dorset police. In it Evans was wearing a suit with a carnation in the buttonhole and smiling stiffly at the camera as though he'd rather be somewhere else. She passed it to Dan, who fished in his pocket for a pair of reading glasses.

'Aye, I'm sure I saw him in the Shepherd's, sitting on his own in the corner with a half of bitter. He looked like a typical walker so I didn't take much notice 'cause we get a lot around here. When I found ... you know, I never put two and two together or I would have said.'

Rachel smiled. 'I'm sure you would. Is there anything else you can tell me?' Her headache was receding now. She stroked the dog again and as she ruffled his silky fur she was rewarded by a wag of his tail.

'Odd,' the farmer said.

'What is?'

'That they were found in Manor Field the same as the other one.'

'What other one?'

'Poor lad who fell and hit his head on that bit of old wall. It was in the papers at the time.'

'When was this?'

'Let me see.' Dan's brow furrowed in concentration as he did an impromptu calculation on his fingers. ''Ninety-five it was. Lot of fuss there was at the time.'

In 1995 Rachel had been a schoolgirl, already eager to join the police and make her mark. When she'd lived at home she known most of the families who farmed near her parents and the inevitable gossip about local goings-on, but Lower Torworthy had been off her patch.

'What was the name of the man who died?'

'Can't rightly remember, my lover,' he said, using the traditional Devon form of address. Rachel thought nothing of it but she knew it had amused Wesley when he'd first arrived in the area. 'But he had something to do with the university in Exeter.'

'A student?'

'Maybe. Lying by the old wall he was ... not far from where that walker was found. There used to be a big house in that field and that bit of wall's all that's left of it. In the old days they used to say the place was cursed.'

In spite of the excitement Neil hadn't forgotten his promise to call on Charlie Perks. But as he drove out of the Exeter suburbs and on to the winding Dartmoor roads his mind was on the mystery of the strange little automaton. When word got out it would cause a sensation – and he needed to find out more about it.

He reached Lower Torworthy but instead of parking outside the Shepherd's Arms, he carried on to Charlie Perks's address.

He pulled up in front of a small, shabby cottage standing on a lane that meandered off the B road to Princebury Hall, although the title 'lane' was probably generous; it was little more than a track and Neil feared for his suspension.

The tiny front garden was better kept than the cottage, with roses still in bloom and a neatly trimmed hedge separating it from the lane. The cottage walls were salmon-pink, stained with lichen, and the front door was a dull shade of red. As with the window frames, the paint on the door had flaked off to reveal greying, half-rotten wood beneath.

There was no bell or knocker so Neil banged on the door with his fist and waited. When he heard footsteps approaching he stood back a little, examining the building. His training told him it was old and constructed of cob like many ancient Devon houses. The walls needed attention and he wondered, not for the first time, what Charlie Perks had done for a living before dedicating his life to metal detecting.

The door was opened by a small, slightly overweight man whose beard and straggly brown hair were peppered with grey. He wore a combat jacket and camouflage trousers which gave him the look of a soldier from a regiment that wasn't too particular about discipline, fitness or appearance.

Charlie looked surprised to see Neil but not displeased. He invited him in at once and offered tea, which Neil accepted gratefully.

The cottage was spotless although the furniture belonged to another era; a time of make do and mend. It was an old person's house with snowy antimacassars draped over the backs of the moquette armchairs and matching settee, relics of the 1950s. The patterned carpet was worn in places but clean and there was a large display of framed photographs on the sideboard showing Charlie as a baby and a schoolboy, and a much younger Charlie with a woman Neil assumed was his mother.

Charlie saw Neil looking at them. 'Mum likes her photos.'

'How is she?' Neil hadn't met her on his previous visits either and he assumed she was upstairs somewhere, completely dependent on her only son.

'We'll have to keep our voices down. She's not been too well.'

'Sorry to hear that.' Neil couldn't think up anything more appropriate to say.

'I keep the house just how she likes it and I sit with her every evening.' A fond smile came to his lips.

'I'm sure she appreciates it.'

Charlie Perks suddenly drew in his breath and smiled, showing a set of uneven, grey teeth. Neil had never seen him smile before and found the sight slightly unsettling. 'What did you want to see me about?'

Neil explained that Wesley wanted him to get in touch. The CSIs needed help and Neil had recommended his services.

Charlie nodded eagerly. He'd be delighted to help and he had a new machine – the latest model – which would be ideal for the job.

When Neil left the cottage he found himself wondering about Charlie's life, stuck there in the back of beyond with his precious machines and his elderly mother, no doubt living in hope of the big discovery one day – an Anglo-Saxon hoard or Viking silver. But he hadn't liked to pry. Some people liked their privacy.

When Wesley and Gerry returned to the incident room, Rachel rose to greet them.

'How did you get on with Jocasta's school friends?' was Wesley's first question.

'I wouldn't describe them as friends. She wasn't the most popular girl in the school – thought she was too sophisti-cated for them.'

'Do you think she was bullied? Girls can be very bitchy, so I've heard.'

'There may have been some subtle bullying going on, although her room-mate Finola said she only had herself to blame. She sneered at the others and that never goes down well. I did learn a couple of interesting things, though. Jocasta told Finola that her father was a creep and her mother suffered with her nerves. She also said she could never take friends home although Finola reckoned she might have made it up to inject some drama into her boring existence. Then there was the suggestion that Jocasta's mother might have a younger lover.'

'Maybe that's why she's avoiding us,' said Wesley. 'But whatever Jeremy Ovorard says, we need to see her.' He looked at his watch. 'The boss has told Ian Evans's local nick in Dorchester that I'll go over at three to speak to his mother.'

'Do you want me to come with you?'

He looked at Rachel and smiled. 'If you're not busy with something else.'

His phone rang and when he saw Belinda Crillow's number on the caller display he hesitated, wondering whether to answer. Then he killed the call and returned the phone to his pocket, feeling another pang of guilt.

Rachel was unusually quiet as they drove to Dorchester, as though she was lost in her own thoughts.

'I've arranged to have a look at Andrea Jameson's apartment with Gerry when we get back,' said Wesley, breaking the silence. 'Someone's already been in and made an initial search but I want to see the place for myself. You know what Gerry always says – find out how someone lived and you're halfway to finding out why they died.'

Rachel didn't answer.

'Something wrong?'

She waited a few seconds before replying. 'I've spoken to Dan Noakes, the farmer who owns the field where the bodies were discovered. He said there was another death there in the nineties. A man died near where Ian Evans was found – a student at your old university apparently.'

This caught Wesley's attention. 'He wasn't shot, was he?'

'No, I think it was a fall – an accident – although Dan was a bit vague about the details. He said the locals think the field's cursed.'

Wesley didn't comment. He'd come across a lot of rural superstitions since he'd arrived from London and he'd never taken any of them too seriously.

They'd reached the outskirts of Dorchester and it wasn't long before Rachel pulled up in front of a small semi in a side road. Spotless net curtains hung at the double-glazed windows and there was a fine display of roses climbing up a trellis beside the freshly painted front door which opened before they had a chance to knock.

The woman who stood facing them was, like her house, small and neat.

'You're the officers from Devon?' she said anxiously, as though she was afraid they'd turn out to be imposters.

'That's right,' said Wesley as they showed her their IDs.

They followed her into a small front lounge where the dark, busy wallpaper gave the room a claustrophobic feeling. Wesley's attention was drawn to three graduation photographs, hanging side by side above the fireplace: two boys and a girl, all smiling proudly and each wielding a scroll like a sceptre. Wesley recognised the young man in the middle photograph as Ian, minus his beard. There was an elaborate bouquet of lilies and white roses on a side table and more flowers on the mantelpiece.

After the initial pleasantries had been exchanged, Wesley asked to see Ian's room and Mrs Evans led them upstairs without a word.

'We'd like to have a look around if we may,' Rachel said gently. 'You don't have to stay if you don't want to.'

'I'll put the kettle on,' the woman said before leaving the room.

They both knew the routine. They were looking for anything that would tell them more about Ian Evans's life.

'He liked walking,' said Rachel after a while. 'He was a member of the local ramblers' group and there's a lot of walking magazines. And birdwatching. There was a pair of binoculars in his rucksack, wasn't there?'

Wesley nodded. He was searching the wardrobe and everything he found confirmed Rachel's verdict. Clothes suitable for the outdoors hung beside office wear: smart jackets, black trousers, shirts and ties. Two lives: one to make a living and one to make that living worthwhile.

There was nothing in Ian's room to suggest anything other than dull respectability. They found a page cut neatly from the travel section of a Sunday newspaper dated a couple of weeks ago, featuring places to stay on Dartmoor. One of those mentioned was Princebury Hall and below a photograph of the building there was a short piece about Xander Southwark – the bad lad who turned his life around and now helped others to do the same. It seemed that he was using his dubious past as his unique selling point. The Shepherd's Arms also featured on the page, described as a suitable pub for walkers; Ian had underlined the phone number twice.

They found no pornographic material on his laptop and all his emails seemed to be from his fellow nature enthusiasts, which suggested that Ian Evans was a middle-aged man who lived with his mother and led an apparently blameless life. The more Wesley discovered about him, the more convinced he was that Andrea Jameson had been the killer's target and it had been Ian's misfortune to witness her murder. The post-mortem hadn't been able to establish which victim had died first but at that moment Wesley would have put money on it having been Andrea.

'We'll get his computer examined properly,' said Wesley with a sigh. 'But I can't see anything remotely suspicious.' He walked around the room, testing the floorboards to see if a loose one might conceal a hiding place. But there was nothing.

'Ian was very keen on walking,' said Wesley once they were sitting in Mrs Evans's front room sipping tea.

'It was his passion – that and nature. He's been like that since he was a little boy.'

'What did he say about his latest trip?'

'He'd been wanting to go walking on Dartmoor for a while so when things were quiet at work ...'

'Did he say why he chose that particular place?'

Mrs Evans shook her head. 'No, but he said he'd found a nice place to stay.'

'He didn't say he was going to meet anyone or ... ?'

'No.' She thought for a moment. 'But he was very quiet before he left. I thought he'd been working too hard. He's very conscientious, you know.'

Wesley flinched inwardly at her use of the present tense.

'Did he ever mention the name Andrea Jameson?'

'Is that the woman ... ?'

Wesley nodded.

'He never mentioned an Andrea. I would have remembered.'

'Did he have girlfriends?' Rachel asked. The question was gentle, almost tentative, as though she feared causing pain.

'He's had a couple. There was a nice girl from church I was hoping he'd ... but ... '

'Where did Ian work?' Wesley asked.

'At Rowberry, Rowberry and Barrow, the solicitors in the middle of town. He dealt with conveyancing. He's always been a bright boy,' she added proudly.

'Has he always lived at home?'

'No, when he finished at university he worked in Exeter for a while but he wasn't keen on the job. I don't think he liked the people he was working with and there was some trouble so he left and took another job in Honiton. Then when his father died he came back home and began working for Rowberry, Rowberry and Barrow. It's a very nice firm and he gets on with everybody. He's very well liked.' She pointed to the bouquet Wesley had noticed before. 'They sent me those. Isn't that kind of them?'

'They're beautiful,' said Rachel.

By the time they'd finished their tea Wesley was satisfied they'd learned everything they could. Since Pam's illness he'd become more sensitive to the grief and worries of others and he knew he'd stay longer if the bereaved mother needed to talk. However, she was expecting her daughter to arrive in half an hour so she'd have company. The daughter was going to move in with her for a while and her other son lived nearby with his family; she wouldn't be alone.

'Do you want to talk to his colleagues or shall we leave that to the local force?' Rachel asked as they left.

Wesley looked at his watch and considered her question. 'We'll send one of our team over to have a word.' He paused. 'Although I'm finding it hard to believe that Ian was the killer's target, aren't you?'

'It's beginning to look that way. So we concentrate on Andrea Jameson?'

'Hopefully by the time we get back to the incident room they'll have tracked down Jason Fitch and Kyle Ball,' he said. 'Then there's Andrea's link to Jocasta Ovorard.'

Rachel's face darkened. 'Think we'll find her dead?'

There was a long silence before Wesley replied, almost in a whisper as if he didn't want to tempt fate.

'It wouldn't surprise me.'

Belinda Crillow had tried Wesley Peterson's number but he hadn't answered.

But now he couldn't ignore what had happened. As she looked at herself in the mirror she saw a thousand jagged images of herself in the broken glass. And the bright redness of her blood.

14

On his return to the incident room in Lower Torworthy Wesley found Gerry pacing up and down, his eyes alight with excitement.

'Jeremy Ovorard provided an old toothbrush of Jocasta's so we could get her DNA,' said Gerry, catching hold of Wesley's elbow and leading him towards his desk.

'We've got a result?'

'Her DNA was found around the front passenger seat in Andrea Jameson's car.'

'Anything to suggest Ian Evans was in the car too?'

'Absolutely nothing, which suggests they either met up at the murder site – possibly by arrangement – or they were complete strangers.'

'I'm beginning to favour the last theory, Gerry. I think Evans was just unlucky. Wrong time, wrong place.'

'I've got the keys to Andrea's apartment. It's already been searched but I think it's time we had a look for ourselves, don't you?'

'What about speaking to Jocasta's mum?'

'Jeremy Ovorard told us to stay away.' Gerry winked. 'But we don't always do as we're told, do we – even by a man who's tipped to be Home Secretary one day. Let's give it another day and if the lass still hasn't turned up . . . '

Wesley was glad to return to Tradmouth, which seemed positively cosmopolitan compared to Lower Torworthy. Nobody took much notice of the colour of his skin in Tradmouth and the other towns along the coast but he'd received some curious looks up in Lower Torworthy and that made him uncomfortable.

Before heading for Andrea Jameson's apartment by the marina they called in at the station to see whether anything new had come in on Jocasta's disappearance. But the flood of interest triggered by Wesley's TV appeal had dwindled to a trickle and his pessimistic feeling that Jocasta was lying dead and undiscovered somewhere on Dartmoor was growing stronger by the minute.

Rob Carter was entering the CID office just as he was leaving.

'Heard anything from Belinda Crillow?' Wesley asked.

'She's called asking for you a few times – won't speak to me.'

Wesley heard a note of relief in Rob's voice. Maybe it had been a mistake to pass Ms Crillow over to someone relatively inexperienced. On the other hand help had been offered and if she wouldn't take it that was her problem. He had more pressing things to deal with at that moment.

It was only a short walk to Andrea's apartment, part of a complex which included a four-star hotel with a spa. Like the others in the small block apartment four overlooked the river.

When Wesley and Gerry climbed the thickly carpeted staircase and let themselves into the flat they found themselves in a luxurious living room, sparsely but expensively furnished in pale hues. Wesley couldn't help wondering what it would look like if some sticky-fingered young children and a muddy dog were unleashed in there for an hour or so.

There was a magnificent view of the river from the massive set of glass doors that could be folded back to access a wide balcony outside. As Wesley opened them the heavy silence was replaced by the chug of boat engines and the clinking of halyards against metal masts. He stood on the balcony watching the yachts on the river, their sails catching the sunlight. A pleasure boat steamed past. Thanks to the kind weather, its top deck was filled with tourists armed with cameras. Some waved as they passed and he waved back.

'How much do you reckon a place like this would go for?' Gerry asked. 'A million?'

Wesley turned to look at him, curious. It wasn't like the DCI to speculate on house prices.

'Wouldn't surprise me,' Wesley answered.

'Party planning must pay well. We're in the wrong job, Wes.'

'Her finances are being looked into so we'll soon know if she was involved in anything dodgy.' Wesley always found it hard to believe that people accumulated wealth by honest means; he put it down to a career spent dealing with villains. 'When they searched this place they took her computer away but they're taking their time getting back to us.'

Gerry didn't answer. He was circling the room, opening cupboards and drawers with a disappointed expression on his face. Wesley stepped back inside, locking the balcony door behind him, and made for the bedroom where he conducted a quick search. Every garment inside the wardrobe bore a designer label and he couldn't help thinking of the other victim's clothes. Everything Ian Evans wore had been from chain stores or outdoor shops and he was struck once more by how little the two victims had in common. The only link between them appeared to be their deaths.

He heard Gerry sigh. 'Don't think we're going to learn much here, Wes,' he shouted through from the next room.

'Why don't we go and have a word with her work colleagues,' said Wesley.

Gerry agreed and as they left the apartment Wesley felt that their journey hadn't been entirely wasted. He was getting a better picture of Andrea Jameson's life, and once he talked to the people who knew her he hoped he'd have more idea of why she died.

Andrea's company had an office in the centre of Tradmouth on the ground floor of a converted sail loft opposite the town's main car park, a stone's throw from the police station.

'Rachel was talking to Dan Noakes, the farmer who found the bodies,' Wesley said as they walked down the esplanade towards their destination. 'He told her someone else had died in that field in the nineteen nineties. A student fell and hit his head on the wall near where Ian Evans was lying.'

'Coincidence?'

'Probably . . . but I might look it up when we get back.'

'If it makes you happy,' said Gerry. 'This must be the place.'

They'd reached the offices of AJ Celebrations and Wesley pressed the intercom key to announce their arrival.

'Looks posh.' Gerry grinned. 'They probably have a "no riff-raff" rule.'

The smiling young woman who greeted them in the reception area was dressed entirely in black and had the over-perfect look of a lifelike female robot Wesley had once seen in a film. When they showed their ID the smile vanished suddenly, to be replaced by a solemn expression that, somehow, looked as false as the smile.

As she led them through an outer office staffed by equally slender and attractive young women, all clad in black, Wesley noted his surroundings. No expense had been spared on the conversion of the ancient sail loft into an ultra-modern office space, remarkably similar in style to Andrea's apartment. He looked round at the faces of the workers, who appeared to be engrossed in their tasks; like a crew who'd just lost their captain but were determined to pull together in order to get the ship back to port safely.

'We're all devastated, of course,' said the woman who introduced herself as Emily Boase, Andrea's second-in-command. 'It came as such a dreadful shock. Andrea was so ... amazing. She built this company up from nothing and now we've got more work than we can handle.'

'You're keeping going?'

'It's what Andrea would have wanted.' She pointed to her desk. 'Next week we've got a wedding in Millicombe and a sixtieth birthday party. The week after we've got another wedding near Neston and—'

'I take it your customers aren't short of a bob or two,' said Gerry.

The young woman looked at him with undisguised curiosity and Wesley guessed Gerry wasn't the kind of person who usually graced the premises. 'We cater for the more discerning client, yes. We have TV stars, media people, top London bankers and lawyers.'

'Aristocracy?' Gerry asked.

Emily smiled sympathetically. 'They can't usually afford our services, I'm afraid. Too busy mending leaking roofs in their ancestral homes.'

'Tell us about Andrea,' Wesley said before they became sidetracked by tales of wealth and stardom.

'Like I said, she was amazing. Some clients can be awkward, believe me, but she always managed to smooth things over.'

'Are you thinking of any awkward clients in particular? Had she fallen out with anybody?'

'Not recently, no.'

Wesley and Gerry exchanged a glance. 'But in the past?'

'There was someone . . . ' she said slowly.

'Who?'

'It was a sixteenth birthday party for a family in Morbay. It was cancelled at the last moment because the birthday girl was having a teenage tantrum but Andrea sent a bill for all the preparation we'd done. We'd gone to a good deal of expense and the caterers needed paying for the food they'd bought and the marquee firm had to be paid.'

'What happened?'

'The father refused to pay because the party hadn't gone ahead and Andrea had to point out to him that it didn't work like that. After our solicitors became involved he paid up eventually but there was some bad feeling.'

'Anything else?'

She hesitated as though she was making a decision. Wesley waited expectantly and eventually his patience was rewarded. 'There was an . . . incident last year. A French millionaire asked us to arrange a party on his yacht and a young student on the catering staff was . . . assaulted by one of his guests.'

'You mean she was raped?' Gerry said bluntly.

Emily bowed her head and gave an almost imperceptible nod.

'I don't remember the case. Was it here in Tradmouth?'

'The yacht was moored here at the time, yes. The girl was paid off by the owner of the yacht and she never made a formal complaint.'

'She should have come forward,' said Wesley, trying to hide his anger at someone being able to get away with wrecking a young woman's life just because he had money.

'Of course she should,' Gerry chipped in. 'We might have been able to make an arrest.'

'The yacht had sailed off to God knows where before she plucked up the courage to tell her parents. Then they blamed us because we oversaw the event and, however much Andrea tried to convince them she had no control over the behaviour of her clients' guests, they kept threatening to sue. They didn't, of course.'

'Your solicitor again?'

'There was no need to involve him on that occasion. Once the parents had calmed down, they saw they didn't have a legal leg to stand on, or even a moral one. What happened was hardly Andrea's fault. They were just looking for someone to blame.'

'If you could let us have the details of these two cases . . . ' Wesley said, his voice cold. He waited while she tapped into her computer and a couple of sheets of paper slid from the printer beside her desk.

'What do you know about Ms Jameson's private life?' Wesley asked as she handed him the printouts.

'I know she was seeing someone.'

'Jason Fitch?'

'I believe his name's Jason, yes. But I didn't know his surname.'

'Ever meet him?'

She shook her head.

'She was on her way to a place on Dartmoor when she was killed.'

Emily smiled. 'The Well-being Centre. I wouldn't have thought all that New Age stuff would be Andrea's cup of tea. She was a hard-headed businesswoman and she'd always been very scathing about that sort of thing.'

'Did she say much about her plans?'

'Not really.'

'She was supposed to be meeting Jason Fitch there.'

'Then that explains it. He was married so I suppose it was a place to meet up.'

'Couldn't they have met at her apartment?'

'No way. His wife found out the address so Andrea always feared she'd turn up there like an avenging fury. From what Andrea told me about her she sounds like a nightmare. I really don't know why this Jason didn't leave her. Perhaps he was scared of her. Or her brother – apparently he has convictions for violence and he's very close to his sister.'

'What did Andrea say about Jason's brother-in-law?'

'I think she was frightened of him.'

'Did she mention that he owned a gun?'

'Definitely not.' She stood in silence for a few seconds as the suggestion sank in. 'Did he kill Andrea?'

'We haven't ruled anything out at the moment. Is there anything else you can tell us?'

Emily shook her head and as Wesley prepared to take his leave he glanced at the printouts in his hand. The name of the family whose daughter had been attacked wasn't familiar but his heart beat faster when he saw the name on the other sheet. Andrea Jameson had argued with the father of an awkward teenage girl who had insisted that the birthday party he'd arranged for her was cancelled at short notice. And that father's name was Jeremy Ovorard.

With the all-too-familiar enthusiasm of a
scientist so excited by his creation that he
pays no heed to its potential dangers, Sir
Matthew embarked upon what appears to be a
programme of healing which involved taking
his little monk 'unto divers sick and dying
and setting him to pray'.

There is no record of the efficacy of
his efforts, apart from a few scribbles
in the parish records against a list of
sick parishioners that say 'healed by the
intercession of my monk'.

Contemporary sources suggest that word of Sir
Matthew's miraculous monk spread rapidly beyond
the village to the surrounding district and
eventually the news reached Oswald DeTorham,
lord of the manor of Lower Torworthy, patron of
the church and owner of the fine manor house
which stood half a mile outside the village,
setting in motion a series of disturbing events
that ultimately led to murder.

15

Neil Watson had gone straight from the university lab to a meeting with developers about a planned rescue dig in the centre of Plymouth. The meeting had gone on longer than expected so when he reached Lower Torworthy he parked outside the Shepherd's Arms and hurried to the church, hoping his volunteers had used their initiative and started without him.

He slowed his pace as he passed the church hall, hoping to see Wesley. But he was out of luck. Then he heard someone calling his name and when he turned he saw Charlie Perks with a metal detector slung over his shoulder like a rifle.

'Charlie. Good to see you,' Neil said, glancing at his watch. 'Have you been in touch with the police?'

Charlie Perks nodded earnestly. 'I've been helping out their Forensics team,' he said with a hint of pride.

'Helping the police with their inquiries.'

Charlie's face remained solemn, as though he hadn't caught on to Neil's feeble joke. 'You could say that, I suppose.'

'Any success?'

'Oh yes. I located their bullets for them. They would have

had a hard job finding them without this little beauty.' He gave Neil a distant smile and touched his machine lovingly, like a mother with a precious baby. Neil had encountered a lot of people like Charlie in his line of work; obsessives who were more at home with artefacts and technology than they were with people.

'I hope you didn't mind me giving the police your name. Only the inspector working on the case is a friend of mine and I thought ...'

'Not at all. I was glad to help,' Charlie replied. 'I've always been interested in forensics and all that.' He hesitated. 'A big house used to stand in that field in the olden days and I reckon the foundations are still there. And there's that bit of old wall.'

'I know. I've been thinking it might be a suitable site for a training excavation. I'll look into it when the police have packed up. Might need your services again.' Neil made a show of checking his watch. 'Sorry, Charlie, better go. I'll be in touch.'

Neil left, knowing that if he hadn't been firm with Charlie he might have become embroiled in a long and probably tedious conversation.

As he neared the church he could see the contractors who'd found the lead box sitting on the churchyard wall drinking tea and sharing jokes while their mini digger lay idle. Neil wondered whether there was anything else of interest in the trench they'd dug. He strode over to them and introduced himself but they assured him nothing else had turned up, although he wasn't sure whether to believe them. He had a fear that they might have pocketed some rich artefact for themselves or discarded something of historical significance because they didn't want any further delay to their work. Not everyone was as honest as Charlie Perks. However, he could hardly stand there and call them liars so he walked off up the church path.

Suddenly the roar of an engine shattered the peace of the afternoon as a motorbike tore out of the small church car park, its leather-clad rider hunched over the handlebars. Neil was sure the bike belonged to the man who'd introduced himself as the curate but he continued inside where he found his little team working away armed with clipboards, torches and cameras.

For a while he watched them shining their torches at oblique angles to make any shallow carvings on the stone walls stand out so they could be photographed and recorded.

Relieved to see them engrossed in their tasks, he headed for the vestry at the far end of the church and gave a token knock on the door.

Oliver Grayling was sitting at his desk and when he turned his head Neil saw that his eyes were bloodshot as though he'd been crying.

It was Friday. A week since, according to the available evidence, Andrea Jameson and Ian Evans had met their deaths; Wesley felt frustrated that every lead they'd followed so far had met a dead end or a delay.

Pam was working that day so Wesley had risen early to make breakfast for the family. As his daughter, Amelia, chatted away at the breakfast table the house phone rang and Pam answered with a weary 'hello' before replacing the receiver, a look of disgust on her face.

'Is it Mr Nobody again, Mum?' Amelia said.

'Yes. I wish he'd go away.'

Wesley put down his toast.

'What do you mean?'

'All yesterday the phone kept ringing but there was nobody there when I answered.' She sounded exasperated as she sat down at the table. 'Number withheld.'

'I answered it a couple of times,' said Michael, who was shovelling cereal into his mouth.

'Put the phone down or unplug it. They'll soon get fed up,' said Wesley, kissing the top of his wife's head. 'Sorry, I've got to go.' He ruffled Michael's hair and gave Amelia a hug before heading to the car. Normally he got his daily dose of exercise by walking down the steep hill to the police station in Tradmouth but today he had to drive out to Lower Torworthy. At least the time spent in the car gave him the opportunity to go over the case in his mind.

He arrived in the incident room before Gerry to find the team hard at work tapping information into computers and making calls. Once at his desk he made a list of everything he needed to do. Someone needed to talk to Ian Evans's colleagues at the Dorchester solicitors and he wanted to ask Jeremy Ovorard about his dispute with Andrea. Speaking to Mrs Ovorard was also high on his list. Then there was the family of the girl who'd been attacked aboard the yacht; the family who'd blamed Andrea Jameson for their daughter's ordeal. Kyle Ball still hadn't been found and his brother-in-law, their main suspect Jason Fitch, had vanished, possibly to his second home in Littlebury. They needed the address and he hoped it wouldn't be long before they found it.

'Has that address in Littlebury been traced yet?' he asked Trish Walton, who was sorting through witness statements.

'Not yet. I think our best bet is to go there and ask around. It's not a big place.'

'Fancy the job?'

Trish nodded eagerly as though this was what she'd been after all along – a chance to get out of the incident room and spend a few hours at the seaside in the weak September sun.

At that moment Gerry came in and as he took off his jacket Wesley handed him the list he'd made.

'What's this, Wes?'

'Lines of inquiry I want to follow up. We need to speak to Jeremy Ovorard again – and his wife. She's worrying me, Gerry.'

'Why?'

'Just a feeling.' In his opinion the missing girl's mother's continued absence from the investigation was odd. 'And the family of the girl who was assaulted aboard the yacht blamed Andrea Jameson for what happened so we'll need to speak to them as well. I'm sending Trish over to Littlebury to chat up the locals and see if she can locate Jason Fitch's holiday home.'

'Good idea. Anything else?'

'I'd like someone to have a word with Ian Evans's work colleagues – just in case.'

'Fair enough. Mind you, Evans didn't seem the type who'd make enemies. Whereas Andrea ... Sounds like a lot of people had it in for her.'

Gerry called for attention and the room fell silent.

'The latest from the CSIs is that the missing bullets have been found with the help of a local metal detectorist,' he began. 'Which means we now know for certain that Andrea Jameson died in the lay-by near the gate leading to the field and her body was moved later. It looks as if she got out of her car, either to enjoy the view or to wait for someone.

That was why she left her handbag inside the car – she never expected it to be out of her sight. Ian Evans died around fifty yards away, not far from where he was found. There's no way of telling who died first but my guess is that she was shot and he happened to be walking through the field and witnessed the whole thing. He was shot in the back so maybe he was running away – or trying to hide behind that old wall.'

'It was important to the killer that they weren't found immediately?' Rachel said.

'He needed time to get away,' Trish said as though this was obvious.

'Trish is right,' said Wesley. 'It's not a busy road by any means but the next person who passed that way would be bound to see Andrea's body lying there. Whereas a parked car . . .'

'Nobody would take much notice.' Gerry finished Wesley's sentence for him.

'Tell you what,' Gerry said to Wesley as he returned to his desk. 'While Trish is doing her bit over in Littlebury why don't we pay Jeremy Ovorard a visit? We can mention his row with Andrea Jameson and see how he reacts.'

Wesley agreed but something else was nagging away at the back of his mind, something about an accident in the field in the 1990s near where Ian Evans was found. He'd been too preoccupied to follow it up but now he wanted to know more.

16

There was no sign of Oliver Grayling when Neil entered the church. Instead two flower arrangers were on duty, preparing for the weekend services. The women, one elderly and one considerably younger, looked up from their lilies and carnations and greeted him with a nod.

'Is Oliver about?' he asked.

The younger woman put down her secateurs. 'He'll be at the vicarage. Do you know where it is?'

Neil said yes and thanked them. He'd visited the vicarage to arrange the graffiti survey and he'd been given tea which, he supposed, was traditional.

Lower Torworthy's new vicarage stood in a cul-de-sac a hundred yards from the church. Unlike its roomy and beautifully proportioned Georgian predecessor – now home to a couple from London who'd given up the world of international banking for the Devon good life – it was a small modern detached house complete with double glazing, pebble-dashed walls and all the character of a cardboard box. Neil supposed that spiritual men weren't meant to bother about their accommodation.

Grayling looked wary as he opened the front door but when he saw Neil standing there he put on a smile and invited him in. Neil was offered a drink but when it arrived he wished he hadn't accepted, as the coffee was powdery and the milk slightly off. Nevertheless he sipped it out of politeness as Grayling asked how the survey was going and when they'd be finished. Neil was non-committal: the work was being done by volunteers from the local Archaeology Society so it depended on their availability, he explained apologetically, hoping they hadn't already overstayed their welcome.

'I've heard that someone from the university did some research on the history of the village – this would be in the nineties.'

'Before my time, I'm afraid. And the old incumbent of this church has gone on to higher things.' Grayling raised his eyes to the ceiling.

'You mean he's ... '

'Oh no, you misunderstand me. The Reverend Collins is now a canon at the cathedral. A well-deserved promotion. He's a good man.'

'I take it you mean Exeter Cathedral?'

Grayling nodded, fidgeting with the front of his black clerical shirt as though something was bothering him; maybe something to do with Canon Collins.

'When I called in at the church last night you looked upset.' Neil thought he might as well be direct.

'I was worried about a sick parishioner,' Grayling said quickly. 'Sometimes you can't help getting emotionally involved.'

Neil was sure he was lying.

'Have you discovered any more about the wooden figure?' Grayling changed the subject skilfully as though he was used to steering conversations in the direction he wanted them to go.

'No, but everyone at the university's very excited about it. It's an important find and I wouldn't be surprised if it ends up in a major museum. I'd like to find out more about it if possible.'

'Canon Collins took an interest in that sort of thing while he was vicar here. I'll give you his address if you like.'

He consulted an address book bulging with scraps of paper and scribbled something on a notebook, then tore out the page and passed it to Neil.

'I haven't seen your curate around much – John Davies.'

'He's . . . gone to another parish.'

Neil knew this was another lie. He thanked Oliver Grayling and returned to the church.

Jeremy Ovorard's white mansion was perched on the hillside above Morbay, near one of the resort's more exclusive beaches. Wesley's tyres crunched on a thick layer of gravel as the car came to a halt in front of the house. As an early warning system it was as effective as an alarm.

Ovorard opened the door a split second after Wesley pressed the bell, almost as if he'd been waiting in the hall for them.

'I hope you've come to say you've found her.' His words sounded more like a criticism than an expression of hope.

'No news yet, I'm afraid,' said Wesley. 'But I assure you we're following every lead.' He saw Gerry give him a slight nod. 'We'd really like to speak to your wife, Mr Ovorard. She might have something valuable to tell us.'

'That's out of the question, I'm afraid.' He looked at his watch. 'I'm about to go to London for a couple of days – a parliamentary committee I really can't get out of. I'm sorry, gentlemen, if you'll excuse me I have a train to catch.'

'Let's not waste time then,' said Gerry. 'Can we come in? Won't keep you long.'

Ovorard nodded meekly and stood aside to let them in, checking his watch again as if to make a point.

'We'd like to talk to you about Andrea Jameson,' said Wesley once they were seated in a cream-and-gold living room decorated in the style favoured by premiership footballers and their glamorous wives. The place looked like a show house on an upmarket development with nothing out of place and little sign of human habitation.

'Andrea who?'

'The woman Jocasta was last seen with in the village of Lower Torworthy up on Dartmoor. She was later found dead half a mile away.'

'The name isn't familiar.'

'I don't think that's true, Mr Ovorard,' Wesley said softly. 'You had a dispute with her about a party you arranged which was later cancelled. She sent in her account for the work she'd done and you refused to pay.'

For a brief moment Ovorard looked uncomfortable. Then the untroubled mask slipped back into place. 'Of course. I'm sorry, I'd forgotten all about it.'

The words were said with confidence but Wesley didn't believe them for one moment.

'You argued with Andrea Jameson.'

Gerry had been watching silently, letting Wesley do all the work, but now he chipped in. 'We've been told things got a bit acrimonious.'

'It was a simple legal matter, Chief Inspector. Nothing personal, I assure you. I dealt mainly with her solicitors.'

'But you must have met Ms Jameson,' said Wesley. 'Tell us what you remember about her.'

'She seemed very efficient and her firm came highly recommended.'

'Is that all?'

'Of course. Our dispute was settled and I assure you I bore her no grudge.'

'You must have been annoyed with Jocasta for causing you all that trouble,' Wesley said, watching Ovorard carefully. The man pressed his lips together in a hard line at the mention of his daughter's name. He'd been annoyed with her all right.

'OK, I admit I was angry at the time because we'd gone to a great deal of trouble to arrange a memorable sixteenth birthday party for her and invited all our friends. It was embarrassing when we had to cancel but we made an excuse that she wasn't well. Gastroenteritis if you must know.' He gave a humourless smile. 'The political variety.'

'One of her former classmates at Widedales said she had a boyfriend.' He was bending the facts but he wanted to see Ovorard's reaction.

The MP's face reddened. 'Whoever told you that was wrong.' He checked his watch again. 'I'm sorry. I really must go.'

Wesley heard a noise; the dull thud of a door banging upstairs. 'In that case we won't keep you. If there's any news about Jocasta you'll be notified at once.'

'Well, he didn't like the idea of his little girl having a boyfriend,' Gerry said as they made their way back to the car.

'If he's away in London for a couple of days it means Jocasta's mum'll be here without her guard dog,' said Wesley. 'You thinking what I'm thinking?'

Gerry looked at him and grinned.

17

There was a message from the incident room to say that Trish Walton's visit to the village of Littlebury had borne fruit. After asking around in the village she'd discovered that Jason Fitch had inherited a bungalow overlooking the sea from his grandmother and that he used it for the occasional weekend away. The woman who ran the village post office said that Fitch and his wife were careful to keep themselves to themselves, quite unlike the former owner of Gull's View, Fitch's grandmother – a Mrs Lingham – who'd been well liked and a mainstay of the local WI.

The next piece of good news was that when Trish had taken a look at the bungalow she'd seen a big SUV registered to Sharon Fitch parked outside.

Wesley drove straight to Littlebury down the narrow country lanes. He'd never been comfortable driving in this terrain, leaving it to Rachel if at all possible because she'd grown up in the area and navigating the high-hedged, single-track roads was second nature to her. But this time he had no choice and his hands tightened on the steering wheel as he instructed Gerry to look out for passing places and approaching vehicles. Gerry, in contrast, looked perfectly relaxed in the passenger seat.

'Let's hope they've got the kettle on when we arrive.'

'Aren't we bringing Jason in for questioning?'

'We'll have time for a cup of tea first,' said Gerry. 'I'm spitting feathers.'

The village of Littlebury consisted of a few streets of pastel cottages, two pubs, a medieval church and a village hall along with a post office cum general store that did a roaring trade in beach equipment in the holiday season. Today, with the fine September sun, there was a small display of bright plastic buckets and spades outside to attract any off-season holidaymakers with small children who happened to pass by. The main road through the village sloped towards a wide expanse of beach and beyond the beach was a small island topped by an impressive art deco hotel. Wesley had visited Monk's Island before in the line of duty but had never set foot inside the hotel. He'd heard it was expensive but perhaps one day he'd treat Pam to a night there.

Gull's View wasn't hard to find. It was a small bungalow with the slightly run-down look Wesley had seen before in properties owned by the elderly who find day-to-day maintenance too much to cope with. It was clear that the Fitches had done little to the exterior since inheriting and Wesley couldn't help wondering what they had planned for it in the future.

The SUV was still outside; a large white BMW which dominated its surroundings. Out of habit Wesley put his hand on the bonnet as he passed. It was cold, which meant the Fitches hadn't ventured far from the house since Trish made her report.

There was no bell so Wesley rapped on the glazed door and waited. After a while a dark shadow appeared in the hallway, distorted by the patterned glass. Wesley held his breath as the door opened to reveal a woman with a bottle-blonde ponytail and tanned limbs. Her jeans were tight enough to leave nothing to the imagination and she wore a skimpy vest top which revealed an array of tattoos on her shoulders and arms. She didn't look pleased at being disturbed.

'Mrs Fitch?'

She nodded cautiously as though she was thinking of denying it.

'I'm DI Peterson and this is DCI Heffernan,' Wesley said, showing his ID. 'We're investigating the death of Andrea Jameson. May we come in?'

Sharon Fitch grunted something under her breath and walked ahead of them into a small parlour. All trace of Fitch's grandmother had been erased and replaced with white walls and simple Scandinavian furniture. The place had an unfinished look; a work in progress.

'What do you want?' Sharon's question was brusque, as though she couldn't wait to get rid of them. They weren't invited to sit.

'We'd like to speak to your husband.'

'You and me both. We had a row and he buggered off.'

'Where to?'

'No idea.'

'You knew Andrea Jameson?'

Sharon turned away and stared out of the window. 'I knew Jason was screwing her. Found texts from her on his phone, didn't I. He said he'd finish it but that's not the first lie he's told, believe me.'

'Andrea Jameson had arranged to join your husband at

Princebury Hall up on Dartmoor last Friday but she was killed before she got there. Your husband didn't turn up either.'

'That's because I finally put my foot down and told him I was leaving if he went. I should have done it years ago.'

'How did he react to that?' Gerry asked. It was the first time he'd spoken and he sounded genuinely curious.

'He went off and sulked for a bit then he came back, which surprised me because I thought he wouldn't be able to resist sniffing around that bitch again. He can never usually help himself. He sulked all day Saturday then on Sunday I told him we were coming here for a few days. Thought it'd do us good to get away.'

'I understand your brother, Kyle, was at your house on Sunday. We've been trying to get in touch with him.'

'You'll be lucky. He's in Spain; he just called in on his way to the airport.'

'When's he back, love?' said Gerry.

'Early next week, he said.'

'Does your brother own a gun?'

'Kyle's been a bad lad in his time but if you're trying to pin this murder on him you're making a big mistake.' She was either genuinely shocked or she was a good actress because she almost had Wesley convinced. Almost but not quite.

'Can you tell us exactly what your husband did last Friday?'

Sharon slumped down on the sofa. 'He was at home till early afternoon catching up with work in his study,' she said, fishing a tissue out of her jeans pocket. 'Then he told me he was going away to Dartmoor for the weekend – he'd already packed without bloody telling me. We had a flaming row, then he drove off – must have been around three o'clock.'

'What time did he come back?'

Wesley held his breath while she made the mental calculation.

'Around seven thirty. Came back with his tail between his legs.' There was a note of triumph in her voice and Wesley suspected she'd enjoyed her moment of victory against her rival.

'What was his explanation?'

'He said he'd been driving around thinking and he'd decided to stand her up.'

'Did he say why?'

'No. But it was a result,' she added with a satisfied smile.

'Does your husband own a gun?'

'Of course not.' She didn't sound altogether convincing.

'We've heard a rumour that your brother, Kyle, has a nickname: the Hit Man.'

She said nothing for a few moments while the implication of Wesley's question sank in. 'He used to work as a DJ at a club in Plymouth. Hit Man – hit records. Get it?' She sounded as though she was addressing a particularly stupid child.

'Did you or your brother ever meet Andrea Jameson?'

'No.'

'What about Kyle?' Gerry asked.

'Not as far as I know.'

'But he knew about her?'

She hesitated. 'I might have mentioned it. Look, Andrea wasn't Jason's only bit on the side. She was one in a long

131

line but he always comes back to me in the end,' she added with satisfaction.

'There are more women?'

'Too right there are. That's one of the things we rowed about.'

'Where's your husband now?'

There was a long silence before she answered. 'I have my suspicions.'

'Will you share them with us?' said Wesley.

Sharon looked him up and down as if she'd noticed him for the first time. 'OK, seeing as you asked so nicely. I think he's with Gemma Whittingstill. She's a nutcase. She threatened me, would you believe.'

Wesley looked at Gerry. 'What form did these threats take?'

'She phoned the house a couple of times and said Jason was leaving me and if I stood in her way she'd kill me. Anyway, I asked our Kyle to go round and have a word. There were no more calls after that,' she added with a satisfied smirk.

'So he's still seeing this Gemma?' Gerry asked. He sounded fascinated by this real-life soap opera.

'Wouldn't surprise me. They've been on and off for ages. He keeps finishing it but she always lures him back somehow. Trouble with Jason is he can never refuse a shag when it's offered. Sex addiction, they call it in the States.' Her eyes lit up. 'If I were you, I'd pay La Whittingstill a visit. She's a jealous cow and if she found out he was planning to go away with Andrea ... '

'Do you know where she lives?'

'In the middle of nowhere off the road to Neston. She's a mad bitch and if it wasn't for our Kyle ... '

She didn't have to finish her sentence. She'd just given them the name of another person who might want Andrea Jameson out of the way for good.

'Ever heard the name Ian Evans?'

'No. Who is he?'

Wesley didn't answer her question.

Letter from Oswald DeTorham
to Sir Matthew

6 November 1531

There is much talk in the district about your monk and
the miracles he performs. My steward Peter's mother
was cured of the falling sickness through his intercession.
I implore you to attend upon my brother Simeon, who is
sick of the fever. He suffers much and is in need of your
prayers and your monk's good offices.

Send word I beg you for I fear Simeon will soon be
called to the presence of Our Lord where his many sins
will be judged and I do not wish him to die unshriven.

I wait upon your word.

Letter from Sir Matthew
to Oswald DeTorham

6 November 1531

*Sir I am grieved to hear of your brother's sickness
and I will attend him without delay. My little
monk is at your disposal and his intercessions
will, I am sure, bring comfort to Simeon.*

*I have feared for Simeon in the past and pray
that my monk's godly influence might close the
door to Satan who would prey upon your brother's
weak soul if care is not taken. I fear there is one in
your household who exerts an evil influence upon
him. Yet I am loath to name him.*

18

Neil had arranged to meet Canon Collins at a small pub in the cathedral close which had a glowing reputation for its real ale. The venue was the canon's idea, which surprised Neil who'd always assumed that clergymen of a certain age went in for sherry.

When Neil entered the pub he recognised Collins at once; not because he'd ever seen the man before but because he was the only person there who was wearing a clerical collar. The clergyman stood to greet him with a hearty handshake before Neil asked what he wanted to drink. His offer was accepted eagerly and when Neil returned from the bar with a pint of the guest ale for Collins and a half for himself, Collins raised his glass in thanks before taking a sip.

'Dr Watson. I'm intrigued. How can I help you?'

'As I told you on the phone I work for the County Archaeological Unit and at the moment I have a team from a local archaeology group conducting a survey of Lower Torworthy church. We're looking for medieval graffiti.'

'Sounds interesting.'

'By graffiti I don't mean naughty choirboys carving their initials on the pews. We're looking for protective symbols and marks made by superstitious parishioners to ward off evil. For instance they used to carve the overlapping letters VV which stands for Virgin of Virgins to honour the Virgin Mary. Then there were daisy wheels and crosses and patterns of five dots. Sometimes, if we're lucky, we find images of ships carved into the stone. We've already found one at Lower Torworthy. We're looking for masons' marks as well, which should tell us whether the same people worked on other churches in the area.' He saw that the canon was watching him with a slight smile on his lips. 'Sorry if I'm boring you. I tend to get carried away.'

'Not at all. It's good to see someone so enthusiastic about church architecture.'

Neil took a photograph of the mechanical figure from his pocket and put it on the table in front of the canon. 'This was found outside the boundary of the churchyard by workmen digging a ditch. It was sealed in a lead box – like a coffin. At first we thought it was a child's burial but when it was opened we found—'

'What is it? A statue?'

'Yes and no. It's an automaton. If you look carefully at the picture you can just make out the machinery where we've removed the flap at the side.'

Collins pushed his glasses down his nose and peered at the photograph. 'So I can. Good heavens. How old is it?'

'Late fifteenth- or early sixteenth-century. We think it was buried to save it from destruction during the Reformation. I've heard rumours that someone was researching the subject while you were vicar of Lower Torworthy. Your successor said you'd be the person to ask.'

Collins's face lit up with recognition. 'I remember helping a young man who was doing his doctorate back in the nineties. Now his name was somewhat unusual. A Northern saint as I recall.' The canon screwed up his face in concentration. 'Alcuin, that was it. Alcuin Garrard. It was tragic. A young man like that, so full of life.'

'What do you mean?'

'He fell and hit his head; one of those freak accidents you sometimes hear about. He was investigating some earthworks in a field – something to do with his research – when he tripped over and that was it. Dead.' He shook his head as though he was despairing of the fragile nature of existence.

'Earthworks?' Neil's archaeological curiosity was working overtime.

'The site of a manor house I believe. It was destroyed by fire in the reign of Henry the Eighth.'

'You're talking about Manor Field?'

'That's right.'

'What exactly was Alcuin researching?'

'That's the interesting thing, Dr Watson. He'd come across some old documents that mentioned a mechanical monk. Apparently one of my sixteenth-century predecessors at Lower Torworthy fancied himself as a bit of an inventor and he made a machine with the help of a clockmaker from Exeter; a sort of robot I suppose. I viewed the story with scepticism but now you've told me about this find of yours . . . '

'Do you know where Alcuin found his primary sources?'

'He used some parish records from the cathedral archives . . . and I remember him saying he'd visited Princebury Hall. I believe it's some kind of health spa nowadays but back then it was owned by a gentleman called Ralph Detoram – a bachelor of advanced years and the last of his family, I understand. Mr Detoram lived alone in that big house and he allowed Alcuin free range of his muniment room – I expect he was glad of the company, especially as Alcuin was taking such an interest in the history of his family. I had the impression they got on well.' He thought for a moment. 'Alcuin also found a couple of things in the vestry cupboard.'

'Did he return them?'

Collins sighed. 'Do you know, I'm not sure he did. He took an old journal away with him if I remember correctly. It had been stuck at the back of the cupboard and forgotten. I'd always intended to have a good sort-out but I'm afraid I never got round to it.' He consulted his watch. 'I'm sorry but my wife's expecting me back. We have people coming over for dinner this evening and she wants me to do some shopping. All hands on deck.' He paused as if he'd just recalled something important. 'Alcuin's accident was in the local papers at the time and I kept the cuttings. I could dig them out for you if you think it would be any help.'

'If it's not too much trouble.'

'Not at all.'

They said their farewells at the pub door. There was just time for Neil to go back to Lower Torworthy and ask Oliver Grayling if he could take a look through the vestry cupboard to see whether Alcuin Garrard had returned the journal. After Canon Collins's revelations he was impatient to follow the trail.

When he reached the church the door was unlocked and he half expected to find his team of volunteers still at work. But they were nowhere to be seen; being Friday evening, they must have knocked off early.

As he walked down the aisle he could hear raised voices coming from the vestry and when he drew closer he could tell the conversation wasn't amicable. He stopped and listened.

'There's no more money. You've had everything.' The voice was Oliver Grayling's and he sounded close to tears.

Neil pushed the vestry door open and the two men turned to face him. Grayling appeared to be in a state of agitation. The man he knew as John Davies, however, seemed completely calm.

'Sorry to interrupt,' Neil said.

Without a word Davies marched out, brushing Neil's arm as he headed for the door.

'What was all that about?' Neil asked once he'd heard the church door slam shut.

Grayling turned his face away.

'Who is that man and why's he giving you a hard time?'

Neil heard a motorbike starting up outside, the noise of the engine shattering the peace of the countryside.

'I can't tell you.'

'If he's threatening you, you should tell the police.'

Grayling's eyes widened in panic. 'No. Under no circumstance must the police be involved.'

Neil sat down. There was a bunch of lilies in a cut-glass vase on the desk and their heady scent made him sneeze. He grabbed a tissue from the box by the vase and looked straight at Grayling.

'You mentioned money. Have you been paying him to keep quiet about something, Oliver?' he asked quietly. 'What is it you've done?'

'I've been to A and E.'

Wesley pressed the phone to his ear and listened. Belinda Crillow had called him several times but he'd let it switch to voice mail until his conscience had finally forced him to answer.

'I'm sorry to hear that. Are you all right?'

'He's been watching the house. I went outside to put something in the bin and he was waiting for me so I ran inside and locked the door. Then I fell against the mirror and it shattered. I cut myself.'

'Did he touch you?'

'I didn't give him the chance. But if I hadn't got away I dread to think what he'd have done.'

'You've told DC Carter?'

'He's not interested. I need you to help me. Please.'

Wesley took a deep breath, annoyed with Rob Carter who probably thought the job of reassuring a frightened woman was beneath him. 'Sorry, I'm in the middle of a murder inquiry at the moment. But I'll call the station and ask them to send someone round immediately.'

'But ...'

Wesley ended the call and when he contacted Tradmouth Police Station the woman constable he spoke to said she'd call at Belinda Crillow's address right away. She sounded efficient and, hopefully, she'd be more sympathetic than Rob. Job done.

19

Wesley had asked Rachel to trace the address of Jason Fitch's alleged jealous lover, Gemma Whittingstill. There was a chance Sharon had given them her name out of revenge or to deflect suspicion from her husband and brother, but they needed to follow it up.

Rachel suspected that if they dug deeply enough into Andrea Jameson's past more skeletons could come rattling out of her cupboard. Wesley had also been wondering whether Gemma was the other woman Jason had taken to Princebury Hall – the one Xander Southwark had refused to name. Rachel would ask when she saw her. Maybe that warrant to search Southwark's records wouldn't be needed after all.

'If Gemma works she should be home by now,' said Rachel as she climbed out of the driving seat. Trish Walton didn't reply; she was already making for the front door of Gemma Whittingstill's isolated cottage.

'Think she lives alone?' Rachel asked as she caught up with her friend.

'There's no record of anybody else living at this address. Bit cut off, isn't it?'

Trish was right. The narrow lane leading to the cottage

had vegetation sprouting from the tarmac; a sign that it was rarely used.

A set of wooden gates separated the lane from the cottage garden and beyond the gates a newish blue Vauxhall Astra was parked in front of a detached garage. Rachel knew that anyone living here would need a car if they wanted to maintain any contact with the outside world.

The cottage itself was freshly painted and looked well kept. There were fashionable white louvred shutters at the windows and the front door was a tasteful sage green.

'Nice little hideaway,' said Trish. 'Think we'll find Jason Fitch lying low here?'

'Certainly looks like a love nest to me. But that's not his car.'

They'd already established that a white Porsche SUV was registered in Fitch's name. Besides, the Astra was hardly his style.

The woman who answered the doorbell was slender with shoulder-length dark hair and immaculate make-up. Her pencil skirt, cream silk blouse and high heels suggested she'd recently arrived home from work.

'Ms Whittingstill?' Rachel said, displaying her ID to the astonished woman. 'We'd like a word about Jason Fitch.'

'He's not here. I haven't seen him for a few days.'

Somehow Rachel hadn't expected Gemma Whittingstill to be so smart and well spoken. When she asked if they could come in, Gemma hesitated for a moment, barring their way. Then she relented and showed them into a living room decorated in a style that, in Rachel's opinion, wasn't in keeping with the cottage. Everything was beige, apart from the garish abstract wallpaper on the fireplace wall. The fireplace itself had been removed and replaced by a square recess which held three fat candles.

Rachel sat down on the low sofa and took out her notebook. 'I believe you've known Mr Fitch for a while.'

'We're close.'

'Are?' Trish picked up on the use of the present tense.

'He told me he couldn't see me for a couple of weeks because things were difficult at home but he'll be back.'

'You've heard about Andrea Jameson?'

'It was on the news.'

'We think she died last Friday and Mr Fitch's movements are unaccounted for between three and seven thirty on that day. Did he come here?'

She hesitated. 'I was at work so if he came here I didn't know about it.'

Rachel suspected she'd been tempted to lie but was wise enough to know that her story could be checked.

'I believe you threatened Mr Fitch's wife.'

She shook her head vigorously. 'It was the other way round. She got her thug of a brother to come round here, which scared the hell out of me. But Jason promised everything would be fine if we just took a break and let things calm down.' She shuddered.

'When was this?'

She thought for a moment. 'A week last Sunday.'

'Did you ever meet Andrea Jameson?'

'No. I knew Jason had a brief fling with her but . . . '

'You weren't aware that he was planning to go away with her last weekend?'

'That can't be true. It was over between them ages ago. Someone's been lying to you.'

Rachel and Trish exchanged a look. It was obvious the woman had no idea about the booking at Princebury Hall. If she'd found out, Rachel wondered how she would have reacted.

'Somebody shot Andrea Jameson. We think it was a targeted attack.'

'Don't look at me,' Gemma said indignantly. 'I've never handled a gun in my life.' She raised her hand, as though she'd suddenly had a brilliant idea. 'Sharon's brother's ex-army and I'm sure he'd be able to get hold of a gun. I wouldn't put anything past him.' She gave a smug nod as though she was satisfied she'd just solved their case for them. 'His name's Kyle Ball and Sharon uses him as her personal attack dog. If she got it into her head that Jason was still seeing Andrea . . .'

'We've been told you were jealous of Andrea.'

'Why should I be jealous of her? Jason ditched her ages ago. He said she'd just been a bit of fun.'

'We need to speak to Jason but he seems to have vanished into thin air.'

'Jason wouldn't shoot Andrea. It wouldn't make sense. Even if she was pestering him to get back with her he would have told her where to go.'

'Unless he had a reason to get rid of her you don't know about,' said Trish.

'I know him better than he knows himself. And once he's sorted things out with that mad wife of his he'll be back here with me. You'll see.'

She sounded confident – the brittle confidence of self-delusion.

'What do you do for a living, Ms Whittingstill?' Rachel asked, purely out of curiosity.

'I'm a solicitor. I work in Neston.'

'You don't fancy living anywhere more . . . central?' Trish asked.

'Jason and I chose this place together. He likes the privacy,' she said with a distant smile, as though she was imagining a future of romantic bliss.

Rachel suddenly felt sorry for Gemma Whittingstill.

'If you know where Jason Fitch is at the moment you should tell us. The sooner we can eliminate him from our inquiries, the better.'

'I can't help you.'

Rachel didn't believe her but she knew there was no point pushing it.

'If you hear from him or have any thoughts about where he might be, please contact me.' She handed her card to Gemma, who took it between her finger and thumb as if it were contaminated.

'Think she's our killer?' she asked Trish as they drove back to the incident room.

'I wouldn't rule anything out just yet,' was the reply.

As soon as Wesley and Gerry reached the incident room Gerry was whisked off to Tradmouth in a patrol car for a meeting with Noreen Fitton. He needed to bring her up to date with developments and Wesley wondered what he would tell her. There'd been developments all right – too many leads which ended nowhere.

Belinda Crillow was still on Wesley's mind and he couldn't banish the uncomfortable feeling that he'd fobbed off a woman who genuinely feared for her life. He tried to reassure himself that he'd had no choice but couldn't quite manage it. He resolved to call the station later, just to make sure everything was being dealt with properly at their end.

At 5.45 Gerry returned, announcing he was hungry as he marched into the incident room. Then he spotted Wesley and took him to one side.

'Let's go and pay Mrs Ovorard a visit. She won't be expecting us to turn up unannounced at teatime. I'm wondering whether she knows where Jocasta is and she's keeping it from her husband. And I want to know why Jeremy's so anxious to keep her out of the investigation.'

'Probably just being protective.' Wesley paused. 'I've heard he's a good MP – sorts out people's problems.'

'Even if he's a cross between the Dalai Lama and Mother Teresa, we've still got a job to do.'

The September sunshine had vanished behind a layer of cloud earlier in the afternoon and there was a chill in the air as they set off for Jeremy Ovorard's house on the far side of Morbay. To Wesley's relief rush hour was over.

Unlike their last visit, it took some time before the door opened, just a crack as though the person inside was expecting trouble.

'Mrs Ovorard?' Wesley said, poking his warrant card through the gap. 'I'm DI Peterson and this is DCI Heffernan. We're sorry to bother you but can we have a quick word about Jocasta?'

The door opened wider and Wesley saw Tabitha Ovorard for the first time. Looking considerably younger than her husband, she had long fair hair like her daughter's. She was dressed in tight white jeans and a white cotton shirt and Wesley's first thought was that Pam would have considered her outfit impractical – but perhaps Mrs Ovorard had someone else to see to the housework.

'Go through to the lounge.' A slight lisp gave her voice a childish quality. 'Would you like something to drink. Tea? Coffee? Something stronger?'

'No thank you. We'll try not to keep you long,' said Wesley, surprised that she hadn't demanded the latest news about her daughter.

When she invited them to sit Wesley sank into the over-sized sofa, feeling like a child nestling in a grown-up's armchair. Gerry, wisely, perched on the edge of the chair opposite.

'I take it Jocasta hasn't contacted you, Mrs Ovorard?'

She shook her head without meeting his gaze. 'Please, call me Tabitha. Mrs Ovorard seems so ... unfriendly, doesn't it.'

Wesley smiled. 'Very well, Tabitha. Can you tell me when you last saw your daughter?'

'Hasn't Jeremy told you?'

'We'd like to hear your version.'

She sighed. 'It was three weeks ago. She was busy with her drama course and ... '

'She came home?'

'No, I met her in Neston for lunch in a strange little café – a hippy place that serves vegan food. She said she was getting on fine with the course. She'd hated school, you see, and I was glad she'd found something she liked at last.'

'You've heard about the woman who was shot up on Dartmoor? Andrea Jameson.'

Tabitha Ovorard began to fidget with a button on her shirt. 'There was something on the news but I didn't take much notice.'

'Hasn't your husband told you that Jocasta was seen getting out of the victim's car?' said Gerry.

Tabitha stared at him as though he'd yelled an obscenity. 'You don't think ... ?'

'She was seen walking away from the car so there's nothing to suggest she was there when ...' said Wesley, trying to calm the mother's fears.

Tabitha pressed her hand to her mouth as if she was trying to suppress a scream. Wesley wished Gerry's question hadn't been so blunt but then nobody could have realised her husband had kept this development from her.

'I'm sorry if this has come as a shock,' said Wesley.

Tabitha took a clean white handkerchief from the pocket of her jeans and dabbed her eyes. It was then he noticed that she hadn't actually been crying and he wondered if the whole thing had been a show put on for their benefit.

'Is it all right if we ask you a few more questions?' he asked gently.

The answer was a brave nod.

'The dead woman's name was Andrea Jameson. I believe you and your husband had dealings with her last year.'

'I don't think so.' She didn't sound sure of herself.

'Let me jog your memory. You'd arranged a birthday party for Jocasta using Andrea Jameson's company. At the last minute Jocasta cried off and the whole thing had to be cancelled. Mrs Jameson presented you with a bill which your husband disputed. Do you remember now?'

She nodded. 'Jeremy was annoyed that she was charging us so much when it hadn't gone ahead.'

'How annoyed?' Gerry asked, leaning forward and looking Tabitha in the face.

She pondered the question for a while. 'He was within his rights. She was ripping us off. People do when you're in the public eye. They think you won't fight back because the publicity will cause embarrassment.'

'Did you meet Mrs Jameson?'

There was a moment of hesitation before she nodded. 'We needed to choose the food and the marquee, that sort of thing. That's all we talked about so I wouldn't say I knew her and when things became ... awkward, everything was done through our solicitor. We didn't go round there and shoot her if that's what you're getting at.' She pouted, like a little girl falsely accused of taking another child's toys.

'When did you last see Andrea Jameson?' Wesley asked.

'I told you, when she came here to discuss the arrangements for the party.'

'You haven't seen her since?'

She shook her head.

'Has your husband seen her since that incident?'

She looked at Wesley. Her face was a mask of innocence, as though she didn't understand the significance of his question. But he could see through the act.

'I'm sure he would have mentioned it if he had.' She shifted in her seat, as though she was preparing to stand up. 'Is that all you wanted to ask me?'

'There's one more thing if you don't mind,' said Wesley. 'A couple of our officers had a chat to the girl who shared a room with Jocasta at Widedales. She told them she thought Jocasta had a boyfriend.'

Tabitha shook her head.

Wesley took a deep breath, knowing that he was about to broach a sensitive subject and that his question would probably be met with indignant denials. 'Her room-mate also said that you and Jocasta don't get on.'

He watched Tabitha and saw her body tense. If she'd been a cat she would have arched her back and bared her claws.

'That's ridiculous.' She'd given the answer Wesley had expected but he pressed on.

'So you and Jocasta are close?'

'I'm her mother.'

'Do you know where she is?'

'Of course not.'

'Are you concealing her whereabouts to get back at your husband for some reason?'

She shook her head vigorously and the curtain of blonde hair fell over her face, hiding her expression.

'Or are you doing it to protect Jocasta? We heard your husband lost his temper with Andrea Jameson. Did he lose it with your daughter too?'

She pushed her hair back and looked up. 'No. Nothing like that.'

'What then?'

She looked away.

'If you know where she is we don't have to share the information with your husband. As long as we're satisfied she's safe and well that'll be the end of the matter as far as we're concerned.'

'I don't know where she is. That's the truth.' The words came out in a whisper.

'I'm sorry to have to ask you this but it might be important. We've heard rumours that you're having a relationship with another man. Is it true?'

She sprang up. 'I'd like you to go now. I'm not feeling well.'

Wesley knew they wouldn't learn anything else that day,

but he also knew Tabitha Ovorard was lying about something. If only he could work out what it was.

'I wonder if they have any staff,' Wesley said on their way to the car.

Gerry stopped and looked back at the house. 'Shouldn't be hard to find out.'

20

It was Saturday morning and Neil had arranged to meet his team of volunteers at the church at 10.30. There was a wedding at 3.30 so time was limited, which disappointed those volunteers who could only make it at weekends; Sundays were out for obvious reasons.

He parked his car, unable to forget the events of the previous day and suddenly apprehensive about seeing Oliver Grayling again. He was sure that the 'curate' John Davies wasn't who he claimed to be and in his imagination saw the man as a blackmailer – or a kidnapper who was holding the vicar's nearest and dearest hostage in some long-disused Dartmoor mine. His instinct was to ask Wesley's advice but Grayling had been adamant that he didn't want the police involved.

Neil's team were waiting for him in the church porch, perusing the parish notices and chatting amongst themselves. When they made their way into the church Neil noticed the flower arranger who'd directed him to the vicarage the other day was busy putting the finishing touches to a large display by the pulpit. She was around his own age, slim in jeans and sweatshirt, with bobbed sandy hair and a pretty face. When he asked her if the vicar was about, she pointed to the vestry.

After telling the others to carry on with the survey, he knocked on the vestry door. He wanted to speak to Grayling in private.

He heard a cheerful 'Come in' and pushed the door open. To his surprise the vicar displayed no sign of embarrassment; it was as though the previous day had never happened.

'Are you OK?' Neil began. 'It's just that after yesterday . . . '

'It was a silly misunderstanding. I'd rather not talk about it.'

'Up to you.'

There was a long silence before Neil changed the subject. 'I saw Canon Collins yesterday.'

'How is he?'

'Fine. He told me a student called Alcuin Garrard found an old journal in the vestry cupboard in the nineteen nineties. I was wondering if it mentioned our mechanical figure.'

'As far as I know the cupboard's full of dusty old hymn books but you're more than welcome to have a look if you wish.'

Neil thanked him and conducted a swift search of the huge cupboard, only to find that Grayling had been right about the hymn books. If Alcuin Garrard had found anything interesting in there, he'd taken it away with him and never returned it. Perhaps death had prevented him.

'There's just one more thing,' Neil said when he'd finished. 'Is it possible to get up on your roof? You often find graffiti in out-of-the-way places. I don't like asking the volunteers so . . . '

'Of course. I'll show you the way.'

Ten minutes later Neil was stepping through a rickety

154

door off the clock chamber near the top of the tower on to the lead roof. There was a high, crenellated parapet between him and the long drop to the ground but, even so, Oliver Grayling made his excuses and returned to the vestry. Neil looked down on to the churchyard and from his lofty position the graves looked tiny, like toys made for a child with a particularly morbid imagination, and Lower Torworthy, tucked into the green Dartmoor landscape, reminded him of a model village he'd visited as a child.

He leaned against the sloping lead watching people come and go from the Shepherd's Arms and the village shop. He could see police cars parked outside the church hall and he wondered whether Wesley was in there – even though it was Saturday he guessed he'd still be working on his double murder.

The sun emerged from behind the clouds and he shielded his eyes. These weren't ideal conditions to see any shallow carvings left by the villagers of days gone by but he began to edge his way carefully around the parapet, his gaze fixed on the ancient stones.

In the sunlight he managed to spot a mason's mark, identical to one he'd seen several times inside the church, and it wasn't long before he came across more marks; the initials of long-dead souls who'd left signs of their presence up there for posterity. He spotted what looked like the imprint of a foot carved into the stone between the lead roof and the parapet along with more protective marks; the same signs to ward off evil that he'd found inside the building. However it wasn't until he was at the far end of the church, just above where the altar stood, that he saw an image that made his pulse race.

It had been incised deep into the stone of the parapet

with a knife or compasses and Neil immediately recognised it as the little mechanical monk they'd found. It was pictured in an attitude of prayer and, although the carving was crude, he could make out its face, tilted upwards towards heaven.

Three feet away someone had carved another figure, similar in shape but twice the size of the first. This too looked like a monk but its cowl half concealed a face that was a deeply incised void. This figure, unlike the first, was covered in protection marks: crosses, daisy wheels, M for Mary; every symbol in the medieval armoury of defence against the devil.

Neil stared at the two images for a while before taking out his phone and photographing them from several angles. If he wasn't mistaken, these were the most exciting carvings in the whole place.

He made his way unsteadily down the tower steps, clinging to the rope which served as a banister. He wanted to share his discovery with somebody and the first person he thought of was Lucy, who was enjoying some retail therapy in Exeter after her long stay in Orkney. However, in her absence he gathered the volunteers around him as soon as he reached the church and when he showed them the photographs the news was greeted with excitement and speculation about the meaning of the larger figure, which had clearly been regarded as evil by whoever had carved it.

He noticed the flower arranger hovering at the edge of the group, standing on tiptoe to see over the shoulder of the man in front of her. Once the volunteers had dispersed with their clipboards and pencils to carry on their work Neil went over to her.

'Like to see the pictures I took up on the roof?'

The woman looked as though she wasn't sure how to answer. Eventually she nodded warily.

He was about to select the photographs when she spoke. 'I heard you talking to Oliver about Alcuin – the student who died.'

'You knew him?'

There was a short silence before she answered. 'I met him during the summer before I went away to uni. Lower Torworthy isn't the most exciting place for a teenager so it was good to have someone to talk to.'

'What did you study?'

'History – at York.'

'Amazing,' said Neil, sensing the presence of a kindred spirit although he couldn't help noticing that she was fidgeting with the secateurs she was holding, as though she was anxious to cut their conversation short. But Neil was intrigued.

'How come you ended up back here?'

'I married one of my fellow students.'

'History?'

'No, computer science. My husband's originally from London and he thinks this is a good place for kids to grow up ...' She sounded doubtful.

'What does he do?'

'We both work from home. He runs a software company and I run a business too – silk flowers.'

'Tell me about Alcuin.'

She glanced over her shoulder. 'There's nothing much to tell. He was doing research for his PhD and he had a terrible accident. That's all really.'

His instincts told him she was holding something back.

157

'Fancy a drink at lunchtime?' he asked, hoping she wouldn't take the invitation the wrong way.

She made a show of looking at her watch. 'I haven't time. Sorry.'

'What's your name, by the way?'

'Sarah. Sarah Shaw.'

He held out his hand and she took it limply. Her hand was moist, as if she was nervous.

'I'm Neil Watson.'

'I know. You're quite famous round here. Nobody's taken so much interest in our little church since . . . '

'Alcuin?'

She didn't reply. Instead she returned to her flowers, working intently as though there was something on her mind. Neil wondered if the subject of Alcuin Garrard had upset her.

Ten minutes later he received a call from Canon Collins to say he'd found the press cuttings and Neil could pick them up any time. Neil thanked Collins and felt a tingle of anticipation. He wanted to know what Alcuin Garrard had found out about the little monk – and whether his researches had turned up any mention of a larger, faceless counterpart.

Wesley sat at his desk going through everything they knew about Andrea Jameson and Ian Evans. After their meeting with Tabitha Ovorard he and Gerry felt there was a lot more to learn about Andrea. Ian, on the other hand, had led an apparently blameless life. Everybody who'd been spoken to – colleagues, friends, relatives, fellow members of his rambling club – told the same story and Wesley was finding it hard to believe that anything in Ian Evans's life, a life many people would have described as dull, could have caused someone to kill him in such a violent and calculated manner.

Nothing untoward had been found on his computer. The tech people had gone through his browsing history and found that he'd visited several sites about Dartmoor, including the websites of Princebury Hall and the Shepherd's Arms. A couple of the sites he'd looked at mentioned the death of the student in Manor Field and Wesley wondered whether he'd been paying a special visit to the spot when he was killed. Perhaps it was a coincidence – there was a public right of way through that field after all – but he thought it was worth trying to establish a connection between the two men who'd died in the same field all those years apart; whether they'd once known each other or were related in some way. He'd ask someone to check.

Then there was Jocasta Ovorard. He hoped she wouldn't be found like Andrea and Ian, lying in an isolated spot with a bullet through her head. Dartmoor was vast and dotted with ancient mine workings, abandoned farm buildings and other places where bodies could lie undiscovered for years. The search with dogs hadn't turned anything up so maybe it was time to extend it beyond the area around the village.

It was going to be another long day and he felt he ought to call Pam to check that she was all right. Rachel had observed that he'd become quite the devoted husband since Pam's illness and he wondered if this meant he hadn't been one before. Perhaps she was right; a devoted husband would never have felt that pull of temptation he'd experienced with Rachel when duty had taken them up north together. Since then he'd made sure that when an overnight stay was involved, he took Gerry instead.

Eventually he found a spare minute to call home and the phone rang out for a while before Pam picked it up and answered with a wary 'hello'.

'It's me. Something the matter?'

'No, I'm fine.'

He could tell she was anything but fine so he repeated the question.

'I've been getting more silent calls. There's definitely somebody on the other end because I can hear him breathing.'

'Are the kids there?'

'No, they're both with friends and my mum's still gallivanting up on Dartmoor.' She hesitated. 'I'm feeling a bit nervous about being on my own, to tell the truth.'

'If you're worried why don't you go next door?' he said. His amiable retired neighbours were the type who'd be good in a crisis. 'I'm sure they—'

'They're away, remember? They dropped their key off on Friday.'

Wesley was annoyed with himself for forgetting.

'What if it goes beyond phone calls?' he heard Pam say. 'What if he's watching the house?'

21

'Right.' Gerry waited for the room to fall silent. 'It's just come to light that Jason Fitch is the proud owner of a forty-foot yacht called *The Silvery Moon* moored in Tradmouth. According to the harbour master there's someone aboard. He's promised to let us know if there's any movement.'

'Strange neither Sharon Fitch nor Gemma Whittingstill mentioned a yacht,' said Wesley, knowing this new development meant that he'd lost any chance of an early finish.

'My thoughts exactly. Let's get down there. I've put the river patrol on standby.'

When Gerry was in this mood there was no stopping him, so Wesley followed in his wake and as they were on their way to the car he received a call from Neil. As soon as he answered he asked Neil where he was. If he could ask him to call in to see Pam, it would allay his worries. Neil, however, said he was in Lower Torworthy and that he'd had an interesting conversation with a flower arranger. This conjured strange images in Wesley's head of his friend garlanded with flowers or arranging to have one of his trenches decorated with a floral display. Then Neil told Wesley he was meeting a clergyman later in the hope of making an interesting discovery which might or might not be linked to Wesley's inquiry. But before he could explain, Wesley said he had to go; he had a suspect to pick up – hopefully. They'd catch up soon.

Once they'd reached Tradmouth they made for the waterfront where they were met by the harbour master, who greeted Gerry like an old friend.

After a short conversation Gerry turned to Wesley. '*The Silvery Moon*'s moored at the marina,' he announced before climbing back into the passenger seat.

'That's near Andrea Jameson's apartment.'

'Handy for a bit of how's-your-father,' said Gerry.

They were met at their destination by three uniformed constables and Wesley could see the police launch stationed on the river nearby as Gerry strode ahead along the jetty. The boss was an experienced sailor, having been an officer in the merchant navy before joining the police. After his wife Kathy's death he'd renovated a thirty-foot yacht to take his mind off his grief so he looked at home amongst the gleaming hulls of the vessels Wesley had heard him describe as gin palaces for the idle rich.

The Silvery Moon, as its name suggested, was shiny and white and Gerry estimated that she must have cost a fortune. They stood aside as the uniforms boarded. Then Gerry leaped aboard, moving with the confidence of an expert. In contrast Wesley, no fan of boats, clambered over the rails gingerly, just in time to hear raised voices coming from the cabin.

He followed Gerry to the cabin where he saw shadowy figures struggling in the confined space. By the time they burst in it was all over and a man was kneeling on the floor, subdued and in handcuffs. The prisoner had a deep tan and tattoos on his bare arms and legs; the sunglasses perched on top of his well-cut hair had been knocked askew in the melee. Wesley supposed many would call him good-looking in a flashy sort of way. He'd seen his type so many times before strutting up and down on the esplanade in the summer months or lounging on the decks of expensive yachts.

'Jason Fitch, I presume?' Gerry said with relish. 'I'm arresting you on suspicion of the murders of Andrea Jameson and Ian Evans.' He recited the familiar words of the caution while Fitch stared up at him, his mouth hanging open to show two rows of unnaturally white teeth.

'This is a joke, right? I never touched Andrea. And I've never heard of this Ian whatever his name is.'

As soon as a constable had hauled Fitch to his feet one of his colleagues appeared from the cabin beyond holding a long object wrapped in canvas.

'I found this, sir,' the young man said eagerly, hoping to impress his superiors.

And Wesley was impressed, because when the constable unwrapped the object he saw that it was a rifle.

Jason Fitch was in the cells and the clock was ticking away the time until they had to decide whether to charge or release him.

'What do you think, Wes?' Gerry said. He was in his office in Tradmouth Police Station, sinking into the worn leather swivel chair that had moulded itself to his body over the years.

Wesley leaned back and closed his eyes. He found it easier to think here than in the makeshift incident room.

'What's his motive?'

'Andrea was making life awkward for him. Making

demands. He already had a wife and Gemma Whittingstill – by the way, neither of them knew about the yacht. He was a devious bugger and maybe Andrea was a complication too far.'

'He'd arranged to meet her at Princebury Hall for a weekend of yoga and motivation and sex. Surely if he was planning to get rid of her . . . '

'Who knows what goes on in people's minds – or what pressure Andrea was putting on him.' Gerry sounded unsure of himself. Usually making an arrest fired him with fresh enthusiasm, but not on this occasion.

'Something wrong?' Wesley asked.

'I was hoping to take a few days off next week to go up to Liverpool. Alison's taking time off work and . . . '

'If Fitch is our man, you'll still be able to make it,' Wesley said with an optimism he didn't really feel.

'Still no sign of Jocasta Ovorard. We were going to have a word with Ovorard's staff, weren't we.'

'According to Morbay nick they've got a cleaner and a part-time gardener. I don't know whether that counts as staff.'

Gerry tapped the side of his nose. 'Cleaners know things. She might be worth talking to.'

'Might be a he,' said Wesley with a grin. 'And gardeners can observe comings and goings. He maybe even had a thing going with Jocasta.'

'You've been reading *Lady Chatterley's Lover* again.'

They started to laugh and Wesley felt a release of tension. For months he'd lived with the worry of Pam's health coupled with pressure at work and the simple act of laughter lifted the shadow from his soul.

But the respite wasn't to last. His phone rang and when

he looked at the caller display he saw Belinda Crillow's number.

'I've told her I'm not dealing with her case but she keeps on calling me,' he said to Gerry, staring at the ringing phone.

'Who did you pass her on to?'

'Rob Carter. He says she hasn't been cooperative.'

From Gerry's office window he could see Rob at his desk, deep in paperwork. He looked fed up, as though he'd rather be out chasing villains up dark alleys.

'He's contacted Ms Crillow several times but she says she'll only speak to me.'

Gerry sighed. 'I'll have a word with her?' he said, stretching out his hand to take the phone.

Wesley passed it over. 'DI Peterson's phone, DCI Heffernan speaking.' Gerry sounded authoritative; the man to sort out any problem.

But the line went dead and Gerry was left shaking his head. 'Looks like it's you she wants, Wes.' He paused and lowered his voice. 'It happened to me once. I was kind to this woman – prostitute she was. I got her away from her pimp, fixed her up with somewhere to stay and listened to her woes. From then on I was the first person she called whenever anything went wrong – and in a life as chaotic as hers that was every other day. In the end Kathy put her foot down. I'd got too involved.'

'What did you do?'

'I put her in touch with a charity and they arranged for her to move out of the area. Never heard from her again. Give it time. It'll sort itself out. You know your trouble, Wes? You're too soft.'

'There have been times when I could have said the same about you.'

'Hard as nails, me. Scourge of every villain this side of the Tamar,' Gerry said with a wink.

Wesley's phone rang again and this time the number was one he didn't recognise. When he answered he heard a male voice. Whoever he was he sounded young – and he was speaking quietly as though he didn't want to be overheard.

'Inspector Peterson? This is Craig Carswell. We met at Tradington Barn when you came to ask about Jo. Remember?'

It took Wesley a few seconds to place the name. Then he recalled the cocky boy with the top knot and wispy beard who had made the introductions. Now he sounded nervous. Perhaps the blasé confidence had been an act he'd put on for the benefit of the others in the group.

'I remember. What can I do for you?'

'You spoke to Kimberley, didn't you?'

'That's right.'

'Well, she doesn't know the whole story. Jo and me . . .'

'You were close?'

'For a short while. Nothing heavy. Look, I haven't been in touch before now because I've been thinking things over.'

'Do you know where she might be?'

'Afraid not.' He hesitated. 'We went our separate ways a week before she left. She gave me the usual crap about it being her not me but I reckon I was just a distraction. I think there'd been someone else all along.'

'Any idea who?'

'Sorry. But she did say something which might be relevant.'

'What was that?' Wesley was doing his best to curb his impatience.

'That it would be good to go off the grid; to become a different person so nobody could ever mess with your head again. I think she had problems.'

'What problems?'

'Don't know. Might have been something to do with her family. She seemed quite bitter about them, specially her dad.'

'Off the grid? You're sure that's what she said?'

'Yes. And I overheard her talking to someone on the phone the day before she left. She called him Luke.'

Wesley sat forward, suddenly alert. 'Luke? Had she ever mentioned that name before?'

'Don't think so.' He paused. 'I heard she was seen with that woman who was shot. You don't think she's . . . ?'

Wesley picked up on the anxiety in his voice and knew that Carswell was thinking the worst.

'That's why we're trying to find her, Craig. If you remember anything else, no matter how trivial it seems, you'll call me, won't you?'

The line went dead just as Gwen from Forensics entered the office, a file tucked under her arm. She made straight for Wesley's desk and he watched her expectantly, hoping she was bringing news that would move the investigation on.

None of the usual pleasantries were exchanged. She came straight to the point. 'Ballistics say the rounds found at the scene of the double shooting probably came from a powerful hunting rifle, something like a Winchester, but there's no match to any legally held firearms in the area.'

'Maybe we should widen the search but it's more likely our killer doesn't hold a licence.' He looked at her and smiled. 'Thanks, Gwen. Leave it with me.'

*

167

Why wouldn't Wesley Peterson speak to her? Didn't he know how frightened she was? Belinda felt a wave of fury and feared she was losing control. Somebody had his phone. Someone was keeping him from talking to her – probably Rob Carter, who treated her as if she was a time-wasting nuisance. He didn't realise it could be a matter of life and death.

Belinda sat on her sofa twisting a strand of hair tight around her finger. Was Carter part of the conspiracy? And if he was, who was behind it? Perhaps it was the wife. Or his boss, DCI Heffernan – the one who'd answered his phone earlier. What was Heffernan doing with his phone anyway?

All sorts of possibilities ran through her head. But she needed to find out for sure.

Letter from Oswald DeTorham
to his cousin Henry Dyce

3 February 1532

Cousin, I write to tell you that my brother Simeon is well again after his long illness, thanks to the good offices of our priest, Sir Matthew, and his strange mechanical monk. I give thanks even though my brother was, before his sickness, much given to wickedness.

Simeon recovers his strength and speaks of journeying to Exeter. I pray he will not seek out trouble now that the Lord has spared his life.

Letter from Henry Dyce
to Oswald DeTorham

5 February 1532

My dear cousin, greetings.

I rejoice at your brother's recovery even though, as you say, he has been wont to cause great trouble to all around him. You say your priest has a mechanical monk which brought about this miracle. I would see this thing for myself and perchance your priest would bring it to my house for Jane is once more with child and it would be a great comfort to her.

I pray Simeon's glimpse of death will cause him to mend his ways. He was ever an untamed soul and such a soul is oft times sought by the devil to do his work. I beg you to watch him closely lest he makes mischief for you and your neighbours.

I hear talk of another matter concerning your household. It is said that your steward Peter consorts with heretics and those who would scorn the teachings of the Holy Church. The devil stalks the world and you must be alert for evil. I fear for Peter's soul as I fear for Simeon's.

22

'All legally held firearms in the area have been checked and eliminated,' said Wesley. 'The murder weapon's off our radar.'

Gerry thought for a few moments. 'Can't say I'm surprised. Neil's metal detector did a good job.'

'It's detectorist, not detector. He's helped Neil out on a lot of digs. Apparently his equipment's the best you can buy.'

'Bit of a nerd then?'

'I couldn't possibly comment,' said Wesley with a smile which vanished when a glance at his list of things to do reminded him that someone needed to visit the family of the girl who'd allegedly been assaulted aboard a yacht during a party organised by Andrea Jameson.

The girl's name was Phoebe Jakes and she lived on the road to Tradmouth Castle in a house with a crenellated tower. He remembered Pam saying it reminded her of something from a fairy tale – a tower overlooking the water with wisteria growing around the door.

Gerry agreed that Wesley should pay the Jakes family a visit while he and Trish Walton interviewed Jason Fitch. Knowing the situation needed delicate handling, Wesley insisted on Rachel going with him, even though he had to wait for her to arrive from the incident room in Lower Torworthy before he could set off.

The day was fine so they decided to walk, which gave them a chance to consider their strategy for an interview which was bound to be awkward and painful for the girl concerned.

When Rachel knocked at the door Wesley hung back, overwhelmed by a strong feeling that they shouldn't be intruding. What had happened to the girl was terrible, and here they were about to question her family on suspicion of murder.

The middle-aged man who answered the door introduced himself as Richard Jakes, Phoebe's father, and asked what they wanted. His attitude was protective, which was hardly surprising, but Wesley knew he shouldn't allow his sympathy to get in the way of the investigation.

'You've heard about the recent shooting up on Dartmoor?' Wesley asked once they were settled in the living room.

'Yes. But I don't see what it has to do with me.'

'Is your daughter at home?' Rachel asked. She'd switched on the sympathetic professional manner Wesley had seen so many times before.

Wesley's eyes were drawn to the large window to his left, which afforded a view over the river to the far bank where stone houses perched on the hillside, nestling amongst the trees. Yachts glided past on the glistening water, a silent moving tableau beyond the glass. If he lived here he'd never leave this room, he thought. Still, a policeman's salary didn't buy views like that in South Devon.

'She's in her room but I don't want to disturb her unless it's absolutely necessary.' Wesley saw the challenge in his eyes.

'That's fine, Mr Jakes,' said Rachel. 'Maybe you could answer some questions for us.' She waited expectantly.

Jakes appeared to relax now the threat to his daughter had passed. 'How can I help you?'

'One of the Dartmoor victims was called Andrea Jameson. I believe you had dealings with her.'

'I'd hardly describe it as dealings. She gave Phoebe a holiday job, that's all. And before you ask, I didn't like the woman. I thought she was a hard bitch.'

'How old was Phoebe when she took the job?'

'Seventeen. She was in the sixth form and she wanted to earn some money over the summer as kids do. Mrs Jameson advertised for waiting staff at the events she organised and Phoebe went for an interview. She loved the work at first.' He stood up and walked over to the window. Even though he had his back to them Wesley could sense the man's anger as the memories resurfaced. His body had tensed and his fists were clenched as though he wanted to punch something – or somebody.

'We've been told about the incident,' Rachel said softly. 'You didn't report it to the police. Why was that?'

'What use would it have been? The man in question had sailed away in his yacht so he was long gone and, besides, she didn't tell us right away so it would have been her word against his even if you had found him. I wasn't going to drag her through all those intrusive questions; making her relive her ordeal time and time again. It would have done more harm than good.'

'If people don't come forward we can't catch the offender

and stop him doing it again to someone else's daughter,' said Rachel.

But Wesley had a daughter of his own so he understood how Jakes felt. You'd move heaven and earth to stop your child suffering, even though you longed to wreak your revenge on the person who hurt them. In the absence of the real perpetrator, had Richard Jakes taken his fury out on Andrea Jameson, the woman responsible for Phoebe being there in the first place?

'You bore a grudge against Mrs Jameson?'

'I thought she had a duty of care towards Phoebe, and I suspect she persuaded her to say nothing about the incident. My daughter's personality changed that night, Inspector. She became withdrawn and frightened. Yes, I bore a grudge against Andrea Jameson but that doesn't mean I killed her.'

'Do you own a firearm?'

'No. You can check. I'm sure you have records.'

'Ever served in the army?'

'I was in the officer cadet corps at school. Why?'

'So you know how to handle a rifle?'

'No. I mean . . . it was a long time ago.'

'Where were you the Friday before last, Mr Jakes?' he said. 'I'm sorry to have to ask but we'd like to eliminate you from our inquiry as soon as possible.'

Jakes hesitated by the window for a few seconds before leaving the room and returning with a large desk diary. He consulted it before passing it to Wesley. 'As you can see I was away at a weekend conference in the South of France.'

'What kind of conference?' Wesley asked, curious. The police conferences he'd attended had been in places like

Leeds or Reading. The sunny climate of the South of France would have made a pleasant change.

'I'm in pharmaceuticals,' he said. 'Look, is that all?'

'What about your wife?'

'She was here. We always make sure somebody's at home with Phoebe these days. I work from home whenever I can.'

'Can we speak to your wife?'

'She's out at the moment. Shopping in Morbay.'

'Is it all right if I talk to Phoebe?' Rachel's question was tentative. 'I promise I'll try not to upset her.'

'That's out of the question, I'm afraid.'

'What's going on?'

The speaker was a girl who must have been in her late teens but looked younger. She was standing in the doorway with one hand resting on the doorframe as if for support. She was small and skinny with curly dark hair and a pinched face.

'Phoebe, darling, these people were just going.'

Rachel stood up and gave the girl a reassuring smile. 'I'd like to ask you a few questions, Phoebe. It'd help us a great deal and we can stop whenever you like.'

'OK.' Her voice sounded surprisingly strong – and determined.

'You don't have to, darling.'

She turned to her father. 'It's fine, Dad. Why don't you go and make a cup of tea or something.'

Her father wavered, as though he couldn't decide on the best course of action, but eventually he left the room, glancing back to make sure everything was all right.

Phoebe sat down and tucked her legs beneath her, her fragile body dwarfed by the marshmallow-like sofa.

'Thank you for speaking to me,' Rachel began.

'Sorry about Dad. He's very protective.'

'That's understandable,' said Wesley. 'Are you sure you're up to this?'

She looked straight at Wesley and her expression suddenly became guarded. 'I saw you on TV. You were talking about that missing girl.'

He could tell she was nervous of him. Whether it was because of his gender or the colour of his skin he couldn't tell.

'That's right. Look, if you'd rather speak to Rachel alone, I quite understand.' He rose from his seat. 'I'll go and help your dad with the tea.'

Once he'd left the room Phoebe made her way over to the window where she stood with her back to Rachel, staring out at the scene beyond the glass. After what seemed like a long time she turned and spoke.

'I overheard you asking about Andrea. She's been murdered, right?'

'Yes.'

'Well I know it wasn't Dad. OK, he was angry with her for sending me on to that boat but it wasn't her fault. She couldn't have known what was going to happen.'

There was something about the way she said it, a hint of uncertainty, that made Rachel uncomfortable.

'It's natural that your father needed someone to blame. Maybe if you'd told him who . . .'

As soon as Rachel had said the words Phoebe's manner changed and she seemed to shrink back into the wall by the window as though she was trying to make herself invisible. 'No,' she whispered, shaking her head.

'Are you afraid of something, Phoebe?' Rachel said softly. 'Or somebody? If you are, we can help you. Honestly.'

'Have you found that girl yet?'

'Not yet,' said Rachel, surprised at the change of subject. 'Why? Do you know her?'

Phoebe shook her head, more vigorously this time.

'We've spoken to one of Andrea Jameson's colleagues. She told us your attacker was somebody on the yacht – a Frenchman who was a friend of the owner.'

'Is that what she said?'

'Isn't it true?'

There was no answer.

'Are you afraid because this man's still around?' said Rachel. 'He wasn't French, was he?'

Phoebe froze and Rachel knew she'd hit a nerve. The attacker hadn't sailed off in that yacht. He was still around and she was afraid of him.

'Have you seen him in the area since the attack?'

Phoebe hugged herself defensively and looked away. 'I thought you wanted to talk about Andrea.'

'What can you tell us about her?'

'She said not to tell anybody. She said no one would believe me.'

'That's not true.'

'Why would anyone believe the word of a silly teenage girl over a man like that? That's what she said.'

'A man like what?'

Rachel watched as a tear rolled down the girl's cheek. 'She said I was a liar and that's what everyone would think.'

'Andrea said that?' Rachel felt angry on the girl's behalf; and if she, a stranger, felt like that she could only imagine how Richard Jakes would react if he ever discovered the truth.

'Did you tell your parents what she said?'

'No. I just wanted to forget about it.' She glanced at the door as though she'd only just realised that her father and Wesley were out there and might be eavesdropping. 'Look, I've told you everything I know. I can't help you.'

Rachel reached out and touched the girl's hand, a gesture of support, but Phoebe flinched as though she'd hit her. Then Rachel handed her a card with her contact details and Phoebe took it and folded it into the smallest possible square before tipping it on to the coffee table.

As they walked back to the police station, Rachel recounted her conversation with Phoebe.

'I don't think it was a success,' she said.

'I don't agree,' said Wesley. 'It's given us a better idea of what Andrea Jameson was like. And, who knows, now she's gone Phoebe might have second thoughts about naming her attacker.'

It was mid-afternoon by the time Wesley reached Lower Torworthy. He'd called in at the police station in Tradmouth on the way back from the Jakeses' house, only to find that Gerry and Trish were still interviewing Jason Fitch. He hadn't had time to wait around until they'd finished.

When he arrived at the church hall he found Neil walking out of the main door; a happy example of perfect timing.

'I've been looking for you but one of your minions said you were in Tradmouth.'

Wesley had to smile. He'd never considered himself the type to have minions.

'I believe Charlie Perks came up trumps.'

'He was a great help – sped things up no end.'

Neil thought for a moment. 'As a matter of fact I want to

speak to him myself. I've got a hunch that figure we found might not be the only one. If there's another wrapped up in lead out there somewhere I need to find it.' He paused. 'I've discovered something that might interest you. In nineteen ninety-five a student was found dead in the field where those people were murdered.'

'I know. What about it?'

Neil produced a plastic folder containing a wad of newspaper cuttings and handed it to Wesley. 'A very nice canon from Exeter Cathedral lent me these.'

Wesley led the way into the church hall and they sat down by the desk that had become his for the duration of the investigation.

'Alcuin Garrard was a PhD student researching the goings on in pre-Reformation Lower Torworthy. My canon was vicar here at the time and he got quite friendly with him.'

Wesley studied the cuttings in the folder. TRAGIC DEATH OF EXETER STUDENT. STUDENT DIES IN FREAK ACCIDENT. It was more or less what he expected to see and similar to the material found in the browsing history of Ian Evans's computer. He was about to hand the folder back to Neil when he stopped himself. 'Mind if I keep these for a couple of days?'

'You don't think it could be connected to your murders, do you?'

'Probably not. But this man was found in the same field so I'm interested. Any more news about your little monk?'

'I found a strange carving on the church roof – the little monk alongside a bigger version, only someone had covered the bigger figure with protection marks to ward off evil. I'm not sure what to make of it.'

'Did Alcuin Garrard finish his thesis?'

'Shouldn't be hard to find out. Hopefully there'll be a copy at the university.'

Neil left the church hall, almost bumping into Paul Johnson who was rushing in as though he had important news. Paul made straight for Wesley's desk and sat down heavily in the seat Neil had just vacated.

'I've just come back from Tradmouth. The gun they found on Jason Fitch's yacht is a two point two – not the weapon we're looking for. He says it's an old rifle he uses for target practice. Claims he's had it for years.'

'I take it the boss knows?'

Paul nodded. 'According to Fitch, when he heard about Andrea Jameson's murder on the news he knew he'd be a suspect so he panicked and legged it. Been lying low ever since.'

'Hardly the behaviour of an innocent man.'

'Says he's got some business deals in the pipeline and he couldn't afford the distraction – that and his missus has been cutting up rough about his tangled love life. He says it was easier to stay on the boat and wait for things to calm down. He bought the boat last year but his missus doesn't know about it. Uses it as a secret hideaway – a shag pad, he says.'

'Was he asked why he didn't turn up at Princebury Hall?'

'His story tallies with his wife's. She gave him an ultimatum so he stood Andrea up to keep the peace. He stormed out and drove round but he swears he didn't go anywhere near Lower Torworthy.'

'Does the boss believe him?'

Paul shrugged. 'If you ask me he's got guilty written all over him.'

'That clinches it then,' said Wesley.

Paul nodded earnestly. He'd never had much of a sense of humour.

Moriarty – named by Wesley after Sherlock Holmes's nemesis – was a cat who enjoyed company and when Pam tried to prise her off her knee the claws came out and dug into her flesh. Gently Pam extricated herself and placed Moriarty on the floor in the kitchen beside her food bowl. She needed to fetch Amelia from her friend's house in Whitely and if she didn't hurry she'd be late.

She wasn't sure what time Wesley would arrive home that evening. The double murder in Lower Torworthy was playing havoc with their domestic life and even her mother had gone AWOL. Della hadn't called her from Princebury Hall so Pam assumed she was having a good time up there. In fact the only calls she'd received that day had been silent and in the end she'd unplugged the phone. If anyone she knew needed to contact her urgently there was always her mobile.

She switched on the burglar alarm and grabbed her car keys before slamming the front door behind her.

As she was about to climb into the driver's seat she sensed something was wrong, looked down and saw that her front tyre was flat. Then she noticed that the back tyre was in the same state and when she circled the car she realised that all four had been attacked. Shaking with panic, she rushed to her neighbours' house and hammered on the front door before remembering they were away.

She tried the other houses nearby but, being Saturday afternoon, nobody was at home. Whoever had vandalised her car had chosen the perfect time.

With trembling hands she took out her phone and called Wesley.

23

By the time Neil returned to the church his volunteers were packing up for the day and the wedding guests were starting to arrive so he was surprised to see Charlie Perks coming towards him down the aisle. Unusually he didn't have his metal detector with him and his hair looked as though it had been washed since their last meeting.

'I've been looking for you,' said Perks.

'That's lucky. I wanted to talk to you as well. You know those workmen found that lead box? Well, I think there might be another.'

Perks caught on fast. 'Where do you want me to start looking?'

'Near where they found the first?'

Perks shook his head and a few flakes of dandruff fluttered on to the shoulders of his combat jacket. 'That was in the street. Too many cables. Signal would be all over the place. You'd never find it and even if you did, you can't just go digging up roads. Council don't take kindly to that sort of thing.'

Neil had been carried away with the excitement of what he'd seen on the roof but he knew Perks was right. 'What do you suggest then?'

'There used to be a manor house on the road to Princebury.' He paused. 'Where all the police are.'

'That's exactly what I was thinking. Once the police have packed up I've got the farmer's approval to do a geophysics survey and sink some test pits. According to old maps and the Historic Environment Record the building that used to be on the site was late medieval. One section of wall's still standing and, judging by the terrain, there could be a lot under the ground. I've suggested the site for a training dig for local archaeology groups and students and the farmer seems happy about it.'

Perks grunted something Neil didn't quite catch, then fumbled in one of his many pockets and brought something out. When he opened his hand Neil saw that the object was a shiny gold ring.

'I need to hand this in. Do you want to take charge of it?'

Neil took the ring from Perks's outstretched palm and examined it. It was large enough to be a man's signet ring and Neil felt a tingle of excitement as he held it, squinting to examine the engraving on the front.

He made for the vestry where the light was better and held the ring up, expecting to see initials or a family crest. But instead he recognised the familiar shape of the small wooden monk they'd found. He studied it for a while, wondering if there'd been some sort of devotional cult in the village, venerating a little machine the people considered miraculous?

'I found it in that field,' said Perks. 'Turned it up when I was helping the cops. What do you make of it?'

In his absorption Neil had almost forgotten about Perks, who was looming in the doorway, blocking his exit.

'I'd like to show it to someone at the university.'

Perks said nothing. He was looking around the vestry, taking in every detail.

'I'll notify the local finds liaison officer and the land-owner as well. You look worried, Charlie.'

'I know it's got to be done and all that but it's the best find I've had in ages and ...'

'Don't worry, I'll take good care of it. Can you show me exactly where you found it?' Neil said, impatient to see where this new treasure had come from.

Perks looked down at his feet like a naughty child caught out doing something he shouldn't. 'It wasn't far from the gate. It's cordoned off with police tape so I don't think we should ...'

Neil experienced a mixture of excitement and frustra-tion. The promising field would be regarded as a crime scene for the time being so no archaeological investigation, however discreet, would be allowed until the police had finished.

Before he could say any more Perks turned to leave. Not for the first time Neil wondered about his life stuck in the middle of nowhere caring for his aged mother, although having another human being to look after was probably better than being alone in the world. For the past months he himself had experienced solitude and he'd had enough of it he thought as he took his phone from his pocket to call Lucy.

Wesley was busy examining a list of Andrea Jameson's contacts gleaned from her computer when he received a call from Gerry telling him to get back to Tradmouth. He needed him to sit in on the next interview with Jason Fitch and the clock was ticking. As Wesley was making for his car his phone rang and when he saw it was Pam he wavered for a moment before answering. If it was some problem with her mother he really didn't have time.

'Someone's slashed my tyres.' Her voice was shaking and he pressed the phone closer to his ear. 'The car was on the drive as usual and when I went out I found it like that. All four tyres.'

'Did any of the neighbours see anything?'

'Most of them are out. No one saw a thing.'

'Have you noticed anyone hanging around?'

'I would have said.' He could tell she was on the verge of tears.

'I'll be there in half an hour,' he said.

If they didn't amass more evidence against Jason Fitch soon Gerry knew they'd have to release him.

He'd taken a break, partly at the request of Fitch's solicitor and partly to give Wesley time to get there. Then Wesley had called to say Pam's car had been vandalised and she was badly shaken. He'd sounded worried and he wasn't the only one: Gerry knew Tradmouth wasn't the sort of place where people's cars were attacked in a respectable residential street, especially when no other vehicles nearby had been touched. It looked as though somebody had a grudge against Wesley, possibly because of his job – or the colour of his skin. The idea that some faceless ill-wisher had been out there watching his friend's house, filled with enough hatred to inflict damage like that, disturbed him. With Wesley and Pam's recent troubles this was the last thing they needed.

He sat there going through all their cases in his mind,

recent and not so recent, but he couldn't think of any obvious suspects, unless it was an irate relative of somebody they'd locked up. Although why pick on Wesley in particular?

Paul Johnson had come down from Lower Torworthy so Gerry allowed him to sit in on the interview in Wesley's absence because time was running out. At least Paul knew when to keep his mouth shut and let Gerry do the talking.

Fitch didn't look particularly refreshed after his break. There were shadows beneath his eyes as though he hadn't slept for days and Gerry hoped that tiredness would lead to him making mistakes. He sat down opposite and when his chair legs scraped on the floor Fitch winced as though the noise hurt his ears.

'Right then, Jason, let's start again, shall we,' said Gerry.

'I've been thinking.' Fitch glanced at his solicitor, who gave him a barely perceptible nod. 'My brother-in-law Kyle. He'd do anything for Sharon so if she got it into her head she wanted to put a stop to me and Andrea ... And he's ex-army so he'd know how to get hold of a weapon – and how to use it.'

'No love lost between you and your brother-in-law then?'

A smirk appeared on Fitch's face. 'No comment. You've tested my rifle, have you?'

Gerry had been wondering how long it would be before that subject came up. 'Yes. It's not the murder weapon.'

'I could have told you that. It's just a bloody toy. Can I go now?'

'When's your brother-in-law due back from Spain?'

'Monday. He's flying into Bristol. Maybe you should be there to pick him up.'

Gerry didn't like being told what to do by suspects but on this occasion he had to agree with him. Kyle Ball had to be brought in, and after a week relaxing in the sun, he hoped he'd be off his guard.

24

By the time Wesley arrived home Pam had already called the garage and he was greeted by the sight of a man in blue overalls, not unlike a crime-scene suit only much grubbier, changing the tyres. The man looked up as he approached.

'This is bad, mate,' he said with what sounded like genuine concern. 'Your missus is right upset.' He looked Wesley up and down. 'You annoyed someone, have you?'

'I'm a police officer so I'm always annoying someone,' Wesley replied.

The man said nothing and returned to his work.

When he opened the door Pam rushed out to greet him and he flung his arms around her, holding her close.

'You must have some idea who did this,' she said, extricating herself from his embrace. 'It must be someone you've arrested sending some sort of twisted message.'

Wesley had already gone through a mental list of all the villains he'd dealt with over the past few years but none seemed to fit the bill. 'I've had threats – it goes with the territory – but there's been nothing recently.'

'Do you think those phone calls are connected? The caller always withholds their number.'

'So do dodgy call centres and banking scams. But I'll

get someone to look into it. Where are the kids?' he asked, experiencing a sudden flutter of panic.

'They're staying at their friends' a bit longer. I didn't want them to see the car like that. They're being brought back later.'

He looked at his watch.

'Have you got to go?' she said, clearly hoping the answer would be no.

'Gerry can manage on his own for a bit longer. I think your mother should come down.' His opinion of Della wasn't high but Pam was her daughter.

'I've tried calling her but I don't think there's a signal where she is.'

'I've got to get back to Lower Torworthy so I'll drive up to Princebury Hall and tell her what's happened.'

Pam looked doubtful and began to make for the kitchen, head bowed, until the sound of his ringtone shattered the silence, at which point he saw Pam freeze. It was Belinda Crillow and he hesitated before answering. Then he told himself that all she probably needed was reassurance.

'Inspector Peterson? Is that you?' She sounded breathless, as though she'd been running. 'When I had the break-in last year you said I could call you any time if I was frightened but whenever I try to call you I get your voice mail,' she said, on the verge of tears.

'Sorry about that but I'm in the middle of an investigation,' he told her as gently as he could. 'DC Carter at Tradmouth Police Station is dealing with your case. I'm sure he—'

'He says there's nothing he can do without more evidence, but I know the man's out there watching. Am I supposed to wait till he attacks me again?'

'I'll have another word. I promise.'

'He's not taking it seriously. He ...'

Wesley could hear the hysteria rising in her voice and he was struck by a disturbing thought. 'You haven't been calling my home number, have you?'

'Of course not.' She sounded hurt and he suddenly felt bad about asking.

'Look, I'll contact the station right away and see what's going on.'

He took a deep breath before calling Rob, who made the point that she hadn't been able to describe her assailant so he was working in the dark. He could almost hear the unspoken words: 'I'm not bloody psychic.'

'I know, Rob, but she's in a right state. Do what you can.'

'How can I when she won't cooperate? She keeps asking for you.'

This wasn't what Wesley wanted to hear. He ended the call and reluctantly left Pam alone with the mechanic, who was still hard at work outside. Before setting off he tried to call Gerry but was told he was interviewing Jason Fitch. It looked as though Gerry was managing fine without him so he drove out to Dartmoor. It was time Della did her bit.

Passing through Lower Torworthy on the way to Princebury Hall, he saw the crime-scene tape fluttering around Manor Field. He found it hard to envisage Fitch meeting Andrea in that spot and shooting her dead along with an innocent walker. Although unexpected things could happen when passions ran high.

When he reached Princebury Hall he tried Della's number but there was no signal. Mobile reception up there was notoriously bad and he wondered how the Hall's guests coped with being cut off from the outside world. Perhaps it was all part of the Princebury Hall experience.

The building seemed deserted as he made his way up the grand central staircase. When he reached Xander Southwark's office he gave a token tap on the door before walking in.

For a second Southwark looked irritated then he swiftly rearranged his features into a calm smile of welcome. Wesley's first thought was that he'd seen that same smile on the faces of conmen and art fraudsters but he knew he mustn't allow his knowledge of the man's past to cloud his judgement.

'Inspector, you've come back to us – presumably with that search warrant your colleague was talking about.' The words were smooth and confident.

'We know the name of Jason Fitch's other lady companion so there's no need for a warrant . . . for the time being.'

Southwark arched his fingers and tilted his head enquiringly like a doctor asking what the trouble was. 'Your colleague could really benefit from one of our courses, you know. He's stressed and overweight. I could do wonders for him – transform his life.'

'I'll take your word for it,' he said, glad Gerry wasn't there to hear. 'But I need to speak to Della Stannard. I've been trying to contact her but . . . '

'I consider our lack of mobile signal a blessing.' Wesley caught a note of self-righteousness in the statement.

'I'm afraid it's a family emergency.'

'You could always have used our landline.'

Wesley had thought of this but rejected it because he'd wanted to take another look at the place Andrea Jameson had been heading for when she died. 'Where can I find Della?'

'You're related?'

'She's my mother-in-law. My wife, her daughter, hasn't been well,' he said, hoping this would satisfy Southwark's curiosity.

Southwark consulted a large chart which took up most of the wall behind the desk. 'She's having a hot stone massage at the moment – finishing at five. If you'd like a herbal tea while you're waiting ...'

He was about to press a key on his desk phone to summon one of his underlings but Wesley interrupted. 'I'd like to ask a few more questions if I may.'

Southwark assumed a patient expression, as though he was indulging an inquisitive child. 'Fire away but I don't see how I can help you.'

'Tell me, Mr Southwark, when were you convicted of fraud?' He knew he should have looked up the case but he hadn't had time. Besides, it might be useful to see what the man himself had to say about it.

'Nineteen ninety-seven – that's a year I'll never forget.' He bowed his head, the picture of penitence.

'Where were you working?'

'Exeter. I considered moving to a different part of the country after my release but that seemed like cowardice. I think people should face up to their wrongdoings, don't you? One thing I've always admired about the Catholic Church is their sacrament of confession. It forces people to acknowledge what they've done. I operate something similar here in our private counselling sessions.'

'But, unlike priests or doctors, you have no obligation to keep what you learn confidential,' said Wesley. 'Perfect opportunity for a spot of blackmail, I should think.'

For the first time Southwark looked uncomfortable. 'If

I suspected any of my staff of abusing their position of trust . . . '

'Did Jason Fitch attend these confession sessions?' Wesley asked.

'Not that I recall.'

'What about Andrea Jameson?'

'No.'

'You told us you didn't know Andrea Jameson personally but according to a list of her clients she organised a party for you a couple of years ago to celebrate the third anniversary of your opening.'

For a split second Southwark looked flustered. If Wesley hadn't been watching the man's face closely, he would have missed it.

'You're absolutely right. She did.'

Wesley's waited expectantly for him to continue.

'Her company came highly recommended.'

'Who by?'

'Jason Fitch if you must know.'

'So you were friendly with him before he became a regular here?'

'Let's say I knew him in a former life. When I was a solicitor he was one of my clients.'

Wesley was surprised by this revelation. He would have thought that anybody who'd had professional dealings with Southwark before his conviction would avoid any further involvement with him. Either Fitch had a very forgiving nature or he was as crooked as Southwark was.

'We'd always hit it off so we stayed in touch.' He smiled. 'Jason might not be a faithful husband, Inspector, but he's been loyal to me over the years.'

'So he's a friend?'

'More of a business acquaintance, I'd say.'

'Do you think he's capable of killing Andrea?'

'Absolutely not. Although I can't say the same for his wife if she finally tired of his philandering.'

An idea sprang into Wesley's head; a connection he hadn't considered before. 'You say you worked in Exeter? Did you ever come across a man called Ian Evans? He was a solicitor too.'

'The name's not familiar. Why do you ask?'

'He's the other victim found with Andrea Jameson. His mother said he used to work in a solicitor's office in Exeter.'

'There are a lot of solicitors in Exeter,' Southwark said, looking at his watch. 'Della should be finishing her massage around now. If you'd like to wait for her in the hall, I'll let her know you're here.'

Wesley had the impression Xander Southwark wanted rid of him. Even though the mention of Ian Evans hadn't appeared to faze him, he suspected the man knew Jason Fitch and Andrea Jameson far better than he cared to admit.

Ten minutes later Wesley met Della in the hall and as soon as she heard his news she fussed a lot then went to her room to pack her bags. Pam needed her.

Once back in the Lower Torworthy incident room Wesley phoned Gerry, who reported that they'd made no progress with Jason Fitch. As soon as he could get a word in, Wesley told him about his meeting with Xander Southwark and his suspicion that he'd known Fitch and Andrea Jameson a lot better than he'd first admitted.

There was something else on his mind, something he hadn't mentioned to Gerry. Alcuin Garrard had died in

Manor Field in 1995 and, even though no connection had as yet been established between Garrard and either of the latest victims, he wanted to find out more.

After looking through Neil's press cuttings he'd called Headquarters to request details of the police investigation. He'd been expecting a long delay so he was pleasantly surprised when he reached his desk and found the file on Garrard's death squatting on top of his paperwork.

He opened the file carefully but, even so, loose papers fluttered to the ground like giant grubby snowflakes and he had to get down on his hands and knees on the dusty wooden floor to retrieve them. Once everything was in place he settled down to read.

Alcuin Garrard had been found dead in Manor Field on the evening of 4 September 1995 and, according to the post-mortem, his injuries were consistent with him falling on uneven ground and hitting his head on an old section of wall. Traces of blood, hair and brain matter had been found on the stones and a small, fallen stone half covered with grass had been dislodged as though somebody had tripped over it, which seemed to confirm the theory. The field was outside the village, hence there were no witnesses to what actually happened, but Alcuin had told several people he was going there in connection with his research. When his body was discovered it was assumed from the first that he'd met with an unfortunate accident so the investigation hadn't been particularly thorough and no alternatives to the fall theory were explored. One passing motorist thought she'd seen a dark-coloured car parked near the field that evening but her testimony was vague and this wasn't followed up.

The contents of the dead student's pockets were listed

but the only thing of interest appeared to be a letter dated three months before his death. A photocopy of the hand-written letter was attached to the list and Wesley saw that it was from a Ralph Detoram. The address at the top of the headed notepaper caught Wesley's attention at once: it was Princebury Hall.

The letter offered Alcuin access to anything in the hall's muniment room that might be of use to him and, from the tone, it sounded as though Detoram was looking forward to his visit. It must have been lonely up there – one elderly man in a big, draughty house. However, the letter ended on a strange note: 'Concerning the other matter, I know you are mistaken. I assure you that I am perfectly satisfied with the status quo and I would rather not enter into further discussion.' Wesley stared at the words, wondering what the 'other matter' could be. As both Alcuin and Ralph Detoram were dead, there was no chance of asking them.

The report mentioned that an eighteen-year-old girl called Sarah Booker had been spoken to in connection with his death. She lived in Lower Torworthy and they'd been seen together in the Shepherd's Arms where he was staying. Sarah had insisted that there'd been no romantic attachment between them and that she knew nothing about his death.

In an ideal world he'd be able to talk to Sarah Booker and ask her about the man she used to drink with in the Shepherd's Arms. But young people tended to leave iso-lated Dartmoor villages for work in livelier locations so she could be anywhere by now.

He flicked through the rest of the file until he came to the photographs taken of the body *in situ*. He stared at the picture of the dead young man, wondering again why

Ian Evans had been looking up details of his death on his computer. And why, given the vastness of the Dartmoor landscape, the two men had been found dead in the same field.

The man who was calling himself John Davies took off his motorcycle helmet before tugging at his clerical collar. When it came away he stuffed it into the pocket of his jacket. It was good to be rid of it but it had the advantage of acting like a cloak of invisibility. A Church of England clergyman was above suspicion, especially in a rural location like Dartmoor.

It also provided the perfect means of learning secrets and this was how he'd made his living since his release from the open prison eighteen months ago. The scheme had come to him in a flash of what Oliver Grayling would no doubt call divine inspiration and there were times when he couldn't help congratulating himself on his brilliance. It was an offence nobody was likely to report so it was as near to the perfect crime as you could get.

He parked the bike and made his way to the front door of the cottage he'd rented cheaply for three months; a shabby place any self-respecting holidaymaker would reject on sight. Weeds sprouted from the gravel path and the paint on the door and window frames had flaked off to reveal the bare wood beneath. The interior was little better but before Davies had a chance to let himself inside, he heard a noise behind him.

He swung round and the world exploded before he fell to the ground.

Extract from draft PhD thesis
written by Alcuin Garrard

July 1995

Sir Matthew's little monk was in great
demand, even beyond the confines of
the village. There are letters from the
DeTorhams' neighbours requesting the monk's
services for the sick and dying. Word spread
as far as Exeter, where a wealthy merchant
wrote to Sir Matthew in June 1532 begging
him to bring his monk to intercede for his
sick child. There is no record of whether
this request was granted.

All was apparently well until early 1533
when several items of correspondence found
amongst the DeTorham family papers at
Princebury Hall hint at something amiss.
There is mention of Oswald's younger brother
Simeon, who would have been in his early
twenties at the time, losing money gaming in
Exeter and getting a village girl with child.

The first mention of a second machine –
a 'big friar' – appeared in June 1533. It
seems that the little monk was a prototype

and Sir Matthew's second creation was more
sophisticated and, it was hoped, more
efficacious.

However, this second machine does not
appear to be received with the enthusiasm
that greeted the first.

25

First thing on Monday morning Neil rang the university's History Department to see whether Professor Laurence Harris was available. He vaguely remembered the professor from his own student days as a tall, upright figure with a shock of grey hair and a distant manner, although he couldn't recall ever actually speaking to the man. He'd heard he had a reputation for irritability and, according to popular legend, one of his students had left his office in tears after having an unsatisfactory essay ripped asunder.

Neil, however, was a student no longer and the prospect of the encounter didn't faze him in the least.

He knocked on the professor's door and heard a curt 'Come in.' Professor Harris was sitting behind his desk, half hidden by books and files. He was no longer the imposing figure of Neil's memory; rather he looked pale and thin. But his manner didn't appear to have changed.

'What is it?'

When Neil introduced himself Harris scowled and carried on scribbling on a notepad, as though an unpromising student had come to hand in an essay that was a week late.

Neil sat down without being invited. 'I'm in charge of a

survey of medieval graffiti in Dartmoor churches and I'm hoping you might be able to help with my research,' he said and waited for the reaction.

The professor's skeletal hand stilled above his notepad and for the first time he raised his head to look at Neil. 'What makes you think that?'

'In nineteen ninety-five you had a postgrad student here called Alcuin Garrard.'

Harris's eyes widened and he dropped his pen.

'He died in an accident, I believe.'

It was a few moments before Harris spoke. 'He fell and hit his head. Chance in a million, they said. Tragic. He was a brilliant student.'

'Who was his supervisor?'

'I was.'

'Had he finished his thesis?'

'Unfortunately not.' The professor turned his head away. Contrary to his reputation for irascibility, he seemed genuinely moved by the subject of Alcuin Garrard's death.

'What was the subject of his thesis?'

'Ecclesiastical life in Pre-Reformation Devon and the effects of Henry the Eighth's reforms on isolated rural communities.' There was no hesitation. Out of all the doctoral theses Harris must have seen during the course of his career, this one had clearly stood out.

'There wouldn't be a draft of his thesis somewhere in the university?'

For a few moments Harris hesitated. 'Not that I'm aware of. His papers might have gone to his family but I believe they emigrated to Australia when he began his studies.'

Neil detected a satisfaction behind his words, as though

the fact that the Alcuin Garrard's work might be lost or inaccessible pleased him in some way.

'I'd like to locate his research notes – if they still exist,' said Neil.

'Then I wish you luck.'

The professor lowered his gaze and returned to his notes, making it clear to Neil that he'd overstayed his welcome – or that the subject of Alcuin Garrard's research was an unwelcome one.

A phone rang in the incident room. It was a normal sound – phones rang all the time – but this particular call brought the work of the investigation team to an abrupt halt as Gerry Heffernan called for quiet.

'There's been another shooting three miles away. Postman found the body of a man outside an isolated cottage.'

For a few seconds the incident room fell silent. Then Wesley spoke.

'Do we know the victim's identity?'

'Not yet.'

'Surely there was a name on the letter the postman was delivering?'

'It was addressed to the landlord. According to the postman, the victim never received any post himself.'

'What about the victim's phone?'

'No sign of it. I'll set the ball rolling and get Colin and the CSI team up there pronto. Hopefully the patrol officers have had the nous to seal off the scene.' Gerry rolled his eyes. He never quite trusted Uniform to get things right if he wasn't there to issue the orders.

While Gerry made his calls Wesley organised his desk

and reached for his coat. The weather in Tradmouth had been pleasant when he'd set off that morning but up on Dartmoor the temperature was a few degrees cooler and a grey mist was veiling the landscape. He saw Rachel watching Gerry expectantly, as though the prospect of another murder excited her.

'Where exactly did you say it was?' she asked once the DCI had finished on the phone.

'Three miles to the north of here,' said Gerry. 'If the postman hadn't called the victim might have been lying there for days. As it is, there was a delivery on Saturday lunchtime so at least that narrows down the time of death a bit.'

When the pair set off Wesley drove as usual. Gerry had taken down the directions and, after a few false leads, they turned on to a lane that was little more than a track.

'You sure this is right?' Wesley said.

'Nothing wrong with my navigation. How's Pam?'

Wesley was surprised by the sudden change of subject. 'Still shaken but she's hiding it well.' He paused. 'Her mother's staying with us for a few days.'

'That must be an ordeal,' said Gerry.

'She wouldn't be anyone's first choice to have around in a crisis but, to be honest, I'm just glad Pam's got someone there.' He paused. 'And I think Della gets lonely ... And the kids think the world of her.'

'Kids always like a disreputable grandma.' Gerry chuckled. 'Mine, God rest her, used to prop up the bar at the Crack drinking pints of Guinness – had her own tankard. Any thoughts on your slashed tyre mystery?'

'I know we deal with some lowlifes but I can't think of anyone who'd do something like that. At least the silent phone calls seem to have stopped.'

'Let's hope that's the end of it.'

Wesley saw a patrol car parked in a passing place next to a rotting wooden gate, half hanging off its hinges. Beyond the gate was a small cottage that looked semi-derelict.

'About as cut off from civilisation as you can get,' Gerry observed. 'Who'd choose to live somewhere like this.'

'I think we're about to find out.'

After reporting to the crime-scene manager they made their way up the gravel path, careful to step on the metal plates put down by the CSIs. They headed towards the action centred on the area in front of the cottage door. At first they couldn't see the dead body lying on the ground for all the living bodies bustling around it in the well-practised choreography of crime-scene investigation.

At the heart of the activity Colin Bowman was squatting next to the dead man, his bag open to reveal the instruments of his trade. Wesley noticed a Harley Davidson motorcycle parked by the cottage wall. Possibly it had been the victim's pride and joy.

Colin greeted them with an affable smile. 'Good morning, gentlemen. You are keeping me busy.'

'Don't blame us, Colin. We're not killing 'em,' Gerry replied. 'What have we got?'

'Male. Late thirties at a guess. Dressed in motorcycle gear. Looks like he'd just taken off his helmet when it happened.' He paused. 'It's the same as the others. Shot to the chest then one to the head to make sure.'

'Another execution,' Wesley said softly.

'Looks that way.'

'Bullets?' Gerry asked.

'There are exit wounds so they won't be far away.' He looked at the cottage. 'Embedded in the wall perhaps.'

'ID?'

'Haven't found any yet. But he has a wallet containing two hundred pounds and some keys, presumably for the cottage and his motorbike. There's something else too.' He looked round and called to a young woman CSI who appeared to be labelling crime-scene bags.

'Have you bagged that collar I found in his pocket yet?'

She nodded and produced a bag. Inside was a stiff white circle and it took Wesley a couple of seconds to recognise it as a clerical collar.

'Looks like a dog collar,' said Gerry, leaning over to see. 'Is our man a vicar?'

Colin unzipped the dead man's leather jacket and pointed to the blue clerical shirt, the fabric stiff with dried blood. 'I think you're right, Gerry. This chap's a clergyman. He'd taken his collar off and stuffed it into his pocket. Perhaps it was uncomfortable under his leathers.'

'We need to take a look in the house,' said Wesley.

The young woman passed him the keys. 'They fit. We've tried. If he was a clergyman it doesn't look like your average vicarage.'

Wesley's sister was married to a vicar and he knew that clergy accommodation can come in all shapes and sizes, but he didn't feel inclined to enlighten her. He made for the front door with Gerry following close behind.

They stepped into a narrow hallway which smelled faintly of old mops. The carpet beneath their feet was worn and filthy and there were no pictures on the grubby woodchip walls. A flight of steep stairs rose ahead of them and the door to their right stood half open, giving a view of a cluttered living room. Wesley pushed the door wide open and walked in.

'He wasn't the house-proud type, was he?' Gerry said as he circled the room, picking up items with his gloved hands and replacing them in disgust.

'If he was a clergyman where are the books? The Bibles and the volumes on theology; every vicarage I've ever been in has shelves full of them.'

'Maybe he keeps them upstairs.'

There was a new-looking large flat-screen TV which looked out of place against the rest of the decor. Above it was a shelf containing a pile of soft porn magazines. Wesley took a couple down and held them up for Gerry to see.

'A naughty vicar, eh? The Sunday papers used to be full of them in the old days,' he added with a touch of nostalgia.

The kitchen yielded little in the way of clues to the dead man's lifestyle. Just tins and a few ready meals in a fridge with black mould around the seal. Wesley made his way upstairs and Gerry followed.

'We're sure he was actually living here? He didn't just come here to visit a parishioner and ended up getting shot? Mistaken identity maybe?'

'The keys were in his pocket but you could be right, Gerry. Maybe he was keeping an eye on the place for someone.'

However, this theory was exploded when Wesley opened the wardrobe and saw a row of clerical shirts dangling from cheap wire hangers. There were black trousers too and a couple of dark jackets. When he opened the drawers he saw three spare clerical collars lying there. 'He lived here all right,' he said, standing aside so that Gerry could see the proof for himself.

'It shouldn't be hard to find out who he's annoyed,' said Wesley. 'Unless . . . '

'Unless what?'

The idea that had just occurred to Wesley was so shocking that he hardly liked to put it into words. 'Unless there's a madman going around shooting people at random.'

Gerry looked at him. 'I hope to God you're wrong, Wes. I really do.'

The broken glass crunched beneath Belinda Crillow's high heels and she took a deep, shuddering breath. She closed her eyes to blot out the sight of the destruction and when she opened them again she clamped her hand across her mouth to suppress a scream of anguish.

She called Wesley Peterson's number first but when she heard his voice mail asking her to leave a message she sank down in the armchair and considered her next move.

Eventually she called DC Carter at her local police station and he promised to come round, although it had taken a few white lies to goad him into action. She told him in a whisper that the intruder was still on the premises: she could hear him smashing things up. She thought he was armed with a knife or machete, or maybe an axe. For the first time Carter sounded genuinely concerned and he promised to send a patrol car right away.

She sat in the silence and waited. First to arrive was a burly uniformed constable with a shaved head whose stab vest gave him the appearance of a robot. Wesley Peterson had been so much gentler; more sympathetic to her plight.

'You OK, love?' the constable asked. 'Where's your intruder?'

'He's gone. You're too late.'

'Tell us what happened,' he said, taking his notebook from his pocket.

She described the incident in as much detail as she could recall. The man had burst in and threatened her. Then he'd searched for something – she wasn't sure what – smashing anything that got in his way. Yes, he was armed with a knife and he was big. Over six foot and wearing a balaclava like before – and he had a local accent. No, she didn't know what he wanted. She'd been too frightened to ask questions. She was sure it was the same man who'd attacked her when she was out jogging, although she had no idea who he was or why he was picking on her. Apart from the break-in at her flat in Tradmouth eighteen months ago she'd had no previous experience of the world of crime.

'Did he say anything else?'

She hesitated, tears brimming. 'He said he knew I'd been talking to Inspector Peterson. He told me to keep my mouth shut or he'd shut it for me.'

'Inspector Peterson? Are you sure?'

'Of course I'm sure.'

'What have you been talking to Inspector Peterson about?'

'Nothing. I've no idea what he meant.'

When she broke down in tears the conversation ground to a halt.

26

According to the landlord the dead man's name was John Davies and he'd taken the cottage on a three-month lease. All he knew was that his tenant was a clergyman looking for a spot of peace and quiet in the countryside and that he paid his rent on time.

If there was anyone who'd know about any clergy in the area, Wesley thought, it would be the vicar of Lower Torworthy. Neil had been spending a lot of time poking around in his church so presumably they were on good terms, which might be to Wesley's advantage.

Colin had booked the post-mortem for the following morning so Wesley hoped that the short delay would give them time to find out more about the victim. Clergymen tended to be public people, he thought, so the information shouldn't be hard to come by.

Once they reached Lower Torworthy Gerry returned to the incident room to bring everyone up to speed with developments. Wesley, however, made straight for the church and stood in the porch for a while, looking at the parish notices and thinking about the man he'd just seen lying dead in front of that dilapidated cottage. From where he was standing he could see the Shepherd's Arms, the pub where Alcuin Garrard had drunk with a girl called Sarah all those years ago. Alcuin had been found dead in the same place as Ian Evans, which suggested a connection. Although at that moment Wesley had no idea what it could be.

The heavy church door opened with a loud creak and as Wesley's eyes adjusted to the dim light in the nave he saw a huddle of people with clipboards and cameras in the south aisle. Neil was amongst them and as soon as he spotted Wesley, he broke away from the others.

'Hi, Wes. What brings you here?'

'Business, I'm afraid.' He paused. 'You won't have heard about Pam's car.'

Neil's smile of greeting vanished. 'Has she had an accident?'

'Someone slashed all her tyres on Saturday afternoon while the car was on our drive.'

Neil swore under his breath. 'Someone you've arrested?' He hesitated, choosing his words carefully. 'Or racially motivated maybe?'

Wesley shrugged his shoulders. 'We've been getting strange phone calls too. I didn't want to leave her on her own so Della's staying with us for a while. She's making herself useful for once because I'm working all hours at the moment. How's the survey going?'

'We should be finished tomorrow. I went to see Professor Harris at the History Department this morning. Do you remember him from our student days?'

'Not really.'

'I had some dealings with his colleagues when I was doing my doctorate and I had the impression Harris wasn't particularly popular. Anyway, I asked him about Alcuin

Garrard because I'm trying to track down his thesis. He was researching this area in the early sixteenth century so I hoped to find some reference to our little monk.'

'And did you?'

'According to Harris he never finished the thesis and he doesn't know what became of his drafts or research notes. I hoped there might be some documents in the church but I haven't found anything. I was told Alcuin found material at Princebury Hall so I went up there.'

'Any help?'

'I saw a guy called Xander Southwark, who told me the builders flung a lot of old stuff into skips when the place was being converted.' Wesley could hear the disgust in Neil's voice. 'He said if he'd known the material was important he'd have saved it, but he didn't sound altogether convincing. I'm still waiting to hear from Annabel. She's promised to look for references in the cathedral archives.'

'I found the police file on Alcuin Garrard's accident. He was friendly with a girl called Sarah Booker shortly before he died but I guess she could be miles away by now.'

'One of the flower arrangers here is called Sarah Shaw and she was brought up in the village. She told me she used to know Alcuin so she could be your woman. No harm in asking.'

'If you see her, will you ask her if her name used to be Booker and, if so, would she be willing to have a word with me?'

'Sure.'

'Thanks. I owe you one.' Much as Wesley wanted to trace Sarah Booker, there were more urgent matters to deal with. 'Is the vicar about?'

'In the vestry.'

Without another word Wesley headed for the vestry where he found Oliver Grayling at his desk bent over a notepad. When Wesley cleared his throat Grayling's head jerked upwards, as though Wesley had caught him doing something he shouldn't.

'Sorry to disturb you but I need a word,' Wesley said. 'This morning a man's body was found three miles from here. He'd been shot and there are similarities to the two deaths in Manor Field. It was another execution-style killing.'

Grayling stared at him. 'That's terrible.' He sounded genuinely shocked. 'But I don't see how I can help you. You say it happened three miles away. Where exactly?'

'An isolated cottage near Three Crosses Farm. It's north of here.'

Wesley saw relief on Grayling's face. 'That particular parish isn't my responsibility. You need to speak to the Reverend Yelland.'

'The dead man was a clergyman. Late thirties, well built, shaved head. Rented the cottage in the name of John Davies.'

'Doesn't ring any bells.' The words came out in a squeak. 'Perhaps he was here on holiday. He isn't necessarily local.'

'I thought it was worth a try.' He gave the man a disarming smile.

'Sorry I can't help you,' Grayling said weakly.

Calls were still coming in about Jocasta Ovorard and were being processed by the team who'd stayed behind in Tradmouth.

The missing girl had been spotted alive and well in all parts of the UK. There had even been a sighting in Spain and Gerry had joked that they should go over themselves and follow it up. But Wesley knew there was no chance of them getting away from Dartmoor until the killer of Andrea Jameson, Ian Evans and the as-yet unidentified man near Three Crosses Farm had been caught.

The phone on his desk began to ring and when he picked it up he heard Rob Carter's voice.

'There's been a break-in at Belinda Crillow's. Few things smashed up and she's badly shaken.' He paused. 'The intruder mentioned your name.'

Wesley's grip tightened on the handset.

'He said he knew she'd been talking to you. It looks like the attack was some kind of warning. He was armed with a knife.'

Wesley had done his best to delegate the problem but now it seemed he was about to become involved whether he liked it or not.

'Description?'

'Same as before. Male. Balaclava. Local accent. She thinks it's the same man who attacked her before but she has no idea who he is.'

'Believe her?'

Rob hesitated. 'No reason not to ... is there? A female PC's there looking after her. Thought I'd better let you know.'

An image of the slashed tyres on Pam's car flashed into Wesley's head. But if Belinda Crillow's intruder was responsible and he knew where he lived, what did he have to gain by going after Belinda?

After speaking to Rob he phoned home and Della answered after three rings.

'Is Pam OK?'

'Of course she is.'

'Nothing unusual's happened?'

When she replied in the negative he asked her to go to the front window and look out. Were there any unusual vehicles? Or any strangers hanging around the close?

'Your neighbours over the road are having a delivery from Sainsbury's. Does that count as unusual?' Wesley heard a note of sarcasm in her voice. Telling her about Belinda Crillow's intruder might make her take the matter more seriously but he couldn't trust her not to panic and make things worse.

'Can I speak to Pam?'

'She's gone into work this afternoon. One of the other teachers called in sick and she offered to cover for her. I told her not to go but she wouldn't listen. You know what she's like.'

As soon as Wesley put the receiver down he was seized by panic. What if Pam had been followed to work? He'd slashed her tyres so he knew her car. Wesley toyed with the idea of calling her mobile but he knew she wouldn't thank him when she had a class full of children clamouring for her attention.

Instead he called Rob back and asked him to return to Belinda Crillow's cottage and ask her more questions. If there hadn't been so much to deal with in the incident room he would have gone himself, he said apologetically, uncomfortable about ignoring the victim's calls.

He crossed over to Gerry, who was busy studying witness statements, and asked if he could have a word.

Gerry sat back, glad of the break. 'Have as many as you like, Wes.'

He told Gerry about Rob's call. 'Seems I was wrong to ignore her.'

Gerry considered the problem for a while before speaking. 'If this thug's after you I can't see where this Belinda Crillow comes into it. Why not approach you direct?'

'Maybe he has – Pam's tyres? Someone seems to think Belinda Crillow's involved with me somehow but I can't think why. I've had no contact with her since her break-in the year before last.'

'Did we make an arrest?'

Wesley sighed. 'Afraid not. But it must be the same man. I'll ask Rob to go through the file. There might be something we missed at the time.'

'Good idea, Wes. But if you ask me, you should keep your distance from Ms Crillow from now on. Let Rob deal with it; it'll do him good to get some experience. And watch your back. Anything suspicious, you call it in right away. That clear?'

Wesley nodded. Gerry was right: Belinda Crillow wasn't his problem.

The officers sent to Bristol Airport to meet Jason Fitch's brother-in-law, Kyle Ball, off his flight had a wasted journey. The so-called 'Hit Man' hadn't been on the flight and further inquiries revealed that he'd returned from Spain late on Saturday evening instead – considerably earlier than planned.

Colin Bowman hadn't yet got back to them to confirm their latest victim's time of death but as soon as Wesley heard about Ball's early arrival he realised that he could well have been in Devon at the time the man at Three Crosses Farm met his end.

Jason Fitch had been released on bail pending further inquiries and his whereabouts at the weekend had already been checked out. Rather than going home to Dukesbridge or joining his wife in their Littlebury cottage, he'd gone to stay with Gemma Whittingstill at their little love nest and she'd been only too ready to vouch for him. Gerry observed that perhaps Gemma's patience might now pay off and he was sure she had good contacts amongst the area's divorce lawyers.

Gerry called Plymouth to request that Kyle Ball be picked up at his address and brought to Tradmouth. They needed to interview him sooner rather than later and, with all the hints about firearms that were flying around, his flat needed to be searched for illegally held weapons.

They were waiting for news when Neil entered the incident room, looking unsure of himself. As soon as Wesley saw him he beckoned him over.

'Looking for me?'

'Word has it that a vicar's been shot.'

'There's been a suspicious death at a cottage three miles north of here and we think the victim's a clergyman. I've already asked Mr Grayling but he says he doesn't know him.'

'Have you got a photo of the dead guy?'

Wesley hesitated before leading Neil to the noticeboard at the far end of the room where photographs of the recent victim had joined those of Andrea Jameson and Ian Evans. The images taken at the crime scene weren't pretty to look at but Neil didn't seem unduly upset by the explicit signs of violence. He studied the pictures of the dead man for a while before turning to Wesley.

'Grayling lied to you. Last Thursday he was leaving the church as I arrived and Oliver seemed upset, as though they'd had some sort of row.'

'Why would the vicar lie to us?'

'That's your department, not mine. I thought me and Lucy might come round one evening – if you're not there we can keep Pam company. She must be feeling jittery after what happened.'

'She's better than she was. Her mum's still staying.'

'I can put up with Della if she can put up with me. Any news on your vandal?'

'No, but the phone calls seem to have stopped.' He wondered whether to mention Belinda Crillow's intruder before deciding against it. 'Can you tell me anything else about the victim?'

'Only that I found him in the church one day and he introduced himself as John Davies – said he was a curate. When I asked Oliver about him later he denied knowing him.'

'Is Grayling in church at the moment?'

'Are you going to question him?'

'He lied to me, Neil. I've got no choice.'

Extract from draft PhD thesis
written by Alcuin Garrard

July 1995

Although in June 1533 we start to find
references to a 'big friar' accompanying Sir
Matthew and his little wooden companion on
his visits, the priest's meticulously kept
parish records contain no mention of its
creation, whereas the construction of the
'little monk' two years earlier is described
in some detail, along with the costs
involved.

The journal of Henry Dyce, cousin to
Oswald DeTorham, contains an interesting
entry dated July 1533.

'My maidservant was sick of a fever,'
Henry writes. 'And as I knew of Sir Matthew's
machine's miraculous powers I sought my
cousin's steward, Peter, wishing him to fetch
the priest. I could not find Peter so I sent
another servant and when Sir Matthew arrived
he had with him his praying monk which was
pulled upon a rough cart by a donkey. There
was also a larger machine upon the cart - a

wooden figure in the habit of a friar which had upon its wooden face such a gentle expression that I knew at once it was a holy thing.'

Later Henry writes that: 'Peter's behaviour of late has been most secretive and yet my cousin will hear no word against his steward.'

27

On Tuesday morning Professor Harris arrived in his office earlier than usual.

He'd had the initial idea when he'd discovered Lower Torworthy's parish records in the archives at Exeter Cathedral but it had been Alcuin Garrard who'd found other primary sources and gathered all the material into one coherent form to bring the dramatic story to life. Alcuin Garrard had had the makings of a brilliant historian and Harris possessed enough self-knowledge to realise that, on Garrard's death, he'd hidden his research out of pure envy.

The visit from Dr Watson of the County Archaeological Unit had triggered an uncharacteristic attack of conscience. Watson had found the thing itself – the little monk mentioned in the early sources – and, with the publicity this was bound to generate, Harris needed to consider his options. Perhaps Watson's discovery would spur him on to complete the work Garrard started all those years ago, but there was still the question of the wrong he had done and the possibility of exposure. Then there was the future to consider – what was left of it, anyway.

Watson had left his number but as Harris's hand hovered

over the phone he began to have second thoughts. A short delay would allow him to read through Garrard's notes again. This latest development might mean Harris's career would end in the blaze of glory that had eluded him all these years. First though he had a visit to make ... and after that he would decide.

When Wesley reached work on Tuesday morning he found a message waiting for him. The latest victim had been identified from his fingerprints as Nathan Rowyard, a small-time crook and conman who'd spent a few short stretches inside. Although Rowyard had no record of violence it was doubtful whether he'd found God and taken holy orders since his last period of incarceration so the clerical get-up was most likely part of some scam he was running.

After breaking the news to Gerry he wrote the dead man's real name beneath his picture on the noticeboard. He hadn't spoken to Oliver Grayling the previous day because the vicar had been called away to Exeter on unspecified business but seeing him was at the top of his list of things to do that morning.

Rowyard's post-mortem was booked for 11.30 so he had time to visit the church and seek out the vicar. Rachel was deep in witness statements but when he asked her to go with him she didn't hesitate to accept his invitation.

'Nice church,' she commented as they entered St Bartholomew's. She walked down the aisle, paying particular attention to the flower arrangements. 'I'm in the middle of choosing flowers at the moment,' she explained. 'St Margaret's is a big church to decorate so it's going to cost a bomb.'

For a long time she'd avoided the subject of her coming

wedding and this was the first time he'd seen her display anything approaching enthusiasm.

'Everything's going OK is it?'

She looked at him and smiled. 'It's fine, Wes. Honestly. I've got over my jitters. And you and Pam . . . You seem solid these days. After her . . . treatment.'

Wesley nodded, surprised at the intensity of her words. 'Something like that makes you realise what's important.'

They stood for a moment facing each other before Rachel broke the silence.

'I never thought I'd marry a farmer.'

'Probably in your blood. It's good to have roots.'

She didn't answer.

They found Oliver Grayling in the vestry and he greeted them with an unconvincing smile which didn't spread to his eyes.

'Sorry to bother you again,' said Wesley. 'May we sit down?'

'Of course.'

Wesley came straight to the point. 'Dr Watson met a man here in the church who introduced himself as John Davies. He claimed to be your curate.'

'He must have got hold of the wrong end of the stick.' He gave another smile which looked more like a grimace.

'The man found dead at a cottage near Three Crosses Farm has been identified as the man Dr Watson met here.' He paused to allow his revelation to sink in. 'He appears to have been posing as a clergyman but his real name was Nathan Rowyard and he had convictions for deception. What exactly was your relationship with Rowyard, Mr Grayling?'

Oliver Grayling looked at Rachel, who was sitting

expectantly with her pen poised over her notebook. 'Can we speak in private, Inspector?'

Rachel stood up. 'I'll be outside,' she said before leaving the room.

Once they were alone Grayling buried his head in his hands and when he eventually looked up Wesley saw that his eyes were filled with tears.

'He was blackmailing me,' he said in a shuddering whisper.

Wesley wasn't sure what he'd been expecting but it certainly hadn't been this. 'I'll need to know the details, I'm afraid.'

'You don't understand, I could lose everything.'

'Have you broken the law?'

Grayling brushed his sleeve across his face and Wesley saw a snail trail of tears on the black cloth. 'Not as you would see it, no.'

'In that case I'll do my best to ensure that whatever you tell me goes no further, providing it doesn't turn out to be relevant to our case.' He arched his fingers. 'Just think of it as making your confession.'

It was a few seconds before Grayling leaned forward and lowered his voice. 'It happened ten years ago when I was curate at a parish in Truro. There was a woman – the wife of a parishioner who'd been badly injured in an industrial accident and was in a coma. She came to me because she wanted someone to talk to but ... Things developed between us. It's not something I'm proud of, Inspector. She was vulnerable and many people would say I took advantage of the situation for my own gratification, although I didn't see it that way at the time. Eventually my vicar found out and I was sent to another parish as far away as possible.'

'It was hushed up.'

'What good would it have done to broadcast it to the world? By that time the lady's husband had died of his injuries and she had children so it was thought best to forget the whole thing. I took a post as curate in a parish near Axminster and I never saw her again, although I heard that she remarried a couple of years later. It was a part of my past I wanted to put behind me but about three weeks ago I received a visit from a man who claimed to be a curate visiting the area. My instincts told me at once that he wasn't genuine. Then he began to talk about my old parish in Truro – how his mother used to clean the church. He said she'd told him some interesting things.'

'Do you remember her?'

Grayling gave a snort of disgust. 'She was always poking her nose into other people's business. My boss, the vicar, spoke to her on several occasions about the evils of gossip – not that it did much good.'

'What was her name?'

'I knew her as Maggie Rowyard. I was vaguely aware she had a son but he never darkened the doors of the church and I think he was always in trouble of one sort or another. When he turned up I asked him if he was Maggie's son and he admitted he was but he said he'd changed his name to Davies.' He hesitated. 'Then he told me he had contacts with a tabloid journalist who'd think all his Christmases had come at once if he got hold of a story about a vicar who'd seduced a vulnerable woman with a dying husband. He soon came to the crux of the matter and said he was going through a hard time and he needed money to pay off his debts, the suggestion being that if I didn't pay up he'd call the journalist and tell him about Truro.'

'How much did he get out of you?'

'I think the total came to around eleven thousand pounds – money I've managed to save over the years plus a small inheritance from my grandmother. In the end I told him my savings were running out but he kept asking for more.'

'You should have come to us.'

'You don't understand. I'd taken advantage of a woman who came to me for help. I was ashamed.'

Wesley sat in silence for a few moments. 'You were weak. It was a mistake and even the best of us can make those.'

'It was unforgivable.'

'You're supposed to believe that God forgives everything.'

Grayling looked surprised; then he nodded.

'Look, I'm afraid I'll have to ask you to make a statement.' The vicar looked devastated but his next question had to be asked. 'Do you own a gun, Mr Grayling?'

'Of course not.'

'Ever served in the forces?'

'I did a brief spell in the army cadets at school.'

'You learned to handle a rifle?'

Grayling hesitated. 'Yes, but ... '

'If you come to the incident room, someone will take your statement.'

'Can't you do it now? Discreetly?'

Wesley couldn't help feeling sorry for Oliver Grayling, although he was only too aware that suspects he'd felt sorry for in the past had sometimes turned out to have blood on their hands. 'I'm afraid I have to go to Tradmouth soon but whoever deals with it, everything you say will be treated in the strictest confidence. I promise.'

Grayling looked as though he was about to object but then he gave a resigned nod.

'I presume you've been asked where you were when Andrea Jameson and Ian Evans were murdered?'

'I gave a statement to one of your constables like everyone else in Lower Torworthy. I was in a meeting with the Bishop of Exeter.'

Wesley smiled to himself. Alibis didn't come much better than that.

'Rowyard's death bears similarities to the double murder and we're working on the theory that the same person is responsible.'

A look of relief passed across Grayling's face. Wesley had seen a similar look on Pam's face when the consultant had given her the all-clear after her cancer diagnosis.

'So I'm ruled out?'

Wesley didn't answer. He couldn't reassure him of anything at that stage in the investigation. He looked at his watch. 'If you come to the church hall at four I'll ask my sergeant to take your statement.' He caught sight of the small arrangement of flowers on the desk. 'While I'm here can you tell me if you have a flower arranger called Sarah?'

'Sarah Shaw. Why?'

'Do you happen to know what her name was before she married?'

'It was Booker. Her family are regulars here and I married Sarah and Paul myself.'

Wesley felt a flutter of excitement. 'Can I have her address?' He knew it might be there somewhere buried in the house-to-house statements taken after the first shootings but hoped this would be a quicker way of finding out.

'The house is called Tarn End Barn – it's a barn conversion at the other end of the village. Can you tell me why you want to talk to her?' He sounded anxious to protect his parishioner against the sort of intrusion he'd just had to endure.

'I want to ask her about something that happened years ago. Nothing to worry about.'

Rachel was waiting for him in the church, sitting in a pew at the front gazing at the stained-glass window above the altar.

'Well?' she said, rising to her feet.

'I'll tell you later.'

As they walked back to the incident room in silence his mind was on Oliver Grayling's revelations. And whether someone had been prepared to kill to prevent their own dark secrets from being revealed to the world.

28

Jeremy Ovorard had been in touch at least twice a day since the TV appeal and each time Gerry had to disappoint him, although he always reassured him that Jocasta's disappearance was still top of their priority list. Gerry had offered the services of a family liaison officer but Tabitha Ovorard had refused on the grounds that she couldn't bear the intrusion. When Wesley said he found this hard to understand Gerry observed that different people react to tragedy in different ways.

Gerry still had a bad feeling about Jocasta. The fields and woods in the vicinity of Lower Torworthy had been searched by tracker dogs but her body hadn't been found. There were a lot of old mine workings on Dartmoor but he'd been assured that there were none in the immediate vicinity – although that didn't mean the killer hadn't transported her body further afield after disposing of her. Then there was the possibility, hard though it was to contemplate, that the killer was holding her prisoner somewhere.

Wesley's arrival interrupted his thoughts.

'Rowyard's PM's in an hour,' Gerry said, looking at his watch. 'Time we set off.'

'Can I have a word in private?' Wesley made for the little

kitchen at the side of the stage and Gerry followed. A young constable was in there making tea for his colleagues, but as soon as he saw the boss enter he finished what he was doing and hurried from the room carrying a tray of mugs, in his haste allowing tea to slop over the rims.

'What is it?' Gerry asked as soon as the door closed.

'Nathan Rowyard was blackmailing the vicar, Oliver Grayling. He handed over eleven grand to hush up an affair he'd had with a woman in one of his previous parishes.'

'Must have been some affair.'

'He slept with her while her husband was in a coma. I don't think the bishop would approve.'

'Probably not. But eleven grand . . .'

'He abused his position and Rowyard's mother was privy to the gossip. That's how her son found out.'

'So we treat Grayling as a suspect. People have killed for less.'

Wesley shook his head. 'He has a cast-iron alibi for the double murder.'

'Rowyard's murder could be a copycat . . .'

'Ballistics have confirmed Rowyard was killed with the same weapon as Jameson and Evans. How would Grayling get hold of it?' Somehow he couldn't see Oliver Grayling as a killer but he knew he could be wrong. 'Know what I'm thinking, Gerry? If Nathan Rowyard was blackmailing Grayling, who's to say he wasn't trying the same trick on the killer?'

'Rowyard's phone records and bank details are being examined and his cottage is being searched. If he was in touch with the killer we'll find out eventually.'

Wesley wondered whether to mention Sarah Shaw and her possible link to the death of Alcuin Garrard all those years ago but Gerry spoke again before he had the chance.

'Someone went to pick Kyle Ball up earlier but he wasn't at his flat. I told Plymouth to let us have him when he shows up.'

'Think he's lying low?'

'The Fitches will have tipped him off that we're looking for him.' Gerry sighed. 'If Andrea Jameson was the killer's target there are an awful lot of people who'd be glad to see her out of the way.' He began to count them off on his fingers. 'There's Jason Fitch, his missus and her brother, Kyle. Then there's her love rival Gemma Whittingstill and Richard Jakes, who blames her for what happened to his daughter. And Jeremy Ovorard, who had a run-in with her over Jocasta's birthday party. We're spoiled for choice.'

'She certainly had a gift for making enemies. And there could be others we don't know about yet.'

Gerry stretched like an animal awakening from sleep. 'Better go and see what Colin has to tell us about Nathan Rowyard. Although I don't anticipate any surprises, do you?'

Before Wesley left the church hall he gave Pam a call. But there was no answer.

As Wesley anticipated, the post-mortem didn't throw up anything unexpected. Colin estimated that Nathan Rowyard died sometime between Saturday evening and Sunday night. Colin always insisted that the super-accurate times of death given on TV cop shows were pure fiction so Wesley nodded politely and accepted his verdict.

As they were leaving the hospital mortuary, Gerry received a call to say that Rowyard's bank account was remarkably healthy. Fifteen thousand pounds in cash had been deposited by Rowyard himself over the past five weeks.

'Fifteen grand,' Wesley said. 'Grayling gave him eleven so where did the other four thousand come from?'

'We're trying to get his mobile records as a matter of urgency so there's a chance we'll find our killer's number, if Rowyard was blackmailing him as well as Grayling.' He paused. 'I can't see Grayling shooting someone like that, can you, Wes? It seems so ... cold-blooded.'

Before Wesley could reply his phone began to ring. For a brief moment Belinda Crillow leaped into his mind. He still felt uneasy that the man who'd broken into her house had mentioned his name. It was something he didn't understand – just like the attack on Pam's car and the silent phone calls she'd been receiving.

This time, however, there was nothing familiar about the female voice on the other end of the line. She sounded wary, but so did a lot of people when they were calling the police.

'Inspector Peterson. A DC Thorne from Morbay Police Station asked me to call you. I clean for the Ovorards.'

'Thanks for calling, Ms ... ?'

'Pepper. Shona Pepper. Look, I'm free this afternoon if you want to meet. I don't drive so can it be somewhere in Morbay? The Blue Lagoon Café on the front's very nice and it shouldn't be too crowded now it's out of season.'

Wesley looked at his watch. 'I'll see you there at two.'

When Wesley entered the Blue Lagoon, setting the bell above the door jangling, he realised he was hungry because he'd missed lunch. With all the developments in the case, food had completely slipped his mind.

The café was cheap, cheerful and empty apart from an elderly couple in the corner. The vivid seaside murals

231

decorating the walls reminded Wesley more of his parents' native Caribbean than the English Riviera.

He was five minutes early so he ordered tea for two and a tuna sandwich for himself. He hoped Shona Pepper drank tea and not coffee. He'd assumed that a cleaner would prefer the former but perhaps he was pandering to stereotypes, he thought guiltily.

At two on the dot a woman pushed the door open and looked round. She was in her twenties, slightly chubby with curly auburn hair, tight jeans and a mouth that smiled readily. Wesley stood up.

'Shona?' he said tentatively. If he'd got it wrong there was a chance she'd think he was trying to pick her up and he was relieved when she gave him a warm smile and hurried to sit down at his table. When she took off her denim jacket he saw a fine display of floral tattoos on her forearms.

'Inspector Peterson, I presume.' There was a friendliness about her which made Wesley warm to her at once.

'That's right. I've ordered tea. Want anything to eat?'

She shook her head. 'I grabbed a butty at home thanks.'

'Thanks for meeting me. Did DC Thorne tell you what this is about?'

'I presume it's about Jocasta.' She tilted her head to one side and looked at him appraisingly. 'I saw you on telly making that appeal with Mr Ovorard. You were good if I may say so.'

Wesley felt the blood rushing to his face. 'Thanks. I was hoping you could help me. You must be near Jocasta's age ...'

She gave a little giggle. 'Flatterer. I'm nearly thirty. Jo's twelve years younger.'

She was flirting and her vivacity was so infectious that

Wesley was sorely tempted to reciprocate. Then he remembered that a young woman was missing, possibly dead, and he was there to do a job.

'But you speak to her when she's home?'

'I reckon I'm the only one who's ever showed any interest in her and I'm only the cleaner.' She said the last three words with heavy irony. 'And don't they let me know it.'

This was better. Wesley hoped the tea wouldn't arrive and break the spell. 'Tell me about the Ovorards.'

'Well, don't believe the concerned politician act.'

'I thought he was one of the good guys.'

'That's what he wants you to think. He's a complete shit – there's only one person Jeremy Ovorard loves and that's Jeremy Ovorard.'

'Has he ever . . . made advances to you?'

She giggled. 'I think I'm a bit long in the tooth for him.' She glanced round the room before continuing. 'Let's just say Jo hasn't brought any mates home for the past couple of years.'

Wesley raised his eyebrows. 'Is that just gossip or have you got evidence?'

Shona shrugged. 'There's no smoke without fire, is there?'

'He seems worried about Jocasta.'

'It wouldn't look good if he didn't play the anxious father, would it?'

Wesley was surprised by her cynicism. So far he'd had no reason to doubt Jeremy Ovorard's sincerity. He'd seen how upset he was when he'd made the appeal and he'd assumed Jocasta had either got herself into genuine danger or that she was a spoiled daughter putting her parents through hell. Now he was beginning to doubt his own judgement.

'What about his wife?'

'He keeps her in the style she's become accustomed to so she turns a blind eye. Tabitha's OK but she's a bit of a princess. Good job she's got me to clean her loos for her – she's got four by the way. One main bathroom, one downstairs cloakroom and two en-suites.' She rolled her eyes at the extravagance.

'How do Mr and Mrs Ovorard get on?'

'They don't. They lead separate lives.'

'And Jocasta?'

Shona tapped the side of her freckled nose. 'She hates her dad and she thinks her mother's a pain in the arse. A dysfunctional family, I think they call it.'

'A family with secrets?'

She considered the question for a few moments. 'Don't all families have secrets? Only some are worse than others,' she added with a knowing wink.

'Like the Ovorards'?'

'I'm just the cleaner. They don't wash their dirty linen in front of me if that's what you're hoping.'

'How long have you worked for them?'

'Four years. I clean for other people as well but the Ovorards have always been regulars. And before you ask I don't claim to know them that well. Some people like to be all pally with their cleaner but they keep their distance.'

'But you must hear things; find things lying round,' said Wesley.

'They're very careful – especially him. He keeps his office locked. He's an MP so he says there are confidential papers in there. But you're right. I've got eyes in my head and I see what's going on.'

'And what do you see?'

'I see Tabitha flirting with the gardener. Not that I blame her. He's really fit.' She bent forward and whispered. 'I found his T-shirt in Tabitha's bedroom a few months back.'

'Her husband didn't notice?'

'Oh, they don't share a bedroom. Tabitha's just wheeled out when he needs a devoted wife to parade in front of the media. Luke's not the only one, I'm sure of that.'

'The gardener's called Luke?'

'Yeah. Luke Wellings.'

Wesley felt like a piece of the jigsaw had just fallen into place. Craig Carswell from the Drama Centre had overheard Jocasta speaking to someone called Luke and the coincidence was too strong to ignore.

'Is Luke . . . friendly with Jocasta?'

Shona gave him a knowing smile. 'I see what you're getting at and you could be right. If you ask me he fancies himself as a bit of a stud. Mother and daughter. Now that'd be a challenge.'

'Have you any evidence?'

Shona considered the question for a moment.

'A couple of weeks before Jo went to that drama course I saw her with Luke in the summerhouse in the garden. I wasn't close enough to hear what they were saying and as soon as they saw me at the back door they shut up.'

'Does he own a motorbike?'

'Yeah. It's his pride and joy. Why?'

Wesley recalled the doodle of the motorbike he'd found at the Drama Centre and felt like punching the air. But as the waitress was just bringing his order, he controlled himself.

'Where can I find him?'

'He lives with his gran.'

'Know the address?'

'It's not far away. I'll show you if you like. But he's not there, he's travelling round the States for a few months. Holiday of a lifetime.'

'When did he leave?'

'About three weeks ago.'

'And nobody connected this with Jocasta's disappearance?'

'You think they've run off together?'

'Would it surprise you?'

She considered the question while Wesley took the first bite of his sandwich. 'I'm sure the idea of screwing mother and daughter would appeal to Luke but I'm not sure he'd want it to get heavy.'

'You seem to know him well.'

Shona's cheeks turned red. 'We had a bit of a fling about a year ago. He's that sort of guy. But we're just mates now.'

'According to a witness Luke might have been in contact with Jocasta while she was in Tradington.' Wesley watched her sip her tea, wondering if she was as unconcerned about Luke's relationship with Tabitha as she claimed. A little jealousy wouldn't have surprised him but she shrugged as though she couldn't care less.

'I might have got it wrong. Mind you I know he's in the States 'cause I got a postcard from him yesterday.' She delved in her bag and took out a postcard of the Statue of Liberty. *Having a great time*, it said on the reverse. *See you soon. Luke xxx.*

'I didn't think people of his age sent postcards any more,' said Wesley.

'It's retro. He likes that sort of thing – very into vinyl records. Even his motorbike's from the fifties. He loves that bike more than any woman – that's one thing I know for sure.'

When it was time to leave Wesley asked Shona to show him where Luke Wellings lived but when he knocked on the door Luke's grandmother confirmed Shona's story. Her grandson was in the States. And he'd gone there alone.

There was nobody about when Pam parked her car in the drive, squeezing it in beside her mother's VW Beetle. Della had parked too far over as usual, failing to anticipate that Pam and Wesley also needed space. As Pam manoeuvred herself out of the driving seat she was engulfed by tiredness. It had been a hard day at school and an imminent inspection only added to the stress.

She was longing to get into the house to put her feet up and she hoped her mother had something planned for dinner. But when Della rushed into the hall to greet her she could tell something was wrong.

'I've been trying to call Wesley but I keep getting his voicemail,' Della said, grasping her daughter's arm and propelling her into the living room.

Pam noticed that the curtains were drawn across the French window, blocking out the view of the garden beyond.

'Someone was in the bushes at the bottom of the garden. I was in here watching the lunchtime news and when I looked up there he was – dressed all in black with his hood up. He shot off through your neighbour's garden – must have found a gap in the hedge.' She took a deep breath. 'If the kids had been here ... '

'They weren't,' Pam said, trying not to let her mother's panic infect her.

'Where are they?'

'Amelia's having tea at a friend's – she's being dropped off later.'

'What about Michael?'

A shadow of fear seized Pam's heart. Michael's school was on the other side of the river. He caught the ferry back to Tradmouth then walked home up the hill from the middle of town, usually with his friend, Nathaniel. 'He won't like it but I'll go down to meet him at the bottom of the hill,' Pam said. 'He'll be with Nathaniel most of the way but once they separate he's on his own.'

'Be careful.'

Pam would have liked to ignore her mother's words of warning but she couldn't. The steep, winding road out of the centre of Tradmouth became quiet as it neared their close at the top of the town, ideal for a stalker to strike.

'Why don't you go round and ask the neighbours if they saw anything?' Pam said, delving in her bag for her keys.

'I've already done it. Next door are still away and nobody else saw anything suspicious.'

Pam was pleasantly surprised at her mother's bout of efficiency. She found her keys then dropped them back in her bag. 'It's not worth taking the car. I'll walk down to meet him.'

'No. Don't do that.' Della's words were barked like an order.

'Why?'

Della hesitated. 'Because I saw a flash of metal. I think he had a knife.'

Extract from draft PhD thesis
written by Alcuin Garrard

July 1995

There are references to the DeTorhams'
steward, Peter, in correspondence found in
the DeTorham muniment room at Princebury
Hall and in the journal of Henry Dyce,
which suggest something amiss. It is said
that he failed to attend mass and the word
'heresy' is mentioned on two occasions –
a serious matter at that time. There is a
strong suggestion that Oswald was anxious to
keep his steward out of trouble and a letter
to his cousin Henry Dyce hints at a bond
between the two men. That letter states that
Oswald and Peter had known each other from
childhood and in other correspondence Oswald
describes his steward as being 'as learned
as myself'.

Most of the written evidence, however,
concerns events in the village of Lower
Torworthy and it appears that the atmosphere
in the village changed with the introduction
of Sir Matthew's 'big friar'. Before 1533 the

priest writes in the parish records about the day-to-day affairs of the community; the many saints and feast days the people of Lower Torworthy came together to celebrate and the use of the 'little monk' to heal and comfort the sick. After that date, however, although there is no mention whatsoever of a 'big friar' in church inventories or the parish records, other documents hint that it has become a focus of unease – even fear – in the locality.

It is necessary, therefore, to consider why any reference to the 'big friar' is omitted from official records and whether something was happening that needed to be concealed; perhaps something the superstitious villagers regarded as evil.

29

When Wesley ended the call he turned his head and saw Gerry watching him.

'Something the matter?'

'Della thinks someone's been watching our house.'

Gerry walked over to Wesley's desk and sat down. It wasn't a conversation he wanted the whole incident room to hear.

'She's always been inclined to overdramatise, hasn't she?'

'I take your point but Pam believes her and Belinda Crillow's attacker mentioned my name. Then there's Pam's tyres.'

'This latest thing'll be some opportunist toe-rag looking for drugs money.' Gerry was doing his best to reassure but he didn't sound altogether convincing.

'It's not easy to get into our garden from the back.'

'Neighbours see anything?'

'Next door are away on holiday.'

'There you are then. An opportunist cut through their garden to try his luck. If I were you I'd make sure next door hasn't been broken into when you get home.'

Wesley knew Gerry was right. It was possible his absent

elderly neighbours had been targeted but he hardly liked to ask Pam or Della to go and check.

Trish Walton's voice interrupted his thoughts. She sounded breathless, as if she'd just received some momentous news she couldn't wait to share.

'There's been a sighting of Jocasta Ovorard in Newquay.'

Wesley found it hard to share her excitement. There had been so many sightings of Jocasta since the appeal and they'd all come to nothing. 'Can you get the local nick to check it out?'

But Trish didn't move. 'The witness who contacted us took a picture on his phone and Newquay emailed it to us. It's her this time, I'm sure it is.'

Wesley followed Trish to her computer where she brought up the image on the screen and stood aside triumphantly to give Wesley a better view. The girl in the picture certainly resembled the photographs he'd seen of Jocasta Ovorard – the poker-straight hair; the sulky expression that suggested she found everything and everybody around her unworthy of her attention. She was sitting alone at an outdoor table in front of a café with a dark drink in her hand and a peevish look on her face. A man's leather jacket was draped over the back of the chair opposite and the café's name was quite clear – The Thirsty Lobster.

'What do you think?' Trish asked.

'Do you have a contact number for the person who took the picture?'

Trish produced a scrap of paper. 'He's down here on a surfing holiday for a couple of weeks. He saw the appeal and he thought he'd better call it in.'

'Good of him.'

Trish smiled. 'He's an off-duty copper from up

north – couldn't break the habit even on holiday. Want me to call him?'

'Yes please. And after you've spoken to him can you call Newquay? If it is her she must be staying somewhere.'

'Are you going to let her father know?'

He couldn't help recalling his conversation with Shona Pepper. Perhaps there was a good reason why Jocasta didn't want to be found. 'Better not get his hopes up until we're sure,' he said.

He needed to tell Gerry about this latest development and found him talking on the phone. Gerry's side of the conversation was monosyllabic and gave nothing away but Wesley could see the light of anticipation in his eyes.

'Kyle Ball's been found and he's being brought in,' said Gerry after he'd finished. 'I said we'd meet him over in Tradmouth in an hour.' He looked at his watch.

'There's been a sighting of Jocasta Ovorard.'

Gerry looked underwhelmed. 'Another one. Where's she got to now? The Amazon jungle?'

'Newquay. An off-duty policeman took a picture on his phone. I think it's her this time. I've asked the local station to follow it up.'

'Good. If we find her safe and well it'll get her dad off our backs.'

An hour later they were back in the interview room at Tradmouth Police Station, the scene of their encounter with Jason Fitch a few days earlier. Fitch's place was now occupied by a man with the face of a belligerent baby and bulging, tattooed muscles. His flesh had turned beetroot-red in the Spanish sun. He looked the type who'd think sunblock was for sissies.

'You've been hard to find, Mr Ball,' Wesley began.

'I've been staying with my girlfriend since I got back. She missed me while I was in Spain. Had to keep the lady happy, didn't I.'

'We'll need your girlfriend's details.'

'What if I don't want to tell you?'

The solicitor by Ball's side – a young man in a sharp suit – gave a small nod of approval. Wesley thought he looked the type who'd encourage his clients to utilise the words 'no comment' at every opportunity.

'Why did you go to Spain?'

'Wanted a bit of sunshine, didn't I.'

Wesley took a deep breath. 'Andrea Jameson.'

Ball shifted uncomfortably in his seat. 'What about her?'

'She was having an affair with your sister's husband Jason Fitch. You must have been angry on your sister's behalf.' It was a statement rather than a question.

'Course I was. She's my sister. So?'

'Ever meet Andrea?'

'No.'

'You've been in the army so you know how to use a rifle.'

He looked wary. 'What of it?'

'Do you possess a firearm?'

'That's illegal.'

'But they're not hard to buy if you know who to ask.'

'No comment.'

'Where were you a week last Friday?' said Gerry.

'I was with Chantalle all that day – my girlfriend. You can ask her. She'll tell you.'

'What about last Saturday? We know you came back from Spain earlier than expected. Why was that?'

'Missing Chantalle, wasn't I. I was at hers last Saturday. Went there straight from the airport.'

'But you won't give us her address so we can't ask her,' said Wesley reasonably.

He could almost see Ball's brain working as he made the calculation.

'OK,' he said eventually. 'But she suffers with her nerves so go easy on her.'

'We'll treat her like a princess,' said Gerry.

As soon as he gave an address on a notorious Plymouth housing estate, Gerry left the room. Wesley knew he'd gone to organise a search warrant but there was no need to mention that to Kyle Ball.

'Do you know a man called Nathan Rowyard?'

'No.'

'Are you sure?'

'Course I am.'

'He used to specialise in blackmail before he was shot at the weekend. Identical MO to Andrea Jameson's murder. We think the same person's responsible.'

'Well, it wasn't me. I've never even heard of him.'

'So he wasn't blackmailing you?'

He snorted as though the idea was ridiculous and as Wesley watched him, the confidence he'd felt at the start of the interview began to melt away. Even so, if there was a connection between Rowyard and Ball it was bound to come to light eventually.

Wesley ended the interview and ignored the solicitor's request that his client should be released. They still had hours yet before they had to either charge him or release him – but he knew the clock was ticking.

There was nothing more they could do until the premises belonging to Kyle Ball's girlfriend were searched – a

245

task they assigned to Chantalle's local station in Plymouth.

Before leaving the station Wesley asked Rob Carter about Belinda Crillow, only to be told that there were no new leads, and when he returned to the incident room in Lower Torworthy with Gerry he spent some time studying the crime-scene pictures on the board, focusing on one in particular.

Then he took a photograph of the dead Alcuin Garrard from the 1995 police file and compared it with the crime-scene pictures of Ian Evans's body. The fact that they'd both died in the same field was probably a coincidence but, on the other hand, he had an uneasy feeling about it. Ever since Oliver Grayling told him that the girl who'd befriended Alcuin all those years ago was still in the village he'd wanted to speak to her and now was as good a time as any.

Gerry looked dubious when he told him where he was going. 'If you think it's worth it.'

Wesley didn't answer. He left the church hall and hurried through the village. It was a pleasant evening but a breeze was getting up, sending the white clouds scudding across the vast sky, and by the time he reached his destination he was glad he'd zipped up his coat. Beside a neatly painted sign bearing the name of the house he saw a larger sign, decorated with painted flowers. Tarn End Flowers – Sarah Shaw's business. A small grey van standing on the drive had an identical logo on the side.

Before ringing the doorbell he looked at his watch. Seven fifteen. It was late to call on her unannounced but, on the other hand, there was a good chance he'd find her at home.

The woman who answered the door was in her late

thirties; fair-haired with a snub nose and a slender figure. Wesley produced his ID and apologised for bothering her so late in the day.

'We've finished eating.' She sounded as though she wasn't sure how to react to the unexpected intrusion. 'Come in,' she said eventually. 'We can go into my workshop. We won't be disturbed in there.'

He could hear a TV blaring in the distance and the chatter of children. No doubt there was a husband somewhere keeping an eye on them.

'I understand you've met a friend of mine. Neil Watson,' he said as she led him into a room that had once been a double garage but was now filled with work tables and buckets of colourful blooms.

A look of relief passed across her face. 'Neil. Oh yes, he's been doing a survey of the church with some volunteers.'

'You told him about a student you knew years ago; a young man who was researching the history of the village.'

The look of relief vanished and he saw her hands clench. She opened her mouth to say something but no sound emerged.

'You'll have heard about the double murder in Manor Field?'

'Of course. An officer came round to take our statements – not that we could tell him anything,' she added in a rush.

'You got to know Alcuin Garrard while he was here researching for his doctorate?'

'Er . . . yes.' She blushed. 'Al was fairly near my own age so . . . Lower Torworthy isn't the most exciting place for anyone that age.'

'You were going out with him?'

247

'Nothing like that. We were just friends.'

'I believe you used to meet him in the Shepherd's Arms.'

'That's right. I had a taste for cider in those days.' There was a brightness in her voice that sounded artificial, as though she was putting on an act for his benefit. 'He used to go on about this mechanical monk he'd found mentioned in some old documents he'd found. Apparently it was credited with all sorts of miraculous cures.'

'Neil discovered it.'

'He told me.'

'Have you seen it?'

'It's at the university at the moment but he's promised to show it me one day.'

She turned away and picked up a flower, fidgeting with its silk petals.

'You must have been upset when Alcuin died.'

'Yes,' she said, her gaze still focused on the flower. 'He was . . . nice.'

'Is there anything else you can tell me? Anything out of the ordinary that happened back then?'

There was a long silence before she replied.

'He used to talk about his great-aunt who was murdered.'

The mention of murder caught Wesley's attention. 'Was anyone arrested?'

'Yes, her carer. She'd been stealing from the old lady. She killed herself before she could be put on trial. Al had been close to his great-aunt and she'd promised to give him something to help with his studies but the carer stole everything. He was really cut up about it.'

'What was his great-aunt's name?'

'Mary, I think. Don't know her surname.'

'Where did she live?'

'Not sure.' There was something guarded about her reply which reinforced Wesley's impression that she was holding something back.

'Do you remember anything else?'

She appeared to consider the question carefully. 'Shortly before he died he was excited because he'd found out there might be a second mechanical monk – a big friar. He said some references to it had been obliterated and it was a mystery.'

Wesley recognised this as a deliberate change of subject but he was intrigued. 'Obliterated?'

'That's what he said.'

'What happened when he died?'

'We were supposed to be meeting in the Shepherd's Arms but he rang to say he'd be late 'cause he was going to Manor Field. Something to do with his research. He never turned up but I thought he'd just got sidetracked – he was like that about his work sometimes. Then he was found the next morning and . . . '

'Why Manor Field?'

She considered the question. 'It was the site of an old manor house. He was researching the family who lived there and a descendant of theirs lent him some old family documents for his research. His name was Ralph Detoram. Al said he was a nice old boy. They got on well.'

'Mr Detoram lived at Princebury Hall?'

She nodded.

'It's a well-being centre now.'

She hesitated. 'Yes, I know.'

'The police report into Alcuin's death mentions that a witness saw a large dark-coloured car parked near the field around the time he died. It was never traced.'

'Al didn't own a car,' she said quickly.

'Did he have any friends who did?'

'I've no idea. I'm sorry. I can't help you.' Her eyes widened. 'You don't think … you don't think these latest murders have anything to do with Al's death, do you?'

Wesley felt obliged to give an honest reply. 'I'm sorry. I don't know.'

Kyle Ball's girlfriend, Chantalle, wasn't the nervous type; quite the reverse. She gave the officers a mouthful when they arrived with the search warrant and watched them, arms folded and uttering a stream of foul-mouthed complaints, as they went through the house. But as soon as they used a stepladder to access the loft of her maisonette she fell silent – and when they emerged from the darkness holding six Winchester rifles, she swore she'd never seen them before in her life.

30

'The rifles from Chantalle's loft have gone to Ballistics,' Gerry said when Wesley arrived at the incident room the next morning.

'Did she say what they were doing there?'

'She said Kyle was looking after them for a mate and she could be telling the truth. According to Plymouth, he has links to the owner of a boat they've been watching for a while – gang importing hunting rifles from the Continent where they're relatively easy to get hold of.'

'So we're treating Ball as our number one suspect?'

'He had access to the weapons so I suppose we have to.' He scratched his head. 'Newquay haven't got back to us about Jocasta Ovorard yet ... if it was her in the picture.'

'I'm pretty sure it was.'

Gerry hesitated. 'Is Pam OK?' He sounded concerned.

'She says she's fine but I can tell she's putting on a brave face.'

'What about Della?'

'Hard to tell with Della. She can make a crisis out of the slightest thing. I reckon it makes her feel important. She's now saying she could have been mistaken about the knife but after what happened to Pam's tyres ...' He paused.

'I'm getting a bad feeling that it's something to do with me – that I've brought something home that could harm my family.'

'You've arrested a lot of people in the course of your career, Wes, but this?'

'Unless it's Della they're after. She's mixed with some strange people in her time.'

'Well, if whoever it is is trying to deliver some sort of message they're bound to make themselves known eventually.'

'That's what I'm afraid of,' Wesley replied almost in a whisper. 'And what on earth does it have to do with Belinda Crillow? Maybe I shouldn't have passed her on to Rob.'

'There's nothing wrong with a bit of delegation. Besides, if our man has got it in for you, it makes sense to keep your distance.'

'Pam's still fragile. She can do without all this.'

'I know, mate.' Gerry put his hand out to touch Wesley's arm in a gesture of sympathy. Then he withdrew it, aware that a group of uniformed constables was watching, and examined his watch.

'Kyle Ball's solicitor's moaning but now the firearms have been found at his girlfriend's place that should shut him up. Once we get the report back from Ballistics we can ask him a few pertinent questions,' Gerry said with satisfaction. 'He hated Andrea Jameson for upsetting his sister and Ian Evans was collateral damage as we've always suspected.'

'What about Nathan Rowyard?'

'Falling out amongst thieves?' Gerry sounded confident. 'No doubt all will become clear in due course.'

'I want to know where that unexplained four grand in Rowyard's bank account came from.'

'If we find out Ball's account's four grand light we'll know. Or maybe Rowyard's victim was Jason Fitch – I'm sure finding four grand to pay off a minor villain wouldn't present him with a problem. Maybe he got Ball to do his dirty work for him ... keep it in the family.'

'If Ball is a hired assassin perhaps that's why Fitch's other girlfriend Gemma Whittingstill hasn't been targeted. Rather than Sharon Fitch using her brother to exact her revenge, it might have been her husband wanting to get rid of an inconvenient mistress. Andrea Jameson sounded like the troublesome type.'

'You could well be right, Wes.' Gerry sat back and patted his large stomach, like a man who'd just enjoyed a good meal.

'I haven't told you about my meeting with Sarah Shaw last night. She used to know Alcuin Garrard, the man found dead in Manor Field in 'ninety-five.'

'Is it relevant?'

Wesley considered the question for a few moments. 'Andrea Jameson, Ian Evans and Alcuin Garrard all died in the same field.'

'Coincidence?'

'Sarah told me Garrard's great-aunt was murdered a few months before he died. She was killed by a carer who'd been stealing from her. I want to find out more.'

'What has this got to do with our recent victims?'

'Not sure yet. But if we don't—'

Before Wesley could say any more the phone on his desk began to ring and he hurried over to answer it, his mind still on Alcuin Garrard and his murdered great-aunt. But when the woman on the other end of the line introduced herself his thoughts returned to the present.

'Inspector Peterson, this is Emily Boase – AJ Celebrations. We spoke last week. Remember?'

'Of course. What can I do for you?' he asked, settling in his seat, his pen poised over his notebook.

'I've found something you might be interested in – a list of guests who were on that yacht when that poor girl was attacked. Would you like to see it?'

'I would. Thank you.' He felt a frisson of excitement. Phoebe Jakes had been in his thoughts on and off but he wasn't sure how her assault fitted into his inquiry – if indeed it did.

'I'll send someone round for the list if that's OK.'

'Fine.' There was a moment of silence, as if she had something else to say. 'It features the usual suspects – businessmen and councillors and a smattering of local VIPs. But there's one name I didn't expect to see – a client I didn't associate with that particular event. We organised a party at Princebury Hall – the place Andrea was going to when she was . . . ' There was a pause, as if she didn't dare utter the word 'murdered' in case it released some terrible curse. 'According to our records the invoice was sent to a Xander Southwark and Mr Southwark's name was on the guest list for the yacht party – although it probably doesn't mean anything,' she added quickly as though afraid she'd just accused an innocent man of something unspeakable.

'You were right to tell me. Thanks,' said Wesley. He hadn't liked Xander Southwark and he'd put this down to his fraudulent past, but perhaps the man was mixed up with darker matters than dipping into clients' funds. 'Tell me, was Jeremy Ovorard a guest at the party?'

'His name's not on the list but . . . '

'But?'

'Well, not everyone who was there would be on the list – not if Andrea gave them a personal invitation.'

The woman had begun to flounder – as though she was regretting her indiscretion. When she said she had to go Wesley decided not to press the matter for now.

As soon as he finished the call he broke the news to Gerry.

'I want to find out more about Xander Southwark,' he said. 'Andrea Jameson was on her way to Princebury Hall when she was killed and she'd organised a party for him, although he claimed he didn't know her personally. He's also on good terms with Jason Fitch.'

'He was a crooked solicitor and they're ten a penny, Wes. I reckon his only crime nowadays is fleecing the gullible up at that Hall of his.' Gerry gave a heavy sigh. 'But if you think it's worth following up we can put it on the list.'

Wesley returned to the report on the death of Alcuin Garrard and fifteen minutes later he called the station to request the file on the murder of the great-aunt, probably called Mary and possibly somewhere in Devon.

He hoped he wasn't wasting his time.

Manor Field was no longer sealed off by police tape so Neil seized the opportunity to visit Dan Noakes's farmhouse to tell him he was beginning an archaeological survey of the field. Dan seemed happy that things were moving, pointing out that, should any treasure be found, as landowner he'd be entitled to half the proceeds. The farmer was a man who knew the law of the treasure trove and he was delighted when Neil told him about the ring Charlie Perks had turned up.

Neil's plans for a training excavation on the site the

following spring were progressing well and he'd already persuaded his contacts at the university that it was an ideal place to let students loose with their trowels once the initial assessments had been done and the Dartmoor winter was over.

He'd also secured the services of Charlie and his metal detector to sweep the area in the hope of finding the big friar depicted in the strange carving on the church roof. If the small monk was buried in lead at the time of the Reformation, surely the larger one would have been interred with similar reverence. According to records he'd found, the manor house that had once stood in the field had been demolished in 1534 after suffering a fire and the usable materials had been salvaged to build Princebury Hall three miles away where the DeTorhams, their name later amended to Detoram, lived until the last of the line died in 2012, after which the place was acquired by Xander Southwark and his Well-being Centre.

He stood in Manor Field watching Charlie sweeping his machine over the ground. So far he'd turned up some barbed wire, a couple of ring pulls and a George V penny. But Neil was waiting for the big one – the powerful signal that would herald the discovery of the second figure, encased in a lead coffin like its little counterpart.

His phone rang and when he saw Annabel's name on the caller display he experienced a surge of optimism.

She came straight to the point. 'Neil, I've just come across a document that mentions your monk. It was written in the early seventeenth century, almost a hundred years after the events it describes.' Neil could hear excitement in her voice. 'It says the manor at Lower Torworthy was destroyed by fire and the good stones taken to build a new house at Princebury. It also claims that the then lord of the manor, one Oswald DeTorham, was forced to abandon Lower Torworthy because of "a mechanical devil which caused great trouble to the people of the village". Any idea what it means?'

'Haven't a clue,' Neil replied. 'But I want to find out.'

Pam had often been irritated by her mother's behaviour in the past but now she was grateful for her company. Wednesday was one of her days off so if it weren't for Della, she'd have been alone in the house with her fears, praying Wesley would come home early for once.

It was only ten o'clock but Della was already making suggestions about how they should fill the day, as though her daughter was a child to be entertained and distracted.

'There's a lovely little café in Neston,' she twittered. 'Their carrot cake's to die for.'

'Sounds good.' Pam would have preferred to spend the morning with a good book but there was no arguing with Della once she'd made up her mind.

'That's settled then. I'll drive.'

Pam had the uncomfortable feeling that her mother's presence was making her revert to a childish state, willing to be ferried about to prearranged activities. She knew she should resent it but there was something comforting about having someone else assuming the burden of responsibility that was usually hers.

Della disappeared upstairs to get ready, leaving Pam staring out of the window. Since the incident with the tyres and the sighting of the stranger in the garden she'd found it hard to relax, although in front of the children she pretended all was well.

She jumped when the insistent chirruping of the phone on the side table shattered the peace of the room. She forced herself to pick it up and at first there was silence. But as she was about to slam the receiver down she heard a voice.

'I'm watching you, bitch. I'm coming to get you.'

Letter from Thomas Chetham
to Henry Dyce

May 1533

*I hear your cousin Oswald is unwell and that his brother
Simeon has assumed charge of the estate. My steward's
sister dwells in Lower Torworthy and she says Simeon
is a bad master without fear of God or man and that the
household prays day and night for their lord's recovery.*

*Word has it the priest Sir Matthew brought his little
monk to pray at Oswald's bedside and with him also was
a big friar, a miraculous machine like the other. When
questioned Sir Matthew would say nothing of the ori-
gins of this new miracle but assured the servants that the
use of both machines would certainly heal their master. I
await news of the truth of this for it is said there is something strange and unnatural afoot.*

*I remain, sir, your loving friend
Thomas Chetham*

31

When Wesley finished speaking to his wife he realised his hands were shaking.

'Something the matter, Wes?'

He saw Gerry looking at him. Not wanting the whole of the incident room to overhear he approached the boss's desk and lowered his voice.

'Pam's had a threatening phone call. Number withheld. Whoever it was said they're watching her and they're coming to get her.'

'No points for originality.'

'You don't need to be original to terrify someone.'

'Look, Wes, you go home. I'll get someone to trace the call.'

Wesley hesitated. Everyone was hard at work, all bent on bringing a triple killer to justice, and if he left now he'd feel he wasn't pulling his weight. On the other hand his wife had been threatened.

'That information you asked for about the murder of Alcuin Garrard's great-aunt hasn't come through yet,' said Gerry as though he'd read his thoughts. 'But it was nineteen ninety-five so it might take some digging out.'

'I'm also waiting for more background on Xander Southwark.'

'There you are then. Grab the chance to get out while you can. I'll call you if anything important comes in. Go on. That's an order.'

With a weak smile, Wesley did as he was told. But as soon as he reached the car his phone rang. It was Tradmouth Police Station and he answered, hoping for news about Jocasta Ovorard, preferably that she'd turned up safe and sound.

But the call had nothing to do with Jocasta or the recent murders. Rob Carter's words on the other end of the line made Wesley's heart sink.

'Belinda Crillow's been attacked again. She insisted on going back to her cottage after the last incident.' He hesitated. 'I reckon she's only got herself to blame. If she'd—'

'What happened?'

'She answered the door and a man pushed his way into her cottage and threatened her with a knife. She sustained cuts to her arm but apart from that she's just shaken. We've got a crime-scene team down there and she's been taken to hospital for a check-up.'

Wesley froze. The violence was escalating.

'She's asking for you again,' Rob continued. 'Says she has something to tell you.'

'If my name's come up I shouldn't get involved.'

'She's insistent. She'll only speak to you.'

Wesley could hear relief in Rob's voice, as though he'd be glad to rid himself of Belinda Crillow once and for all.

Wesley sighed. 'Is she still at the hospital?'

'They've released her and she's staying at a B and B for the night while the CSIs finish at her house.'

'I'll speak to her as soon as I can. This needs sorting out.'

As soon as he arrived home he was greeted by Della, who appeared to be in a state of panic while Pam sat calmly at the kitchen table, sipping coffee.

Before he could talk to his wife, Della took his arm and dragged him into the hall. 'She's taking it too well. She's in denial.'

For once Wesley had to agree with his mother-in-law. 'I'm going to ask our crime prevention people to install a panic button and I'll get a patrol to keep an eye on the house. In the meantime can I ask you to stay a bit longer – just till this is sorted out?'

A satisfied look appeared on Della's face, as though this was what she'd been angling for all along. Without waiting for her reply he joined Pam in the kitchen and sat down. 'Did you recognise the voice on the phone?'

'I think it was disguised. I couldn't even tell whether it was a man or a woman.' She began to twist a strand of hair in her fingers, something she did when she was tense.

'I'll ask someone to trace our incoming calls. Should have done it ages ago when the silent calls started.' He put out his hand to touch hers and she grasped it tightly.

'I'm frightened, Wes,' she said in a whisper. 'I don't feel safe here any more. And the kids ... What if he does something ...'

'Michael always comes home with Nathaniel – and I'll pick Amelia up on the days you're not at work if you like.'

'There's no need. She'll be with Jane and she won't mind bringing her to the door. I don't want the kids to see I'm frightened.' She looked at him intently. 'You must have some idea who's doing this? It must be someone with a grudge against you. I don't move in that sort of world but you do.'

She was right. Over the course of his working life he'd encountered people who'd think nothing of terrorising an innocent woman in her own home to get back at the man who'd helped to put them behind bars. But try as he might he couldn't think of anybody who might be responsible for recent events.

'I'll speak to Gerry again; see if he can think of anyone – someone who's recently been released from prison perhaps.' He suddenly thought of Belinda Crillow and the man who'd attacked her. His name had been mentioned. He needed to talk to her as soon as possible to see if she could provide a better description.

'I'll call in at the station and arrange things,' he said, squeezing Pam's hand.

'I need to get out of the house. Della suggested lunch in Neston but I'll have to back in time for the kids. I don't want them to know about this, Wes. They've been through enough with my operation and ... '

'Hopefully the sight of a patrol car parked outside will put our friend off. And I'll see about that panic button.'

They both stood up and he took her in his arms. 'Sorry.'

'What for?'

'For bringing my work home like this.'

Perhaps it had been a mistake to choose Newquay as their hideaway. The weather was good for September so the place was still full of surfers. And they all had eyes in their heads and access to social media.

Going off-grid had been Luke's suggestion. No mobile usage; no cash cards or credit cards; taking casual work with no questions asked to get the money to live on once the cash they'd taken with them ran out. He'd seen it on some reality show and Jocasta had agreed it was a great idea. She'd laughed when she'd watched her father making the TV appeal, pretending he was too distressed to carry on speaking. He'd let the police inspector sitting next to him do most of the talking. The inspector was black, rather good-looking with a sympathetic manner, and he'd sounded a lot more sincere.

There was an ancient portable TV in the little flat above the chip shop Luke had blagged for the duration in return for working a few shifts, and he liked to watch the local news – just to see what they were saying about them. It had been a laugh at first, keeping one step ahead of the cops, then one day the news bulletin announced that they were looking for her because she might be a vital witness in a murder case. That was when things turned serious.

Luke had asked her whether she wanted to speak to the police but she'd been adamant that she knew nothing about the murder apart from what she'd seen on the TV. She'd sensed that Luke hadn't believed her but he hadn't argued.

It was almost time for him to start his shift in the chippy. Jocasta had found herself work in a souvenir shop on the beach selling buckets and spades and general holiday tat and he reckoned she had a better deal, even though she had to start earlier in the morning. At least she didn't smell of chip oil all the time and she didn't have to endure the heat that built up in the glass-fronted shop over the evening.

Maybe they'd move on soon. Somewhere exciting like London – although the last thing Jo wanted was to bump into her father. She hated him with a vehemence Luke couldn't quite understand. Every time he'd tried to find out more from Tabitha during the rather satisfying times they'd spent in bed together, she'd changed the subject.

He was coming down the stairs from the flat when he heard the boss's voice. The owner of Pride's Fish and Chips was a small wiry man with thin black hair that looked as if it had been plastered across his scalp with oil from his fryers.

'I wanted a word with you. That girl who's staying with you, she looks familiar.'

The man was staring at him and Luke found his unblinking gaze disconcerting.

'She was here in Newquay last season,' Luke lied with confidence. 'Maybe you saw her then.'

'That'll be it.' The man's lips twitched upwards in a cold smile and he examined the cheap watch on his hairy wrist. 'Better get to work. Those cod aren't going to batter themselves.'

As Luke followed him into the shop he felt uneasy.

Wesley's instincts screamed at him that seeing Belinda Crillow might be a bad mistake. But he needed to know whether her ordeal at the hands of a faceless attacker had anything to do with what had happened to Pam.

He found her at the backstreet B and B near the town centre where she'd taken refuge while the CSIs went over her cottage. Rob Carter had advised her to get better locks fitted while she was there and Wesley imagined that she wouldn't feel safe until this was done. He wondered whether Pam was beginning to feel like that about their own home. His house was a sanctuary; somewhere he could escape the world of crime; somewhere his children could grow up safely. It was precious and he couldn't bear the thought of it being tainted by violence.

He'd arranged to meet Belinda in the little lounge at the front of the house but when he arrived he was given a message by the landlady, delivered impatiently as though she had better things to do. Belinda felt too nervous to come down so could he go to her room. Suddenly he wished he'd brought someone else with him – Rachel perhaps – but she'd asked to see him alone.

When he tapped on her door it was opened immediately. Belinda Crillow's left arm, he noticed, was bandaged and there was a dressing on her right hand. The black eye she'd sustained in the previous attack was now a vivid shade of yellow. He'd thought her attractive when they'd first met and her injuries gave her an added vulnerability. She looked fragile; in need of protection.

'You asked to see me,' he said, trying to remain businesslike.

'Would you like a cup of tea?' She gestured towards the tray of tea-making equipment provided by the landlady.

Wesley declined her offer and remained standing.

'Have you remembered anything else about the man who attacked you?'

Belinda shook her head.

'What exactly did he say? Please think hard.'

She gazed up at the ceiling, making a great effort to remember. 'It was something like: "You've been blabbing to Peterson again. You need to shut your mouth." He said it was my final warning. Next time he'd kill me.'

She looked at him appealingly. For a moment she reminded him of a puppy in an animal shelter begging to be given a loving home, but he banished the thought from his mind. She was a grown woman and she might be in serious danger.

'I said I hadn't told you anything but he wouldn't listen.' She took a step closer to him. 'I'm frightened, Wesley. I need protection.'

'My colleague DC Carter . . . '

'I don't feel safe with him. Will you stay with me?'

The hysteria rose in her voice as she moved even closer to him, her eyes fixed on his, pleading. He feared the situation was hurtling out of his control.

'You'll be safe here for the time being and I'll have another word with the station.'

'If you were here . . . ' She clasped his arm tightly and he could feel her fingers pressing through the cloth of his jacket like talons.

He removed her hand gently, holding it in his for a few moments. 'I'll arrange for a female officer to stay with you if you want. And if you remember anything else – or if you have any more trouble – call the station right away. Promise.'

'Stay with me . . . please.'

He could sense her despair but what she suggested was out of the question.

He called the station, asking them to send a female officer round at once. He needed to go.

32

'You've got to nip this in the bud now,' was Gerry's verdict when Wesley reported back.

'If it's the same person who's been targeting Pam . . .'

'I've gone through all our old cases in my head and I can't think of anyone who fits this particular bill. Can you?'

Wesley shook his head.

'Could it be someone you offended before you came to Devon – someone you nicked in London while you were working in the Met?'

'I was a DS in the Art and Antiques Squad and to be honest, Gerry, I can't remember anybody I arrested being that scary. And I certainly didn't receive any threats. I'd remember.'

Wesley knew further speculation was futile. He'd done all he could – until the adversary made his next move.

As he returned to his desk his attention was drawn to the crime-scene photographs on the wall. Alcuin Garrard, Ian Evans and Andrea Jameson had met their deaths in the same field but so far he'd found nothing to suggest this wasn't just a coincidence. But Dartmoor was a huge area so why that particular place? It was a question that kept running through his mind and he was grateful for anything that distracted him from his more personal problems.

The Xander Southwark fraud case file he'd requested was waiting for him, balanced on top of his computer keyboard. When he flicked through it he learned that Southwark had been a partner in a successful law firm; handsome, charming and with a taste for the high life. His clients had trusted him implicitly, probably because he had a silver tongue and a good line in persuasion. Wesley had long ago given up trusting anybody with the gift of the gab but he knew how well it worked with many victims, especially the elderly. Southwark had been methodical in his fraudulent activities. He'd selected elderly clients with few relations – or relations who lived at a distance and took no interest – and, after obtaining power of attorney over their affairs, he systematically plundered their accounts, in several cases altering wills in his favour. When asked, the clients in question said they thought he was wonderful – such a kind and trustworthy young man who did a lot for charity and the community.

Wesley searched the file for familiar names but there were none he recognised. One thing, however, shone through all the statements – wherever Xander Southwark went he made friends and influenced people. It was only after an irate relative from Canada questioned the fact that her mother had left her nothing in her will, naming instead her trusted solicitor as her main beneficiary, that Southwark's wrongdoings came to light.

Once his crimes were discovered, however, people began to come forward with accusations. As well as plundering the accounts of elderly clients, his secretary accused him of starting an affair with an impressionable young girl who was on work experience in his office. No complaint, however, was ever made so the allegation was put down to spite – or even envy – on the secretary's part.

As Wesley read on he formed an image of the man in his mind. Ruthless, risk-taking and arrogant to the point of recklessness.

He stared at the list of party guests provided by Andrea Jameson's assistant and Xander Southwark's name stood out as though it had been printed there in large scarlet letters. Rachel was engrossed in paperwork and Wesley thought she looked as though she needed a break.

Forty-five minutes later they pulled up outside Phoebe Jakes's house. He'd briefed Rachel during the drive and it would be up to her to do the talking.

The call from the chip-shop proprietor in Newquay came in at four o'clock, an hour and a half after Wesley and Rachel had left the incident room. When DC Paul Johnson heard what the man had to say he immediately transferred him to DCI Heffernan, who was soon barking excited questions into the phone.

'You absolutely sure it's her?' Paul overheard him saying, disappointed that he couldn't hear the answer.

'We'll get someone there right away. Where are they now?'

Again Paul listened but all he could hear was a tantalising silence.

Phoebe Jakes was still adamant that she didn't know her attacker's identity. She said he'd come up behind her and pushed her into a pitch-dark cabin and all she knew was that he was strong and smelled of expensive aftershave – she didn't know which brand. After the ordeal she'd been paralysed with fear; too shaken to move until Andrea Jameson had come to find her, demanding why she wasn't handing round the drinks.

Wesley let Rachel do the talking, noting how Phoebe shot him nervous looks every now and then. When Rachel showed her the picture of Xander Southwark they'd taken from the files, he was certain he'd seen a reaction. Then she'd glanced at her mother who was sitting next to her with a protective arm around her shoulders and shaken her head vigorously. It definitely wasn't him.

Wesley wasn't convinced by her refusal to name Southwark as her attacker but he said nothing and struggled to control the pent-up anger he felt; an anger he suspected was born of prejudice. He'd met Southwark's type before.

On the way back to Lower Torworthy he suggested that they drive straight to Princebury Hall to speak to Southwark. Rachel, however, advised against it.

'Phoebe didn't name him and even if she had it would be her word against his. Can you imagine her in a witness box?'

He acknowledged that Rachel was right. They needed more on Xander Southwark if they were to take the matter any further.

His phone rang. It was the station to say that a female constable had been sent to look after Belinda Crillow, who wasn't being very cooperative, insisting that only Wesley could deal with her case.

'Who was that?' Rachel asked, fixing her eyes on the narrow lane ahead.

Wesley explained. 'I might have been too hard on her. She's terrified.'

'You can't keep running every time she snaps her fingers.' She hesitated. 'You don't think she's becoming obsessed with you?'

Wesley shook his head.

For a few moments Rachel said nothing, then: 'Has it occurred to you that she might have made up the bit about the attacker mentioning your name to get your attention? I know Rob might not be God's gift to sympathetic policing but he's doing his best. I think Belinda Crillow sees you as her knight in shining armour.'

'How do you explain the incidents at my home?'

'Ex-con out for revenge? If he really intended to harm you or your family, he'd have done it by now. He's either letting off steam or sending you a warning.'

'What about?'

'Who knows?' It had started to drizzle so she flicked on the wipers. 'It all started when we began this investigation, didn't it? You think it could be the killer?'

Wesley had considered a lot of possibilities but not this one.

'Or someone who doesn't want you to dig too deeply into his background. Xander Southwark?'

Wesley shook his head. 'I don't think it's his style. Besides, I'm not the only officer on the case so why pick on me?'

Rachel didn't have an answer.

As soon as they arrived at the incident room Wesley sensed excitement in the air. When Gerry greeted him with a wide grin he found out why.

'We've found Jocasta Ovorard. She ran off with her mum's toy boy and they've been living under the radar in Newquay only to be rumbled by an observant chip-shop owner who gave Luke a cash-in-hand job and free accommodation above the shop. He'd been watching the local news and decided to call it in.'

'Don't suppose Jocasta's too pleased.'

'On the contrary, according to the patrol who picked her up she seemed relieved. Slumming it above a chippy loses its glamour after a while. And the excitement of running off with your mum's personal stud no doubt wears thin when you have to live with his dirty underwear,' he added with a chuckle.

'Have her parents been told?'

'Yes. She's being brought back to Tradmouth and Jeremy Ovorard's meeting up with us later.'

'What about Tabitha?'

'Thanks to Luke I imagine relations between mother and daughter will be a bit strained.'

'He was supposed to be in the States. The cleaner, Shona Pepper, had a postcard from him.'

'According to the officers in Newquay he's been very chatty. He gave a couple of postcards to a mate to post while he was over that side of the pond to throw everyone off the scent. I'll give him and Jocasta their due, they planned it well. By the way, the results on the rifles in Chantalle's loft have come back from Ballistics. There's no match to the bullets found at the murder scenes, which puts us back to square one. Mind you, Kyle Ball's been looking after them for a mate so we can get him for something.'

'And it's possible he used one of the consignment for the killings then got rid of it.'

'You're right, Wes. Can't rule him out just yet.'

When Wesley returned to his desk he found an extra file there that hadn't been there before. It was brown, curled around the edges with a faint musty odour, and when he opened it he saw the papers concerned the death of Mary Tilson – spinster; aged eighty-four: the only murder that matched the case mentioned by Sarah Shaw.

Miss Tilson lived alone but her great-nephew, Alcuin Garrard, was studying in Exeter and called round to see her whenever he could. When Wesley saw the name he smiled to himself. Alcuin's visits had become infrequent in the months leading up to her death but, according to the neighbours, they were on good terms.

When Mary Tilson died suddenly her post-mortem revealed that she had been smothered with a pillow found nearby and the obvious suspect was Mary's carer, Judith Westminster, who called on the old lady four times a day. Judith had been suspected of theft in the past and Mary had complained to Alcuin about things going missing. However, Mary was forgetful so her allegations weren't taken too seriously, especially as Alcuin wasn't aware of Judith Westminster's history of petty pilfering. Whenever he was there Judith played the devoted carer to perfection so he put his great-aunt's suspicions down to a touch of paranoia.

Judith visited Mary late one evening to get her ready for bed – something confirmed by a neighbour who'd seen her car outside – and when the old lady was found dead the next morning she immediately came under suspicion.

According to the file, Alcuin Garrard had been only too ready to accuse his great-aunt's carer. He had been fond of the old woman and had given evidence against her alleged murderer, even accusing her of stealing several thousand pounds missing from his great-aunt's bank account. The money was never found but Judith had run up considerable debts which had mysteriously been paid in the months before Mary's death. Consequently Mary Tilson hadn't had much money to leave to her family.

Wesley sat back in his seat. He'd hoped to find some connection between Alcuin Garrard and either Andrea Jameson or Ian Evans, but there was nothing.

His musings were interrupted by Gerry's voice. 'Jocasta's home with her mum. I said we'd go over and have a word. You up for it?'

Wesley closed the file and stood up.

They found Jocasta Ovorard at home in Morbay but there
was no sign of her mother. Instead it was her father who
greeted Wesley and Gerry at the front door, his face solemn.

33

They found Jocasta Ovorard at home in Morbay but there
was no sign of her mother. Instead it was her father who
greeted Wesley and Gerry at the front door, his face solemn.

'You must be relieved, Mr Ovorard,' said Gerry
cheerfully.

'Of course.' The man's exasperated expression suggested
the reunion hadn't been altogether amicable.

'How is your daughter?' Wesley asked.

Ovorard didn't answer the question. 'I take it the man
concerned will face charges.'

'That's still to be decided,' said Gerry with uncharacteristic caution. 'Can we speak to Jocasta? Promise we won't
keep her long.' He gave the MP a hopeful smile but Wesley
knew he wasn't going to take no for an answer.

Without a word Ovorard showed them into the living
room before returning to the hall and shouting up the
stairs, 'Jocasta, darling. The police want a word with you.
Nothing to worry about. Can you come down, please?'

The words sounded normal and reasonable but Wesley
caught the tension in his voice, as though he was expecting
his daughter to tell him to get lost.

To Wesley's surprise she entered the room half a minute

later, head bowed meekly, as though she was embarrassed by the whole incident. Her father touched her arm as she entered and Wesley saw her pull away as though his touch had caused her pain.

Gerry gave her his best avuncular smile. 'We're glad to see you back home safe and well, love.'

'Yes,' Wesley said. 'Everyone was very worried about you.'

Jeremy Ovorard was hovering by the door, as though he was reluctant to leave. At a nod from Gerry, Wesley went over to him and whispered in his ear. 'If we could have a word with Jocasta alone, Mr Ovorard ...'

Ovorard looked as though he was about to object but eventually he left the room. As soon as Wesley closed the door behind him Jocasta looked considerably more relaxed.

'Sorry to be a nuisance, love. You must be shattered.' Gerry was doing his best to sound sympathetic.

'Luke won't get into trouble, will he? I mean, he didn't abduct me or anything. I wanted to go. I needed to get away from all this crap.' With a sweep of her hand she indicated that she considered the crap to be her parents' house and everything – and probably everyone – in it. 'My father says he wants to bring charges but ...'

'You're not a minor below the age of consent,' Wesley said. 'And you went of your own accord. Am I right?'

There was no mistaking the relief on Jocasta's face. 'I thought it would be great to be with Luke and we planned it all down to the last detail.' She suddenly frowned. 'Although I hadn't imagined it would be so boring in Newquay – working in that shop day in day out and Luke stuck in the chip shop all evening. I thought we'd be surfing all the time. Luke said it would be cool.'

'Life isn't all champagne and roses,' Gerry mumbled.

'Where is Luke?'

'He's at Morbay Police Station answering some questions,' said Wesley. 'Although I don't think he'll be there long – unless you want to press charges.'

As he'd expected, she shook her head vigorously.

'In that case I think we can put the whole incident behind us,' he said. 'But we'd still like a chat if that's OK.'

Her expression turned defiant. 'So I went off with Luke and we lived off the grid for a while. I know that sort of thing gets up the authorities' noses 'cause they like to keep track of everyone. I hate the bloody establishment.'

'Your father's part of the establishment,' Wesley said, watching her face.

'Too right he is.'

'So this was a way of getting back at him?'

There was no answer but Wesley knew his words had hit home. Jocasta's disappearance had been a political statement born of personal animosity.

'Can we move on to something else?' he said, glancing at Gerry. 'You were seen getting out of a red Mercedes in the village of Lower Torworthy on Friday the fourteenth of September.'

She suddenly looked uncomfortable. 'Yeah, I was meeting Luke there.'

'Lower Torworthy seems an odd place to meet.'

She smiled. 'Me and Luke had been holed up just outside Holne in a cottage belonging to a friend of his but the friend was coming back so we had to shift. Luke stayed to see his mate but he said it was best if I made myself scarce. I said I'd go on ahead and meet him later. At first I thought I'd get a bus then I realised I might be spotted and besides, they have CCTV on buses these days. I decided to hitch-hike.'

Wesley was about to point out the risks then thought better of it.

'I was only going to accept lifts with women. I'm not stupid,' she said as though she'd read his thoughts.

'The woman who gave you a lift to Lower Torworthy . . . '

'Andrea. She saw me by the road and recognised me.'

'You made a lot of trouble for her when she arranged that party for you – caused her to fall out with your father. How did the journey go?' Gerry asked, curious.

'She was cool. She stopped and asked me what I was doing. I made her swear not to tell Dad she'd seen me and she said that was no problem 'cause there was no love lost between them. She told me she was on her way to some spa I think it was. Said she was meeting someone there.'

'Have you heard she was murdered shortly after you saw her?'

'Yeah, I heard,' she said after a short silence.

'So you might have been the last person to see her alive,' said Wesley, letting the words sink in.

She shook her head as though she didn't believe what he was saying.

'Were you aware of a car or motorcycle following her car?'

She shook her head again. 'When Andrea told me she wasn't going on much further I spotted this old red phone box and told her to drop me off outside the pub. I called Luke right away. It only took him a quarter of an hour to get there.'

'I thought you were doing without phones,' said Wesley.

'We did . . . but Luke's mate's cottage had a landline.' She

279

wrinkled her nose as though a landline was some strange relic of the past.

'Anything else you can tell us?'

'When me and Luke set off on the Norton I saw Andrea's car parked on a grass verge just outside the village. I told Luke to pull over just out of sight because I wanted to see what she was up to.'

'So you saw her?'

'Yeah, but she didn't see me.'

'What made you curious?'

Jocasta blushed. 'I wanted to see if the person she was meeting was my dad. He was screwing her, you know.'

'I didn't know.' Wesley glanced at Gerry. This was something new.

'It started while she was arranging my party. That's why I pulled out. I couldn't stand seeing him all over her.'

'I was under the impression they fell out when she presented him with the bill for a party that hadn't gone ahead.'

'She did and they had a big row about it – or at least that's what I was told. If you ask me, there was more to it.'

'What?'

'Don't know. I wondered if they'd made up since. My mother thought they had.'

Wesley sighed. Tabitha Ovorard had only given them half a story. It also gave her one of the oldest motives of all for the murder of Andrea Jameson – jealousy.

Wesley leaned forward. There was a lot riding on the answer to the question he was about to ask.

'You say you and Luke parked by the field. Can you tell me exactly what happened?'

'When we drove past Andrea was standing near her car so we went on a bit and stopped round the bend. It was then

I heard a bang and then another. Luke said it sounded like shots but he told me lots of farmers use guns in the country so it was nothing to worry about.'

'Are you telling us you saw Andrea being shot?'

'No. We'd parked out of sight and I hid behind some bushes so I could see what she was up to. She was standing by the gate staring into the field as though she'd seen something interesting.'

Wesley's heart beat faster. 'Was this before or after you heard the shots?'

'After. Luke said we should go 'cause it was none of our business. He went back to the bike and started revving the engine.'

'Did you hear any more shots after that?'

'I told you, Luke was revving the bike and I got on the back. I couldn't hear anything over that racket.'

'You should have come forward with this information, love. It could be important,' said Gerry.

'And let my dad know where I was? Anyway, I didn't see anything.'

'But you definitely heard two shots while Andrea was standing there alive and well?'

'Yes. Is it important?'

'It could be very important. I'll send someone round to take your statement.'

She gave a resigned shrug and Wesley knew it was time they left.

When they opened the living-room door Tabitha Ovorard was standing in the hall as though she'd been waiting for them to leave. She ignored them and dashed towards her daughter, arms outstretched, but Jocasta dodged her embrace and Wesley saw a look of devastation on Tabitha's face. It seemed wrong to intrude on her pain so he hurried out after Gerry.

'What if we've been looking at this case the wrong way round?' he said as they walked to the car. 'If we believe Jocasta – and we've no reason not to – Andrea was alive when the first two shots rang out. What if Ian Evans was the target? What if Andrea Jameson saw him being killed and she was the collateral damage?'

Letter from Oswald DeTorham
to Sir Matthew

9 June 1533

By your good prayers and thanks be to God I am recovered from the fever that afflicted me. I would know
the true nature of this new machine of which the whole
village speaks, for in my fever I was unaware of its
presence.

   The 'little monk' has brought much comfort to your
flock in their afflictions but I hear word that people
fear this new miracle, and Peter my steward says that
Mistress Rowland has not spoken since you left her
alone with it and is sore afraid to leave the confines of the
farm. Some say Peter is wont to defy the Holy Church
and yet I trust his word in this and would speak with
you on the matter for some are saying the 'big friar' is
Satan himself.

Letter from Oswald DeTorham
to Henry Dyce

20 June 1533

Cousin, Sir Matthew showed me the 'big friar' many
say they fear. It was a figure dressed in the plain grey
habit of a Franciscan and upon examination I found it
to be nought but wood and cloth with a wooden mask of
gentle countenance and I am satisfied that the tales told
to you were born of the fevered imaginings of the sick.

This was no man but a mere machine.

34

A subdued Luke Wellings confirmed Jocasta's story. He too had heard two shots ring out, around half a minute apart, while Andrea Jameson was standing near her car but he'd thought little of it.

Every farmer in the area had been questioned during the initial house-to-house inquiries, along with anybody else who owned a legal firearm of any kind, but nobody had admitted to having been out shooting that day.

'What will you tell the chief super?' Wesley asked as they returned to the station in Tradmouth.

'I'll boast about our success in reuniting Jocasta with her worried parents,' Gerry said with a grin. 'That should get her in a good mood for the rest of it.'

'I think Jocasta's statement changes everything, don't you?'

'Unless she's lying to protect someone. Her father perhaps? Or even her mother? If Ovorard was involved with Andrea it opens up a load of possibilities.'

'Ovorard was at a constituency meeting. I've already checked. Besides, I don't think Jocasta would lie for him. As for Tabitha, somehow I can't see her murdering a love rival in a jealous rage.'

'But if he was going to leave her for Andrea – or maybe if Andrea knew something that would bring everything crashing down around her ears: a major scandal for instance.'

Wesley knew this was a possibility – but his instincts still told him that Ian Evans should now become the focus of their investigation.

When they reached the CID office Wesley was greeted by an eager Rob Carter, who looked as though he had news.

'There's a cottage practically next door to Belinda Crillow's. It's a holiday home and it's empty at the moment but the owners installed CCTV. I've got their permission to go through the footage.' As Rob often did, he sounded pleased with himself.

'Good. Keep me posted,' Wesley said. The problem of Belinda Crillow had been festering in the back of his mind. Perhaps now they'd make progress at last.

Neil Watson knew he was in danger of becoming obsessed with Manor Field's tantalising lumps and bumps and remnants of wall. Now that Charlie Perks had swept the field with his metal detector and the team had begun the geophysics survey, the prospect of a dig on the site was beginning to excite him; and he knew Lucy was feeling the same. It was so good to have her back from Orkney.

He called Wesley but there was no reply so he tried his home number, wondering if it was one of Pam's days off work. She answered after two rings with a wary 'hello'. Then he remembered the anonymous calls she'd been receiving.

'It's Neil. How are things?'

'I've just had a particularly nasty call.' The words came out in a rush as though she needed to tell someone. 'Told me I was a bitch and I was going to get what was coming to me.'

He could hear the panic in her voice. 'Where is Wes?'

'At work and he'll be late back tonight. Della's here but she's going out in an hour – one of her Arts Committee meetings.'

'OK if I come over later?'

'That'd be great. Thanks.' She sounded relieved.

As soon as he'd said goodbye his phone rang again. This time it was Annabel from the county archives – and she sounded excited.

'I've located Lower Torworthy's parish records at last. They weren't where they should be,' she added sadly, as though this was a failure on her part. 'I must say the priest at the time kept them meticulously. Sir Matthew, his name was. He says: "I oft times carry with me to the sick and dying my little monk who says prayers for their souls". Earlier he says he paid for it out of his own pocket and made it with the help of a clockmaker from Exeter. There are records of donations made by grateful parishioners.'

'It's the big monk I'm most curious about.'

'I'm coming to that,' said Annabel with an uncharacteristic hint of impatience. 'There's no mention of it in the parish records.'

'Nothing at all?'

'Odd, don't you think?'

'Mmm. Funnily enough I'm standing on the site of the DeTorhams' old manor house at the moment. A metal detectorist I know has gone over this field. I was hoping the big friar would be buried in lead like his little counterpart but there's nothing.'

'I'll get these records scanned and send them over to

287

you.' She paused. 'Do you think there was something dubious about this big friar?'

'That's what I intend to find out,' said Neil.

As yet there'd been no word from Rob about the CCTV which, he claimed, was in a perfect position to capture any comings and goings at Belinda Crillow's cottage. Wesley was waiting impatiently for the result. Whoever was terrorising Belinda might also be threatening his family so a picture of the tormentor might help clear up the business once and for all. All the threats had been made to Pam and not directly to himself so perhaps they saw her as his vulnerable spot.

He sat in the incident room staring at the notes he'd made. If Ian Evans was the killer's intended target all along and Andrea Jameson had simply been in the wrong place at the wrong time, they needed to start concentrating on Evans's life, which meant another trip to Dorchester to speak to his family and colleagues.

Gerry was on the phone and Wesley could tell that the conversation was annoying him. He saw him slam the receiver down and mutter something under his breath.

'Something the matter?' Wesley said, strolling over to join him.

'Jeremy Ovorard wants us to arrest Luke Wellings for abduction. I told him Jocasta went with him of her own accord but he's trying to make out Luke put pressure on her. If you ask me, he wants the lad to suffer for screwing his wife and running off with his daughter.'

'I take it there'll be no charges?'

'Aunty Noreen says we should consider passing it on to the CPS but that's only 'cause she doesn't want to get on the wrong side of an MP, especially one who's tipped to be a future home secretary with power over her precious budget.' Gerry leaned back in his seat. 'Anything new?'

'After hearing what Jocasta and Luke had to say about the shots I think we have to start looking at things from a different angle. I think Ian Evans might have been the killer's intended target all along.'

Gerry nodded in agreement.

'We should go over to Dorchester to ask more questions.' He checked the time. 'It's four thirty now so we'd better make it first thing tomorrow morning.' He thought for a moment. 'In the meantime I'll give Evans's employers a call. There's something I want to ask them.'

Gerry made his way over to the wall where the crime-scene pictures were displayed and stood gazing at the images. There were scrawled comments on the huge whiteboard they'd brought over from Tradmouth and Gerry took a felt-tip pen from his pocket to add something beneath the picture of Ian Evans: 'Possible target'.

A couple of minutes later Wesley called Rowberry, Rowberry and Barrow and when he was put through to the senior partner he asked the questions that had been on his mind since Jocasta Ovorard had made her statement.

'What can you tell me about Ian Evans's background? And who has he worked for in the past?'

35

They'd have an early start in the morning so, on Gerry's suggestion, Wesley decided to call it a day. He arrived home at six to find Neil waiting for him in the living room.

Pam seemed relaxed as she and the children listened to Neil's account of the mystery of the Little Monk and his mysterious bigger counterpart. She'd received no more calls that day and Wesley hoped this meant their tormentor was growing tired of whatever sick game he was playing.

When he'd parked on the drive he'd taken time to check the close but he'd seen nothing out of the ordinary. It had been confirmed that all the anonymous calls had been made from an unregistered mobile and, even though the crime prevention officer had visited and a panic button had been installed by the front door, the insidious presence of their faceless enemy gave him a restless night.

In his sleepless hours he went over the case in his head. How was Nathan Rowyard, petty criminal, conman and blackmailer, connected to Ian Evans, an apparently blameless small-town solicitor, and Andrea Jameson? Try as he might, he couldn't think what the connection could be.

The next morning he departed with a backward glance at the house, just to make sure the persecutor didn't emerge from the bushes as soon as his car pulled off. Pam had told him not to worry and sometimes he thought she was braver than he was, especially when he remembered how she'd dealt with her cancer diagnosis.

When he arrived at the station Gerry greeted him at the door of the CID office, rubbing his hands in anticipation. 'Are we off to Dorchester then?'

'Yes. When I spoke to Evans's boss yesterday he gave me the name of the solicitors he used to work for in Honiton. We'll pay them a visit later but first I want to speak to his current colleagues in Dorchester. Last time they spouted the usual platitudes but I want to dig a bit deeper. We should speak to his family again too. He lived at home with his mum so she might have known if he had any enemies.' He thought for a moment. 'There was absolutely nothing on his computer, apart from that stuff about Lower Torworthy and the death of Alcuin Garrard. Perhaps that's why Evans was in that field – but is it that why he was killed?'

'Have we found any link between Evans and Garrard?' Wesley shook his head.

'There's one possibility we're ignoring, Wes. What if it is some random nutcase like you said the other day? You get these mass shootings sometimes; no reason behind it apart from a general hatred of the human race.'

This was a theory Wesley had considered briefly and then dismissed. The calculated nature of the crime had convinced him that it was no random act of violence.

He shook his head again. 'It's beginning to look as if Ian was targeted and Andrea stumbled on the scene by accident.'

'What about Nathan Rowyard?' asked Gerry.

'Probably picked the wrong person to blackmail. We still

haven't found the source of that four grand in his account. I've asked someone to trace his movements. We need to find out who he met during the last weeks of his life.'

'We know about the vicar – Oliver Grayling. But I can't see him shooting Ian and Andrea, can you?'

'Who knows what people are capable of when they're desperate?'

Gerry didn't reply and as they drove to Dorchester he relaxed and admired the countryside flashing past the window.

They reached the offices of Rowberry, Rowberry and Barrow at exactly ten o'clock and were shown into the office of James Barrow, the senior partner Wesley had spoken to the previous day. He was a large, amiable man who reminded Wesley of a benevolent gorilla.

'I've got Ian's HR records out for you,' he began, handing Gerry a thin file. 'He came with excellent references and his work's been exemplary. Ian was an unambitious man, quite content to beaver away at routine conveyancing and wills until retirement. Don't get me wrong, he was well qualified and highly intelligent but he didn't seem to crave anything more ... challenging.'

'Have you any idea why that was?'

This was a question Barrow clearly hadn't expected. He picked up the fountain pen lying on his desk blotter and turned it over and over in his fingers.

Eventually he looked up. 'Ian worked here for twelve years and never put a foot wrong. Same with his previous employer, Bach and Whitcombe in Honiton. Look at his references.'

Gerry handed the file to Wesley, who did as he suggested. The reference from Mr Paul Whitcombe glowed with praise. Ian Evans was a reliable and trustworthy employee who worked to the highest standard. Whitcombe was very sorry to lose his services but quite understood the personal reasons he'd given when he'd handed in his notice and wished him well in the future. However, the final sentence struck Wesley as odd: *I have never for one moment had reason to doubt Ian Evans's integrity.*

James Barrow frowned. 'I did ask Mr Whitcombe why he'd added that particular sentence but all he'd say was that any rumours we might hear regarding Ian's past would be completely false. He wouldn't elaborate. Said it wouldn't be fair on Ian.'

'According to this he was with Bach and Whitcombe for eight years. Where did he work before that?'

Mr Barrow dropped his pen. 'The file doesn't say. I believe Bach and Whitcombe's still going strong in Honiton so perhaps you should pay them a visit.'

Gerry grunted. Wesley knew he didn't like to be told how to do his job.

'Thank you for your help,' Wesley said politely, ushering his boss out of the office.

He'd just caught the whiff of something out of the ordinary; the first indication that Ian Evans's life had been anything other than faultlessly boring. He was keen to get on the trail; but first they needed to speak to the dead man's mother.

Wesley was pleased to find that Mrs Evans had company in the form of one of her daughters; a chubby woman with short brown hair who introduced herself as Shirley. There was a strong resemblance between her and her late brother and for a few moments he found this disconcerting.

'Is there any news?' Shirley asked as she showed them

into the lounge where her mother was sitting, a tissue clutched in her hand. There were used tissues scattered around her on the settee like the shed plumage of some large white bird.

'We're following a few new leads,' Wesley replied before turning his attention to her mother. 'We're sorry to bother you again, Mrs Evans,' he said, sitting down opposite her.

She looked at Gerry. 'You've not brought that nice girl with you.'

'DS Tracey's busy in the incident room. This is Detective Chief Inspector Gerry Heffernan. He's in charge of the case.'

As he'd hoped, Mrs Evans looked impressed, as though she was glad the senior officer was taking a personal interest.

'We'd like to ask a few more questions if that's OK,' Wesley said, glancing at Shirley, who was hovering by the door. As soon as her mother nodded her assent she joined her on the settee and touched the older woman's gnarled hand.

'Anything that'll help you find out who did this to Ian.' Mrs Evans's voice was weak but Wesley could tell the words came from the heart.

'Ian worked at a firm of solicitors in Honiton called Bach and Whitcombe before he moved back to Dorchester twelve years ago.'

'That's right.'

'What about before that – when he'd just left university.'

'He went to Leeds, you know. Got an upper second. He was a clever boy. Then he went to law college in Chester. Did very well.'

'And after that?'

'He got a job in Exeter as a trainee solicitor. A girl he'd

met in Chester was working in Exeter for another firm so he followed her down to Devon. I didn't see much of him in those days. Young people don't have much time for their parents when they're just setting off in life, do they?'

Wesley nodded. With luck, it was something he and Pam would have to face one day.

He suddenly had an idea. 'While Ian was in Exeter did he share a house with any other young men?' If he'd known Alcuin Garrard at the time that would be link.

But Mrs Evans shook her head. 'No. He shared with his girlfriend.'

'What was her name?' Gerry asked the question that had been on Wesley's lips.

'Diana. Diana Ruffwood. He brought her home a few times. She was a very nice girl.'

'I take it they broke up?'

'Yes, but he didn't tell me any details – just that she'd moved out of their flat.' She paused, as though she was wondering how much to share. 'After that he changed. He lost his . . . zest for life.'

'Mum's right,' Shirley said. 'I blamed Diana but Ian said it had nothing to do with her. He said they were still friends and that it was his fault.' She glanced at her mother. 'I wondered whether something had happened at work, because that was around the time he left his first firm and took the job in Honiton. He'd been very ambitious at first but the job in Honiton was just routine stuff. I asked him why but he refused to talk about it.'

'What was the name of the Exeter firm?' Wesley asked, his pen poised over his notebook.

'I can't remember,' the mother said, casting a desperate look at her daughter.

'I think it began with a J but it was around the time I got married so I had other things on my mind.' Shirley hesitated. 'I've been going through his things but I didn't find any reference to it. Maybe he had a bad experience there. Maybe it was something he wanted to forget.'

36

Wesley and Gerry grabbed a sandwich in Honiton and ate in the car because they didn't want to waste time. Gerry scoffed his quickly and when he'd finished he brushed the crumbs off his jacket and asked after Pam. He sounded concerned but Wesley assured him that she was safe at work that day and her mother would be there when she arrived home. All bases had been covered, including the panic button.

'Anything more on Belinda Crillow?'

Before Wesley could reply he heard his ringtone. It was Rob Carter and he had news – or rather he didn't.

He came straight to the point. 'I've been through that CCTV footage from Crillow's neighbour's cottage and there's nothing on it, apart from the postman. Certainly no intruder.'

'He might have spotted the CCTV camera on an earlier recce and gone round the back,' Gerry said when he heard the news.

'Still seems odd.'

'You don't think she's making it all up? Attention-seeking?'

'Those injuries were real enough. And she's terrified.'

'Or says she is.'

Wesley finished his sandwich, folding the wrapping neatly and stuffing it in the ashtray before climbing out of the car. They'd parked down the street from Bach and Whitcombe's offices, just out of sight in case any of the employees happened to be looking out of the window.

As luck would have it the receptionist who greeted them was the chatty type and as she walked with them down the corridor she explained that the senior partner, Paul Whitcombe, had been there for years, which was what Wesley wanted to hear.

Whitcombe was a tall, distinguished-looking man with a good-humoured smile. Family photographs stood beside a selection of sporting trophies on the bookcase opposite the window and his desk was stacked with files which he shifted out of the way so he could see the two policemen sitting opposite. When he asked how he could help them his smile of greeting vanished and he assumed a solemn expression, as though they were bereaved relatives there to discuss a contentious will.

'Just over a week ago the body of one of your former employees was discovered in a field on Dartmoor,' Gerry said bluntly. 'He'd been shot.'

'I read about it. Terrible business. I wondered whether to send my condolences to his family but . . . '

'You remember Ian Evans?'

'Quite well as a matter of fact. He was a nice quiet chap, good at his job and very thorough, although he lacked ambition. I'm not sure whether that was because of what happened . . . ' His voice trailed off.

'Sorry, Mr Whitcombe, I'm not sure what you're talking about,' Wesley said.

'I thought it would be in your records.'

'Why don't you tell us your version?' said Gerry, not wanting to admit to ignorance.

'There's not much to tell really. He'd been working for an Exeter firm and when he applied for a position here I was told that he'd been uncomfortable about certain things that were going on there and wanted to move. When I contacted his employer I found out that the partner he was working for had been arrested for fraud and there were hints – not solid accusations you understand; we are lawyers after all – but hints that Ian was aware of the irregularities. After the arrest Ian went off sick for a while; then he resigned, which made me cautious. His employer had no evidence to substantiate the veiled allegations but mud sticks, doesn't it?'

'If there was a question mark over his integrity I'm surprised you took him on,' said Wesley.

For a few seconds Paul Whitcombe said nothing, weighing up his answer carefully. When he finally spoke he lowered his voice.

'One of my staff here had known him very well for a number of years and she assured me that the accusations were completely false. She begged me to meet him for myself and I must admit when I did I was impressed. He'd been badly shaken by events at his old firm and had suffered what I can only describe as some kind of breakdown, hence the sick leave. Anyway, I decided to trust my instincts and employ him on a trial basis. He worked very well with clients and colleagues but I think the episode in Exeter robbed him of his confidence and any ambition he had once had. He admitted to me much later that it had made him wary of people. When his father died he moved to

Dorchester to look after his mother and I had no hesitation in providing him with excellent references.'

'Can you tell us the name of the firm he worked for in Exeter?'

Whitcombe searched through the files on his desk, eventually selecting a thin folder. He opened it and began to read. Wesley, who had some practice in reading upside down, saw that it was Ian Evans's personal file.

'Ah yes, the firm was Jellicoe and Travers – now defunct.'

'What was the name of the partner who was jailed for fraud?' Wesley thought he could guess but he wanted it confirmed.

'Alexander Southwark. He must be out of jail by now. Wonder what happened to him.'

Wesley and Gerry exchanged a glance. Perhaps it was Southwark himself who started the rumours about the young employee, Ian Evans, who was too junior and powerless to answer back. Evans would have been the ideal scapegoat to deflect suspicion from himself.

Alexander Southwark had transformed himself into Xander and now he was up at Princebury Hall, a couple of miles from where Ian Evans met his death.

'Who recommended Ian for the job here?'

'Diana Ruffwood. She used to work for me. Nice woman. Very capable.'

'Ian's mother mentioned her.'

'I believe she and Ian were close at one time but he broke off their relationship after the trouble in Exeter. Ian was a sensitive man and I can only imagine he considered himself unworthy of her, despite the fact that he was innocent. I think she was still fond of him for a while but eventually she must have given up. About a year after Ian started here she met someone else, got married and moved away. I understand she lives in Tradmouth now.'

'Do you know her married name?'

'Smith.'

As soon as they left the offices of Bach and Whitcombe Wesley made a call to the police station at Tradmouth to ask them to trace a Mrs Diana Smith, née Ruffwood.

Wesley was sure he'd heard the name somewhere before.

Extract from draft PhD thesis
written by Alcuin Garrard

July 1995

After the first tantalising mention of the 'big friar' records become sparse. However, a senior cleric in Exeter writes to Oswald DeTorham in February 1534.

'Word has reached me that the machine the priest has lately created is present when he hears the confessions of the sick and there is talk that the people go in fear of it.'

The letter mentions no specific cases but the Exeter cleric is clearly worried by the rumours of what is happening in Lower Torworthy. There is no record of Oswald's reply.

An entry in the journal of Oswald's cousin, Henry Dyce, dated January 1534 states that Sir Matthew and both his machines visited one of Henry's tenants who later came to him 'in much distress' claiming that the 'big friar - that thing with the wooden face - moved in such a lifelike way that he would swear it was a living man and his wife was sore afraid and would not be alone with it'.

The truth of this, however, was uncertain as Sir Matthew left with the thing before he could be challenged. At this stage it appears that the seemingly blameless parish priest was heavily involved in whatever deception was going on.

37

It was just after 3.30 when they returned to the incident room and Wesley knew that if the station managed to trace Diana, it might be a late night. However for the first time since the case began his frustration gave way to hope.

'Fancy going to Princebury Hall to poke the hornet's nest?' The sound of Gerry's voice made him jump.

'I want to speak to Diana first. We need to be sure of our facts before we go barging in.'

Gerry shrugged his shoulders and sloped off like a child whose friend hadn't been allowed out to play.

The file on Alcuin Garrard's death was still on Wesley's desk and he stared at it, lost in thought. Garrard's great-aunt's money had vanished and Xander Southwark – or Alexander as he called himself in those days – had been jailed for defrauding the estates of several elderly clients in 1997. What if he'd been Mary Tilson's solicitor and done something similar with her assets two years earlier without being caught? He was about to pick up the file when he saw Rachel walking over to join him.

'Something wrong?' she said.

'We've found a link between Xander Southwark and Ian Evans.'

'And Southwark's connected with Andrea Jameson as well. What about Nathan Rowyard?'

'Can you get someone to check whether Southwark and Rowyard were in prison together? Or maybe Rowyard was a client of Southwark's at some point.'

'Sure.'

As soon as she left his phone rang. It was Pam and she sounded worried.

'I've just got home and Maureen opposite said she saw someone going round the side of our house this lunchtime. She called the police but by the time they got here whoever it was had gone.'

'I wasn't told.' Wesley felt annoyed at the laxity of the patrol officers who'd gone to investigate. He should have been their first point of contact.

'They said they'd let you know.'

For the first time he noticed a piece of paper on his desk amidst the files and paperwork. He unfolded it, cursing himself for not seeing it before – but he'd been too busy thinking about Xander Southwark.

It was a scribbled message asking him to get in touch with Tradmouth regarding a suspected intruder at his home. He screwed it up and threw it at the bin with some force.

'And there's something else. I can't find Moriarty. She always meets me by the front door but there's no sign of her. I've looked everywhere.'

'She'll turn up soon.' He was fond of the cat and he felt a twinge of worry.

'Amelia's upset and my mother's out scouring the area.'

'I'll be home as soon as I can.'

He saw Gerry watching him. 'What's up?'

'Someone was seen hanging round our house and the cat's gone missing.'

'Cats can go walkabout for hours.'

'I know, but ours always hangs around by the front door when Pam gets home, nagging for food. After everything that's happened Pam's convinced herself . . . '

'OK, Wes. You get home and see what's going on. We can manage for an hour or so.'

Before he could pick up his coat Rachel hurried over, a look of triumph on her face. 'I've found Diana Smith. She does live in Tradmouth.'

'That was quick.'

'She wasn't hard to find. She's a big noise in the Traders' Association – gave up the law a few years ago and now she runs a bakery opposite the market – the posh kind where a small fancy loaf costs five times what you'd pay in the supermarket.'

Wesley now knew why the name was familiar. He must have passed Loaf by Diana Smith many times but, as with many overfamiliar things, he hadn't paid much attention to it.

'Do you want to pay her a visit?' She passed him a piece of paper with the woman's home address written on it in Rachel's neat handwriting.

'Fancy coming with me? Only I'll have to call in at my house first. Bit of a crisis.'

'More funny phone calls?'

'The cat's gone missing.'

'Cats do their own thing.'

He went on to explain about the neighbour's sighting of an intruder.

'Pam's really upset. All this is getting to her.'

Rachel followed Wesley to the car and offered to drive. She enjoyed driving down the country lanes but she knew he didn't. Besides, he looked as if his mind wouldn't be focused on the road.

When Wesley and Rachel arrived Pam was doing her best to stay calm, but Amelia was tearful and even Michael had let down his guard and kept asking what they could do to find their pet.

Rachel advised checking nearby sheds and outhouses. It was a practical suggestion which went down well, since at least the children would feel as if they were doing something constructive. Wesley found it strange to see Pam and Rachel sitting side by side deep in conversation and he felt a pang of something he hadn't experienced for a while: shame and embarrassment that he'd been attracted to Rachel. It had taken all the self-discipline he could muster to banish the temptation. The memory flashed back into his head and made him turn away to gaze out of the window, hoping to catch a glimpse of the elegant black cat who had inveigled her way into the heart of the family. But there was no sign of her.

It was almost five by the time Wesley and Rachel finally got round to visiting Diana Smith. When they reached her small baker's shop, Wesley feared she'd already have packed up and gone home and he was relieved when he saw an OPEN sign on the shop door and the proprietor wiping down the empty shelves.

Diana Smith, née Ruffwood, wore a floral apron over jeans and striped Breton top, the sort favoured by the yachting set who probably provided her main source of income. She was small, with a pleasant face and tied-back brown hair, and she smiled as they introduced themselves; the sort of cautious smile Wesley had often seen before on the faces of people who had no idea why the police would come calling.

'I understand you used to be friends with Ian Evans,' Wesley began once they were seated in the shop's little back room. In contrast to the self-consciously rustic decor of the shop, the room was homely with a well-worn sofa and an array of mismatched mugs upside down on the sink drainer.

It took Diana a few seconds to answer. 'Yes, Ian and I were close at one time.'

'Did you know he'd been murdered?' said Rachel.

Diana winced at the bluntness of her words before shaking her head in disbelief. 'I heard on the news that an Ian Evans had been identified as one of the victims of that shooting up on Dartmoor but it's not an unusual name and it seemed so unlike the Ian I knew to get involved in anything like that, so I never associated it with ...' Her voice trailed off and Wesley saw that her eyes were moist with unshed tears. She tore a tissue from the box beside her and dabbed at them before blowing her nose.

'I'm sorry. It's definitely the Ian Evans you knew,' said Wesley. 'I realise this has come as a shock but would you mind if we ask you some questions?'

She took a deep, shuddering breath. 'I haven't seen or heard from Ian for years so I don't see how I can help.' She gazed down at her hands. 'I knew him in another life.'

'You were a solicitor?'

'That's right. Some years ago I felt I needed a change of direction so I gave up the law and opened this place. I've always had a passion for baking and I've no regrets about the path my life's taken, Inspector,' she said with a sad smile. 'But I often wondered what became of Ian. I can't believe he's dead, I really can't.'

'He was working in Dorchester – living with his mother.'

'He never married?'

Wesley shook his head.

'There was a time when I thought ... '

'That you and him ... ?'

She looked Wesley in the eye. 'I saw it as a possibility once but ... '

'What went wrong?'

'Everything.'

Rachel was about to say something but Wesley gave her a small signal to wait. His patience was rewarded when Diana took a deep breath and began her explanation.

'We met in Chester when we were studying to become solicitors and when we finished we both got jobs as trainees in Exeter at separate firms – junior dogsbodies straight out of law school.'

'You were going out together?'

She nodded. 'Ian worked at a firm called Jellicoe and Travers, mostly dealing with wills and related matters. His boss was a man called Alexander Southwark and Ian was really impressed with him at first – said he was charming and good with elderly clients who thought he was wonderful and recommended him to their friends. Then slowly Ian started to realise Southwark was taking risks and that there was a lot going on that he kept to himself – files locked away that Ian wasn't allowed to see, that sort of thing. Later Southwark was found guilty of fraud – milking clients' accounts and altering wills in his favour. I believe he got away with a fortune before he was caught. According to Ian, he was extremely plausible.'

'And Ian?'

'He worked directly for Southwark but even so I'm absolutely sure he had no idea what was really going on. And even if he'd had his suspicions, nobody would have believed him.'

'How did Ian react when Southwark was arrested?'

'I'd left Exeter by then to work in Honiton but we were still in touch, although we didn't see each other quite so often.' She sighed. 'We were drifting apart but even so, when Southwark was arrested I was the first person Ian turned to. To be honest, I was shocked by the change in him. Southwark had tried to lay the blame on him and the fraud officers refused to believe he hadn't been aware of what was happening so he endured hours of questioning. To cut a long story short he had a breakdown and I let him stay at my place because I couldn't bear to think of him being on his own and he said he was too ashamed to go back to his family in Dorchester. When he was better I got him taken on at my firm in Honiton. It was a small firm – friendly. I thought it would suit him better.'

'We've spoken to Paul Whitcombe.'

She smiled. 'How is he?'

'Very well.'

'That's good to hear. He's a nice man. Ian was ... damaged, traumatised, and Paul allowed him to take on undemanding work because that was all Ian felt capable of doing.'

'You and Ian never got back together?'

'I would have done but he insisted he wasn't worthy of me and nothing I said would convince him otherwise. In the end he moved into a place of his own and I gave up, I suppose. Then I met my husband and ... ' She gave a long

310

sigh. 'Ian had been so ambitious when he first started at Jellicoe and Travers – far more ambitious than I ever was. As far as I'm concerned Alexander Southwark destroyed him.'

'Southwark's running a well-being centre up on Dartmoor now,' said Wesley.

Diana gave a bitter laugh. 'Well-being? How inappropriate. The man's a snake – and Ian got bitten.'

'How long did Ian work for Southwark?'

'We left law school in nineteen ninety-five and it was his first job. He stuck at it – until Southwark's arrest in nineteen ninety-seven. Maybe he should have got out sooner but we can all be wise with hindsight, can't we.'

'Is there anything else you can tell me about the goings-on at Jellicoe and Travers?'

She stood up. 'Tea?'

'Yes please.' Wesley saw Rachel sneak a look at her watch but he had the feeling Diana's memories couldn't be rushed and that the tea-making ritual might help.

When the steaming mugs were in front of them his patience was rewarded.

'Ian wasn't privy to Southwark's financial dealings and he was very discreet about work matters but I do remember him saying something about Southwark and a young temp who worked there – a student I think. He used the words *droit de seigneur*.'

'You mean Southwark was guilty of sexual harassment as well as fraud,' said Rachel with disapproval.

Diana shrugged sadly. 'According to Ian, the girl was flattered. Sometimes people are their own worst enemies.'

'Anything else you can tell us?' Wesley butted in before Rachel could vent her indignation. Then he had an idea; a long shot but worth a try. 'Did Ian ever mention the name Mary Tilson? She was an elderly lady murdered by her carer in nineteen ninety-five.'

Diana frowned, trying to retrieve a memory. A few seconds later she spoke. 'Yes. Ian had only just started and Southwark sent him to see her and pick up some documents. As you can imagine he was shocked when he heard she'd been murdered. A few weeks after she died her nephew came into the office but Ian was told to take an early lunch so he never found out what he wanted.'

Wesley took a deep breath. 'Was the nephew called Alcuin Garrard?'

'That's right. I remember because the name was so unusual.'

'Garrard was found dead shortly after the incident you mentioned. Accidental death according to the coroner.'

'Yes, I remember Ian saying the nephew died in some sort of freak accident but I didn't know any details.'

Wesley paused. 'Ian's body was found near the place Alcuin died.'

Diana stared at him as if the revelation had robbed her of the power of speech.

'What did Ian say about Southwark's arrest?'

'He wouldn't talk about it. I begged him to confide in me, but it was as if a light had gone out inside him. I couldn't get through to him any more.'

'Can you think why he'd want to visit the scene of Alcuin Garrard's death?'

At first she shook her head but after a few moments she spoke again, almost in a whisper.

'Ian was always conscientious. If he suspected Garrard's death wasn't an accident and he'd found new information he might have thought he could do something ... I don't know.'

As Wesley left the bakery, an idea was forming in his head. A letter from Ralph Detoram, the owner of Princebury Hall, had been found in Alcuin Garrard's pocket. According to the file, Mr Detoram had been asked about it at the time but he'd insisted it was a personal matter of no importance and nobody had bothered to dig further. As Wesley recalled Detoram's claim that Alcuin was mistaken about some unspecified matter, he was becoming more and more convinced that Alcuin Garrard's death wasn't as straightforward as everybody had assumed at the time.

Belinda Crillow felt the cold metal of the blade being drawn across her flesh and let out a loud sob.

As if in answer she heard another sound; an insistent crying that sounded like a hungry baby in its urgency.

Five minutes later it was over.

38

Wesley was returning to the police station with Rachel when he received Belinda Crillow's call.

He passed his phone to Rachel. 'Will you answer?'

She gave him an enquiring look before taking it from him. 'Inspector Peterson's phone.'

There was silence on the other end of the line for a while until a cracked, faint voice uttered Wesley's name. Rachel pressed the phone close to her ear, trying to make out what was being said, but she couldn't decipher the whispers that sounded like the voice of a suffering ghost.

She turned to Wesley. 'Something's wrong.'

'She's at the B and B, isn't she?'

Rachel made a couple of calls. After the second she turned to Wesley, worry clouding her face.

'According to the landlady she insisted on going back home earlier today. I think she's in trouble, Wes.'

They picked a car up at the station and drove to the little cluster of cottages that made up the hamlet Belinda Crillow called home, using the blue light on the unmarked car to clear the way. When they arrived Wesley banged on Belinda Crillow's front door with his fists.

The curtains were drawn across, hiding the interior.

It looked like a house in mourning and Wesley's senses screamed that something was badly wrong.

'Are we going in?' said Rachel.

Wesley hesitated. 'Hold on a moment. I want to check something.'

He moved out of earshot and called Pam's number. He had that feeling again, an icy grip of alarm on his heart. He waited for five seconds. Ten seconds, the grip tightening with each passing moment.

'Hi.'

'Are you OK?' he asked in a breathless rush.

'Yeah. What time will you be home?'

The normality of the question almost brought on tears of relief.

'I'll do my best to be back before the kids go to bed.'

'I'd better go. Someone's at the door. Could be Neil – he said he'd call in if he got the chance.' The line went dead before he could utter a warning: check who it is before you answer the door.

He could hear Rachel battering her fists on the front door and when there was no reply she pressed her face to the window, trying to peep through a small gap in the curtains.

'Does she have a car?' Rachel asked.

'An oldish Fiesta. Dark blue.'

'It's not here now.'

Wesley said nothing for a few moments, weighing up the implications. Then he made a decision. 'We should break in. Agreed?'

'Agreed. We can't take any chances.'

Wesley darted around the side of the house, seeking out its weaknesses. For a woman who claimed to have been

315

threatened she was remarkably lax with her security, he thought as he lifted a plant pot by the back door and found a key underneath. He tried the key in the back door and when it opened smoothly he stepped into Belinda Crillow's kitchen, Rachel following close behind.

There wasn't a thing out of place and the room had been scrubbed clean; the kind of clean Pam would have called obsessive.

Rachel headed for the hall and he followed, first into the living room where he'd been before and then into the dining room where a table was set for two; an intimate dinner *à deux* with sparkling glassware and tasteful white crockery.

'She's expecting company,' Rachel observed. 'Or perhaps it was her dinner companion who caused the trouble – if it is trouble.'

'No sign of cooking.'

'Takeaway?'

Rachel's suggestion was feasible. Even high-end restaurants delivered nowadays. He began to climb the stairs with a growing feeling of dread. There was a faint sound, perhaps of a baby crying in one of the nearby cottages.

He made for the front bedroom, uncomfortable about intruding on such an intimate space. But it had to be done and, besides, Rachel was with him. When they searched the room they found nothing out of the ordinary. Belinda's clothes hung in a wardrobe that seemed remarkably empty compared to Pam's tightly packed space where clothes emerged so creased they needed ironing twice. The drawers were the same: everything arranged with a precision that verged on the military.

The small bedroom yielded nothing and by the time

they reached the room at the back they were satisfied Belinda Crillow wasn't at home. If she was in trouble she was in trouble somewhere else.

The sound of the crying baby was there again, muffled and faint, and when Wesley approached the back bedroom door he realised the noise was coming from inside the room. He tried the door but it was locked.

He put his shoulder against the door and pushed. Once. Twice. On his third attempt the door gave way and he staggered into the room.

To his astonishment a cat shot out; a dark furry blur dashing past his legs before vanishing down the stairs. When Wesley looked inside the room he saw that it was empty apart from an expensive-looking cat bed and a litter tray at one end and a small double bowl of food and water at the other. A carrying basket stood on a chest of drawers by the window.

'Did you know she had a cat?' said Rachel.

Wesley didn't reply. He was too busy calling the cat, using her name: 'Moriarty.'

He began to descend the stairs and saw Moriarty in the hall looking up at him as if to say, 'You took your time.'

'Are you absolutely sure that's Moriarty?' asked Rachel from the top of the stairs after he had scooped the cat up in his arms.

'She's wearing her collar,' he said, burying his face in the soft fur as the cat's loud purr vibrated through his hands.

'What the hell's Belinda Crillow doing with your cat?'

Wesley's hand froze on the black fur. 'That's what I'd like to know. I'll have to take her home. The kids are going frantic.'

'Don't you think we should find Belinda first and ask her what's going on?'

Without answering Wesley returned to the back bedroom and looked around, still with the cat nestled in his arms. The alcove to the right of the chimney breast was curtained off; with his free hand he tugged the curtain to one side and heard Rachel swear under her breath behind him.

Wesley stared at the photographs pinned to the wall with drawing pins, too stunned to speak. Some had been taken in the police station car park and others outside the incident room in Lower Torworthy.

'You've got a bloody stalker, Wes,' said Rachel. 'She's been following you. And these photos of Pam – isn't that outside your house? This is getting weirder by the minute.'

Wesley felt as though he'd been punched; as though he couldn't trust his own judgement any more. 'Our neighbours are overfond of those bloody leylandii, which are a security hazard in my opinion,' he said, trying his best to keep calm. 'Whoever's taken these pictures has hidden themselves in the bushes.'

He studied the pictures with growing horror: Pam leaving the house, dangling her car keys; Pam opening the passenger door for Amelia; Pam opening the front door to Della ... and Neil. Wesley kissing his wife goodbye on the doorstep with Pam in her dressing gown. This was their private life but an intruder had been there watching their every move from the shadows, even taking their pet. What if it was one of the children next? The thought made him feel sick. Belinda wasn't here and his family could be in danger.

The cat wriggled from his arms, only to be scooped up by Rachel who, having been raised on a farm, was used to animals of all varieties. She instructed Wesley to retrieve

318

the carrying basket. They didn't want to risk this particular prisoner making a run for it.

Once Moriarty was safely incarcerated in her basket, protesting loudly at the indignity, Rachel called for back-up. Wesley wanted Belinda Crillow's house searched and secured. And he wanted her picked up.

Once their work in Lower Torworthy had ended for the day Neil returned with Lucy to his Exeter flat and found a message on his answerphone.

He listened to the disembodied voice floating through the silent air as Lucy staggered into the flat with the bagful of shopping they'd bought on the way home.

'This is Professor Laurence Harris for Dr Neil Watson. Can you contact me on ...' He went on the recite a telephone number – a landline with a local code. 'I need to speak to you urgently. Thank you.'

The professor's feeble voice trailed away. When Neil had visited his office he hadn't looked well but he'd been confident, even aggressive. Now, however, he sounded like a different man and Neil wondered what had happened to bring about the dramatic transformation.

His curiosity made him phone straight away and his call was answered after two rings, as though Harris had been sitting by the phone waiting for his response.

An hour later Neil was sitting in the living room of Professor Harris's Victorian semi ten minutes' walk from Neil's flat. The professor lived alone, he explained. His wife had left him several years before and his two children had grown and fled the nest long ago. All of a sudden Neil found himself feeling sorry for the man who lived in cluttered bachelor solitude in a house far too large for one.

319

'I expect you want to know why I've asked you here,' the professor began. He didn't give Neil a chance to reply. 'I did something in the past that I'm rather ashamed of and now I need to make my confession.' He inhaled deeply, as though hungry for air, and immediately fell into a paroxysm of coughing, turning his head away.

'Alcuin was a brilliant student,' he continued once he'd recovered. 'When I became his supervisor for his doctorate I admit I was looking forward to it. Then he showed me his work.'

'Good?'

'He'd chosen a subject I'd wanted to research myself. I'd found the records kept by Sir Matthew At Wood, the parish priest of Lower Torworthy, in the cathedral archives several years before and I was planning to write a book on the subject.

'It felt at the time as though he'd stolen my idea, although I'm sure it was just coincidence because Sir Matthew's writings were available to anybody who cared to search for them.'

'I've read them myself.'

Harris bowed his head and when he looked up Neil noticed that his eyes were bloodshot, as though he'd been crying. 'I watched Alcuin Garrard produce a brilliant thesis on a subject I'd thought of as my own, even discovering an account of a bizarre crime that wasn't mentioned in Sir Matthew's records. I hadn't realised that professional jealousy could be such a fierce emotion.'

Neil remembered that Alcuin Garrard had been found dead in Manor Field and although the authorities had treated it as an accident, he'd harboured a niggle of suspicion that there might be a more sinister explanation. His heart rate quickened as he wondered whether he was about to hear a confession to murder.

But instead the professor stood up and walked over to a mahogany chest of drawers on the far side of the room. It was a heavy piece of furniture, Victorian to match the age of the house, and when the bottom drawer was opened Neil heard the grating of wood against wood. Harris took something from the drawer, a cardboard folder bulging with papers, and handed it to Neil.

Neil opened the file and when he scanned the contents he realised he was holding Alcuin Garrard's thesis. The name Oswald DeTorham caught his eye along with mentions of Oswald's younger brother, Simeon, and the steward, Peter. Then he noticed the word 'monk' cropping up with increasing frequency.

'Alcuin found other sources apart from Sir Matthew's records,' Harris said quietly. 'Contemporary letters and a journal. Pure gold.'

'What became of them?'

Harris hesitated. 'They're in the drawer if you care to have a look. Alcuin became friendly with an old gentleman who lived at Princebury Hall on Dartmoor – a descendant of the DeTorham family, I believe. He allowed Alcuin access to his muniment room. I'd have given anything for such an opportunity.'

Neil delved into the drawer and pulled out two large box files filled with ancient documents, too fragile to be stored in such a haphazard manner. With great care he began to read snatches, still legible after five centuries. Then, tempted though he was to continue, he placed them carefully to one side, resolving to give them into Annabel's care at the earliest opportunity.

He picked up Alcuin's thesis again and turned the pages until he came to an account of the fire which destroyed the manor in 1534. Aware that Harris was watching him, he closed the file. 'I'd like to show the documents to a friend at the County Archives if I may.'

Harris sighed. 'That would be for the best. They need conserving properly. Knowing they're here makes me uncomfortable if you want the truth.'

'May I borrow the thesis?' he asked, hoping the answer would be positive.

'Yes, and after you've read it I want you to submit it to the university authorities.'

Neil looked at him, puzzled.

'It's time I put a stop to the deception, Dr Watson. Alcuin Garrard was never awarded his doctorate because I failed to submit his thesis after his death. I suppressed it because I intended to use his research myself but in the end my conscience wouldn't let me. Alcuin's work has sat in that drawer since nineteen ninety-five because he made me feel inadequate.'

The tortured look on Harris's face suggested that his sin of omission had eaten away at his soul for over twenty years.

'Why are you telling me all this now?' Neil said after a long silence.

The professor walked over to the window and stared out at the street. It was dusk and the street lights were already glowing feebly, gathering their strength for the night.

'I received the results of a number of hospital tests yesterday and the upshot is that my heart's giving out. According to the quacks I don't have long unless I have a transplant and I don't think that's going to happen.' His words were regretful rather than anguished. He sounded like a man

resigned to his fate. 'I don't want to leave this world bur-
dened with the memory of what I did but I want to ask a
favour of you.'

'Anything,' Neil said, stunned by the man's revelation.

'Please wait until I'm gone before submitting Alcuin's
thesis. I couldn't bear my colleagues to . . .'

Neil nodded. He understood.

'But by all means use the information Alcuin found for
your own research. It's what he would have wanted.'

'Thank you.'

'And I want to make one thing absolutely clear before
you go.'

'What's that?'

'I was bitterly jealous of Alcuin Garrard but I had nothing to do with his death. I might be weak, vain and spiteful,
Dr Watson, but I'm not a violent man.'

39

Wesley tried to ring Pam but there was no reply. Rachel put her foot down, the cat complaining loudly from the carrying basket, as all sorts of scenarios flashed through Wesley's mind, each one more dreadful than the last. Without doubt Belinda Crillow had kidnapped his family pet, slashed Pam's tyres and bombarded her with threatening calls. She was disturbed, obsessed – and she wished Pam harm.

Rachel was concentrating on the road, staring ahead with her mouth set in a determined line. They'd soon be at their destination and Wesley felt a knot of dread clutching his stomach.

'Look, she didn't harm the cat,' Rachel said, as though she'd read his thoughts. 'She's playing games.'

Wesley knew her words were meant to reassure but they didn't make him feel any better.

As they turned into his close he could see Pam's car in the drive with a dark blue Fiesta parked behind, blocking it in. There was no sign of the patrol car he'd ordered.

In spite of the cat's vociferous objections they left her in the car and when Rachel opened the boot she took out two stab vests.

'OK, let's go in,' Wesley said once the vests were on.

'We're not waiting for back-up?'

Wesley ignored the question and ran to the door, his hands shaking as he turned the key in the lock. Once inside the house he stood and listened, aware of Rachel standing close behind him. He could feel her breath on his neck.

He could hear muffled female voices behind the closed living-room door, speaking softly. Then he heard a voice he wasn't expecting. Amelia was at the top of the stairs shouting, 'Daddy, Daddy.' When she started to come down he darted up to meet her taking the steps two at a time.

'Go back to your room, love,' he whispered, brushing the top of her head with a kiss. 'Where's Michael?'

'At Nathaniel's.'

'And Della?'

'She's gone to the shops. Who's that lady with Mum?'

'When did she arrive?'

'She was waiting when me and Mum got home. Mum asked her to go but she wouldn't so Mum told me to go upstairs and not to come down. I'm hungry. When's dinner?'

Wesley's heart ached at the innocence of her question. She had no idea Pam was in danger – and he wanted to keep it that way.

'Can you do me a favour, darling? Do as Mum told you and stay upstairs. I'll talk to the lady and everything'll be fine. We'll have dinner later. And I've got good news. I've found Moriarty. She's OK.'

Amelia gave a little cry of relief and excitement. 'Can I see her?'

'Soon, I promise.'

His daughter was bright and old enough to know when adults were fobbing her off. But, to Wesley's relief, she didn't argue and retraced her steps, giving him and Rachel a questioning backward glance as she walked across the landing to her room.

He took a deep breath and pushed the living-room door open, glad that Rachel was behind him providing support.

Pam was standing with her back to the fireplace, her fearful gaze fixed on the woman a few feet away. Belinda Crillow turned her head as he entered the room. Her eyes were wide and she was smiling, almost flirting.

'I've been waiting for you,' she said in a nervous rush. 'Where have you been?'

'You called me. I thought you were in trouble.'

She waved her hand in Pam's direction and he noticed the cuts to her left arm, thin red lines traced on the flesh. 'I was explaining to this woman that we want to be together.'

'You slashed my tyres.' Pam sounded remarkably calm.

Belinda ignored her. 'I'm making us something special to eat tonight. I thought we'd have a bit of a celebration.'

Pam drew herself up to her full height. 'I want you to go. So does Wesley.'

Wesley shot his wife a warning glance. 'Please, Belinda, can we talk about this another time.'

'No. It's time we were honest. Tell her she has to leave. Please.'

There was a note of hysteria in her voice, as though she was on the verge of losing control. It would only take one wrong word to push her over the edge. Then he saw the knife in her hand, held at waist height and pointed at Pam's stomach. A vegetable knife: small but sharp and potentially lethal. Rachel positioned herself behind her and Pam caught on quickly, staring directly at Belinda, doing her best to keep her attention.

'I'll need time to move out?' Pam said calmly. 'Me and the children need to find somewhere to live.' She glanced at her husband and he gave her a small nod of approval. Appeasement was their only option for the time being. 'Why don't you give Wesley that knife? Please.'

Wesley edged forward a little. 'Please, Belinda. There's no need for this. Let Pam go and she'll put the kettle on for us, eh. We can talk about it over a cup of tea.'

His heart was racing but he forced himself to stay calm, knowing that if he said or did the wrong thing the results could be devastating. But just as he thought Belinda was going to do as he suggested, she shook her head and the knife stayed where it was.

'I don't want tea,' she said like a petulant child. 'This woman's been making your life a misery. She's keeping us apart.'

'You're right,' said Wesley. 'But surely you can see she needs time to make arrangements. Give me the knife. Please.'

He heard the whine of approaching police sirens and saw Belinda's hand tighten on the weapon. Then, without warning, she swung round and slashed at Rachel, who was standing behind her, catching the stab vest she'd had the foresight to wear. When Belinda saw what she'd done she froze in panic, giving Pam the chance to shoot out of reach and put the sofa between her and her would-be attacker.

Wesley saw Rachel, handcuffs at the ready, creeping forward like a hunter stalking her prey.

'I'm sorry, Belinda,' he said gently. 'You'll have to go with the officers now. They'll look after you – make sure you're safe.'

She screamed like a wounded animal, repeating the

word 'no' several times before lunging at Wesley, who caught her wrist, sending the knife clattering to the floor. Belinda collapsed, sobbing, as Rachel darted forward to make the arrest but somehow the prisoner managed to slide from her grasp and hurtle out of the room.

'Amelia's upstairs.' Pam's words were screamed; the raw, primitive sound of a mother protecting her young.

Wesley and Rachel reacted immediately. They rushed into the hall and saw Belinda vanish through the open front door.

'Where's that bloody patrol car?' Rachel shouted. They'd expected to see it outside but there was no sign of it.

Belinda Crillow had reached her car and Wesley heard the engine start up just as a familiar figure emerged from the car that had drawn up opposite. The dark-blue Fiesta's engine revved like a racing car and shot off, flinging the other vehicle's former occupant upward like a rag doll.

Pam's scream coincided with a loud metallic bang that shook the air. Belinda Crillow had driven straight into the side of the patrol car as it turned into the close.

Extract from draft PhD thesis
written by Alcuin Garrard

July 1995

Henry Dyce's journal, along with other
correspondence discovered at Princebury Hall,
hints at an increasing atmosphere of fear in
Lower Torworthy and beyond. By 1534 parishioners
are requesting the services of Sir Matthew's
'little monk' less and less whereas previously
the machine had been hailed as a miracle worker
and in great demand. The evidence suggests that
this was connected to the increasing use of the
'big friar' alongside its smaller counterpart.
There is also a tantalising mention of Peter,
Oswald DeTorham's steward, 'going once more to
London and returning with divers books which he
hid from others'.

In 1534 Henry Dyce writes in his journal:

'My wife fell sick after the birth of our
child so I sent word to Sir Matthew and he came
at once. I requested that he bring his "little
monk" but he also brought the "big friar",
saying that two machines for prayer would be
more efficacious.

'Once in my wife's chamber the machines were set moving, raising their arms to heaven and beating their wooden breasts. The larger figure's movements, I noted, were fluid and most human-like and once again I marvelled at the miraculous nature of Sir Matthew's creation.

'Sir Matthew bent to hear my wife's confession and as I stepped back into the shadows I observed that the "big friar" had crept forward as my wife mouthed her sins, her voice feeble but clear. Then I heard a strange sound, like a man sneezing, and the "big friar" shook. At once my neighbour's fear was brought to mind.'

40

'How is she?' Gerry's face was solemn. Wesley's mother-in-law Della had often been the subject of the DCI's teasing, but all that had changed overnight.

'In intensive care. Pam's with her.'

'Crillow just ran her over?'

'She was trying to get away but God knows what was going through her head. I should have seen the signs. If I'd dealt with it instead of passing her case on to Rob I might have realised what was going on.'

Gerry put a comforting hand on Wesley's arm. 'You couldn't have known it would go this far. We had three murders and a missing girl on our hands so you had no choice.'

'I'd helped her when she had that break-in and when she saw me on TV making the Jocasta Ovorard appeal the memory turned into an obsession. You have to feel sorry for her. She needs help.'

'Typical. She persecutes your wife and almost kills your mother-in-law and you still see things from her point of view. Still, I expect the psychiatric report will recommend she gets treatment rather than prison.' Gerry sounded exasperated. He looked at his watch. 'We need to speak to Xander Southwark about Ian Evans's days at Jellicoe and

Travers. If Ian suspected there was something dodgy about Alcuin Garrard's death ... '

The events of the previous evening had almost driven the case out of Wesley's mind and now he was glad to have the distraction of work – anything that didn't remind him of Belinda Crillow. Even though she'd tried to harm his family the thought of her loneliness and desperation depressed him. 'I need to check something first,' he said.

He found the file on Alcuin's death beneath a pile of papers on his desk and, after studying the letter found in the dead man's pocket, he asked one of the DCs to contact the Probate Registry for him. He needed to confirm the suspicions that were forming in his head.

On the main road half a mile from Princebury Hall Wesley saw flashing blue lights on the road ahead. It was an accident. An SUV had come off the road and turned on its side; probably driving too fast in the drizzle that had dampened the tarmac. He carried on past, refusing to be one of those rubberneckers who slows down and causes more problems, but the sight of that car triggered a tantalising flicker of recognition, there for a moment then gone. Maybe whatever it was would come back to him in time.

'Probably speeding. Some idiots never learn,' said Gerry.

'Think we should have stopped?'

'Nah. Leave it to Traffic.'

When they reached their destination it was hard to read Xander Southwark's thoughts as they were shown into his office. He wore an expression of polite concern but Wesley thought he must have become a master of pretence over the years. Perhaps that's why he'd succeeded in fleecing so many of his clients before he was eventually caught.

'I'm always happy to help the police,' Southwark said smoothly. 'Only I can't add anything to what I told you last time – or the time before. You're becoming regular visitors, gentlemen. Perhaps I can tempt you to sample our facilities.' His lips formed a mirthless smile that reminded Wesley of the serpent in the Garden of Eden depicted in the west window of Lower Torworthy church.

'On my last visit I asked if you knew Ian Evans.' Wesley watched Southwark's face closely. 'You said you didn't recognise the name.'

Southwark gave a little shrug.

'Evans used to work for Jellicoe and Travers, the law firm where you were a partner.'

'It was a large firm. I can't be expected to remember everyone who ever worked there.' Wesley detected a new wariness in Southwark's voice.

'Evans was a trainee solicitor at the time, fresh out of law school. He worked in your department and he became involved in the case of an elderly client of yours who was murdered – smothered by her carer … allegedly. You sent him to her house to fetch some papers.'

'Who on earth told you that?'

'Is it true?'

Southwark assumed a mournful expression. 'I presume you're talking about Miss Tilson. She was a lovely lady. What happened to her was tragic.'

'The carer who was arrested for her murder hanged herself in her cell. She always protested her innocence.'

'Surely the fact that she killed herself confirms her guilt. She was either overcome with remorse or she couldn't face the consequences of her actions.'

'Why did you tell us you'd never heard of Ian Evans?'

Gerry's question sounded threatening but Wesley suspected this was the intention.

'Evans is a common name.' He sat back, looking pleased with himself. 'I have a faint recollection of him now but I confess he'd slipped my mind. Between you and me he wasn't very memorable.'

'Memorable enough to be murdered,' said Wesley. He glanced at Gerry before dropping his bombshell. 'On our previous visit we asked you about Andrea Jameson but we now think Ian Evans was the killer's target.' He paused. 'You tried to point the finger of blame at Evans when you were investigated for fraud in nineteen ninety-seven.'

'I honestly don't remember.'

'To return to the case of Mary Tilson: her great-nephew, Alcuin Garrard, came to see you after her death, no doubt wondering where her money had disappeared to. You had power of attorney for Miss Tilson, I believe. Don't deny it because it's a matter of official record.'

Southwark's eyes narrowed. 'Miss Tilson's carer was helping herself to her money and valuables. You can't prove otherwise after all this time and you know it.'

This was a new Xander Southwark. The serpent was showing his fangs.

'Did you steal Mary Tilson's money, Mr Southwark?'

'The police knew the carer had been pinching the old lady's stuff. She had a record for dishonesty – open and shut case. You're on a fishing expedition but you're wasting your time. I served my sentence and there's absolutely no evidence against me as far as the Tilson case is concerned. This is beginning to look like harassment.'

Wesley put his face close to Southwark's, angry that he was trying to portray himself as the victim. 'Talking of harassment, I believe you were involved in an inappropriate relationship with a junior member of your staff.'

'I don't know where you heard that but it's a lie.' He sounded indignant but Wesley knew he'd touched a nerve.

'You attended a party aboard a yacht in Tradmouth marina. It was arranged by Andrea Jameson's company.'

He sighed. 'I'm invited to a lot of parties, Inspector. And as I knew Jason . . . '

'A young waitress was assaulted at this particular party. Her name was Phoebe Jakes.'

'That's dreadful . . . but I don't see what it has to do with me,' was the calm reply.

'We think the girl will be able to identify her attacker.'

'Good. I hope you catch him.' He made a show of examining his watch. 'I have an appointment in fifteen minutes so if you're not going to arrest me, I'd be grateful if you'd leave.'

But Wesley hadn't finished. 'Do you know a man called Nathan Rowyard?'

'No.'

'He'd been posing as a clergyman using the name John Davies.'

'In that case I definitely don't know him.'

'He was murdered not far from here and we think Andrea Jameson's and Ian Evans's killer was responsible for his death as well.'

'We don't have TV or newspapers here at Princebury Hall so I'm not aware of the case,' he said smugly.

'Where were you last weekend – late Saturday and early Sunday?'

'I was here. Ask any of my staff.'

'I presume you have a car,' said Gerry. 'You could have slipped out without anyone seeing.'

'I don't drive. I know it's unusual these days but I was involved in an accident some years ago. I sustained leg injuries and it left me with a fear of driving so I haven't been behind a wheel since. And you can check with all the local taxi firms; I didn't take a cab and nobody here, guest or staff, gave me a lift.' He smiled, satisfied. 'I'm sorry to disappoint you. If that's all . . .'

'I'd like to arrest that man for being in possession of an offensive personality,' said Gerry on their way back to the car.

Wesley didn't reply. He was too busy texting Pam to see if there was any news on Della's condition. But Pam replied in two words – no change.

Neil had intended to spend the previous evening poring over Alcuin Garrard's thesis but events dictated otherwise. He had called Wesley to tell him about his new discovery, only to find that his friend was at home looking after the children while Pam was at the hospital. Wesley explained that there'd been an incident at his house: Pam had been threatened with a knife and Della had been run over by the culprit's car and was now in intensive care. When Neil asked what he could do to help Wesley asked him to take the children over to his sister's in the nearby village of Belsham so he could join Pam at her mother's bedside. Neil and Lucy drove straight down and delivered Michael and Amelia to the vicarage where Wesley's sister Maritia lived with her husband and baby son. It was almost midnight by the time they arrived back in Exeter but Neil felt he'd done his good deed for the day.

First thing the next morning he arrived in Lower Torworthy. There was somebody he wanted to speak to before he joined the geophysics team in Manor Field.

He made straight for the church and found the door unlocked. As his eyesight adjusted to the gloom he saw Sarah Shaw beside the pulpit, carefully inserting blooms into a large flower arrangement. He watched as she stood back to assess her handiwork before removing a couple of stems and replacing them further up. He recognised a perfectionist when he saw one.

'Hello.'

She swung round, startled, and he was tempted to tell her what he'd discovered about Alcuin's research. But there was somebody else who needed to be told first.

'Is Oliver around?' he asked, strolling down the aisle towards her.

'At the vicarage as far as I know.' She looked as if she was about to say something else but returned to her flowers.

Neil headed for the vicarage where he found Oliver Grayling drying his breakfast dishes. An open laptop stood on the kitchen table and Neil assumed he'd been working on a sermon. But whatever it was, Grayling seemed glad of the interruption.

'I've found Alcuin Garrard's thesis,' Neil said as he made himself comfortable on one of the kitchen chairs. 'He discovered a box full of documents at Princebury Hall when he was given access by Ralph Detoram and he located a will dated January fifteen sixty-nine which tells the whole story.' He grinned. 'It's a lurid tale of deception and blackmail ending in murder. Want to hear it?'

The vicar sat down opposite him, looking more relaxed

337

than he had during Neil's previous visits, perhaps because the bogus curate was no longer around.

Neil took a deep breath and began. 'The DeTorhams were lords of the manor and patrons of the living with power to choose the vicar, which was probably why there were certain things Sir Matthew left out of the parish records.'

'He wanted to keep on the right side of the local bigwigs.'

'That's right. Alcuin found letters to and from various members of the DeTorham family in the early fifteen thirties and there were some from the young lord of the manor, Oswald. Oswald wrote to his cousin Henry Dyce confiding his worries about his younger brother Simeon. By the sound of it Simeon had always been trouble and when the vicar Sir Matthew created his little monk ...'

'The one we found?'

'Yes. Everything started well but after a couple of years Simeon DeTorham had an idea. Somehow he persuaded or threatened the priest to take along another prayer machine as well – a big friar to accompany the small version. I'd hoped to find it using a metal detector but that was before I realised that the big friar's actually buried in the church. I'll show you.'

The two men made their way back to the church where Neil led the way to the little chapel to the right of the altar which housed a number of DeTorham tombs. In the chapel Oswald's effigy, splendid in ruff and doublet, lay beside that of his wife while effigies of their eight children knelt piously around the base of the tomb. Neil knew from his research that Oswald had died peacefully in his bed in fifteen sixty-nine. Or perhaps his end hadn't been so peaceful – perhaps he had been tormented by the thought of the terrible deed he'd committed all those years before.

The vicar watched as Neil squatted down beside a small, worn memorial stone let into the chapel floor.

'Simeon DeTorham. Fifteen thirty-four. No other details.'

'I've always assumed it was the grave of a child,' said Grayling.

'Simeon was an adult – and he was murdered.'

'Can you prove that?'

'Alcuin did. I wondered why our graffiti survey found so many protective marks around his memorial stone.' He pointed at the ground. 'You can see the shape of an eye with three lines through it – the Holy Trinity cancelling out the evil eye, and crosses formed of five dots representing the five wounds of Christ. The people of Lower Torworthy went to a great deal of trouble to protect themselves against what they saw as an evil soul. If you're looking for your big friar here he is. Simeon hit on a great scam. He went around with the vicar pretending to be the big friar and he'd listen in to people's confessions. If they recovered he'd blackmail them – or put the squeeze on their relatives if they didn't. As far as his victims were concerned, he had an almost supernatural knowledge of their wrongdoings because initially they had no idea the big friar was anything but a machine like its small counterpart.'

'I'm surprised the priest went along with it,' said Grayling with a hint of disgust.

'Think about it. The DeTorham family held sway over the village. Simeon had knowledge and he used it to control the inhabitants, possibly even his elder brother, Oswald. The priest, Sir Matthew, was local, the son of a carpenter, and, according to Alcuin's thesis, Simeon knew about an incident in his past which gave him a hold over him and so ensured his cooperation. In the parish records Sir Matthew describes the creation of the little monk in detail but there's absolutely no mention of the big friar.'

'Because it was Simeon?'

Neil nodded.

'What happened to him?'

'He died in the fire at the manor house, along with the DeTorhams' steward, Peter. After the fire Oswald moved to Princebury Hall. It always seemed odd to me that he had a house built two miles away instead of rebuilding the manor house.'

'His brother had died there,' a woman's voice said. 'There would have been too many memories. Then there was the possibility that the site was cursed.' Neil turned and saw Sarah Shaw standing at the chapel entrance. He hadn't realised she was still in the church.

The vicar looked at her, then at Neil. 'Can I have a word in private, Dr Watson?'

Sarah showed no sign of being put out by Grayling's dismissal as Neil followed the vicar to the vestry.

'Something's been weighing on my mind,' Grayling said as they sat down. 'I thought I should maybe mention it to the police but ...'

'What is it?'

'I don't think I was the only person around here Nathan Rowyard was blackmailing,' he said after a long silence.

'Why's that?'

'I'd forgotten until now but on one occasion when he came here he said he had to go because he had somebody else to see. Somebody nearby.'

'You should tell the police. It might be important.'

Oliver Grayling nodded. 'That inspector's a friend of yours, isn't he?'

'Would you like me to speak to him?'

Grayling looked as though Neil had lifted a terrible burden from his shoulders.

41

Wesley put the phone down. Neil's call had confirmed the suspicions that had been buzzing around in his head. So far he'd found no link between the sham curate-cum-blackmailer, Nathan Rowyard, and Ian Evans – or Andrea Jameson for that matter. If it hadn't been for his execution-style murder he would have assumed that Rowyard's death was unrelated but, as it was, the similarities were too obvious to ignore.

Slowly things were starting to make sense. Rowyard had been hanging round Lower Torworthy for a while, using Oliver Grayling as a human cash machine, so if he'd seen something suspicious on the day of the double murder and then tried to extort money from the killer, that would explain why he was murdered. Wesley looked for Gerry, eager to test his theory. The DCI, however, was nowhere to be seen.

The delay didn't bother Wesley because he had other things on his mind. The file on the death of Mary Tilson was lying open on his desk and there was something he wanted to check; something Xander Southwark had said during their last meeting.

The DC who'd contacted the Probate Registry had come

back with the news that he'd traced Ralph Detoram's will and Wesley smiled to himself as he read the copy, surprised that it hadn't been changed after the main beneficiary came under suspicion of fraud. No wonder Xander Southwark had been able to afford to open the Well-being Centre: he must have used all his persuasive powers to ensure the old man's will went unaltered. Wesley made some phone calls to the station and once he'd finished he went through the Mary Tilson file again, checking everything twice and making notes. The timing fitted perfectly.

When Gerry appeared from the direction of the church hall's lavatories Wesley hurried over to meet him.

'I think we've got him, Gerry,' he said, waving a sheet of paper in front of the DCI's nose.

'There wasn't much forensic evidence connected with the murder of Mary Tilson and what there was had been ignored at the time because the police were so confident they had the culprit.'

'I don't suppose anything still exists in some exhibit store somewhere?' Gerry asked as if he expected the answer to be no.

'I've been making some calls,' said Wesley. 'And it turns out the pillow used to kill Mary is still stored in the basement of her local station. There was no way they could get anything from it at the time but with recent improvements in DNA analysis . . . '

'Get it sent to the lab, Wes. Even if nothing's found we don't have to let our suspect know that, do we,' said Gerry with a hint of mischief. 'You're sure about the date of that accident?'

'Absolutely. I think Mary Tilson was killed because she

was getting wise to what was going on with her finances. And there's something else: Ralph Detoram's will named Xander Southwark as his sole beneficiary. Southwark told us he'd acquired Princebury Hall through an inheritance but it didn't occur to me for one moment that he'd actually inherited the place. There was a letter from Mr Detoram in Alcuin Garrard's pocket when he was found. I think Alcuin tried to warn the old man about Southwark but he refused to believe him.'

'So we bring him in?'

Wesley considered the question for a moment. 'While we were up at Princebury Hall I noticed a CCTV camera at the front gate. I've sent someone to collect the footage for the time of the double murder and the shooting of Nathan Rowyard, if it still exists. The Reverend Grayling thinks Rowyard was blackmailing someone else as well, which would explain the mysterious four grand.'

'Has he any idea who Rowyard's second victim was?'

'No. But he told Grayling he was going to see them so they must be local.'

Gerry paused. 'What's the latest on Della?'

Gerry's question brought the memories flooding back. 'No change.'

'And Pam?'

'Bearing up.'

The next few hours passed slowly as Wesley tried to concentrate on the case. The pillow that had been the instrument of Mary Tilson's death had been sent to the lab and the CCTV footage from Princebury Hall had been brought in and was being examined by Trish Walton in the AV room at Tradmouth Police Station. It was a gamble but one Wesley considered worth taking.

At three o'clock Gerry told Wesley to return to Tradmouth. He could check on Della, keep Pam company and call in at the station to see what progress Trish was making, if any. More evidence was needed before he acted.

It was a job Trish Walton hated – going through hour upon hour of footage, watching the tedious comings and goings on the dates of the three murders. When there was no sign of their main suspect leaving the premises at the appropriate times, she did as Wesley requested and began to go through earlier disks. She wasn't sure why he wanted it done but she braced herself for an afternoon of mind-numbing boredom while the September sun shone outside.

After a while her concentration started to waver and she almost missed a small grey van pulling up at the gates of the Hall, only to be met by a familiar figure who looked around furtively before getting into the van's passenger seat.

Trish froze the image and scrolled back. It was him all right – she recognised him from the photo on the incident-room wall: Xander Southwark.

The registration number of the van was clearly visible, and once she'd entered it into the system she called Wesley.

Wesley was at the hospital sitting beside Pam while the machines keeping Della alive beeped with reassuring regularity. He held his wife's hand but there was nothing he could say to comfort her, apart from telling her that Belinda Crillow was now in a secure psychiatric unit and would never threaten their family again.

Not being allowed to use his mobile on the ward, he went outside every so often to check his calls and at 5.30

he found a message from Trish. When he called her back she revealed the identity of the van's owner and he asked her to make some checks. After twenty minutes the answer came back and he felt a thrill of triumph. He'd found the missing link; the connection that made sense of everything. He needed to get someone up to Princebury Hall as soon as possible.

Extract from draft PhD thesis
written by Alcuin Garrard

July 1995

Henry Dyce then continues his story.

'I leaped forward and smote the thing
that let out a most human cry. I tore at the
robes and the mask fell to reveal the face
of a man. As Sir Matthew groaned I beheld my
cousin, Simeon, in the rough grey robes of a
friar and I demanded of him the meaning of
the outrage.'

According to correspondence between Oswald
DeTorham and Henry Dyce, Simeon DeTorham was
fond of gaming and found himself in debt to
an Exeter moneylender. It seems likely that
when he saw the success of Sir Matthew's
'little monk' he hit upon a scheme to
extort money from his brother's tenants and
neighbours.

There is the question, of course, of how
he secured Sir Matthew's cooperation. First
of all, the priest was dependent on the
DeTorham family for his living - secondly
there are hints that he knew something about

347

Sir Matthew's past that enabled him to put pressure on the priest. There are references in the coroner's records to the death of Sir Matthew's cousin in 1518. The inquest concluded that the cousin, aged twenty, drowned in the river while fishing but nothing was proved against Matthew, although he and his cousin were prone to arguing. It is possible that Matthew's decision to enter the priesthood was a penance for committing murder and if Simeon DeTorham had his suspicions he might have used them to his advantage.

Simeon disguised himself as the friar and used the information he overheard during the confessions of the sick to blackmail them or their relatives. There is no record of anybody challenging him but perhaps, in that society, it was difficult to refuse the demands of the lord of the manor's brother.

The scheme came to an end when Simeon died along with Oswald's steward, Peter, in the fire which destroyed Lower Torworthy Manor. In his journal Henry Dyce speculates that the fire was started deliberately, perhaps by one of Simeon's blackmail victims – but he admits he had no evidence for this theory.

However, the will of Oswald DeTorham, discovered in the cathedral archives in Exeter, clarifies the matter.

42

For the first time Xander Southwark seemed unsure of himself. Back at Princebury Hall he'd been in charge but Tradmouth Police Station was Wesley and Gerry's territory, and they'd chosen the bleakest interview room available to unsettle him further.

'What did you say to the person in this van?' Wesley pushed a still image from the CCTV over the table towards him. Southwark had brought his solicitor but the young woman looked uncomfortable. Wesley wondered whether she knew about his murky history in the world of the law.

When Southwark didn't reply, Wesley continued. 'We know about the connection between Mary Tilson's carer – the woman accused of her murder – and the person on the CCTV footage. Only the carer didn't kill Mary, did she? Mary died to cover up the fact that her solicitor had been using his power of attorney to milk her bank account until it was almost empty. And that solicitor was you, wasn't it, Mr Southwark?'

Southwark held up his hands, the ghost of a smile on his lips. 'I admit that I borrowed from clients' accounts but I served time for it.'

'Not for Mary's case you didn't.'

Southwark shrugged. 'You can't prove anything now and you know it.'

'I'll repeat the question – what exactly did you tell the driver of the van?'

'I agreed to meet because I thought it'd get him off my back. He kept going on about how his mum had been accused of something she hadn't done and died because of it. He said he'd found out I'd been the old lady's solicitor and he tried to blame me for what happened. He concluded, quite wrongly, that as I'd been convicted of fraud in nineteen ninety-seven I must have stolen from Miss Tilson too – which was absolute nonsense. Anyway, it was over twenty years ago so I don't know why he couldn't just let it go.'

'How did the meeting end?'

'Amicably. I managed to persuade him I had nothing to do with his mother's death.'

Wesley leaned forward, putting his face close to Xander's. He could smell mint on his breath. 'I think you pointed the finger at someone else to get him off your back – someone junior who worked for you at the time. You'd tried to implicate him when you were arrested for fraud but it hadn't worked.'

There was no answer.

'When you named Ian Evans you signed his death warrant. How did you know he was in Lower Torworthy?'

'I didn't.'

'We've been going through the CCTV footage from Princebury Hall's entrance and there's one vehicle that turns up regularly – a small van with a flower design on the side belonging to a Sarah Shaw.'

'She does flower arrangements for the Hall. What of it?'

'I didn't notice any flowers when I was up there. And

when she was Sarah Booker she worked for you. Don't deny it because we've checked.'

'So?'

'You had an affair with her, didn't you.'

'No comment.'

'She was only eighteen back then but the relationship's still going on, isn't it, Mr Southwark?'

There was no reply.

'Sarah had a temp job at Jellicoe and Travers before she went away to university and Ian Evans was working there at the same time. Did Sarah recognise him in the village and tell you he'd turned up? You'd tried to shift the blame for your fraudulent activities on to Evans all those years ago. You saw him as a useful scapegoat back then and you thought you'd try the same tactic again.'

'You can't prove a thing, Inspector.'

Wesley stood up, sending his chair clattering backwards. Gerry did likewise.

'When can I go?' Southwark's question sounded confident, with a hint of boredom. But Wesley could see he was starting to panic.

'You're not going anywhere,' Gerry barked as he followed Wesley from the room.

Wesley stood in the lay-by where Andrea Jameson's car had been found, gazing into Manor Field just as she must have done before she met her death. He could see Neil squatting by a newly dug test pit but he didn't call out to greet his friend. He'd hoped his target would be there but he was nowhere to be seen.

'Have you called for back-up? The Armed Response Unit?' Gerry asked.

'I'll ask them to meet us there. I want this done discreetly. No sirens,' he said before getting into the car to make the call.

He set off slowly, feeling apprehensive. Their quarry had a firearm – a powerful hunting rifle according to Ballistics. At the moment they were the hunters but he knew how quickly the situation could reverse.

It wasn't far to their destination; just a mile down the main road then down a narrow track. When Wesley pulled up he saw the small grey van he'd watched on the CCTV footage; the one Xander Southwark had been filmed getting into the day before the double murder.

Wesley could feel his heart beating faster as he headed for the front door with Gerry by his side.

'Shouldn't we wait for back-up?'

'According to Neil there's an old lady living here so I want to keep things low key if possible. Neil said it's his mum – but that's impossible.'

'A gran maybe ... or an aunty?' Gerry suggested as he rapped on the door with his fist.

To Wesley's surprise the door creaked open and he saw Gerry hesitate before he stepped inside, shouting out a greeting, making it sound as if it was a casual call. But there was no answer.

Gerry opened the living-room door and Wesley looked in, dreading what he might see. But the room was empty, although there was a half-drunk mug of tea on a side table – still warm.

'He can't be far away,' Wesley whispered, gesturing towards the kitchen. But that was empty too, with unwashed dishes in the sink and a smell of stale cooking in the air.

This left upstairs. Wesley stopped at the foot of the

uncarpeted staircase and listened. But all he could hear was Gerry breathing behind him. He started to climb, aware of his footsteps clattering on the bare wood. If somebody was up there they'd have plenty of warning.

He reached the landing and again all he could hear was distant birdsong. Gerry gestured towards the nearest door and Wesley pushed it open with his foot. It was a plain room with a neatly made single bed topped by an old-fashioned quilt; a room from the 1950s, immaculate with an almost military austerity.

The next door led on to an inhospitable green-tiled bathroom, unaltered since its installation in the middle of the last century. Wesley paused before trying the final door and he felt Gerry nudge his arm.

The contrast to the first bedroom was marked. This was a fussy, feminine room with clothes laid out on the double bed and a pair of tights draped over the back of the chair by the window. The wardrobe door stood open to reveal the clothes inside and the dressing table was strewn with make-up and bottles of perfume. Wesley stood in the doorway and stared, breathing in the scent of decay.

'Looks like she's popped out and she'll be back any minute,' said Gerry in a low whisper.

'Doesn't look like an old lady's room,' Wesley said. 'Do you agree?'

'Depends on the old lady,' said Gerry. 'Where is she?'

Wesley took a deep breath. 'Dead. This is a shrine. Let's get out of here.'

Gerry led the way downstairs. 'Where now?'

'His equipment's not in the house but he must keep it somewhere.'

Wesley found the back door unlocked. It led on to a

353

small garden with a large brick outhouse at the end. The outhouse door stood open and as they approached Wesley could hear the sound of voices, then music; something from the 1960s. The radio was on.

'We need that back-up, Wes. If we're wrong Aunty Noreen's going to moan about wasting her precious resources but we can't take the risk.'

'The ARU should be here in ten minutes. Let's hang on till then.'

They started to retrace their steps but before they could reach the house a figure appeared in the doorway. Now they had no choice but to play for time and hope for the best.

Wesley fixed a smile to his face and stepped forward. 'Sorry to bother you, Charlie.'

Charlie Perks gaped at him. He was holding a metal detector and Wesley could see others behind him hanging from specially made holders around the outhouse walls like a small robot army ready to be activated for battle.

'Can we have a word?'

Perks squared up to them and slung his metal detector slung over his shoulder like a rifle. 'What about?'

Wesley hadn't expected the aggression in his voice.

'I'd like to ask you about your mother. She died in nineteen ninety-five, I believe?'

Perks stared at the two policemen as though they were alien beings.

Wesley moved forward. The back of the outbuilding was in shadow and he couldn't make out what was by the far wall. 'What was your mother's name?' he asked gently.

Perks took a deep breath. 'Judy.'

'It was Judith Westminster. We've been doing some

detecting ourselves,' said Gerry, nodding at the machine. Wesley cursed his flippancy. The situation needed tact.

'Why ask if you already know?' Perks turned his back on them and walked into the outhouse.

'This was your mother's cottage?' Wesley shouted at his disappearing back.

Perks stopped abruptly. 'I inherited it when she ... passed away. What about it?'

'She was Mary Tilson's carer, wasn't she, Charlie? She was accused of Miss Tilson's murder. Arrested for a crime she never committed.'

Perks swung round, his face suddenly animated. 'The old lady's solicitor said she'd been pinching things. They found jewellery but she didn't know how it got here.'

'Why wait so long to look for the truth?' Wesley asked.

'When she passed away I was only a kid so I moved to Birmingham to live with my dad – they'd split up when I was very little. A year ago Dad died and there was nothing to keep me in Birmingham so I came back here to her cottage. It was exactly as she'd left it – hadn't been touched since ... I feel close to her here. She speaks to me – says she wants me to clear her name.'

'And have you?'

Perks nodded vigorously. 'Yes. I know who really killed Miss Tilson.'

'And you hold that person responsible for your mother's death too.'

Perks looked at Wesley gratefully, as though he was glad he understood. But Wesley's next words would shatter his assumptions.

'You tracked down Miss Tilson's lawyer and he told you a trainee solicitor called Ian Evans visited Mary Tilson regularly on his instructions. He told you this young man insinuated himself into Miss Tilson's life and stole from her. He said Evans planted the jewellery he'd taken in your mother's cottage when he thought he was about to come under suspicion. Xander Southwark suspected Evans was guilty but he had no evidence so he couldn't say anything. A while later he was arrested himself so even if he had found evidence nobody would have believed him. Is that what Southwark told you?'

Perks looked astonished, as though Wesley had pulled off a remarkable conjuring trick. 'That's right. Evans killed the old woman when she caught him stealing but it was my mum who got the blame.'

'Southwark lied to you, Charlie,' said Wesley. 'Ian Evans was completely innocent. Southwark was convicted of fraud in early nineteen ninety-seven but eighteen months before that he'd killed Miss Tilson when she became suspicious and challenged him. Your mother was a handy scapegoat ... as was Ian Evans when you came looking for the truth years later.'

Perks took a step back into the shadows. 'You're lying,' he hissed like a cornered animal.

'You went to see Southwark to find out what really happened and he told you Evans was staying at the Shepherd's Arms in Lower Torworthy. A woman who used to work at Southwark's firm had seen Evans in the village and recognised him.' He paused. 'But you killed the wrong man, Charlie.'

'No.'

'And you also killed a woman who'd stopped in the layby – an innocent witness.'

'I had no choice.'

'And what about Nathan Rowyard? Did he see you in Manor Field that day? Was he blackmailing you?'

'I gave him everything I had – all my savings – but he wanted more.'

'So you killed him as well. You're a good shot, Charlie.'

'I joined the army when I left school. You never forget your training,' he said with pride. 'And I've got the best equipment there is – an Owen rifle made in the States in the nineteen thirties; a real beauty.' He spoke lovingly, as a father might speak about a favourite child.

There was no sign of the back-up Gerry had ordered but Wesley reckoned the suspect would come quietly now. He held out his right hand to the man, feeling for the handcuffs he'd put in his back pocket with his left.

'Where's the rifle?'

He didn't answer.

'Put the metal detector down, Charlie. It'll be safe here. We'll make sure the door's secure.' Wesley made a calculated guess that the man would need to be reassured about the safety of his mechanical pride and joy. For a moment he thought his ploy had worked. Perks cradled the metal detector in both arms then placed it carefully in its own holder on the wall.

Now his eyes had adjusted to the light in the outhouse Wesley could see mysterious shapes shrouded in sheets at the back of the building. But he was unprepared when Charlie Perks lunged backwards and grabbed something from beneath the covers. It took him a split second to register that it was a rifle, complete with a telescopic sight; the wood of the stock polished to a shine. And Perks was pointing it in their direction.

'Don't be stupid, Charlie,' Gerry said. 'Put it down.'

Wesley heard the squeal of tyres outside and knew the ARU had arrived. He sent up a silent prayer that they'd use their initiative and come round the back of the house. In the meantime they needed to keep the man talking.

'Tell me how you got Ian Evans to the field.'

'Mr Southwark said he was staying at the Shepherd's Arms so I waited outside in the van. I've stalked animals before so I'm good at it.' His lips twitched upwards in a grim smile. 'When he walked to Manor Field I followed him and hid myself. He stopped by that old bit of wall – had a really good look at it. He didn't know what had hit him.' A gratified look appeared on the killer's face as though he was delighted with his own cleverness.

'You killed him near the spot where Mary Tilson's great-nephew died.'

He shook his head. 'I don't know anything about that.'

Wesley had the feeling he was telling the truth.

'What about the woman, Andrea Jameson?'

'I turned round and she was standing there looking straight at me. I couldn't let her go, could I?' He took a deep, shuddering breath. 'I got justice for Mum so she can rest in peace now. That's all that matters.'

'But Ian Evans had nothing to do with your mother's death. He was set up.'

'You're lying. Mr Southwark knew he'd done it. He told me.'

'And you believed him?'

Perks looked confused, swinging his rifle between Wesley and Gerry. Both men stood perfectly still.

'Mr Southwark had no reason to lie. Why would he.'

'He had every reason if he'd killed Mary Tilson himself.'

'He wasn't anywhere near the old lady's house when she died. He was at home in Exeter. He said.'

Wesley and Gerry looked at each other. 'I've spoken to our Traffic Division,' said Wesley. 'Southwark was involved in a motor accident late on the night Mary Tilson died. The collision took place ten minutes from her house but when he was interviewed about Miss Tilson's death he told the police he'd been in Exeter all that night and his accident happened the following evening. They didn't bother checking out his story because they were so convinced of your mother's guilt. It was sloppy policing and others paid the price for it.'

'You're lying.' The words came out in a whine just as Wesley heard a sound behind him. He saw Gerry turn his head but he didn't move.

He heard the click of the ARU's weapons being readied for firing and held his breath. They were flitting like shadows around the garden. Suddenly chaos broke out as voices barked instructions.

'Put down your weapon and put your hands in the air.'

'On the floor. Now.'

Charlie Perks raised his rifle and Wesley froze and shut his eyes. Then he heard the clatter of the weapon hitting the ground and felt the air move as the firearms officers surged forward.

He felt Gerry's arm on his, clinging on, and when he opened his eyes he saw Perks on the floor, his arms pinioned behind his back.

'Let's get back to the village,' Gerry mumbled. 'I need a drink.'

Wesley nodded. A drink in the Shepherd's Arms was just what he needed.

Extract from the will
of Oswald DeTorham

The seventh day of January in the eleventh year of the reign of our Sovereign Lady Queen Elizabeth.

I wish to set out the truth of my great sin and I trust the Lord will judge me when I stand before Him.

I confess that I used the fire in which my brother and my steward died to conceal a terrible deed of which I most heartily repent.

My brother Simeon was without fear of God or man, and his grave debts made him desperate. My cousin, Henry Dyce, accused Simeon of great wickedness but, when challenged, Simeon swore by all that is holy that Henry was mistaken and that the guilty one was Peter, my steward, who was suspected by all the village of heretical and ungodly ways.

Simeon told me that Peter deceived our priest into allowing him to assume the guise of a friar in order to overhear the confessions of the sinful and gain power over them. I accepted my brother's word and challenged Peter who denied all but Simeon urged me to press the matter. Peter persisted in his denial, saying he hated the little monk and the superstition of the people and that he desired nothing more than to prove the falsehood of the diabolical machine as he called it, and in my anger I struck him and he fell.

I then went to Simeon's chamber, only to find the robes of a friar and a wooden mask laid upon his bed. I knew at once he had deceived me and when I told him what I had done he laughed and said Peter was a fool and a heretic and, besides, was only a servant.

Fury rose within me and I drew my dagger to stab my mocking brother through the heart. As he fell he upset a candle which caught the drapes of his bed and soon the flames caught hold. Seeing a chance to conceal my crime I fled, leaving some time before seeking help so the raging fire would consume all proof of my wrongdoing. To my eternal regret I forgot about Peter, thinking he would recover and flee the fire as I had, not knowing that my blow had rendered him senseless so he perished and I beg the Lord's forgiveness for my most grievous error.

43

Shortly after Della was brought out of her induced coma a few days later she began issuing her orders to Pam. She wanted magazines. She wanted books. She wanted chocolate. For the first time in his life Wesley was glad to see her back on form.

Now all Wesley had to do was make sure the case against Charlie Perks would stand up to the scrutiny of the Crown Prosecution Service and Gerry had no doubts that it would.

Xander Southwark had been arrested and questioned but the evidence of his car accident on the night of Mary Tilson's death was purely circumstantial, especially when he insisted he'd merely made a mistake about the date. There was still no way they could make a murder charge stick, even after he'd confessed to playing fast and loose with Mary Tilson's bank account. He insisted that Ian Evans killed Miss Tilson because she'd caught him stealing her jewellery which he'd later planted at Judith Westminster's cottage. When asked why he hadn't brought this to the attention of the police at the time, he said that he'd thought Judith's arrest and suicide confirmed her guilt so he'd had no reason to voice a nebulous suspicion about a junior employee. It might even have made him look foolish.

Southwark's version of events was so persuasive that Wesley almost started to believe it himself and Gerry reckoned they had no choice but to let the matter drop. Southwark might face additional fraud charges but in the meantime he could go on running the Princebury Hall Well-being Centre untroubled by the law.

The equipment in the temporary incident room was being packed up to be returned to Tradmouth. Lower Torworthy would soon have its church hall back; the village would return to normal and Neil would be able to continue his investigation of the manor house site undisturbed. Even so, Wesley couldn't shake off the feeling that there was unfinished business. They'd arrested the killer of Ian Evans, Andrea Jameson and Nathan Rowyard but another truth was buried out there somewhere – like that little mechanical monk the workmen found. He knew all about the big friar, the automaton that would never come to light because it had never existed in the first place, and he wondered if this case was like that. Was he looking for something that wasn't there?

His phone rang but he didn't recognise the caller's number. Since Belinda Crillow's campaign of harassment he'd become wary of strange calls and he experienced a split second of apprehension. When he answered he heard a woman's voice and it took him a while to place it.

'Is that Inspector Peterson?'

When Wesley answered in the affirmative, the woman continued. 'This is Sarah Shaw. We spoke recently . . . about Alcuin.'

'I remember.'

Sarah Shaw had been questioned about her unwitting part in the murders of Ian Evans and Andrea Jameson but no charges had been brought. Although she had been Xander Southwark's lover Wesley wondered whether, by being taken in by his charm, she was just another of his victims. Perhaps he was being too charitable. Gerry had often said it was a weakness of his.

'Can we meet in the Shepherd's Arms in half an hour?'

Wesley's curiosity made him agree and half an hour later he was sitting beside Sarah in the lounge bar, an orange juice in front of him because he was driving. She'd chosen white wine which she drank thirstily, as though she was in need of Dutch courage.

'What can I do for you?' he asked, watching her face.

'I'm not seeing Xander any more.'

'Any particular reason?'

She blushed and bowed her head. 'When I told him I'd seen Ian Evans he used the information to get that Charlie Perks off his back, didn't he?'

'Looks that way.'

She sighed. 'I realise now that he used me and people died as a result. And I was too stupid to see it.'

'We all make mistakes.' Wesley paused to take a sip of juice before asking his next question. 'Did you speak to Ian Evans when you saw him in the village?'

She gave a small, reluctant nod. 'I was leaving the church and he recognised me. He asked me if I remembered him but I told him I didn't – which was a lie. Then he asked me if I still saw Xander . . . only he called him Alexander. He doesn't like being called Alexander any more. Says that was part of his old life.'

'What did you say?'

'I told him I hadn't seen Xander since my time at Jellicoe and Travers and I think he believed me.' She paused, turning her glass round and round in her fingers. 'I love my husband ... and my kids. But I met Xander again when he opened the Well-being Centre and he offered me something I hadn't had for years. He made me feel like a desirable woman again rather than a mum in jeans juggling my own business and the school run. He asked me up to the Hall for a drink and we ended up in bed together. I used to lie to my husband – I'd tell him I was meeting friends or making deliveries when I was really going up there to meet Xander. I became very good at lying.'

Wesley looked straight at her. 'It didn't make you happy, did it?'

She gave a weak smile and shook her head. Then she looked at him. 'Inspector ...'

'Wesley, please.'

'Look, Wesley, there's something I haven't mentioned. You know I first met Xander when I worked at Jellicoe and Travers.'

'Yes.'

'I was ... seeing him when I met Alcuin.'

'I guessed,' said Wesley.

She bowed her head. 'It never occurred to me at the time but recently I've started wondering whether Xander had something to do with Al's death. I know they said it was an accident – but what if it wasn't?'

Wesley waited for her to carry on.

'It was me who told Xander about Alcuin's suspicions. Al confided in me; he said he thought his aunt's solicitor knew more about her death than he admitted. Of course he had no idea that me and Xander were ... close.' There was a moment of hesitation, as though she found it hard to carry on. 'I ... I told Xander everything Al said. I betrayed his trust.'

There was a long silence and Wesley waited, watching her face. He could see she was hurting, racked with regret, and he guessed she'd put any nagging suspicions she'd had about Alcuin's death out of her mind for years. But now she couldn't ignore them any more.

Then she spoke again in a hushed whisper. 'There's something I've never told anybody before.' She took another drink, draining her glass. 'I think Xander might have been near Manor Field on the evening Al died.'

Wesley sat forward, giving her his full attention. 'You saw him there?'

She shook her head. 'When Al didn't turn up here I went to the field to see if he was there; I wanted him to show me the site of the old manor house.'

'You lied to the police?'

'I didn't lie exactly – I just didn't mention it. Anyway, I walked there but there was no sign of him. Then I saw a car in the lay-by and I thought it looked like Xander's so I turned back because the last thing I wanted was for anyone to see us together. When I asked Xander about it he said it couldn't have been his because he'd been in Exeter all evening.' She looked at him nervously. 'When they said Al's death was an accident it was easier to believe him. Besides, I didn't want my parents to know about me and Xander. He was a lot older than me and they would have gone mad.'

'I think it's time the truth came out, don't you.'

'Can you promise I won't get into trouble for withholding information?' She sounded frightened now; scared of losing the life she'd built for herself – a life she was prepared to put at risk for a few hours of excitement with Xander Southwark.

Wesley made the promise, although he couldn't assure

her that her evidence wouldn't be needed in a future court case. Her mistakes might catch up with her whether she liked it or not, and he just hoped it wouldn't destroy her family.

As he drove home an idea came into his head. If he was right justice would be done – for Mary Tilson and Judith Westminster – and now he could add Alcuin Garrard to the list.

Bringing Xander Southwark to justice had been like wrestling with an eel – just when they thought they had something on him he slipped from their grasp. But now Gerry was happy that they had enough to charge him and Sarah Shaw's statement that she'd seen a car like his at Manor Field around the time of Alcuin Garrard's death and her revelation that she'd told him Ian Evans was in Lower Torworthy would, he hoped, clinch it. But Southwark's solicitor was confident he'd be acquitted if the case came to trial, claiming all the prosecution evidence was circumstantial. Besides, even if he had told Charlie Perks that Ian Evans was responsible for his mother's death, how could he possibly have known how Perks would react? Wesley knew he had a point.

He arrived home early. Since the traumatic events of a couple of weeks before the household had returned to normal – normal apart from the fact that Pam had insisted on Della staying with them to recuperate. Wesley hadn't argued. He'd been the one who unwittingly brought Belinda Crillow into their lives so he couldn't help feeling responsible in some way.

Over the past week or so he'd met up with Neil several times during the evenings so as to give Pam and her mother some space. He'd also met Gerry for a drink at the Tradmouth Arms next door to his waterfront home. It turned out that Gerry had two pieces of news. First of all his long-lost daughter Alison was coming for Christmas, although he hadn't yet broken the news to his other daughter, Rosie, who could be relied on to react badly – it was a problem he'd have to consider carefully. Also, and perhaps more importantly, he'd asked Joyce to make an honest man of him, as he put it, although as yet they hadn't thought about a date.

'It's Rachel's wedding in a couple of weeks. St Margaret's. I've threatened to sing in the choir but she says it won't be necessary,' he told Wesley with a wicked grin.

Wesley was happy for Gerry but when he walked home that night he had a feeling that something still wasn't right.

Then first thing the next day Rachel received a call from Phoebe Jakes's mother asking her to call at the house. Phoebe was prepared to identify her attacker.

Rachel went to see her. Just the two of them in private – woman to woman. Expecting Phoebe to name Xander Southwark, Rachel did her best to hide her surprise when she finally revealed the identity of the man who'd assaulted her.

Phoebe had recognised the man who'd cornered her in an empty cabin from the TV and when she'd watched him sitting beside Inspector Peterson appealing for information about his missing daughter, she'd felt physically sick. But now she was willing to make a statement.

When Jeremy Ovorard was brought in for questioning, Rachel almost felt the victory was personal.

44

At least when you're on remand you can wear your own clothes, Xander Southwark thought. And his were expensive because he'd always liked the best: that's why he'd risked so much. He was a gambler by nature and most of the time he'd won. Now it looked as though he was on a losing streak but he'd get over it just as he had before. He reckoned he could wriggle out of the new charges, no problem. After all, it was his word against Sarah Shaw's. She'd had a crush on him as a teenager when she'd worked at Jellicoe and Travers and when they'd met again years later she'd rekindled their relationship to relieve the boredom of her rural existence. She'd flung herself at him and then had second thoughts so her word was hardly reliable. A good barrister would destroy her in the witness box.

He had plans for when he got out. Perhaps the Wellbeing Centre had run its course but those tapes he'd made during the counselling sessions might come in useful one day – once sufficient time had elapsed. It was surprising what secrets people would reveal to perfect strangers, given the right encouragement.

He'd managed to get hold of a mobile. He knew the ins and outs of prison life and he knew what he had to do to get what he wanted. He knew Sarah's number too and he keyed it in, a small smile on his lips. At least he'd have something waiting for him when he got out – and he would get out.

'Sarah. It's Xander.'

There was silence on the other end of the line but he thought he could sense her fear.

'I understand you've been talking to the police. You do realise that lying to them is a crime and you can go to prison. Perverting the course of justice they call it.'

'I didn't lie. '

She sounded scared. This was perfect. He left a brief silence before his next attack. 'Does your husband know about us?'

'No … I … '

'I've got friends who'd be only too happy to tell him, and I used to be a keen photographer back in the day.' He let the implication sink in. 'So why don't you tell the police you made a mistake about seeing my car near Manor Field back in nineteen ninety-five. And as for telling me that you'd seen Ian Evans in the village … well, we all get a bit forgetful, don't we? If you don't want your kids to see evidence of your … exciting past, maybe you can make a little donation to my coming-out fund – say five grand for starters. I know your husband's worth a bob or two.'

The phone was slammed down but Xander was confident his message had got through. She wasn't to know he'd lied about the existence of photographs and as he returned to his cell he felt pleased with himself. Without Sarah's testimony, any charges were unlikely to stick.

A couple of hours later he was told that his solicitor wanted to see him. There'd been a development. His stride towards the spartan room where they were to meet was jaunty. He could smell triumph. A gambler always can.

The solicitor's face was solemn but then she was a miserable cow at the best of times.

'Sit down, Xander, I've got some news.'

'One of the witnesses has withdrawn her statement. The charges are being dropped.'

It came as a shock when she shook her head. 'No statements have been withdrawn. And the police have new forensic evidence. The pillow used to smother Mary Tilson was found in an exhibits store and it's been examined for DNA – they have new techniques nowadays that can detect the minutest trace.' She paused. 'According to the police your DNA was found on it. We'll do our best, Xander, but it's not looking good.'

Xander Southwark buried his head in his hands. Every gambler loses eventually.

He stood in his glass case – the little wooden man with the benign face, an enlarged photograph of his metal innards displayed behind him. His hand was raised as if to bless the onlookers who now came to gape at him, just as they'd done when he'd been created in 1531. Back then his people had been needy – now they were merely curious.

Pam bent to speak to her mother, who was sitting in her wheelchair, uncharacteristically quiet. 'What do you think?'

'It gives me the creeps. I hate machines . . . always have.'

Wesley had been concentrating on pushing his mother-in-law's wheelchair but now he broke his silence. 'Machines are only as good or bad as the person who controls them.'

'Take me home,' Della ordered with an imperious wave of her arm.

As Wesley pushed the chair down the museum's ramp he felt the pressure of Pam's hand on his sleeve.

'It's going to be all right,' she said softly.

He smiled. 'Yeah. Of course it is.'

Author note

One of the most common things I'm asked is: 'Where do you get your ideas from?' Sometimes it's not an easy question to answer but in the case of *The Mechanical Devil* an award-winning book provided my initial inspiration. *Voices of Morbath* by Professor Eamon Duffy of Cambridge University is a detailed account of life in a remote Dartmoor village in the sixteenth century written by the village's garrulous parish priest, Sir Christopher Trychay. Sir Christopher arrived in his parish in 1520 and his writings cover the upheavals caused by the religious reforms of Henry VIII (and later his son, Edward VI) which resulted in the destruction of a centuries-old way of parish life. In *The Mechanical Devil* I have concentrated on the early 1530s, just before the Reformation began, when something like Sir Matthew's 'little monk' would have been a highly desirable addition to the religious armoury of any parish church. However, the character of Peter the Steward who visits London where he encounters the 'new learning' (influenced by the teachings of Martin Luther) is a symbol of things to come.

The notion of creating an automaton as an aid to prayer is not as far-fetched as it might appear to the modern mind.

In the Smithsonian Institute in Washington DC there is a fifteen-inch-high figure made of poplar wood and iron in the form of a friar. It was made in the sixteenth century by the Spanish clockmaker Juanelo Turriano to please God and to provide instant prayer and supplication at the turn of a key. It was commissioned by King Philip II of Spain (of Armada fame) who promised God a miracle if his son, Don Carlos, recovered after a life-threatening fall. Once wound up, a spring propels the friar forward, moving its lips as if praying and beating its breast. Its left arm raises and lowers a cross and rosary and from time to time it kisses the cross, its eyes following the movement. Don Carlos did recover from his fall, saying he'd seen a vision of a Franciscan friar carrying a small wooden cross, but the effect of the little 'miracle worker' wasn't to last: Don Carlos was mentally unstable and was imprisoned by his father in 1568, eventually dying in solitary confinement. These events are depicted in Verdi's opera bearing his name.

King Philip's little friar was by no means the earliest example of an intricate mechanical figure. The history of automata stretches back to the time of the Ancient Greeks, who were seemingly obsessed by the idea of creating mechanical beings, something reflected by references in Greek mythology to gods creating moving statues. The Greeks had advanced engineering skills and very probably made partially animated statues for use in ceremonies (worked by levers and possibly also steam and water). The Ancient Egyptians too were reputed to have harnessed the power of pneumatics to make moving and musical figures.

Some illuminated medieval manuscripts depict mechanical figures guarding tombs and in 1470 an artificial eagle made by Johannes Muller was said to have flown to greet the Emperor Maximilian when he entered Nuremberg. Leonardo da Vinci made a mechanical lion for Louis XII of France which approached the king and opened its chest to reveal a fleur-de-lis emblem. In the eighteenth century Jacques de Vaucanson produced elaborate automata including a realistic flute player five feet ten inches tall which had (with the help of a current of air and a complex mechanism) a repertoire of twelve tunes.

Throughout the eighteenth and nineteenth centuries automata became ever more popular and sophisticated but one in particular caught my attention when I was researching *The Mechanical Devil*. The Turk was made by Wolfgang von Kempelen, a Hungarian author and inventor, in 1769 and presented to the Empress Maria Theresa of Austria. It was a life-sized chess player with beard and turban which sat behind a desk and won games against all comers (including Napoleon and Benjamin Franklin). The Turk became an international source of fascination and toured many countries, including America, before eventually being exposed as an elaborate hoax (with a chess master concealed inside the machine).

In 1836 Edgar Allan Poe wrote an essay called 'Maelzel's Chess Player', exposing the Turk as a fraud. Poe went on to write *The Murders in the Rue Morgue*, one of the earliest detective stories, and perhaps he was inspired to write mysteries by the case of the Turk's deception. Who knows?

On a personal note, I couldn't resist including a mention of an R G Owen rifle as recently I've discovered that the famous gunsmith, Robert Griffith Owen (originally from Anglesey but later of Ohio, USA) was my great-uncle, my grandmother's older brother. It's amazing what you find when you explore the family tree.